# LANIE SPEROS

## & The Omega Contingency

### Chris Contes

Lanie Speros & The Omega Contingency, First Edition

Copyright © 2021 Chris Contes

ISBN: 978-1-66782-972-2 eBook 978-1-66782-973-9

Cover artwork and page illustrations by Snežana Panić
AutoCAD floorplans by Author
Photography by Joanne West

Special thanks to Connie, Summer, James, Ava, & Soula. Without your assistance, this story couldn't be a successful one.

*For My Boys*

# CONTENTS

CHAPTER 1
**Stranger at the Mine**................................................................. 1

CHAPTER 2
**The Mysterious Pit**.................................................................17

CHAPTER 3
**Road Trip**.............................................................................31

CHAPTER 4
**Suspicious Traveler**...............................................................44

CHAPTER 5
**Parker's Auto Salvage** ..........................................................52

CHAPTER 6
**What's in the Box?** ...............................................................71

CHAPTER 7
**Too Many Coincidences** ........................................................87

CHAPTER 8
**The Incident at Ash Fork**.................................................... 103

CHAPTER 9
**Why We Fight** ..................................................................... 115

CHAPTER 10
**The Corridor**...................................................................... 121

CHAPTER 11
**Emergency Kits** .................................................................. 152

CHAPTER 12
**Revelation at the Red Rocks**................................................ 163

CHAPTER 13
**The Executive Suite**............................................................ 175

CHAPTER 14
**Enough is Enough** .............................................................. 185

CHAPTER 15
**The Omega Director**............................................................ 204

CHAPTER 16
**What's Next?** ...................................................................... 218

CHAPTER 17
**The Site** ............................................................................. 226

CHAPTER 18
**A New Face** .................................................................................. 246

CHAPTER 19
**The Harvest Formal** ...................................................................... 258

CHAPTER 20
**Dangerous Exploration** ................................................................ 278

CHAPTER 21
**The North Gate** ............................................................................ 309

CHAPTER 22
**The Vault** ...................................................................................... 330

CHAPTER 23
**Unhappy Travelers** ........................................................................ 355

CHAPTER 24
**The Return Home** ......................................................................... 368

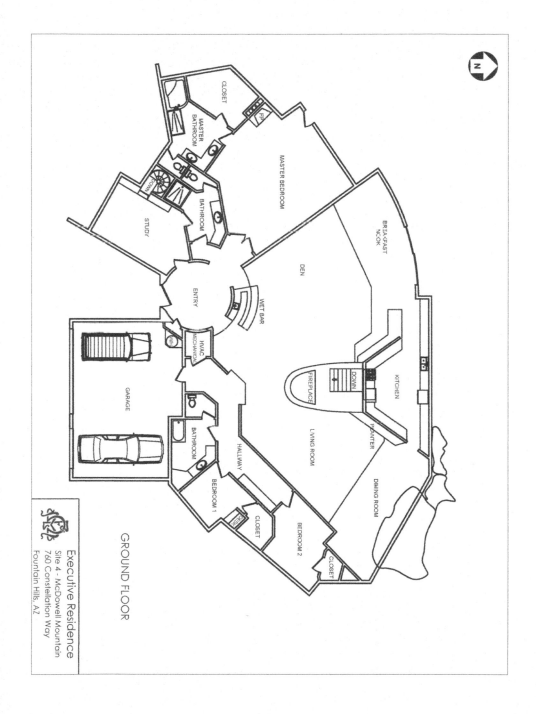

GROUND FLOOR

Executive Residence
Site 4 - McDowell Mountain
760 Constellation Way
Fountain Hills, AZ

Chapter 1

# STRANGER AT THE MINE

Blood was just starting to surface in the abrasion on Lanie's forearm when she realized she'd hit the boulder harder than she thought. Through the hole in her shirt sleeve, she examined the two-inch scrape, then let her arm fall. *No big deal.*

Dropping back to her knees in the dirt, Lanie sucked in a breath of dry, fragrant air. The lantana and sage shrubs in the rocky desert contributed not just their scent but also their color to her surroundings. That particular evening was a beautiful example of fall in Fountain Hills, Arizona. The weather had cooled but not enough to require a sweater. Arizona's epic sunsets were especially colorful during the fall, and Lanie had spent the previous evening watching the fan of orange and pink rays from the hilltop in her backyard. But that evening she wasn't watching the setting sun. Instead, she was pulling broken sticks and brush from the front suspension of her Polaris ATV.

The dust was still settling on the landscape around her. Lanie had just emerged from the unpaved fire road in the canyon and was practicing her drift steering on the trails behind her yard. She'd overcorrected on the second half of the turn and spun off the path, wedging the ACE 150 against a boulder. She cast aside a thorny tumbleweed branch and flapped her right arm, trying to shake the searing pain from her elbow. She'd nearly crushed her arm between the four wheeler's roll bar and the boulder face and knew she was lucky that only her elbow got smacked.

Lanie was disgusted with herself, since she'd made the same S-turn at least twenty times before. Squinting in the softening sunlight, she peered down the trail behind her. Nobody was approaching yet. Her view shifted to the abandoned mine entry over the next ridge, where her friend Hudson had been riding earlier. He wasn't there either. The mine's timber-framed entrance was sealed with stacked boulders and was the only place in the mountainous territory behind her house that was off limits.

She climbed back into the Polaris's single seat and started the engine. Her helmet was stuffed in the compartment behind her, and she thought of how furious her dad would be if he saw her riding without it. But on the last section of narrow trail up to her yard she could only creep at walking speed; Lanie knew a helmet wasn't necessary. What concerned her more was the cracked plastic fender fairing on the Polaris. A scraped helmet or a bruised elbow was one thing, but damage to the quad usually meant she got her key taken away for a week. Feathering the throttle, she eased the Polaris back onto the trail and climbed to the hilltop with all four tires scratching for traction.

The hilltop was her new thoughtful spot—the place Lanie Speros would sit when she wanted to ponder issues without noise or interference. She parked under the gnarled mesquite tree and shut off the engine. As the quiet of the desert returned, Lanie sat on the sloped sandstone rock near the tree and pulled one knee up to her chest. The city lights of Phoenix and Scottsdale were starting to twinkle in the distance. Fall spans a short three weeks in the Phoenix metro area, and the furnace-like summer heat had already slipped away. Just after Halloween, the mornings would get icy as winter muscled in.

Hudson Newman was Lanie's new best friend, and she was still waiting for him. She hadn't driven to the mine fence with him; they'd been apart for the last half hour. He had an older four-wheeled Yamaha whose engine would often stall—then refuse to restart. Lanie dug in the storage compartment on the Polaris and pulled out a dusty set of binoculars. She used her shirt sleeve to clean the lenses, then focused them on the distant mine entrance. It looked as desolate and formidable as always. Near the blocked entry, the mine shaft's rusted elevator headframe stood in stoic silence, its tower-like iron structure as permanent and unchanging as the red rocks around it.

Lanie had resumed her visual sweep of the mine site when a human figure appeared in her lenses—close enough for Lanie to see he was watching her. She gasped in surprise, dropping the binoculars away from her face. He knew she'd seen him—and had turned away. Lanie raised the binoculars to her eyes again, but the man was gone. A shiver wiggled up her spine as she considered how out of place the older man looked, standing alone at the remote site. She scanned the surrounding area looking for him—or even a vehicle he may have been driving—but found nothing.

Seconds later, Hudson appeared from behind a ledge near the mine trail. He wasn't far off, but he was pushing instead of riding. Lanie rolled her eyes and pulled her helmet over her dense, brownish-black curly hair. The trails and fire road behind her neighborhood were County land, and—at age thirteen—Lanie was underage and shouldn't have been operating a motorized vehicle. However, she wasn't any more of a violator than the other kids in the neighborhood who terrorized the same trails with dirt bikes.

In less than a minute she had descended into the valley, barreling through the S-turn again. With a delicate grip, she swished the steering wheel left, then right, nailing the tricky switchbacks. More satisfied, she hung the back end of the Polaris out in a long drift, then spun around a few yards ahead of Hudson.

"Did that old beater stall again?" she asked.

"We can't all have big-bucks fuel-injected ATVs," Hudson panted, waving off the dust.

"Here, hook yourself up," she replied.

Lanie tossed out the end of an orange nylon tow strap, which landed nowhere near Hudson. He looked exasperated but didn't say anything as he recovered the hook. Anyone who knew Lanie never asked her to toss or catch anything. As good a driver as she was, her hand-eye coordination for any type of ball sport was appalling.

She kept the strap permanently attached to the back of the Polaris now, as she seemed to have to *tow* Hudson more than *ride* with him. He was right, Lanie's Polaris was expensive. She owned it only because she'd won it in a sponsored competition with her old race team in Tucson. Lanie had been relieved to withdraw from the team when her family moved to the Phoenix area. She hadn't won many races and wasn't interested in competition anyway—the driving was what she liked. The machines felt like an extension of her own limbs. She loved the sensation of the little tugs on the steering wheel when a tire crossed a groove and the tactile feedback from the suspension links as they followed the features of the earth underneath.

For Lanie, the dynamics of a moving vehicle provided a primal stimulation. She couldn't explain why she liked driving but figured her satisfaction from the command of an instrument was what talented pianists felt when they played their favorite music.

Hudson knew the drill. He anchored the strap's metal hook around his front skid bar and held it until Lanie drew in the slack with the Polaris.

"I don't think your dad can handle carburetor work," Lanie said. "You should just leave this thing at my house so my dad and I can work on it."

Mr. Newman was a brilliant guy, but Hudson was the first to admit that his dad wasn't a mechanic. "Fine," he said. "It would be nice to ride instead of push—"

4

He hadn't finished his sentence when Lanie throttled the Polaris, yanking him up the trail in a storm of dust and gravel. Back at the hilltop boundary of her yard, Lanie stopped short and Hudson piled into the back of her.

"You can coast down into the yard—just leave it in front of the stable," Lanie said, pointing to the small, shabby building near the house below.

Hudson pulled his helmet and goggles off and looked down the trail behind them. "This last section is awesome; you guys have the best yard on the block."

Lanie nodded in agreement. Hudson's house didn't back up to the County preserve, so he came to Lanie's to get onto the trail.

"There was a strange guy down by the mine," Lanie said, pointing toward the fenced compound. "I saw him with my binoculars when I was looking for you. He was *inside* the fence—and he was watching me."

"Probably a hiker," Hudson said. "He probably thought *you* were spying on *him*."

"No way. This guy was old—like in his sixties—and he was dressed like he worked in an office. You know, with a collared shirt and dress shoes. You didn't see anyone? Or any trucks down there?

"Nope," Hudson said, taking the binoculars from Lanie. "If he was dressed like that, he was doing the wrong kinda hike. It's tough to get in there."

They were both still looking at the mine compound when Lanie heard movement on the dirt behind her. They turned to see Hudson's Yamaha rolling down the hill toward Lanie's back patio.

"Did you seriously leave it in neutral?!" Lanie said.

Sprinting down the hill behind the quad, Hudson didn't respond; his guilt was obvious. There was no way the two friends were going to catch up with the Yamaha on foot. They still needed to take some sort of action, however, because his quad was on a trajectory to plow through the glass doors on the back of the house—and into the Speros den.

The tow hook was still attached to the Yamaha, and the slack in the tow strap was being rapidly uncoiled from the back of the Polaris. Lanie knew the hook on the Yamaha would break when the thirty feet of slack was taken up—it wouldn't stop the runaway vehicle. With her gloved hand, she grabbed the fluttering strap just ahead of her Polaris and guided it over a tree stump several feet to her left. The heat of the strap sliding across her glove was just starting to burn her hand when she let go. Then she pushed the sole of her hiking boot against the strap, creating a tension like what a car's fan belt would require. She tensed up, knowing the strap was going to kick her foot back when the slack ran out.

Lanie absorbed as much of the energy as she could through her bent knee when the strap yanked her Polaris, then the hook snapped from the front of Hudson's Yamaha as expected. Lanie ducked as the broken strap whipped overhead on its return. When she stood back up, she saw her plan had worked as anticipated. The wayside stump had pulled the front of the quad to the left, toward her little brother's playground and sandbox.

With a bowling-pin-like crash, the Yamaha scored a perfect strike. Lanie gritted her teeth and watched with hunched shoulders as the playground's spiral slide and ladder fell. The little plastic clubhouse at the top of the slide collapsed on the overturned ATV, and the whole play structure was reduced to a scrambled heap.

"Oh man, I'm so sorry!" Hudson stood breathless at the foot of the hill, with his hands on his knees.

Lanie pulled her gloves off as she approached, examining the wreckage. "Well, that could have gone worse. C'mon, let's get it outta that pile."

The two friends stacked the playground's remains at the edge of the sandbox and pushed the Yamaha onto the patio. Besides its malfunctioning carburetor, it now had a flat tire as well.

"Good job, Bozo," Lanie said, while she stood looking over the maimed playground. Hudson shrugged, as he'd already apologized.

"Ahh well, Isaiah didn't use the playground anyway," Lanie said of her little brother. "My dad was gonna take the slide and clubhouse down. This might have saved him a Saturday of work," she said through a snicker. "C'mon, your helmet is still up on the hill."

A familiar voice called out over Lanie's shoulder. "That was a nice save, young lady."

The two friends looked up to see the Speros' elderly next-neighbor standing on the edge of the arroyo that divided their backyards.

"Oh! Hi, Mr. Rinnas. I didn't see you," Lanie said, looking guilty.

"That quad probably would have gone clean through the living room—Lanie's cool thinking probably saved your skin," Mr. Rinnas said, smirking at Hudson.

"Yeah... must be the engineer in her genes," Hudson replied with a sheepish, crooked smile.

Turning toward his house, Mr. Rinnas added, "Don't worry, Lanie, I'm not gonna say anything to your pop. Just don't get yourselves hurt." He winked, then ambled away.

Hudson followed Lanie back up the meandering path through the jacaranda trees. In the second week of October, sunsets came earlier, and the orange glow was disappearing behind the mountains on the other side of the valley. Hudson had been carrying something under his arm earlier on the trail, and Lanie spotted it in the dirt next to his helmet.

"What did you pick up?" she asked, pointing.

Hudson rushed ahead, scooping it up. "Check it out, I got this from the old truck down by the mine." He offered Lanie a weathered glovebox door, with its rusty hinge still attached. "It's got a cool logo printed on it."

Lanie sat on the boulder near the mesquite tree, turning the panel over in her hand. The ornate three-color emblem on the face was the same image that the truck had stenciled on its bullet-perforated cab doors. "You'd be in trouble if your mom knew you were over the fence."

"Yeah, I know; I didn't go near the mine entry anyway," he replied.

"I didn't think anything was left inside the cab. It's a cool find," Lanie said, handing the piece back. "I'll bet that stranger was watching you when you were there."

"Well that's kinda creepy, thanks a lot," Hudson replied. "It's a half-mile hike from the trailhead to get out there; I don't know where he would've come from."

The County Park Service had sealed the mine entrance years earlier after local teenagers had broken through the original iron gates. One of the teens had been nearly killed in a fall, after which the residents complained to the Park Rangers. That story was common knowledge in Lanie's small neighborhood—and was the most believable of the many that circulated about the mine. Larry Rinnas had lived in the neighborhood longer than any other resident... and was a purveyor of all the tales.

Hudson wiped the dust from his glasses using a soiled finger and examined the faded logo on the piece. "A cactus fell on part of the fence," he said. "That old Chevy has other junk in it too—if you climb through the smashed fence you can get to the truck pretty quick."

Lanie was familiar with the old truck's location. She'd hiked into the canyon with her dad to check it out during the previous spring. Lanie's dad figured that the truck had been there since the mid-60's, when the foothills behind their yard were absorbed into the surrounding mountain preserve. Mr. Rinnas had told them several stories about suspicious activities at the mine back before the growth of the city forced its closure.

On the days that he came over to see what the Speroses were working on in their garage, Mr. Rinnas would tell random stories about the history of their neighborhood on Constellation Way. Mr. Speros wasn't sold on the fantastic yarns about the operations at the old mine, but he and Lanie both liked the stories about the neighborhood when it was new. Mr. Rinnas had lived in his house since 1965 and even knew the history of the Speroses' own home, which was built in 1959.

His more unbelievable stories were versions of a conspiracy theory about how the mine had been converted into a top-secret military site during the Cold War, complete with hidden missile silos. Whenever Mr. Rinnas finished a story, Lanie's dad would append his own warnings about staying away from the fenced compound. "There could be other unprotected shafts in the hills too," he would say. "You could fall into one, and nobody would ever find you."

At thirteen, Lanie wondered what age she'd have to be before her dad trusted her common sense. The mountains of Arizona were full of old mines and their ventilation shafts—she knew what to look out for. Lanie didn't know much about the Cold War, but in her mind's eye she imagined underground rooms with gray computers that filled a whole wall. They'd have buttons, flashing lights, and spinning reels of memory tape—like the spy movies she'd seen. The idea that any such rooms were under the hills behind her house sounded ridiculous. Her mind snapped back into the present when Hudson spoke up.

"That truck isn't as old as the mine—didn't you say it was a 1957?" Hudson asked.

"Yeah, I think it's a '56 or '57," Lanie said. "But the whole front end is missing... I can't tell for sure."

Despite his responsible demeanor, Hudson's imagination was wild. Adventurous speculation was one of his favorite pursuits. "If that old mine is from the 1920s, why would there be a truck from the '50s abandoned out front? 'Cause I thought the mine closed way before then. Maybe—*just maybe*—Mr. Rinnas is right about the military bunker," he said. A suspicious smile was growing on his face.

"Uh oh, here we go with your theories," Lanie said. "That truck probably was abandoned by the mining company with the other junk when they left the site, and nobody ever bothered to haul it away." There wasn't much left of the truck; only its body shell, doors, and a rotted wooden flat-bed remained.

"But still, if we had the right tools, I think it would be cool to go in there and see if there's any old mining equipment or lanterns," Hudson said, looking for a reaction from Lanie.

"I wanna know what's in there too, but I don't wanna get grounded, or eaten by a mountain lion," she said. "And anyway, we couldn't get past the rocks they piled in the entry."

Realizing he wasn't going to talk Lanie into a mine exploration adventure, Hudson gave up the topic. Lanie drew in a deep breath and let her mind and eyes wander. She spun around on the boulder, facing the neighborhood. Her dad wasn't home yet; the house was empty.

The home her dad picked on Constellation Way was larger than their old house in Tucson. Their new house had a mysterious and unique curb appeal, one that piqued Lanie's interest the first time she walked up the front door's staggered concrete path. When she and Isaiah had first seen the house, they weren't sure what to think. It was surrounded by natural Sonoran Desert landscaping, nearly hidden from the street. It's copper-sheathed roof had turned a sage green over the years, and the patina matched the canopy of mature mesquite and palo verde trees that surrounded it.

Seeming to have pushed itself up out of the rocky hillside, the house had broad, flat roofs with long wall segments made of jagged stone. It straddled a red rock formation on the hillside, and some of the giant boulders behind the dining room formed the back walls of the house. There were sheets of window glass that stretched from floor to ceiling, most of which met the walls at a right angle, so that the *outside* walls continued *inside* in some rooms. It didn't look like a home to Lanie at first; it reminded her of the structures she used to make by standing up playing cards on the floor in her bedroom.

From where she sat, Lanie could see the whole form of the house below. Its sections of roof looked like a circular series of fallen dominoes. From the front yard the building looked as though it sat flat on the desert floor. But from behind, half of the house stood on a series of sandstone ledges in the arroyo that separated their yard from the Rinnas'. The home's architecture was enigmatic and elusive, and Lanie loved every part of it.

The sun had disappeared, and the air was getting chilly. Lanie bumped Hudson with her elbow. "Let's go back to the house; my dad's gonna be home soon."

"I'm starvin'; maybe we can get a snack?" Hudson's appetite didn't align with his small stature; he was always eating or looking for food.

Lanie climbed into the Polaris and coasted down the hill to the stable without the engine. Hudson sat on the back, dangling his legs from the rear deck. The home's previous owners had kept horses in the stable, but the Speroses kept modern transportation parked inside. She inched the Polaris up to the nose of the dust-layered Citroën DS sedan that was awaiting restoration in the back of the stall. Inside the house, Lanie washed the dust off her hands in the kitchen's copper sink basin. She tossed the hand towel to Hudson.

"Dry off the countertop when you're done, or my dad will freak," Lanie reminded as she nudged her glasses up with the knuckle of her thumb.

"Yeah, got it, boss," Hudson responded.

There were just as many rules at Hudson's house, so Lanie didn't feel bad about nagging him. The kitchen was one of the most unique parts of the Speros home. The builder sourced the house's construction materials from the local desert, and the kitchen was no exception. The polished knotty surfaces of the mesquite countertops had been well preserved by the original owners, so Lanie's dad was very protective. The grooves and knotholes in the wood had been filled with a glittering resin, which made the wood glow like a distant galaxy in the evening sun rays through the skylight.

Hudson had disappeared behind the bar in the sunken living room and popped up with a can of soda from the mini fridge. The curved bar split the entryway from the living room and den, positioning it as the social hub of the home's interior. Made of teak paneling and pearlescent Formica, the bar reminded Lanie of old Las Vegas casinos she'd seen in photos. While the bar was the social center of the house, the home's most dominant and imposing feature was the massive fireplace.

Built with native rocks, the fireplace stretched from the white carpet on the floor to the beamed ceiling, extending up through the roof like the raked funnel of a cruise ship. The hearth started at the kitchen, extending through the den—then around the wall into the dining room. There was a wide firebox at the end of the structure, which was open on three sides so that the same fire warmed both the den and living room. Lanie had settled onto the cushioned hearth with two bags of chips. She held one up to Hudson, but he'd barely sat down when his watch buzzed, indicating he'd been called home by his mom. "Already?" Lanie asked, checking the clock over the kitchen table.

"Yeah, we're meeting my dad's business partner for dinner. I gotta pretend to be well-mannered for the next three hours."

"You gonna come to work on the quad tomorrow?" she inquired.

"Yeah. Gotta go. See ya, punk!" He shoved past Lanie, then grabbed his dusty glove box door and bolted out across the back patio. At the same time, the door to the garage slammed open (indicating that Isaiah was making his entrance).

"We're HO-OME!" her brother called as he burst into the room with his backpack dragging behind. "Hi, Lay-Lay!" he said and plopped his daycare rigging down near the bar. Isaiah was the only person Lanie allowed to shorten her name.

"Hi, buddy," she said, wrapping her arm around Isaiah's chest from behind. "How was your day?"

"It was OK. I used the potty four times," he said, holding up five fingers.

Mr. Speros appeared next, carrying his worn leather bag as well as a sack of groceries. He kissed Lanie's curled mop of hair, then hurried off to the restroom after the long drive.

In April that year, her dad had taken a new job managing a test engineering team at a car company's desert proving ground in the Phoenix area. Mr. Speros held a similar job at a commercial truck test track in Tucson, but he'd been laid off when the site was closed to make room for new housing developments. Even though Lanie had to leave her friends behind in Tucson, her dad's new job had effectively been a promotion, so Lanie embraced the change and was excited to move to a bigger house with a huge yard.

An added benefit to their move was that her dad managed test and development work on cars that wouldn't be in dealerships for three years or more, and she looked forward to seeing the camouflaged prototype vehicles he'd often drive home. The secretive test vehicles had their front and rear covered in black vinyl masks, to hide their futuristic styling.

Lanie knew she'd be asked to assist in dinner prep, so she started unloading the bag her dad brought home and preheated the oven. Mr. Speros was a great cook, but on busy nights, frozen meals like lasagna or salmon filets were all he could manage. Between her family's move and getting adjusted to a new school, Lanie had forgotten about their upcoming fall vacation. So she was excited when her dad brought the topic up around the dinner table that night.

The Speroses' vacations were most often road trips because the family liked to make stops along the way to see interesting places that were off the main highways. It was also their tradition to stop at auto salvage yards when the route permitted, and Lanie's favorite wrecking yard in Fresno, California, was on the itinerary for their upcoming trip.

Exploring rows of forlorn salvage cars was Lanie's own form of archaeology. When she was in third grade, she'd climb behind the wheel of her dad's '59 Nash Rambler where it sat in their backyard in Tucson. She'd wonder what the Rambler looked like when it was new and where it had gone during its younger years, with its original owners. Her dad had since finished the restoration of the two-tone gold Nash, just like he had with their '87 Jeep Wagoneer. Even though both were in showroom-new condition, she kept photo albums of what they used to look like—before they'd been rescued.

The third car in the Speros household was a Slate Green 1996 Cadillac Fleetwood that was driven by Lanie's mom. The Cadillac was their most modern vehicle, primarily used as the Sunday driver in the Speros fleet. The pristine Fleetwood hadn't been restored; it was the car that Mr. Speros had spent months searching for as a fortieth birthday surprise for his wife. Even though Mrs. Speros was gone, the car remained as part of the family.

None of these vehicles were the mode of transport for their upcoming trip though; the Speroses would be using the family's motorhome. They were traveling to camp in the Sequoia Forest, high in California's Sierra Nevada mountains. Lanie and Isaiah enjoyed the campfires and hikes in the woods as much as Mr. Speros, but Lanie looked forward to the trips more for the road journey and wayside stops. She was also excited because Hudson was going along on the trip.

Originally, she'd asked to invite both Hudson and his twin sister Helen. Once Lanie had described what the trip plans would be, however, Helen was less enthusiastic. The dusty, rusted vehicles that interested her brother and Lanie looked like common junk to Helen. Helen also didn't want to spend her long weekend eating gas station snacks and bunking in the Speroses' motorhome.

It had been tough to convince Hudson's parents that hanging out in a car junkyard was a good idea. Hudson had pleaded to go on his own, with little success. To put his parents at ease, Lanie had to talk Mr. Speros into visiting the Newmans to affirm that he knew the yard owner personally— and that the trip would be safe.

Hudson's dad, Wallace (never Wally) was an electrical engineer who ran his own design firm. Lanie thought he was unnecessarily strict with Hudson and Helen. The twins had an intense home schedule that included structured time for homework, chores, mealtimes, even free time. Hudson said this was what his dad preferred after his years of service with a construction battalion called the Seabees in the U.S. Navy. He'd worked on huge nuclear power plants and generating stations, and—just like those projects—most details of home life were planned and with purpose.

Hudson didn't seem to object to having his days scheduled, but he did complain to Lanie that his dad didn't understand his interests and hobbies. Mr. Newman wanted Hudson to "toughen up" and spend less time at his workbench and more time doing strenuous outdoor activities. For these reasons, Lanie was sure he'd be supportive of sending Hudson on the trip, and she could tell as much when they all met. But before offering his approval, Mr. Newman deferred to his wife.

If you asked Pauline—Hudson's mom—about any activities outside the home, she invariably would point out ways in which they could cause death or dismemberment. Mrs. Newman wasn't over-the-top protective, but Hudson was usually required to wrap himself in some sort of padding and head protection for any activity other than walking.

The two friends were both surprised, then, when Mrs. Newman was the first to offer her endorsement of the trip. She'd made Hudson promise to adhere to a list of specific safety rules, but at least the deal was done. Hudson and Lanie had been preparing for the trip for a couple weeks, and Hudson was excited to get out on the road to see what RVing was all about. He'd been tent camping with his own family, but Lanie laughed at the comparison, informing Hudson that he wouldn't have to work as hard—or get as dirty on their upcoming trip in the motorhome. Unaware of the perilous adventures that lay ahead, Lanie assured Hudson that RV travel was safe, comfortable, and relaxing.

## Chapter 2

# THE MYƒTERIOUƒ PIT

Lanie was a few weeks into her fall semester as an eighth grader at Superstition Canyon Junior High. The transition to a new school hadn't been as bad as she was expecting. Mr. Speros had been concerned that she would rebel—or become a discipline problem—at the new school without her old friends, but Lanie knew better. Making friends would be inevitable because school was really just a continuous social event that also happened to incorporate learning.

When the fall semester started, Lanie wasn't completely new to Superstition Canyon anyway—her dad had enrolled her in the summer school program. He worked long hours at his new job that summer; it was the busiest season for automotive testing in the desert. Since Isaiah was just starting preschool, Lanie would walk him home and supervise him after her summer sessions each day.

Those summer school sessions were where she'd met Hudson. They'd been tasked to work together on a wind turbine science project. Lanie's ability to think mechanically and create technical sketches meshed perfectly with Hudson's talent for tinkering and scratch building. That first day in class, Hudson caught Lanie sketching a car's multi-link suspension and asked to thumb through her notebook of mechanical drawings.

It took Lanie only a moment to realize that they were going to work well together, and their friendship had developed quickly. Lanie could visualize a concept in her mind and draw it, then Hudson would figure out how to build it. Hudson had an approachable appearance with honest, cheerful brown eyes that complemented his easygoing personality—and Lanie always felt comfortable being herself around him.

Hudson's sister, Helen, turned out to be just as cool. Lanie shared a love of adventure and suspense novels with Helen, and they swapped the books they read. Helen was also Lanie's fashion adviser and social director. Hudson's sister was popular at Superstition Canyon, with a wide circle of friends—most of whom Lanie didn't hang out with. Instead, Lanie spent most of her time with Hudson, as they were both uninterested in their social status at school. They were also both car geeks. Calling vehicles an "interest" was an offensive understatement to Lanie. She preferred "passion," or "lifestyle," and wasn't hesitant to justify her logic. Hudson, on the other hand, was not born into an automotive family—he had adopted a love of motor vehicles on his own.

The two friends also shared the need to wear glasses, but Lanie picked large red-rimmed frames that circled lower on her face so she didn't have to bend her neck to read. Her long hair tended to shroud one side of her face, and she liked the contrast of the red frames against her dark curls.

Hudson was more sensitive about his glasses and wore a thin, rimless type that always seemed to be bent. His fine sandy hair was never styled. Instead, it pointed straight down in every direction from the top of his scalp. It wasn't that Hudson was sloppy—in fact, quite the contrary. His clothing was always clean and well-coordinated, his hair always neatly trimmed above his ears and collar, and his workbench at home was as tidy and organized as a surgeon's worktable. One of Lanie's secret nerd pleasures was to shift items around on his desk when he wasn't looking, then watch to see how long it would take him to catch on.

By Thursday afternoon Lanie had taken her last mid-term test, and she exhaled in relief after she slipped out of her last class of the day. With mid-terms wrapping up, the students and faculty were already diverting attention to fall celebrations. Harvest and Halloween decorations were hung in the hallways and classrooms. The huge cottonwood trees all over campus were losing their leaves, coating the lawns between buildings with a crunchy yellow carpet. Adding to the seasonal excitement was the school's upcoming five-day weekend. It was a school policy at Superstition Canyon to close Friday through Tuesday the week before Halloween in order to allow for district conferences and parent—teacher meetings. On the way out of the courtyard after school, Hudson trotted to catch up to Lanie, who had already connected with Helen.

"Were you both gonna leave without me?" he asked, looking offended.

"You know where our house is, don't you?" Helen snipped.

"We waited, don't worry," Lanie added.

Helen kept walking and resumed the discussion she'd started before Hudson arrived. "I still can't believe my parents are going for this trip... My mom must really be comfortable with you guys. Bring some scissors, though, 'cause when you pick Hudson up, he may be coated in bubble wrap."

"Mom's getting better," Hudson said. "She's letting me ride the quad on my own now... That was a HUGE deal."

"You'd also better take some ear plugs for the road," Helen said to Lanie. "The boy here snores."

"At least I won't make everyone in the motorhome gag when I take my shoes off," Hudson shot back, crossing a sensitive border.

Helen's face turned red, and she glared at her brother. "Hey, jerk-wad, you know I can't help that!"

"C'mon, it's fine—I'd go on a trip with both of you." Lanie wedged herself between the twins. "You both sound like two old ladies when you pick on each other—just chill."

"I'm already packed," Hudson added.

Helen laughed. "Good thing your RV is huge. I think he packed every tool he owns."

"I told you, we've got tools in the motorhome," Lanie said, turning to Hudson. "I don't know why you think you'll need them."

"They're not tools; they're my survival equipment," Hudson clarified. "Good for camping trips."

"OK, whatever, we'll make room," Lanie said. "Just be ready to go at 6 a.m.; my dad will get nuts if we blow his departure schedule."

Lanie split from the twins as she passed their house and waved good-bye. Up the street, she found her dad was home early, assembling trip items in the three-car garage. He was packing spare quarts of motor oil and other fluids for the motorhome while Mr. Rinnas chewed his ear.

"… so I said, '*keep* your brake fluid flush; I know when I'm being hustled!'" He was complaining to Lanie's dad about his most recent visit to the Lincoln dealership.

Mr. Rinnas's own red '94 Chrysler Concorde was in fair shape—Lanie helped him maintain it. But Rose Rinnas's 1978 Lincoln Town Car was his wife's pride and joy, and they took it to the dealership to be serviced religiously, even though it had very few miles on it. Still, Lanie respected their fastidious care of the baby blue land yacht. That afternoon, Mr. Rinnas's brown toupee was more at odds with his natural grayed sideburns than usual. *He must have forgotten to keep up with his hair coloring routine*, Lanie thought as she choked back a smile.

"Well, hello there, little lady!" Mr. Rinnas boomed either because he was hard of hearing or he thought Lanie was.

"Hi, Mr. Rinnas, how are you?"

"Oh, I'm dandy. Just chewin' your old man's ear about my trip to the service center today. You'd think those youngsters at the dealership would have more respect for a classic—" he cut himself off, remembering he'd already complained to Lanie on the topic. "Anyway, I hear you're all heading out of town. Don't worry, Rose and I will keep an eye on the place while you're gone. OH! I almost forgot; I have something for you!"

Lanie extended her neck to see what their neighbor was pulling from his pocket. He extracted a small silvery plastic bag and pressed it into Lanie's hand. She turned it over and found it was the circuit board for her 1980s vintage radio—controlled Ford Bronco. Mr. Rinnas was semi-retired from Motorola and had years of experience in repairing printed circuits. Even when his hands were too unsteady for a soldering job, he always had a work acquaintance who could fill in.

"Oh wow! Thanks, Mr. Rinnas!" Lanie unwrapped the piece then rummaged for the old joy-sticked controller on the workbench. She'd bought the Bronco on eBay and was getting it fixed up to flip for a profit... it was one of the ways she boosted her allowance.

"Another historic toy saved from the recycling bin," Mr. Speros mused. "Thanks for keeping my garage cluttered with Lanie's junk store finds," he said to his neighbor.

Mr. Rinnas slapped him on the back and smiled, then patted Lanie's shoulder. "Just happy to be useful," he said to them. "When you're my age, feeling useful is more important than you might think."

He waved, then headed out of the garage. Lanie watched as he disappeared into the landscaped trail between their houses.

"I'm surprised he's still working at all," Mr. Speros said, once he was sure Mr. Rinnas was out of earshot. "He's almost eighty; It's impressive that he's able to keep up with all the younger folks and new technology at Motorola." The same thing had occurred to Lanie.

Before dinner, Lanie's dad was busy loading food and supplies into the RV. Their motorhome—like their cars—was old: a 1995 model that was big and boxy, with a huge windshield and contoured cladding around its lower sides.

21

"Old and well maintained can be as good as new," Lanie's dad often said whenever anyone asked why he didn't drive new cars. But their motorhome wasn't simply old and well maintained; Lanie and Isaiah thought it had more style than newer RVs. It was white and long (forty feet), with a metallic ocean-blue wave that ran along the sides. On the nose below the windshield were wide letters that spelled "COUNTRY COACH," and lettering above each front wheel said "MAGNA." Unlike newer motorhomes, which tended to be very serious with black, taupe, and gray color schemes, Lanie thought their RV was much more cheerful. Its big semi-truck wheels were made of polished aluminum. Keeping up the Alcoa wheels' luster was a laborious chore that Mr. Speros paid Lanie to perform.

That evening, her dad had started the motorhome to check its engine, air suspension, brakes, and other systems, since it had been sitting through the summer. The Cummins diesel engine at the rear burbled its low, sleepy cadence while Mr. Speros walked around the coach. His routine would take most of the evening, so Lanie pressed on with her own preparations in the house. Most of her work involved moving the tubs of clothes and supplies to the patio so her dad could load them more easily. Isaiah's role was to gather his toys and stay out of the way, as well as pack up Buster, his blue betta fish. Betta fish are loners, and Buster was as happy swimming in his little tank at home as he was on the road. He traveled in a little plastic aquarium with blue gravel and a fake plant.

"Lanie and Isaiah!" Mr. Speros yelled from the doorway of the motorhome. The two siblings converged at the corner of the house. "Lanie, spot for me while I back this thing up. Isaiah! Get me the phone charging cords out of the Rambler."

Isaiah tossed down a pouch of fish flakes and shuffled toward the garage.

"Alright, stay back, I'm moving the coach," Mr. Speros said. While Isaiah was retrieving his assigned items, Lanie's dad backed the motorhome away from its spot on the side of the house. He was positioning the tail of the vehicle closer to the patio to speed loading. Lanie stood behind at a safe distance, waving him back.

Just as the left rear dual wheels approached the patio, Isaiah ran out of the sliding door. "Stop, Isaiah!" Lanie cried, dropping her basket of sheets. She grabbed his arm before he ran into the motorhome's path. Just as Lanie yelled, her dad spotted Isaiah in the side view mirror and stomped the brake pedal. The air brakes yelped and hissed, and the RV lurched to a stop. Before her dad appeared in the doorway, she knew that she and Isaiah would both get yelled at.

"Are you two kidding me! How many times have I told you to watch what's going on when I'm moving the motorhome! You *know* I can't see you well! And Lanie!" he turned a finger to her, "You know your job as spotter is to watch for Isaiah!"

"I know, Dad, sorry, *GEEZ!*" she moaned. She'd obviously spotted Isaiah as her job required but knew it was best not to argue.

Isaiah drooped his head like a scolded dog and handed over the items he'd retrieved. Lanie shot him a disapproving glance for having gotten her into trouble, then scrambled his hair with her fingers. As she reached down to pick up a plastic tub of canned food, she felt and heard a loud pop that sounded like two logs being smacked together. The sound came from the earth below. Isaiah heard it too, and the pair stood looking at each other for a moment.

Lanie shrugged, then picked up the tub. Before she could lift the tub up the motorhome's steps, she heard a second, smaller pop, followed by the sound of shuffling gravel. She felt the ground shift under her feet and became scared because the motorhome seemed to be moving.

"Dad! DAD!" Lanie yelled, stepping away from the RV.

Isaiah wasn't sure what to make of the situation and ran farther into the yard. When her dad reached the doorway, the motorhome began to tilt to its left side as the popping sounds and crunching gravel got louder. Mr. Speros jumped off the top step and into the yard next to Lanie, but by this time the noises had stopped. The motorhome had settled but was leaning toward the house. They both ran behind the RV to the patio and found the left rear dual wheels were hanging in a hole that wasn't there before.

"What in the *world*...," muttered Lanie's dad as he squeezed his forehead. Lanie wasn't sure what to think, but her dad was calm—and that was reassuring. He held his arm up to block her as she tried to walk toward the wheel. "Wait... I don't know if it will sink more—stay back."

Isaiah emerged from between the jacaranda trees near his sandbox and reported, "Dad, you backed the motorhome into a hole."

—

"I don't know, a sinkhole, I suppose?" Lanie heard her dad say as he talked on his cell phone. He was pacing around behind the motorhome. "Well, either way I can't drive it out—it needs to be lifted." He was on the phone with a towing service. Briefly covering the bottom of his phone, he instructed Lanie to heat up leftovers for herself and Isaiah. "We might not be leaving in the morning," he said. "We have to figure this out first. Maybe we can get on the road in a day or two."

The disappointment hadn't sunk in yet as Lanie trudged into the house to call Hudson. "Oh man, REALLY?!" he yelled into the phone as Lanie held it away from her ear.

"Yeah, I know, we don't know what's going on yet. Dad says maybe we can still leave tomorrow if we can get the motorhome out and make sure there are no other issues with the yard."

"OK, well, I wanna know what's down in the hole—call me back tonight, even if it's late," he directed.

"Yeah, OK. Bye," she replied, then hung up. She turned and found Isaiah sitting at the breakfast bar. He was being unusually quiet and patient.

"Are you hungry, buddy? I'll heat up some food. What sounds good?"

"Chickanuggits," he responded without delay.

Chicken nuggets was Isaiah's one-word menu request that was usually at the top of his list. He wasn't picky; nuggets could come from the freezer, a fast food drive-through, or even a convenience store food warmer. They didn't even necessarily need to be made of chicken, as Mr. Speros had once accidentally bought tofu nuggets... and Isaiah didn't seem to notice the difference.

"We don't have any nuggets," Lanie said, then turned to rummage in the refrigerator. She microwaved a leftover chicken breast and baked beans for Isaiah, but she didn't feel like eating. Instead, she stood by the kitchen window and watched her dad probing at the dirt around the corner of the motorhome. The stacked granite stones holding up the patio roof obscured her view of the hole, but she could tell that the underside of the coach was sitting on the surrounding landscape. *Weird.* That was the only word Lanie could think of. *Maybe the previous owner's dead dog, entombed in a crate? Nah, hole's too big.* She smirked as the image of a crusty buried armored van full of money crossed her mind. *Yeah, right.*

When Lanie returned to the patio, she heard the *beep-beep* of a truck backing up the drive beside their house. A large, semi-like tow truck was creeping through the gates in the fence. It had three axles in the back, and a long, crane-like boom. There were two men in orange vests—one stood at the back of the motorhome and the other was directing the tow truck driver.

"It's a good thing you've got a couple acres back here," said one of the men to her father. "Otherwise we'd have had a heck of a time getting the wrecker in the right spot."

The second workman, a scruffy round-faced man with a big belly said, "Is there anything under the yard or the patio? Like a basement?"

Her dad shook his head. "Not that I'm aware of."

Grunting as he dropped to one knee, the round-faced man stretched thick yellow straps around the tires that had fallen into the hole. The night air had cooled, and Lanie hugged Isaiah from behind for warmth as they watched the men rig the straps and chains. Slowly the boom lifted the corner of the motorhome out of the hole, and the men slid sections of square wood under the rear wheels so it could be driven out of the area. Lanie's dad crept the motorhome forward while leaning through the window, and everyone rushed forward as the hole was exposed.

"It's a cave!" exclaimed Isaiah as he pointed down into the darkness of the hole.

"I don't think so, son," said the driver of the tow truck. "It looks like a room or a pit, I see a wall."

By then, Mr. Speros had parked the motorhome out of the way. He, too, stood looking into the hole. Sensing a new presence over her shoulder, Lanie looked up to see Mr. Rinnas. She jumped in surprise, as she hadn't heard him come up behind her. He didn't say anything, which was uncharacteristic. But he did pat her on the back as he leaned over, trying to get a look into the hole.

The sun had set, and flashlights were shone down into the hole, which was about four feet in diameter. The truck driver was right—in the flashlight beams, the group could see vertical stone walls. The earth around the hole was sloped as though a slab underneath had partially collapsed into the pit. A musty smell was flowing up around them in a draft of frigid air. Realizing that there was growing curiosity from the crew, Mr. Speros thanked the group of men and started ushering them toward the front yard to settle the bill.

"You two," Mr. Speros pointed at Lanie and her brother, "inside, please. Do not come out here until I come back. We don't know what's going on here yet... the ground could be unstable." Turning to Mr. Rinnas, he said, "I'm sorry, Larry, I'll have to fill you in a little later."

"No problem... I see you have your hands full; I'll pop back over another time." Mr. Rinnas vanished into the dark toward the rocky basin that divided their yards. Lanie resented being classified with the same risk as a four-year-old, but she went inside with Isaiah anyway. As she stood in the den looking toward the living room, it occurred to her that the stone she had seen on the wall in the pit looked just like the blackish-red stones of the walls in the house. She tilted her head in curiosity. A few moments later her dad came in, wiping dust from his hands.

Before he could speak, Lanie flagged him from where she stood near the bar and slapped the stacked stones in the wall. "Dad, look!"

Mr. Speros's face was blank for a moment, then his eyebrows arched. "Oh, wow, you're right—look at that!"

She studied her dad's face for clues as he scanned the stonework in the den, trying to interpret his expression. Mr. Speros was in his mid-forties, and there were already streaks of gray showing in his wavy black hair. He was fit but not the type of person to check his appearance in the mirror, though Lanie's friends told her he was handsome. Her dad's face was articulate and expressive; it was an efficiency feature—enabling his engineering mind to use fewer words to make its points. As a result, her dad also couldn't hide his moods or thoughts. If he was concerned, his eyebrows would turn up at their outside edges, and she'd see his jaw muscles tighten.

Without saying anything, Mr. Speros stepped down into the den and walked over to the monolithic fireplace. He followed the stonework around the living room and into the dining room. The hearth was over twenty feet long and most of it had upholstered cushions, except for right in front of the firebox. On the dining room side of the fireplace was a long ledge full of houseplants instead of a hearth, which stretched to the back side of the kitchen.

"Whatcha looking for?" she asked.

"Probably nothing," her dad replied. "Just curious what relation all of this rockwork is to the pit in the yard." After a few moments of consideration, he said, "Ahhh... whatever," and waved his hand at the mantle. "I need to cover up that hole so nobody falls in. We'll figure out what to do with it later."

In the backyard, Mr. Speros had set up a work light on a yellow stand. Against the black backdrop of the yard, Lanie watched him drag a couple old sheets of plywood over the hole. He moved the patio chairs into a circle around the plywood, then stretched yellow caution ribbon around the chair backs. While her dad washed his hands at the kitchen sink, Lanie sat at the breakfast bar and stared, waiting for details.

"That's a fancy setup you arranged out there," she said. "OSHA would approve."

Mr. Speros squinted his eyes at Lanie as he dried his hands. "Just like your mom, an unemployed comedian," he said, masking a grin. "My guess is that there's an old septic pit or drainage basin under that part of the yard. I don't think it's a cellar or anything like that. Mr. Rinnas said that some of the residents who built these custom homes sixty-five years ago put in bomb shelters that they could hide in if there was a war." Her dad looked skeptical. "But I doubt that's what it is. The hole isn't big enough to see much, though, and it's unstable. I'll need a long ladder to check it out safely. Like I said, you two are to be nowhere near it, understand?" He turned to the den. "You hear that, Isaiah?"

"Yah, Dada," muttered Isaiah, without turning from the TV screen.

Lanie also nodded but asked, "Will we be able to open it up and go down there?"

"I don't know. We'll probably have to rent a tractor and fill it in. I'll check with the city after our trip to see if there are any drawings or permits for anything buried in the yard."

"Oh, we're still going tomorrow?!" Lanie sat straight up and didn't hide her smile.

"Yeah, we'll go. That pit has been there many years. It's not going anywhere. I'd rather take our vacation and deal with it later."

"We're still going!" she said into the phone a few minutes later.

"Awesome. OK, I'll be ready at oh-six-hundred," Hudson said. "What's down there?"

"I dunno, but I think it's a room—the walls are rock, just like the ones inside our house. My Dad is playing it down like it's an old septic pit or something, but I'll bet it's a room."

"Weird," Hudson said on the other end. "OK, well, I wanna check it out with you when we get home. See ya in the morning."

"Later," Lanie said.

By then it was after nine o'clock and Lanie rushed through her shower routine. Wrapped in her flannel pajamas, she sat down at the old built-in desk in her bedroom's reading niche. Lanie had already stowed her schoolbooks and cleared her desk but remembered that she'd forgotten to pack her pocket journal. At the back of her desktop, a small cubby with a sliding teak door was built into the stone wall. About the size of a breadbox, the curious cubby was lined in scuffed stainless steel. Lanie used the little compartment to store her stapler, calculator, and other routine items. She pulled her journal from under her calculator and jammed it into her over-loaded duffel bag. The cubby's sliding wooden door was spring-loaded, and it slipped itself closed when Lanie turned from her desk.

Once Isaiah had been tucked in, Lanie's dad came in to say good-night. "Bright and early tomorrow, before dawn we're on the road," he reminded her.

"I know, I'm ready," she replied, displaying her biggest cheesy smile.

"I know that smile," he said, sitting down on Lanie's hope chest. "You stole that from your mom. I usually saw that smile only when she was hiding a surprise, or about to ask me to do something." This was not a news flash to Lanie, and she used her smile as a tool just like her mom did. Her long lashes, dimples, and toothy smile also came from her mom. She liked to think that her mom's mixed Greek and Portuguese looks paired well with the thin, sloping Greek nose she got from her dad.

"Dad, do you think this house is hiding secrets?" she asked.

"All houses have secrets."

"Yeah, I know that, but you know what I mean..."

"Yes, I know what you mean." Mr. Speros paused, choosing his words. Then he glanced at the stone reading alcove in the corner of Lanie's room. "Yes, from an architectural perspective, I think this house is holding *many* secrets. I knew it the day we drove up in front of it for the first time."

Lanie was surprised by this casual revelation, but she didn't get a chance to ask what he meant. Just then a low reverberating howl began to fill the hallway outside her bedroom. She and her dad both turned to look. Within a few seconds, the sound had abated—as it always did.

"What the heck is making that sound, Dad? It's creepy."

"I don't know... I already checked the furnace and the window seals," Mr. Speros said with a look of resignation. "Maybe a draft across the top of the chimney." He stared blankly into the hallway for a moment, then refocused on Lanie. "OK, goodnight, kiddo. Hopefully that pit in the yard is the last of our trip surprises," he said, kissing her forehead. "Get to sleep."

"Night, Dad."

## Chapter 3

# ROAD TRIP

Consistent with family road trip tradition, Mr. Speros banged on bedroom doorways at 5:15 a.m., calling, "Up, up, let's go!"

Outside, the small orange lights around the roof of the motorhome were lit against the navy-blue dawn skyline. The idling engine sounded like drumming fingers, impatient to depart. Yawning as she stepped through the back door, Lanie pushed her glasses up with her knuckle and hitched the strap of her bag over her shoulder. The coach door swung open as she approached, and the stairs below the door lowered.

"Good morning!" her dad's voice boomed as he reached down from the doorway to grab her bag. Her dad tended to be slightly obnoxious in the mornings after he'd had his coffee. Lanie wasn't an early riser, so her best response was a grunt as she plopped into the passenger seat up front. Isaiah was chattering to himself as he stomped up the steps carrying Buster's small, trapezoidal aquarium. He placed it in the kitchen sink, then settled into the chair at the reading table behind the passenger seat.

With the house and yard gate locked up, Mr. Speros let the coach crawl off the gravel and onto the empty road. Before they got to the traffic light at the entry to their hillside neighborhood, they stopped at the Newman residence. Lanie saw the reflection of Hudson's glasses in the wide living room window as they pulled up. In a flash he emerged through the doorway, trotting down the terraced steps to the street. In her gray robe, Hudson's mom trailed behind him. She stuck her head in to issue final instructions and warnings as Hudson boarded.

"Remember what I told you about helping out—and manners," she said. Her brunette hair was still damp from her early shower.

"Yeah, Ma, I'm all over it."

"Call me if there are any issues," she told Mr. Speros. "We'll keep our phones on through the night."

Mr. Speros gave Hudson's mom the thumbs-up and they all set off. When the rising sun crested the mountains to the east, they had reached Black Canyon City, Arizona, and stopped to top off the motorhome with fuel. By nine o'clock they were floating along the open highway north of a city called Prescott. After some haggling, Lanie agreed to let Hudson split her copilot duties by sharing the front seat in shifts. Up front, she felt like she was on the bridge of a ship—the huge windshield provided a captain's view of the highway. Reading was easier at the small table against the window though, where there was less glare from the sun, so Lanie didn't mind swapping seats. Making way for Hudson to slide past, Lanie pulled her book from the overhead cabinet and sat at the reading table with Isaiah.

The interior decor of the Magna was dated, and Lanie loved it. Her mom used to watch reruns of 1980s shows like *Designing Women, Falcon Crest,* and *Golden Girls,* and the Magna's interior had been conceived during the same generation. Muted floral patterns of mauve, teal, and sage green were set against honey-colored oak cabinetry trimmed with polished brass hardware. There were beveled mirror panels on some walls and floral-print wallpaper on others. The coach was a time capsule—one that happened to be mobile, with comfortable velour seating. More importantly, though, the Magna reminded Lanie of a time when her family was still complete.

"OK, keep your eye out for old cars in barns and tucked behind fences," Lanie advised her guest. "When we get closer to Ash Fork, there will be more classics." Since this was Hudson's first legitimate road trip, he was still adjusting to the novelty of seeing the small towns and isolated homesteads pass outside the windows. By then, the expansive, open desert north of Phoenix had transitioned to the scrubby oak and juniper trees of northern Arizona. It was a landscape that Lanie thought was unique to the Southwest: a low, gnarly forest that had agreed to meet the desert's environmental demands. Near lunch time, Mr. Speros exited Interstate 40 and began slowing for a turn. Lanie had since moved to the sofa behind the driver's seat and looked up from her book to see a green sign pass the windows outside.

"Sweet, we're stopping in Seligman!" she called out to Hudson, slamming her book. She'd told him about her favorite wayside stop at school the week before. Hudson started tying his shoelaces as he looked at the town growing from the tall brush ahead.

Once an important stop on US Route 66, Seligman had shrunk to become a stalwart historical town only a few miles off the more modern I-40. But for Lanie, it was a living museum. More than just vintage cars and gas stations, Seligman had the personality of American motoring's historic origins. It still had its old motels, where the gleaming chrome on travelers' cars was visible just outside their room window at night. Diners, bars, and shops all were within walking distance, lit by garish neon signs. There were burger cafes with old dollar bills and photos stapled to their walls, and (best of all) little souvenir shops.

Lanie didn't have much interest in the touristy stuff that the European visitors bought; she would push to the back of shelves and go into corners of the shops where the dusty local items lay. Old Tonka trucks, scratched Matchbox cars, hubcaps, license plates, and fender emblems from cars that were long deceased—these were the treasures Lanie sought. Mr. Speros enjoyed looking at the old automobilia as much as Lanie, but more important to him was the opportunity to get a decent cup of coffee. Not yet showing the symptoms of automotive fever at age four, Isaiah didn't care about Seligman's history. But he still had fun looking at the gag gifts and homemade candy that each of the shops seemed to have.

The group parked on a side street in the shade of a dilapidated white brick building and prepped for a quick lunch. Lanie and Hudson assembled sandwiches for the group while Mr. Speros checked the RV's tires and other vitals. He also used the opportunity to call Sabine, his new girlfriend. She was the first—and only—girlfriend that he'd had since Lanie's mom passed away.

At first, Lanie had been upset and apprehensive that her dad was dating. But after Mr. Speros had been out on a couple dates, Lanie realized she'd been a little selfish. He was too young to be single the rest of his life, and Lanie truly did want her dad to be happy. She watched him through the kitchen window as he checked tire pressures. He was smiling as he held the phone to his ear, and that was comforting to Lanie. Though it had been three years since her mom died, Lanie remembered how listless and distant her dad had been during the first months after the funeral. For a long time his personality—and even his appearance—seemed colored with a cloudy gray. But Mr. Speros's vibrance and positivity had bounced back lately, and Lanie knew that Sabine was part of the reason why.

Eager to explore, Hudson and Lanie hustled through lunch then disembarked onto the crumbling sidewalk. For Hudson—whose parents preferred to fly anywhere over 200 miles—the road trip experience was delightfully foreign. He and Lanie shielded their eyes from the glare of the high sun, surveying the landscape. "I love this town," Lanie said. "C'mon, let's look around."

While Mr. Speros was situating some luggage that had shifted in one of the Magna's storage bays, Lanie walked around the side of one of the shops and into knee-high brown grass. Hudson stood along Route 66, observing the quiet building facades and weedy, picket-fenced yards. After a few moments of poking around, Lanie scored and called out to Hudson.

"Hudson, come back here, look!"

Shuffling his way through the dry brush, Hudson found Lanie crouched over something in the dirt behind a sagging garage. She straightened up as he approached, and her exaggerated smile gave away that she'd found something she liked. Hudson looked down at a large, rusty iron casting lying on oil-stained earth.

"It's an old engine... so what? They're all over," he said as he panned the area.

"Not just an *engine*," she said. "It's a big Cadillac V12, probably from a 1930s touring car." Satisfied with her find, Lanie continued to probe the engine, trying to tilt it to get a better look.

"You're getting your hands covered in old nasty grease," Hudson noted.

"You should try it; it's not gonna hurt you," she grunted. "Help me pull it over—I wanna see if it has both valve covers."

Their discussion was interrupted by a group of orange BNSF freight locomotives which thundered past only yards from where they stood. The train's rumbling consist of tank cars brought a flurry of turbulent dust and litter. After a long minute, the last railcar disappeared—then their surroundings were silent again. Hudson had reluctantly crouched over the engine and grabbed a corner when they both were startled by Mr. Speros.

"Hey! You two better not be flipping over old junk under the hot sun—that's a great way to meet a rattlesnake," he said.

"I just wanted to get a better look," Lanie said, standing up straight. "Check out what we found!"

"Well, that is something," her dad remarked, stooping over the lump of iron. "If the rest of the car were with it, I'd be a little more excited. C'mon, let's go, you two," he said and turned back toward the street. Lanie reluctantly abandoned her discovery and followed the group.

35

Up the block in a clapboard building which had only trace remains of paint, there was a gift shop that doubled as a coffee bar. The shop didn't stock much except Route 66 mugs and keychains, so Lanie stayed on the front porch while her dad waited for his usual iced Americano. The porch roof leaned as though it were about to collapse, but it had been like that every time Lanie had seen it.

The yard between Route 66 and the porch was full of various old car hoods and doors arranged to be inviting to visitors looking for a photo opportunity. Mixed in with the junk was a lone ash tree, around whose trunk was an iron bench—the only shaded space besides the porch. Hudson and Isaiah sat on the old bench scooping the shaved ice they'd gotten in the coffee shop. Lanie sat on a defunct soda cooler on the porch and let her legs swing.

Only the breeze through the twisted ash tree could be heard, along with the occasional buzz of desert insects. Lanie flopped her tangled mane over her left ear and used her fingers to comb out some leaves that had blown in when the train passed. The silence of Seligman was contrasted by the stage-like wash of desert sunlight, which seemed to radiate from every-where—even the pavement. *No actors on this stage*, Lanie thought. But it did have an elaborate set decoration of faded sign panels and long-neglected shop fronts.

A spotless black Tesla Model S had been parked just up the block and began coasting away. Its darkly tinted windows made its occupants anonymous. It took Lanie a few moments to realize how out of place the car looked. There were no electric vehicle charging stations in Seligman, and even long-range EVs like the Model S were still relatively uncommon in remote towns.

Across the road a white tour bus pulled to a stop at the curb, and a stream of people started emerging from the coach's front door like bees leaving a hive. Many had large floppy hats while others wore oversize sun-glasses. Hudson had joined Lanie on the porch and they both watched as the sun-shocked tourists broke up into wayward groups to shop and take photos. The screen door of the coffee shop slammed next, and Lanie turned to see her dad standing with his coffee, adjusting his sunglasses. He was looking at the disorganized groups across the street as well.

"Ready?" he asked Lanie. She slid off the cooler and walked to the street. With Isaiah straggling behind, they all headed toward the motorhome.

Half a block down, Lanie passed an antique shop's canopy-shaded display window and something within caught her eye. She put her hands and face up to the glass to avert the sun's glare. On a shelf behind the window display of old train hardware was a little metal box about the size of a toaster. The box was coated in dull silver paint, and its corners were chipped and rusty. There was a chrome handle on top, and its lid was pitched like a small toolbox. Above the lid's chrome latch, a combination lock was built in.

What had drawn her attention, however, was the logo on the front—she recognized it right away. It was the same logo as those on either door of the abandoned truck in the canyon behind her house. A stylized calligraphic "M" intertwined with an "E" and Greek character Omega. Lanie's ears felt hot and an anxious, urgent feeling washed over her. The coincidence was too outlandish.

As her dad passed by, Lanie grabbed his shirt sleeve. "Look!" Everyone stopped to peer in.

"What am I looking at?" Mr. Speros asked.

"Look there! That box with the logo on it—it's the same as the truck near the mine," she said, sounding surprised that he didn't recognize it.

"I suppose," he said. "I never really paid any attention; that truck has been pretty much stripped bare."

"Oh man, she's right, that's the logo!" Hudson said, "Sharp eye, good catch!"

"I wanna go in and look," Lanie said.

"OK, go ahead," Mr. Speros said. "Just meet us back at the motorhome in fifteen minutes; we need to get back on the road." He and Isaiah kept on walking. Lanie's and Hudson's eyes locked. She recognized the crooked look of intrigue on his face, though most people would have assumed he was trying to pass gas.

"C'mon, let's see what's in it," she said, grabbing Hudson's wrist.

Lanie had to yank hard on the old Dutch door of the shop, dislodging paint flakes as she flung it wide for Hudson to follow. The rooms were dusty and cobwebbed and the air was stifling. On the right, as she entered, Lanie found a grim-faced, heavyset old woman sitting behind a long glass case. Her bun of frizzy hair was as unkempt as the shop around her. She stared at the two young friends with a look that was mostly disdain, the rest boredom.

Since a greeting seemed superfluous, Lanie just got to the point. "Can I take a look in that other room?" she asked, pointing to the windowed portion of the storefront. The woman waved her on without a word. The three of them were the only people in the shop, though Lanie's nose told her that unseen rodents lived there as well.

The mismatched shelving was packed. Most of the items seemed to be related to either railroad or mining history. Feeling confident in his junk store shopping skills, Hudson asked in his most adult voice, "How much for this old Adlake lantern?" The railroad lantern puffed a cloud of soot as he tipped it.

"Seventeen bucks," the shopkeeper said.

"With a missing glass lens?" Hudson asked, feeling cheeky.

"Sixteen fifty," she countered, maintaining her unimpressed expression. Hudson's eyebrows flattened out when he realized further negotiation would be fruitless, and he dug into his pocket. As he peeled some worn bills out of his wallet, a small crash and clang sounded from the room next door.

"What's goin' on in there?!" the shopkeeper yelled, without taking her eyes off Hudson. Lanie emerged from the back room with the box and a small broken oil lamp. She set both on the counter next to Hudson's lantern and flashed a timid smile at the shopkeeper. The woman glanced at the oil lamp with a raised eyebrow.

"You broke it, you bought it—ten dollars," she said.

"The price tag on it says seven dollars," complained Lanie.

Looking disgusted, the shopkeeper whipped open a used paper bag for her to put the sad oil lamp into. "Fifteen for the lockbox," said the woman as Lanie pushed it toward the register.

"Do you know how to open it, or know what's in it?" Lanie asked.

"Nope. See Bud." Before Lanie could ask who "Bud" was, the shopkeeper yelled the name loud enough to startle pedestrians who were passing outside.

An elderly man in a denim jumpsuit and weathered long-sleeve shirt emerged from a room at the back of the shop. As he approached, his wiry gray hair was blown from one side to the other by a floor fan. He chewed on his gums with his lips pinched shut, but his eyes were kind.

"What's in the box, she wants to know!" the crabby woman yelled into the side of Bud's face.

Happy to provide a history lesson, Bud hooked his arm behind him, gesturing for Lanie to follow. He led her to the corner at the back of the store. On the wall next to a battered china hutch was a faded aerial photograph of a large, open-pit mine. Overlaid on the photo were diagrams of roads, tunnels, and equipment areas.

"Myriad Exploration Group," Bud sputtered through loose dentures, "was a big mining and geological outfit that had sites all over the southwest before the war." Thumping the photograph, he said, "This is the Hualapai strip mine site, about twelve miles from here, on the reservation—up toward Grand Canyon." Bud smelled of chewing tobacco and moth balls.

While Hudson examined the photograph, Bud lifted the lockbox from Lanie's hand and shook it.

"Never did find out what was in here. I got it in a big lot of junk that I bought at auction when they closed the Hualapai site back in the early sixties. I was a laborer there for years before the site closed." Handing it back to Lanie, he said, "I didn't wanna break it trying to open it. Probably just notes from a mine executive's desk, or financial records, or some such paperwork."

Lanie stared down at the box, questioning her purchase.

Seeing Lanie's expression, Bud added, "There wouldn't be any cash or anything valuable in there, young lady. Otherwise they wouldn't have left it lying in a crate of other office surplus."

Lanie explained that there was an abandoned mine near her house outside of Phoenix that was owned by the same company. She was trying not to look too deflated, but Bud caught on anyway.

"You're talking about McDowell Mountain," he said. "It was most active in the early twenties, when Fountain Hills was only a settlement. The Hualapai and Fort McDowell mine sites were managed from the same corporate office in Prescott." Bud scratched his back and one of his cuff buttons dropped to the floor. "The site by your house closed earlier than Hualapai. I have plenty of stuff from the Hualapai mine—look around the shop more if you want... probably not much from McDowell though."

He ambled over to a dairy crate on the floor, slowly crouched, and began tossing items out. An old stapler, a haggard desk clock with no hands, and a fountain pen well. At last he produced a thick metal plate and handed it to Lanie. It was heavy, with dirty green felt covering the bottom. Turning it over, she found that it was an elaborate desk plaque or paper-weight. There was an engraved picture of three mountain peaks before a rising sun. At the base of the peaks was a mine headframe and entry. Below the engraving was text in block letters:

## MYRIAD FORT MCDOWELL – 1950

Lanie recognized the peaks right away as those on the horizon behind her house. "Wow, that's cool!" she exclaimed, turning it over in her soiled hands.

"You can have it," Bud said with a wink. "Eunice already stiffed you fifteen bucks for the box." He turned back to the faded wall photo. "When Myriad went belly-up in 1961, it was a big surprise to all of us," he said, staring into the distance. "With all the copper in the ground here, we couldn't believe that they were closing up shop. Most figured that something happened at one of the sites that got the executives in trouble with the Gov." Lanie assumed he meant the federal government.

"Either way, they had to close up, and all of us scattered to the wind. It was very hush-hush. Even the management at our site wasn't given any details... just told us to clean out our lockers, then they locked the gates. Months later there was an auction for some of what was left at the mine, but by then there had been hundreds of trucks in and out, hauling things away. They were doing construction too, but we never did find out what was happening. They just sealed the place up." Bud turned and shuffled off, and Lanie thanked him as he retreated. He waved his hand without turning back.

Lanie stepped out into the sun carrying her two questionable purchases and her free paperweight. She felt silly, having spent so much of her trip savings on random junk. But she also felt like she needed to do it. Hudson smiled at her as they walked; her expression was probably easy to read.

"I can help you put the oil lamp back together. It's a cool one from an old private rail car," he said. "At least you'll have something useful for your twenty bucks then," he snickered.

"Twenty-*TWO*," she replied. Lanie wrinkled her lips in disappointment.

When they climbed back into the motorhome, they found Isaiah napping.

"You spent your hard-earned allowance on that thing?" her dad asked. "Usually you come back with stuff like car parts, or old leather-bound books. I hope it didn't cost you much."

Lanie didn't have a good explanation, so she just washed up and slumped into her seat as the motorhome passed the town limits. After thirty minutes on the road, she scooped up the old box and turned it over on her lap. The combination dial was seized; it wouldn't spin. She figured that if she had the combination, the chrome button below the dial would pop up, unlocking the lid. The box wasn't heavy, but she could tell it had stiff cards and other items inside, as they slid when she tipped the box back and forth. The steel was coated with a silvery-gray crinkle finish that she had seen on some antique car parts and trim.

Hudson dampened a paper towel in the sink and tossed it to Lanie. She missed the interception and had to peel it off the dashboard. Her dad rolled his eyes then refocused on the road ahead. Wiping the dust off to get a better look at the logo, Lanie noted how ornate it was. The gold-outlined, intertwined characters in the Myriad logo looked much older than typical 1950s art—more like the Art Nouveau designs she'd seen on early twentieth-century car ads. On the bottom of the box a series of small numbers and letters was stamped into the steel:

```
0115-AZ-OMEGA4-MM
CONFIDENTIAL
```

"I'll bet if we whack it with a hammer—or pry on it with a screwdriver—we can get it open," Hudson offered.

"Maybe. We can try with my dad's tools at the campsite."

She handed the box to Hudson for inspection and gazed through the window. About a half-mile off Route 66, another freight train charged through the desert at the same speed they were traveling. Lanie couldn't see the crew in the lead locomotive's windows. The whole train looked like a monstrous, speed-focused snake advancing alongside their motorhome. She sat back into the seat and closed her eyes, thinking of her conversation with Bud. Lanie couldn't be sure but was almost certain that Bud had been expecting someone to be looking for the box. He'd been standing behind a rusty file cabinet—with the hint of a smile on his face—watching Lanie leave.

## Chapter 4

# SUSPICIOUS TRAVELER

Late that afternoon Lanie awoke with the setting sun burning through her eyelids. She shaded her eyes and squinted through the windshield, trying to ascertain their location.

"You were out for a couple hours," her dad said. "Seligman must have worn you guys down." Lanie turned around and saw Hudson sprawled out on the sofa asleep with his mouth wide open.

"He's snoring!" Isaiah said as he swiped his finger around the screen of his weathered iPad.

Lanie put her glasses on and scanned the desolate sandy desert around the highway. "Where are we?"

"Getting into California City. We'll be at the campground in about an hour," Mr. Speros replied.

As they passed a road sign confirming the mileage to their next destination, Lanie saw a white, late model Dodge Durango SUV stopped in a turnout on the roadside. The driver's door was open, and a white-haired man stood with his arm over the door, talking on his cell phone. He watched the motorhome as it sped past. "Did that guy need help?" Lanie asked her dad.

"I don't think so. He just passed us going over eighty a few minutes ago. He has his phone anyway."

Lanie got up and went to the narrow pantry next to the stove and dug out a handful of granola bars. She also grabbed a bottle of her cold-brew coffee from the refrigerator and headed back toward the front seat. Passing Hudson, she kicked his dangling shoe and tossed a granola bar on his chest. "Wake up! We're almost to the campground." Before sitting down, she handed Isaiah a bar as well.

"Thank you, Lay-Lay," he said without looking up.

Hudson rubbed the sleep from his eyes, observing the arid landscape in a daze while he unwrapped his bar. Lanie settled back into her seat and stripped off her boots and socks. She propped her feet up on the face of the dash and wiggled her toes in the sun. Her ankles were stiff, since she'd fallen asleep with her boots on. She searched out some music on the satellite radio that they could all agree on, which usually meant classic rock, if her dad was around.

"Ooh yeah, that's the jams right there," Lanie's dad said as she came across a song by Journey. Mr. Speros spun the volume up and started slapping the steering wheel but spared the other travelers his singing.

Lanie reclined in the seat, smiling. "Road Trip!" she said, shoving both hands up high as though she were on a roller coaster.

"Road Trip!" Hudson repeated, grinning.

By the time they'd arrived in Tehachapi, the travelers were in good spirits and looking forward to some outdoor time. The campground was familiar to Lanie, as the Speroses used it as an overnight stop on most of their trips into northern California. At the entrance was a large country store made of red timbers with a green tin roof. It always reminded Lanie of Isaiah's Lincoln Log toys. The store was surrounded by tall pine trees and manicured green lawns, and a retired wooden farm wagon stood in the grass at the entry, its bed filled with blooming fall flowers.

Mr. Speros returned from the office carrying slips of paper that had their campsite directions and the usual information—like the Wi-Fi password and reminders about picking up your dog's poop.

As he climbed in, he said, "The staff told me that there's rain coming tonight; we need to get the site packed up before we go to bed."

Lanie and Hudson had been sitting at the dinette booth playing card games. Looking through the window, Lanie saw the occasional flash of lightning along the southwestern horizon. "While Dad sets up the motorhome at the site, we should go get a pizza. I'll show you the camp store," she told Hudson.

Lanie's dad steered the Magna's nose into a wide arc and pulled into their space next to a shiny Airstream trailer. He pulled out the parking brake knob and the brakes hissed—which was Isaiah's signal to bolt for the door.

"Hold on Isaiah, you need your jacket!" Lanie shouted. Getting Isaiah into a coat was like trying to put an octopus into a sandwich bag. "Sit still!" she growled as he craned his head to see the nearby playground. As soon as she released him, Isaiah shot off into the pine trees between the RV sites to join the other kids.

"I figure we have about an hour before the rain starts," Mr. Speros leaned from the coach's door, sizing up the threatening sky. "Don't disappear; just grab dinner and come straight back please."

"OK," Lanie and Hudson said in unison.

"Come on, you'll like the camp store," Lanie said. The smell of pumpkin spice, apple, and roasted pecans greeted the two friends when they passed through the country store's rough-hewn wooden doors. There was a food bar, a big display of local fruits, nuts, and preserves, and a long row of old-fashioned arcade games along the front windows. Hudson's eyes were immediately drawn to the vintage games, and he grunted with excitement.

"Oh wow, these are just like the games at the mini-golf place my parents used to take us to!" he said.

"I figured you'd be excited about that," Lanie said, nudging him toward the arcade. "Go on, I'll be there in a minute." She was happy inside, knowing that Hudson was enjoying himself.

He wandered off to peruse the selection of games while Lanie ordered the pizza for dinner. The store was empty of customers except for a man with white hair in a black jacket standing near the ATM in the foyer. Lanie guessed he was in his early fifties. When her eyes met his, he turned back to the cash machine. Lanie rounded up the other materials she had been sent for and walked down the row of used books on her way to the cashier.

Light fixtures fashioned from animal antlers and hammered iron hung overhead, providing barely enough light to shop by. As Lanie stood looking over the tattered paperbacks, she noticed a white Dodge Durango with tinted windows in the parking lot outside. Her spine stiffened and she looked over at the ATM to see if the man she'd seen on the shoulder of the highway was the same person—but he was gone. An uncomfortable chill crossed her shoulders as she surveyed the SUV, but she told herself she was being irrational.

"Did you see anybody in here?" she asked Hudson, who was focused on a game's green matrix of graphics.

"No, why?"

"I think I saw that guy who was standing on the roadside earlier—with the Durango."

Hudson glanced up at the vehicle. It was backed into the space out front and its dark windows hid its interior; they couldn't see if anyone was inside. "Maybe they're just headed our direction. It could be a coincidence."

As they watched, the Durango's taillights lit, and the SUV slowly left the parking lot. Nobody had gotten in or out. Lanie saw curiosity in

Hudson's face then. But neither of them knew what to make of the situation, so the topic dropped.

Sprinkles of rain were blowing in the wind when Lanie and Hudson reached the row of young trees that shaded the motorhome. Lanie set out plates on the heather-colored Corian tabletop, then waved to her dad at the playground from the doorway, signaling dinner was ready. Hudson filled water glasses and set out flatware for dinner but had returned to inspecting his railroad lantern purchase. There were small lights in the cabinet over the reading table, which were perfect for the work the two friends were focused on.

Lanie pulled out the lockbox and pried at the lid with a screwdriver. There were no gaps big enough to insert the tool's tip, so instead she tried to free the lock knob. The hub in the center of the knob contained a small key slot. Years of dust had accumulated in the gap around the dial's circumference, and it wouldn't budge. Lanie used a pair of pliers to try and turn the black Bakelite dial but the brittle plastic shattered after her second attempt.

"Dang!" she shouted as Hudson looked up.

"Oh well," Hudson said, "you might as well bust it open now. Is there a hammer in the toolbox?"

"You think a hammer is the right tool for too many jobs," Lanie replied, looking over the top of her glasses.

Just then, Mr. Speros and Isaiah entered, streaked with rain.

"Pizza time!" yelled Isaiah in his outdoor voice. "The playground is nice here. There was a girl named Marina!"

"Wash up, c'mon." Mr. Speros aimed Isaiah at the sink and gave him a bump. He turned to Lanie and Hudson, then wrinkled his nose, sniffing. "You two need a washup, too—one of you smells like moth balls."

Hudson cackled. "That's Lanie and her mystery box!"

Looking offended, Lanie sniffed her sweater sleeve, then under her arm. "I don't smell anything; you're nuts." But she shuffled into the bathroom to clean up anyway.

All four travelers sat in the cozy dinette booth, sharing pizza and salad as the foul weather intensified outside. An occasional wind gust would twitch the motorhome. "Apparently this storm system will continue for a few days, off and on," Mr. Speros said. "The worst of it is supposed to hit central California Sunday into Monday, which is when we'll be at the campsite in the woods."

"Do you think we'll still be able to hike or do any exploring?" Lanie asked.

"Maybe. Too early to tell."

"Didn't you check the forecast before we left?" she asked.

Mr. Speros clinked his fork onto the plate, looking annoyed. "No, I changed this motorhome's twelve gallons of oil and fluids and did a hundred other things. You have a computer; maybe *you* should get on the interwebs and check the weather for us next time."

Lanie and Hudson exchanged a cautioned glance, then Lanie clamped her lips shut.

After dinner was cleared, Mr. Speros gave the directives for setting up sleeping quarters. The dinette table folded flat into the seat to make a small bed, which was where Isaiah slept. The sofa against the driver's side wall converted to the bunk beds where Lanie and Hudson were to sleep. The sofa's lower cushion lifted straight up on four telescoping posts, then the back slid down to form the lower bunk's mattress. Hudson was impressed with the sofa's mechanical gymnastics, so Lanie showed him how to operate it.

Lanie was anxious to wash off the day's grime, so she locked herself into the bathroom and took a quick hot shower. Afterward she wrapped herself in a towel and stood at the mirror. "You lucky," her grandma Speros would say in her thick Greek accent. "You have the oily hair of a Greek goddess!" Her grandmother used to come over daily to help during the first couple years after Lanie lost her mom. She'd untangle Lanie's unruly curls at bedtime, then her dad's mom would tell stories about her own "exotic" looks when she was younger.

Lanie had inherited her mom's dense hair, and after her tenth birthday, she'd let it grow long. Unfortunately, the daily maintenance routine was cumbersome. Some days, her curls collected dirt and debris like a feather duster. She was happy to be clean but hadn't finished drying when her dad knocked on the wall—the signal that she needed to pick up the pace.

After Isaiah fell asleep, Mr. Speros retreated to his bedroom at the back of the Magna, where Lanie figured he'd catch up with Sabine on the phone. The two friends sat up at the reading table, talking about the day's events. Hudson had given the Durango and its white-haired driver some more thought.

"We probably ought to be on the lookout for any other weird coincidences," he said. "That guy was checking us out when we drove past today."

"Yeah, I agree," Lanie said. She brought up the Myriad Exploration stories that Bud had told them in Seligman.

"These mine stories don't make sense," Hudson said. "Why would a company shut down two profitable mines that were cranking out gold and copper? Mr. Rinnas said that teenagers used to go into the one by our house in the '70s to smoke and have parties—and he used to call the sheriff." Hudson chuckled, then forced his face into a suspicious squint. "He also said that four-wheel-drive trucks with US Government plates used to come and go *all the time* before that—just like what Bud told us about the mine where he worked."

"Mr. Rinnas's story facts don't always line up," Lanie said, kinking her lip. "I wonder if he actually remembers everything in the right order anymore. I don't know how he worked his day job at Motorola if he was always up on the hill snooping on the canyon with binoculars."

"Says the girl who was watching the same mine with binoculars last weekend," Hudson snickered. "What are we doing tomorrow again?"

"We're stopping at the salvage yard near Fresno, remember? That's my happy place—I can't wait to show you. There's a row of newer Fox-body Mustangs you'll like."

"Oh yeah—sweet." Hudson's bent smile returned; '80s-vintage Ford Mustangs were a favorite of his.

In a loud whisper, Lanie's dad called from around the corner of the kitchen "Hey, get to bed; you'll wake Isaiah." Lanie switched off the overhead light and the two fumbled into their bunks. The rain still fell outside, but it was softer. The distant thunder had bypassed them. Lanie drifted off to sleep while thinking of Bud and the antique shop in Seligman.

# Chapter 5

# PARKER'S AUTO SALVAGE

The following morning, Lanie's dad let the group sleep in. He had started bacon in the oven and pancakes on the stove; breakfast was his specialty. The smell of fresh coffee filled the coach, and the gurgling of the percolator woke Lanie first. On motorhome trips she liked to have a short cup of her own before they got on the road. Lanie didn't drink much caffeine, but for Mr. Speros, coffee was a routine—a way of life. Having grown up in a first-generation Greek American household, he drank coffee daily by age nine—at least that's what he told Lanie. Neither he nor Lanie liked the soupy, strong coffee that her grandparents drank though; he and Lanie preferred the "American dishwater," as her grandfather would say.

Lanie sat in the driver's seat leaning against the steering wheel, with the mug held up to her nose as she stared out at the misty campground. Beyond the campground's perimeter of pine and oak trees, a John Deere harvester was idling on the edge of a green field. It seemed hesitant, pondering whether it would sink if it stepped into the soggy furrows. Hudson stirred and sat up, hitting his head on the bunk overhead with a metallic *thunk*.

Lanie snickered at his misfortune, then muffled herself.

"Easy, dude, these bunks are low," Mr. Speros said. Lanie offered Hudson a hand and pulled him up.

"Did you sleep OK?" she asked.

"Oh yeah. I was out cold," Hudson replied. He slid into the seat next to Lanie.

"Coffee?" Lanie pointed over her shoulder at the pot.

"Nah, that stuff goofs me up. I want summa that bacon though," he said, surveying Mr. Speros's progress at the stove.

It wasn't long before Isaiah woke, after which the day's events commenced at full volume. Bunks were stowed, breakfast was cleared, and a fresh pot of coffee was started for the road.

As they rode along, Hudson used his mom's smartphone to upload photos to show off their journey's progress. Neither he nor Lanie had their own cell phones yet, though not because they hadn't asked for them. The best Hudson had managed was a smartwatch that was linked to his parents' mobile service. It allowed him to communicate with them and to access some apps, but not much more.

The span of highway between Tehachapi and Bakersfield, California, was an hour's drive, and the travelers were ahead of schedule, so her dad pulled into a truck stop east of town for fuel. Isaiah and the two friends took the opportunity to shop, perusing the snack aisles in the convenience store like critics surveying art at an exposition. Hudson selected some packaged cakes and Danishes that looked so sweet, Lanie's stomach twitched.

"Are you seriously gonna eat all of those today?" she inquired with her eyebrows raised, looking down from the side of her eye. "After eating a pile of bacon and pancakes this morning? Geez, you cow, I dunno how you stay so skinny."

"Like what you picked is health food?" He nudged her basket of sandwich cookies and beef jerky. "*That's* why you have oily skin," Hudson said, lifting the jerky package with his pinky extended. "It's not 'cause you're

Greek. You could lube the motorhome's axles with the grease in that jerky stick."

Lanie relaxed her judgmental eyebrows and grabbed her jerky. She was tall for her age and didn't need to watch her weight yet, but her grandmother would warn her when she visited, "You watch out, koúkla—you're almost to the age where you hips will grow faster than you hair." Koúkla meant "doll" in Greek, and Lanie was thankful none of her friends were typically around at the same time as her grandmother. Her dad's mother was as outspoken as her mom—no body part or biological function was off limits during a discussion.

Lanie helped Isaiah pile his own sugary selections on the checkout counter and paid for the lot, then they headed out across the fuel pump islands among the idling semi-trucks. The grilles of the trucks stood high over Hudson's head, and he stared up at the emblems and hood ornaments as the threesome walked. He appeared to be uncomfortable with his proximity to the huge machines. Lanie was used to being near the big trucks and their drivers, though. On their many trips, most truck drivers were courteous to her and Isaiah, while some seemed to be offended that her family's motorhome was taking up space at the diesel pumps.

Just after lunch, the Magna coasted up in front of Parker's Auto Salvage. Nine miles off the highway, the salvage yard was free of the city traffic, isolated among wide, flat tracts of farmland. Railroad tracks formed the western edge of the vast yard and an irrigation canal split it down the middle. The motorhome crept over the un-gated railroad crossing as Lanie laced up her boots.

"You need to bring a bottle of water," she advised Hudson. "And definitely your hat." She grabbed her own broad-rimmed canvas gardening hat. It was festooned with lapel pins of small car emblems and road signs. Her ragged hat was decidedly dork-tastic, but Lanie never wore it around Helen—or anywhere that she needed to be concerned about fashion police.

The group of four entered the old metal building and found Mr. Parker sitting at the counter, surrounded by mounds of dusty parts and handwritten receipts, just as Lanie had described to Hudson. Lanie could not remember any living human who looked older—or more weathered—than Mr. Parker. The proprietor's leathery skin sagged from his thin frame and his big blue eyes were bloodshot. His drooping jowls were lifted by a tired smile as the travelers entered. The human incarnation of a junkyard dog, Murray Parker didn't smile, except for when Lanie visited. At least that's what his yard supervisor, Edgardo, had said on their last visit.

In fact, the first time Lanie met Mr. Parker, he'd scowled down at her over the counter, then asked Mr. Speros why the young lady had been brought to a wrecking yard. Lanie had held up her dog-eared copy of a barn-find classic car book in which his salvage yard was featured. She'd turned straight to the page that showed a 1950 Nash Ambassador that sat in a shed near his shop. That was the first time she'd seen Mr. Parker smile. He'd given her a baseball cap with his yard logo and waved her into his world beyond the gate, and Lanie felt like she'd been admitted to the Emerald City.

She'd been back three times since and Mr. Parker knew her by name. Crusty, cobwebbed components with soiled paper tags sat on racks which stood in rows behind him, disappearing into the darkness at the back of the building. Even entry through the front door required careful steps past the more recently accumulated debris. He pushed aside a Packard's tube-type radio so that he could lean over the counter to shake Lanie's hand. Mr. Speros shook his hand next, then introduced Hudson.

"Good morning, Murray! These are your new generation of customers," Lanie's dad said, extending his arm to the two friends.

"I guess they are, aren't they?" Mr. Parker replied in his gravelly voice. "'Mornin', Ms. Lanie." He nodded at Lanie, then gave Hudson a hat of his own, wrapped in dusty plastic. "Welcome, my boy. What are we all lookin' for today?"

"Dad's '87 Wagoneer is missing the trim from the left rear quarter panel," Lanie said. "Also, we need the body control module for a 1995 or '96 Cadillac Fleetwood."

"Oh, do you?" Mr. Parker replied, touching his fingers to his forehead. At nearly ninety, he moved slowly. In fact, Lanie had never seen him rise from his stool. Instead, he'd grab his two-way radio and call the yard supervisor, which is what he did that day.

"ED!" he shouted into the dirt-encrusted radio.

"*GO AHEAD!*" was Ed's distant reply over the air.

"Cadillac Fleetwood, '96, electric parts! Also, Wagoneer trim!"

The response over the radio was swift and loud. "*Murray, I told you I'm in the east end with a customer pulling a transmission for at least an hour!*"

Lanie noticed that everyone who worked for Mr. Parker either yelled at him or complained about him (or both) when she visited.

Having been rejected by his yard super, Mr. Parker called another of his employees. After some profanity-laced objections, he got a commitment from someone named Ricky to appear at the front counter.

A few minutes later, an extremely dirty young man sauntered up to the group. He'd emerged from the stacks behind Mr. Parker, wearing a sleeveless tee shirt which was stained so completely, Lanie could not ascertain its original color. His jeans were so soiled with grease and dirt that they shined.

"Ricky's my newbie," Mr. Parker said. "He knows the yard zones well, but not *which* cars are *where*."

"It's OK, I know where the donor cars are," Lanie said.

"The young lady knows where to go," Mr. Parker relayed to Ricky, who looked unimpressed.

Through his sparse teeth, Ricky muttered, "C'mon. Ain't 'nuf room for all ya, though."

"If it's alright, only these two are going in, Murray," said Mr. Speros, placing hands on the two friends' shoulders. "I need to keep an eye on the little one in the RV." He nodded to Isaiah, who was fingering a dusty gumball machine near the door.

"Follow Ricky," Mr. Parker said to Lanie.

Outside the office, cottony cumulus clouds obscured the sun every few minutes, but the temperature was just right. The two friends hustled to catch up with Ricky, who had climbed into his yard car—a hammered Mazda long-bed pickup that likely hadn't seen a paved road in years.

"Y'all can ride in the bed," Ricky said, and he slapped his calloused palm on the toolbox behind the cab.

In Lanie's experience this was a far better option than sitting on the dirt-layered hamburger wrappers, empty water bottles, and mixed automotive flotsam that littered the interior of Parker's yard vehicles. The truck's tailgate had long since been liberated, so Lanie was able to step straight into the bed over the bumper, then she offered Hudson a hand. They had both barely seated themselves onto the toolbox when Ricky let out the clutch, and they zoomed off into the rows of derelict vehicles. Lanie and Hudson were seated facing backward and the pickup bucked and twisted as they navigated the rutted dirt paths. From their perch on the toolbox, Lanie's waist was at the pickup's roof level, allowing her and Hudson a panoramic view of the 200-acre yard.

Rows of deceased cars passed on either side like crops in a field, stretching to the horizon. Lanie felt like she had arrived at her vacation home. Hudson beamed, his neck snapping back and forth as he tried to identify the makes and models that were passing by. "Whatcha think?" Lanie said, smiling with her nose wrinkled under the sun. Hudson didn't have any words yet; he just smiled back and offered his fist. Lanie bumped it and they pressed their shoulders together for stability.

The clusters and rows of cars were supposed to be grouped by manufacturer, though the lack of organization in the yard left many vehicles orphaned—far from their relatives. When the rows of Cadillacs appeared on the driver's side, she thumped her palm on the roof of the cab. Ricky stood on the brakes, and Hudson threw his arm across Lanie's lap as she began to tumble backwards toward the hood.

"Sheesh," Hudson said, helping Lanie to sit up.

"Thanks, that was kinda close!" she said, adjusting her glasses.

They jumped off the pickup and Ricky followed with his tool bag. "Here!" Lanie veered over to a sad-looking dark red Fleetwood Brougham with a peeling vinyl top. Aside from its chalky paint and sun-hardened maroon leather upholstery, the car was intact.

"This one has good donor parts for my mom's Caddy," Lanie said. She grabbed the keys from the top of the dashboard and released the trunk latch. The hinges creaked in protest as the lid swung upward. Once she'd pointed out the requisite black box deep within the trunk, Ricky climbed in to remove it. Lanie then clambered up onto the hood and stood looking out over the rows.

"I think the Jeeps are way over there," Lanie said, pointing to the southern horizon.

"How do you know your way around this place?" Hudson asked. "It's like a corn maze."

Lanie hopped down next to him, stirring up the dusty soil. "If I see a car I recognize, I remember others that were near," she said. "Plus, I've been here a few times."

Ricky had finished pulling the module from inside the trunk and asked what was needed from the Jeep.

"The fake woodgrain trim that goes behind the left rear wheel," Lanie responded. "There's a black one with the part I need over there, past the row of Dodges," she said, pointing in the general direction the Jeep lay.

Ricky threw his bag into the cab of the truck and flopped onto the threadbare seat. "Are we goin'?"

"If you wanna pull it off, we can just meet you up at the office," Lanie said. She knew the yard laborers preferred to work alone—without the supervisory eyes of the customer overhead.

"OK. Y'all know yer way out?" he asked.

"We're good," Lanie replied with a thumbs-up.

Not needing any convincing, Ricky started the pickup and blazed off in a cloud of dust.

"He was our ride outta here. How are we gonna get back?" Hudson asked, waving his hand to clear the air.

"We're gonna walk. That's why I told you to bring your water. The only way to see the cars you wanna see is to walk."

Hudson pursed his lips, gauging the distance to the entry gate. Lanie struck off down the row. "C'mon, I'll show you the Mustangs," and she swiped at the air ahead, motioning for Hudson to follow.

The salvage yard was even quieter than Seligman—there were no audible signals from birds or bugs, nor a breeze through open car windows. Even though the day was cool, the sun was intense. Lanie's hiking boots—like Hudson's—were coated in a uniform layer of dust, and she tried not to drag her feet to stir up any more than necessary. She rubbed some sunscreen into her forearms then handed the small tube to Hudson. He'd stopped to peer into a Jaguar XJ12 sedan that sat above the weeds, its body propped up on tireless wheels. He picked at its peeling wood veneers and flipped down its once-glossy burled walnut tray tables in the back seat. The delicate wool carpeting on the floor was layered in years of sediment, deposited by the seasonal wind and rain.

"It is just crazy," Hudson said, after a moment of silence. "I mean, people spent so much money on these cars when they were new, then after a while they're just dumped." Lanie studied his expression as he pondered how a stately British sedan had been so unloved that it now lay in a Fresno field.

"Yeah, and that's just one of the thousands of cars here. They all have their own story," Lanie said, turning away. "C'mon, the Mustangs are still a ways off." She uncapped her bottle and filled her cheeks with water.

Near the farthest corner of the yard from the entrance was where Lanie and Hudson found the row of Ford Mustangs. They were hidden beyond a group of retired service trucks. Behind the row, the irrigation canal flowed in a raised earthen channel. Hudson picked a path amongst the trucks and pushed his way through the tall, dry brush. The trucks were similar to the service vehicles that city public works crews would use; their beds had been replaced with steel enclosures that had many storage compartments on either side. Lanie thought they looked like oversized mobile jewelry boxes. Hudson walked up on sloped canal bank where a faded silver Chevrolet service truck lay at an angle. He had to lean against the truck so that he wouldn't slip on the dry berm.

Lanie picked the low path around the truck, through more brush. The water in the canal was green, with long strands of algae coating either bank; she didn't like standing near the edge. Debris and drowned rabbits would occasionally float past and the water didn't smell any better than it looked, so Hudson tried to keep close to the truck as well. As he slid along the cab, Hudson stopped in his tracks and gasped.

"Lanie, look!"

Surprised, Lanie jumped and spun around. "What?!"

Through the cab of the silver truck she saw Hudson was pointing down at the door. Lanie's eyes dropped to the early-sixties sculpted sheet metal on her side—and found the Myriad Exploration Group logo.

"Whoa," Lanie whispered, and her eyes met Hudson's. He was watching her face through the truck's cobwebbed cab, his hands clamped over the window edge. They were both quiet, each processing their own thoughts.

"Did you know this truck was here?" he said.

"No way. Each time we've been here, I've never come back to this area."

Hudson's eyes wandered the side of the truck and his consideration of the irony transitioned to curiosity. "We gotta go through this thing; who knows what's in it?" He began pulling on the door latches of the service bed. "Some of these compartments are locked," he said. "This is weird—lots of coincidences. It even has Arizona license plates."

The irony was not lost on Lanie either, but she was unnerved. These finds were more than just a casual coincidence—they were meant to find them, Lanie was sure. The now-familiar logo was printed below the stainless-steel molding, about Lanie's knee height. Above the molding, intricate gold-leaf "SUPERVISOR" lettering was outlined in dark green. It reminded her of the type of paintwork done on fire trucks. The door handle on the passenger side of the truck was missing, so Lanie reached in through the open window and pulled the interior handle. She let the cab door fall wide open, scanning the interior. There were no keys in the ignition and the cab was clear of items. Lanie picked up a petrified radiator hose from under the truck to use as a web remover and swung it around the interior to clear a path to the glovebox. Inside the glovebox she found an oversize, rusty ring of keys.

"Hudson, I have the keys!" She extended her hand through the driver's window.

"Sweet, come out and see if you can open some of these locked doors." He was tossing items out into the dirt. "There's a lot of junk in here, mostly electrical parts. Contactors and lighting parts... probably an electrical maintenance supervisor's truck."

Hudson's dad was teaching him the basics of high voltage systems at home. Hudson complained about having to learn the rules of grounding, current flow, and other functions at first. But that day he seemed proud of his ability to recognize the items he was finding.

Lanie climbed out of the driver's door and stood next to him. "What's this doodad?" she asked, holding up a gray box with two spring-loaded tabs protruding from its side. It was very heavy for its size.

"That's a security door release. It can unlatch a door electrically by remote. My dad says he puts lots of these in power plants so that people can unlock doors without a key."

"Why would a mine need these?" Lanie wondered out loud. She tossed it back into the truck, where it banged around in the compartment. "Not much else in here, huh?" She began trying the various keys in the compartment door locks. One small brass key opened the remaining locks on the truck, but most compartments were empty.

"Geez, so the rest of these keys must be for a building or something," she said, flipping the key set into one of the newly opened compartments.

"Hey, wait," Hudson said, grabbing Lanie's forearm, "doesn't your lockbox have a keyhole in it?"

Lanie's eyebrows arched, and her lips circled. "Oh!" She reached deep into the compartment to snatch the key ring back up. With her head inside the compartment, the reflection of polished metal glinted in the corner of her eye. Contorting her back, she looked up to the ceiling. A small, rectangular chrome box was mounted just inside the door hinge—out of sight to anyone standing next to the truck.

"What did you find?" Hudson dropped to his knees, following Lanie's glance.

She grabbed the box and it dropped into her hand. "It's magnetic— like a spare key locker." Not any bigger than a deck of cards, the lid had a colorful Myriad logo printed on the left, with an engraving to the right that read:

### EXECUTIVE STAFF

Lanie pushed her thumb on the lid and the box slid open. Inside, she found what resembled a polished copper letter opener, but it was much shorter, about three inches in length. The shank was inlaid with turquoise, but the shank's head was forked with a "V" shaped groove. In the "V" was a red crystal triangle fit with jeweler's precision. The copper blade end was shield-shaped and had a pair of notches cut into either edge. Hudson craned his neck to get a closer look as the copper and red reflected onto Lanie's cheeks.

"Wow," Lanie said. "I don't know what this is, but it's beautiful."

"It looks like one of those little fancy knives to spread marmalade," Hudson joked.

"Look, this red crystal has some sort of etching on it."

Hudson took the piece from Lanie and held it up toward the sky. "Yeah, you're right, but it's tiny—I can't read it. We need a magnifying glass."

"No, we don't... look!" Lanie pointed at the side of the truck, where a red image was being projected. The sun was magnified through the red crystal, and a series of twelve characters shone as white in the projection. The characters were grouped in four sets of three, and each character looked like a jumble of segmented numbers and letters that were stacked on top of each other.

"What kinda language is that?" Hudson wondered, moving the blade so that the digits would focus.

"I don't think it's a different language," Lanie said. "Look, some of the lines and dashes are a different shade... This first one looks like an R on top of a number 6... or is that a G? I think you need a special lamp to see the code."

"Ohhh, wow, you're right, good call. Well, it's of no use to us right now," Hudson chuckled. "This is freaky. This truck has been here for years," he said, looking over rusty patina that was starting to show through the thinning paint. "Why are these Myriad things falling in our lap on this trip?" He handed their artifact back to Lanie. "Remember what I keep telling you? We're meant to rediscover whatever is in that mine! I have a feeling about it."

Lanie nodded. She had the same feeling—that they were being given clues toward a bigger discovery—and the back of her neck tingled. Suddenly, Hudson's adventure theories didn't seem outlandish. "I think something big is gonna happen. I've never seen this logo before, and it's suddenly popping up all over," she said, turning to Hudson. "We gotta figure out how to get down into that pit when we get home." She slipped the copper blade back into its box and stuffed it into her pocket.

"Your dad is never gonna let us go down there, and I'm not even gonna *tell* my parents about it," Hudson said. His expression soured. "We may be on our own, unless your dad cooperates."

"My dad! Shoot!" Lanie twisted to look back toward the yard office. "He's gonna be mad, we've been gone for ages." She hooked the key ring to her belt loop, and they resumed their hike to the yard entrance. Lanie shot a last look back at the sad truck, wishing it could talk to her. As they walked the canal bank, Lanie paused to adjust her hat, waving some cobwebs from its brim. That's when she heard footsteps. Hudson stopped and turned back, seeing Lanie's wide eyes. She was looking around.

"What? What's wrong?"

"I heard steps!" she said, holding up her index finger as if to silence him.

When the steps returned, both friends heard them and Hudson said, "Those are animal footsteps!"

Only a second later the source of the sound appeared. A gigantic dog emerged from between a pair of Plymouths at the foot of the canal berm. Lanie recognized it as a Great Dane, and it was watching them with its head tilted. A pulse of panic spread through Lanie's veins, but she remained frozen. Hudson turned away, motioning for Lanie to follow. The dog detected their intent to flee and began charging up the berm toward them, barking.

Hudson's look of surprise had turned to terror, and he started to run. Lanie's mind raced as the dog came closer; she didn't feel in control of her own movement. Escape paths flashed around her, but her body reacted before her brain approved the plan, and she turned... and leapt into the center of the canal. Her hat flew high above her head when she plunged into the murky water.

She pinched her eyes and mouth shut. Her shoulders bunched up as the cold water surrounded her. Expecting to sink, Lanie flailed her arms, slapping at the water. But just as she submerged, her feet hit the narrow canal floor. She rammed her boots into the soft mud at the bottom, and her head and chest shot up out of the water. Gasping with fright, Lanie watched as the Great Dane flung itself into the canal upstream and began to paddle toward her. She was being carried by the canal's current and Lanie knew that she needed to get herself together if she wanted to escape.

Stifling the urge to scream, she dug at the water to reach the bank. Only a few yards downstream, the canal was cascading over a dam-like steel weir into a swirling pit, where the water was carried underground. Fear filled her chest as she was swept toward the small waterfall. She knew the canal walls were vertical in the pit, and there was no ladder to climb out.

The dog was approaching, paddling at a furious pace. Lanie calmed herself as best she could, figuring that the animal could inflict less damage if they were both in the water. Hudson had first retreated onto the roof of a van near the canal bank, but when he saw Lanie's situation he bolted down to the water's edge.

He ran along the bank, yelling "WAIT, WAIT! I'LL GET YOU!" He searched frantically for any long item he could extend, which Lanie could grab.

Lanie reached up the bank toward Hudson, but the dog was upon her. Her eyes were wide as she felt its huge jaws close around her right arm. Something unexpected happened after that. The dog's grip didn't hurt; it was forcing her upward. She looked over her shoulder to see the Dane's broad nose blowing muddy water onto her glasses. Its paws scraped and clawed at the canal's apron as it wrenched Lanie up the slippery bank. Only the dog's eyes and flattened ears were above the water, and they were not threatening.

Lanie realized in an instant that she had been very stupid, and control of her muscles came roaring back. She grabbed at the jagged concrete edge of the canal above the waterline and pulled herself up, since her boots found no traction below. The strands of algae on the water's edge tangled with her hair as she emerged. Hudson lay on his chest on the canal bank, locking arms with Lanie to resist the current that tugged at her hips. Her dog savior used its broad head to push her torso, and she rolled up into the dust on the bank.

Knowing she was safe, Lanie turned and yelled, "Grab him!" She reached down and gripped the dog's front paw.

Hudson was shocked. "Wait, WHAT?!"

Seeing that the dog was frightened, Hudson rolled over and grabbed its other front paw. They both pulled with all their might, and the Great Dane surged out of the water onto Lanie and Hudson in a smelly, muddy pile. Lanie had a terrible taste in her mouth and her lips curled after she sat up. The panting Dane stood next to her, its tail wagging so enthusiastically that its whole body shook. A huge tongue emerged from the dog's dripping jowls, and it slapped against Lanie's cheek, lifting her glasses off her head. The smelly animal then crowded against her and sat down, shaking off a mist of funky water.

Hudson had recovered his wits and jumped up, ready to tackle their assailant.

"It's ok, it's ok," Lanie said, and she couldn't help but smile. "He's nice." She threw her arms around the dog's neck in a great hug, then rubbed its mane in a display of thanks. "You're a *good* boy, huh! *GO*-OD boy!"

Hudson collapsed to his knees and forced out a dramatic sigh as he wiped the mud from his face. He tilted his head over, examining the dog at chest level.

"She!" he said, leaning back. "It's a girl dog."

Lanie suddenly shrieked and rolled in the dirt as though her shoulders were on fire, then jammed her hand under her shirt. "Ahh, Hudson! Something's crawling up my back, get it! GET IT!"

Hudson held his hands up in alarm, momentarily pausing as Lanie writhed in the dirt. Then he grimaced and shoved his hand up her shirt back. He was immediately pinched and yanked his hand back out.

"YIPE! Ow-ow-oww! He howled.

Lanie spun to see that an angry crawfish had clamped the tender skin between Hudson's thumb and forefinger. He flung his hand high, and the crustacean sailed out amongst the deceased vehicles.

Hudson began inspecting his injury while Lanie crouched over him. The dog had run off to find the crawfish and returned, licking its droopy lips. "It's OK... I'm alright," Hudson said, wagging the pain from his hand. "That's enough... Let's just get outta here."

Several minutes later, Lanie, Hudson, and their new friend neared the yard office with the sun behind them. As they shuffled along the dusty path, Lanie looked at Hudson and the dog and twisted her lips. *We must be quite a sight*, she thought. Hudson's hair stood up in tufts and he had spatters of dry mud all over his sun-reddened cheeks. His glasses had a hazy film from the canal water, and green smears of algae were mixed with mud on his jeans and tee shirt.

Lanie's hair was matted and her hat had washed over the canal weir, lost forever. Her entire body felt both slippery and gritty at the same time, and she knew she smelled offensive. Mud was caked on her skin and packed in the folds of her clothes. Marlene (as the Great Dane's collar tag read) was no worse for the wear; her salt-and-pepper coat was already grimy before their swim.

Hudson hadn't said much on the walk up and his expression didn't give away his mood. He stared straight ahead, lost in his own thoughts. Lanie felt like a terrible host and friend.

"I'm really sorry," she said, searching for his reaction, "for that fiasco back there."

Hudson jerked his head up, his thoughts interrupted.

"Are you serious?" he said. "Today was freakin' *awesome!*" He threw his arm around Lanie's shoulders before she had a chance to react. "I love this place! When you Speroses travel, you really get crazy!"

As if in agreement with Hudson, Marlene woofed at her new friends, then sneezed into the dirt, raising a small cloud of dust. Lanie smiled in relief. She didn't bother to tell Hudson that her trips were never *this* exciting. Her spirits rose as they resumed their walk, and her road trip enthusiasm returned. Sweeping her vision over the automotive graveyard in the yellowing afternoon, she thought about their adventures—and what would be next.

## Chapter 6

# WHAT'S IN THE BOX?

As they anticipated, Lanie and Hudson were obliged to sit for a lecture after Mr. Speros listened to their explanation. He'd seen them when they emerged from the yard office and was standing in the doorway with his jaws clenched and lips sealed tight. It was a look Lanie knew well. At first, she was upset with her dad. Their story had a happy ending, after all. Nobody was badly hurt, they got the parts they needed, and she and Hudson agreed it had been a good experience.

"That's a narrow way to look at this," her dad scolded. "I trusted you to be careful, and I told Mr. Parker he could trust that you'd be no trouble in his yard. I also trusted you to manage your time and be a good lead for Hudson. I'd say you failed all the way around." Mr. Speros rarely yelled; he didn't need to—his words and logic carried his point more effectively than raising his voice.

"I was wrong," he had said to them both after a period of silence. "I shouldn't have sent you in there alone. There's a reason why kids aren't left to run loose in a junk yard. I accept responsibility for that. Either one of you could have been drowned, or at least hospitalized." He seemed to be playing the possibilities out in his head as he spoke. Hudson said nothing—Lanie was sure he was expected to keep quiet and apologize when required.

"You're right, it was a mess," she said. "But it was *my* fault; Hudson was sticking to the rules and he was following my lead... I'm the dumb one who jumped into the canal."

"What possessed you to jump into the canal? I just don't understand why you thought that was a good idea—it wasn't a good show of common sense," Mr. Speros said, studying her disheveled appearance. "I didn't expect that from you."

That remark hurt. Lanie bit the corner of her lip and cast her eyes down at her hands. She knew her dad was more upset with himself than her, though, and she felt ashamed. He was just beginning to give Lanie more latitude to do things on her own and this would set her back months.

They'd gotten underway after Mr. Speros made a few more points. Lanie and Hudson accepted their admonishment, and, after some time, their moods rebounded. They were ready to get on with their vacation. They were, however, told that they'd have to change their clothes before the trip could resume.

Using the restroom and snack hunting were excepted from the seatbelt rule while riding on the open highway. But showers were definitely *not* allowed, so the two adventurers were forced to ride along while smelling their own swampy odor, with the grit in their hair and crevices. Hudson didn't seem to mind, but Lanie's skin crawled in discomfort. She breathed through her mouth so she didn't have to smell her hair.

Because of the delay at the salvage yard, the sun was setting as they neared Merced, California. The heavy weather that Mr. Speros had been told to expect hadn't materialized—the evening was cool and clear. Gold Mountain Springs was the name of the campground they would be staying at. It was a larger facility where the RV sites were spread out between the sequoia trees. The secluded campground was designed to accommodate the big RVs that wouldn't fit in the Forest Service sites in the nearby Yosemite National Park.

When they arrived, night had fallen. Aside from the lit roadway at the main office, the campsite was dark, hidden from the starlight under the canopy of giant sequoias. Mr. Speros sized up the surroundings at their site, then positioned the motorhome so it could be backed into their spot. Lanie and Hudson watched through the windows for a view of the campground, but nothing was visible outside the beam of the headlights.

"OK, c'mon up, Lanie," her dad said as he shifted into neutral.

He pulled out the parking brake knob and stood, letting Lanie slide into the seat. "Watch my signals. I need the tail of the motorhome hanging over the back of the site, so we're clear of the road."

Lanie nodded and motored the driver's seat forward so she could reach the pedals. Hudson stood over Lanie's shoulder to watch. When she saw her dad appear in the rearview camera's monitor, she pressed the wide, flat brake pedal and pushed in the parking brake release. Mr. Speros motioned toward himself with both arms. Lanie pushed the R button on the left console and the motorhome started creeping backward. As she inched the coach back, Lanie feathered the brake pedal. Each time she applied pressure, the air brakes would respond with little *Yip! Yip!* noises. When the Magna was positioned as Mr. Speros liked, he crossed his arms over his chest. Lanie shifted into neutral and set the parking brake, then stood up and stretched as though she'd just driven several hours.

"Oh brother," said Hudson. "I hope you're not worn out from all that driving."

"I could do 200 miles if I *needed* to," she smiled and walked past with her nose turned up. "You can start turning on the lights," she advised. Mr. Speros stayed outside to make the water and power connections, and Lanie switched on the hot water heater in anticipation of a shower. "How are you doing?" she asked Hudson. "Did that last twisty road section goof your stomach up?"

"Nah, I'm good. Hungry though," Hudson replied.

Isaiah was sitting up, looking groggy; he'd been asleep for a couple hours. Lanie sat next to him and smoothed his hair. "I'm hungry too," he said, rubbing his eyes.

"I think we're gonna cook chicken cordon bleu tonight, it's tradition," Lanie said to Hudson. "You can help, so we can get it done quickly."

Mr. Speros had been on the phone with Lanie's grandparents as he worked outside, catching them up on trip plans and current events. After a brief conversation he handed the phone through the door to Lanie. "Gram wants to say hi."

Lanie beamed as she took the phone, then ran back to the bedroom, where she could talk privately.

"Gram!" she said, sitting cross-legged on the carpet. Wise in her advancing age, the elder Mrs. Speros always had timely advice for her granddaughter. But the most important thing, Lanie thought, was that her grandma didn't judge; she let Lanie be her own person. She also didn't preach—her advice was more like a recommendation, though she'd always imply Lanie would be dumb not to follow it.

"How are you, koúkla?" the voice over the phone said.

"Good! Trip is going fine... mostly."

"I heard you had some interesting adventures with you friend," her grandma said. Her Greek accent either clipped the "r" from "your," or she didn't know it was supposed to be there.

"Yeah, it was a weird day." She reviewed the canal disaster and admitted how silly she felt. "Dad said it was a lack of common sense," Lanie said of her unplanned swim with the dog.

"Well, listen, koúkla, you need to understand something," her grandma responded. "Don't be too hard on youself. You are at the age where you really start to learn to be a woman, and common sense comes with those changes. Don't worry, you probably learned a lot today."

Before Lanie could interject, her grandma continued, "Let me tell you something else. There are plenty of adults with no common sense who make child-like decisions every single day. And, there are plenty of kids who are forced to make decisions that adults must make. Losing your *ma-ma* added too many adult years to you childhood; don't worry about acting like an adult yet—it will come to you."

*Ma-ma* was the Greek term for *mom,* and Lanie always grew emotional when her grandma spoke of her. "I know, Gram, it's just that I feel like I should be smarter. I don't feel like I'm thirteen. Today I felt like I was Isaiah's age."

"You're *barely* thirteen, Lanie, and you are stronger in spirit and character than any other teenager I've met," her grandma said. "Don't worry about today; it's passing. Think about tomorrow. Next time a challenge comes at you like a *bull,* assume you're stronger and smarter—and face it head-on! You'll think clearer—and with a clear head you will make better decisions. You'll be fine. Wrestle the bull."

Likely not wanting to sound too inspirational, Lanie's grandma added, "But don't take on any more big dogs, please; be smart enough to stay out of those types of situations. Give you dad a break; he's an engineer and he thinks like one—sometimes his brain has no filter. Now go have more fun."

"Thanks, Gram, you're awesome. I love you."

Lanie ended the call and glanced up at the family photo that hung on the oak-paneled wall of the bedroom. The glossy image was the last photo her family had taken together. In it, Lanie stood between her parents in a grassy field and her mom wore a long, sleeveless white dress. She was holding Isaiah, swaddled in his infant blanket, and the Magna stood in the background. It was the weekend they'd flown to Colorado to buy the motorhome and started their first RV trip.

Mr. Speros finished setting up camp just after seven o'clock. In the narrow patches of sky between the trees, millions of stars fought for space.

Hudson stood gazing straight up as he leaned against their campsite's picnic table. He was bundled in his hooded sweater, though he looked cold in his shorts and flip-flops. There were other RVs at the campsite, but it wasn't crowded. The potential for bad weather had likely scared off some guests. Still, Lanie heard occasional laughter and could see pinpoints of dancing flames between the trees at other sites.

Eager to show off the techniques he'd learned in survival camp over the summer, Hudson had started their own campfire. Lanie turned in slow circles, letting the radiating energy warm her jeans. The two friends had been quiet since Lanie stepped outside, and Lanie watched Hudson's face.

"Whatcha thinkin' about?" she asked.

"I like it here; it's peaceful—like the desert. But it's a different kind of peace."

Lanie knew what he meant. "The forest is more like a bunch of people who are being quiet, holding hands—that's what I always used to think."

That made sense to Hudson. "Yeah, it's like they're surrounding us, like hosts. The desert doesn't have that—you're on your own there." After a few more moments he added, "I can see why people camp in RVs now. You can't do this kind of vacation at hotels. And, you can go from place to place on a longer trip, and still feel at home."

Lanie had explained RV traveling to him before the trip in similar words, but she noticed that he'd found his own opinion now. "Yup" was all she replied.

"Hey Lanie?" Hudson said.

"I'm still sitting here, Hudson."

"Do you know what you're gonna do when you get older?"

"You mean, like my job?" she asked, squinting through the campfire smoke at him. "No, but whatever I do, it will involve cars. Why?"

"Dunno," Hudson replied at first, but then decided to elaborate. "Well... my dad asks me what I want to do. He's trying to find classes I can take to... uhh... *develop my talent*," he said, holding up his fingers to quote his dad.

"We're in junior high," Lanie said. "My cousin has been in college for two years and he still doesn't know what he's going to major in. I think you've got some time."

"Are you gonna be an engineer, like your dad?" Hudson asked.

"Maybe," she replied. "But the type of mechanical engineering work I wanna do isn't what most of them do... at least that's what my dad says. Kinda like designing roller coasters—lots of kids say they want to do it, but only a tiny percentage of engineers get jobs like that. I like the engineering of restoration, you know, designing systems to make old things work like new."

"So... like running a shop that does resto-mod cars?" Hudson snickered. "I think roller coaster jobs are more common than restoration shop gigs."

"I guess," Lanie said. "I dunno. I figure some career will kinda fit me by the time I get done with high school. You could probably take over your dad's business."

"That's what he'd like me to do, I'm sure," Hudson said. "Seems kinda boring, but I know I could do it."

"The electrical control system stuff you work on could be a side business," Lanie proposed. "You know, like the motor controller you made to run my plastic V8 engine model. That setup was awesome."

"You mean the one that over sped your engine and blew it up?" Hudson said, looking guilty.

"That was a ton of fun," Lanie said, giggling. "My dad found one of the piston rods in the rafters of the garage when he was putting Christmas decorations away."

"I got you in trouble," Hudson said.

"You only saw his reaction when he got home from work," Lanie said. "Later, he was kinda impressed—once I showed him the coupling we built to connect the engine model to the vacuum cleaner motor."

Isaiah was sitting on his small folding chair, working on making s'mores. If he was quiet more than a few minutes, he was either up to no good or extremely focused. "How're you doin' there, buddy? Do you need help?" Lanie asked.

"I can't get the chocolate melted; it's getting all over," he replied. He was getting frustrated, so Lanie helped him stack the graham crackers and chocolate, but he was already a sticky mess. Lanie licked her fingers and turned to Hudson.

"Do you want any?" Lanie offered him a skewer. "I'm not big on s'mores—I just like to roast the marshmallows."

"Of course I do!" Hudson said, sliding his chair closer. He loaded up his skewer with marshmallows so that it looked like a kebab.

Lanie watched from the corner of her eye. "How do you think you're gonna roast those without roasting your hand too?"

"Watch the master," he said. He wrapped a piece of the graham cracker cardboard box in tin foil, then slipped it over the shank of the skewer as a makeshift heat shield.

Lanie sighed and rolled her eyes. "You know, it's ok to just do things the normal way sometimes."

"Normal is for chumps," Hudson said as he poked a darkened marshmallow.

Mr. Speros stuck his head through the door after they'd emptied the bowl of s'mores supplies. "Nice fire. Good work Hudson. Who are my meal prep assistants?"

"Oh, that would be Hudson tonight." Lanie smiled, volunteering her friend.

It was bright and warm inside and Mr. Speros had outdated rock ballads playing on the satellite radio.

"Can I take a shower now, Dad? I'm really gross," Lanie pleaded with her fingers locked together under her chin.

"Yeah, go ahead. Your scummy buddy will help with dinner," he said, waving Hudson over. He slid a knife and cutting board across the counter. "You can cut cheese into cubes for me."

Staring down at the tinted water dripping in the shower basin around her feet, Lanie couldn't think of any other time that she'd actually seen dirt running off her body as she washed. The steaming water felt wonderful, and it reset her senses. When she rejoined the rest of the group in the kitchen, she could smell the sizzling Canadian bacon and melted cheese. During dinner, Lanie and Hudson realized they had forgotten to tell her father about the truck they'd found at the salvage yard. Spitting the story out between bites, Lanie spoke of the ring of keys, the hidden copper blade, and the Arizona license plates on the old Chevy.

"... And I think the truck was a 1960; it was newer than the one by our house."

"Pretty incredible. Imagine the coincidence," Mr. Speros said of the truck's location. He turned the copper blade over in his hand, then passed it back to Lanie. "I sure wish we had more of the back story on this Myriad company. It would clear up a lot of questions about our house and the neighborhood."

"Mr. Rinnas could probably relax then too," Lanie said, only half joking.

While Hudson showered after dinner, Lanie cleaned the table and helped with the dishes. She was waiting for him to return before she tried to unlock the box with the keys. Sharing discoveries was a courtesy the two friends extended to each other, though they'd never actually discussed the agreement. Lanie smiled to herself as she wiped off the table, thinking of how Mr. Parker hadn't charged them for anything except the Jeep trim once he'd seen the condition of the two friends. He'd laughed so hard, he'd slid off his stool. Lanie snorted as Hudson sat next to her, buffing his damp hair with a towel.

"What's funny?" he said.

"Nothin'. Just thinking about the junk yard. We were a real mess."

Hudson grinned, recalling the day. "You looked like an old horror film swamp monster climbing out of that canal. I figured if I told you what you looked like, you woulda slugged me."

"Nah, but I'm glad we don't have any pics," she said. "Oh yeah, let's check the keys!"

Hudson produced the lockbox from the drawer under the dinette seat and Lanie grabbed the keys out of the cabinet overhead. One by one, she poked the keys at the crusty lock. Most of the keys were just too big to be for a small lock, while two slid into the cylinder. The first key wouldn't turn, but the second did.

"Shoot," Lanie said, twisting her wrist. "It turns... this key works! But the latch won't release—it's sticking."

"Easy, don't snap the key off!" Hudson said.

Daintily, Lanie jiggled the key back and forth until it began to rotate. The chrome hasp suddenly popped up. "Yes! There it goes!" Lanie said with a proud grin.

"What are you two doing in here? What's the yelling about?" Mr. Speros asked, striding in from the bedroom.

"Nothing's wrong—we're good," Lanie said, flashing a fake grin.

Her dad pursed his lips and his eyes narrowed to slits. "You both should be getting ready for bed, not monkeying around with this junk." He turned to walk back to the bedroom. "I'm trying to get Isaiah into his pajamas. Wrap it up in here."

Ignoring the directive, Lanie said, "Wait!" She held up the open lockbox for Mr. Speros to see. His curiosity overcame his sense of parental obligation, and he sat on the sofa opposite the reading table.

"Alright, let's see what you've got."

Trying not to seem ceremonial, Lanie set the box on the table and forced the lid's rusty hinge all the way open. She craned her head over the open box at the same time as Hudson, and their heads thunked together like two melons.

"Ahh!" Lanie said under her breath, holding her forehead. Her dad shook his head then motioned to speed it up.

She dumped the box over, spreading its contents on the table as Hudson rubbed his own brow. Dust and grains of sand scattered on the table with the other objects. There was a stack of thick cards with handwritten tables printed on them along with a black plastic case about the size of one that might hold reading glasses. There were also two curious rectangular plastic cards that were a little thicker than credit cards. They were off-white and both had a series of square holes punched along one of the sides. One had a diagonal red stripe across its corner.

"Huh." Hudson said, picking the cards up. He held them together so that their edges were aligned. "The holes don't line up," he said and tossed them on the table.

"They look like punch cards," Mr. Speros said. "The kind that used to be used for coded access to an early computer system."

Lanie shrugged and went through the other objects. There was a group of three keys on a ring and a yellowed envelope that had been bent to fit inside the box. Hudson grabbed the black plastic box, while Lanie pulled out the contents of the envelope.

"It's a building layout," Lanie said, unfolding a large sheet of paper. She passed it to her dad. "What's in there?" she asked, turning to Hudson. Lifting the clasps on the box, Hudson pulled out a series of small vellum sleeves with notched corners. Each sleeve appeared to have film negatives in it.

"Those look like microfiche," Mr. Speros said, reaching out to take them from Hudson.

"Micro-what?" Lanie asked, kinking her upper lip.

"Before computers could hold images or drawings, information was stored on film strips like these," he said, holding one up to the light. "See? Look through the light. There are images on here."

"Aww, cool," said Hudson, holding up one of his own.

"How can we view them?" Lanie asked.

"You need a special projector—it's like a desktop computer with a monitor. Instead of a keyboard, though, there's a little glass table. You put these under the sheet of glass and the tiny image is magnified on the screen."

He put the films back in the sleeve and handed it to Hudson. "I haven't seen a reader for a long time, but some public libraries still have them. You guys can check when we get home."

Hudson tucked the films back into the black box. "What's on those cards?"

Lanie picked up the small stack of monogrammed notecards. Each of the five cards had a different heading that appeared to be the name of a location. A series of coded digits was handwritten in columns beneath the headings.

"Two of them are for the Hualapai mine," she said, handing the pair to Hudson. "Two say 'Tonopah,' and the other says 'McDowell Mountain.'"

"The columns underneath look like coordinates or places at each location," Hudson observed.

Lanie saw that the McDowell Mountain card was formatted the same way.

<table>
<tr><td colspan="2">M. Leistra<br>ELECTRICAL — McDowell Mountain – 6/62</td></tr>
<tr><td>Grid Substation</td><td>LL36</td></tr>
<tr><td>12KV Terminal Center</td><td>LL3ER</td></tr>
<tr><td>Atom Rectifier Plant</td><td>LL20</td></tr>
<tr><td>Circulation Motor Control Center</td><td>LL28</td></tr>
<tr><td>Command Center Backup Generator</td><td>LL3ER</td></tr>
<tr><td>Executive Control Center Switchgear</td><td>LL3ER</td></tr>
<tr><td>Elevator Control Bus Room</td><td>LL12</td></tr>
<tr><td>Cash Vault Capacitor Banks</td><td>LL16CC</td></tr>
</table>

"These don't make any sense to me. Dad, whatcha think?"

Mr. Speros pulled out his reading glasses and scanned the card. "This is electrical equipment—big stuff for high-voltage systems."

"Yeah," Hudson chimed in. "I'll bet this is equipment that was inside the mine. But what are the letters and numbers?"

"They look like levels," Mr. Speros said as he swiped his finger across handwritten line LL36. "As in, 'Lower Level thirty-six.'" He handed the card back to Lanie. "I can't imagine what an 'Atom Rectifier Plant' is, or why it would be needed at a mine. Very odd."

Lanie's dad spread the drawing out on the sofa and switched on the overhead light. "Looks like a floorplan. A series of floorplans, rather." Lanie and Hudson settled on their knees and hung their heads over the drawing as Mr. Speros traced corridors and passageways with his finger. "I'd guess that this is a mine layout. There are larger rooms and spaces separated by long corridors."

Lanie's and Hudson's eyes connected with excitement over the promising development.

"It's not very useful though," Mr. Speros continued. "The drawing has no title block with a scale or information, and there are no annotations, other than some room names. This is as cryptic as the cards—not very informative unless you're the person who was making the notes."

"Well, McDowell Mountain must be the mine by our house," Lanie said. "The lockbox is marked 'AZ-MM' on the bottom, and the guy in Seligman said that some of the stuff he had were from their offices."

"Like I said, no way to tell from this drawing," Mr. Speros repeated. "But certainly possible. The McDowell Mountains stretch for miles behind Fountain Hills. I'm sure there are multiple old mines hidden back there."

Handing the sheet to Lanie, her dad stood up and headed to the back of the coach. "C'mon; you guys need to get some sleep."

As she stuffed the envelope and other items back into the lockbox, Lanie glanced up at Hudson, who had been quiet. He was sitting back in the shadows, deep in thought.

"Uh-oh, what's goin' on in your head?" Lanie said.

When Mr. Speros was out of sight, he whispered, "I'll bet that hole in your yard is a passage, connecting these clues. That drawing is *not* for a mine," he said, pointing at the lockbox. "I've seen mine layouts and they don't look like that. And, there's a vault! Who knows what could be in it!"

Lanie grinned, holding up the box with the copper blade. "I wonder if this is a *vault* key?"

Hudson's eyes widened. "Holy cow, you might be right!" Leaning forward into the light, he added, "I'll bet you a million bucks you can walk from inside your house straight into that mine complex."

His last statement took Lanie by surprise, even though she was used to Hudson's grand theories. She chuffed, showing her skepticism. "That sounds pretty awesome, but not likely." She stopped short of trying to discredit his theory, though. Even Lanie was growing more suspicious about the history of the houses on her cul-de-sac.

She thought of the Mindehanis' house to the left of her own. The Speroses' shy Sri Lankan neighbors had lived in the neighborhood only a couple years longer than Lanie's family, but the Mindehanis had renovated their house when they moved in. Their home was originally built in the mid-seventies, though, and was constructed by an entirely different builder than the Speros house. On the other hand, Mr. Rinnas's home, which was to the Speroses' right, had been built by the same developer.

Seeing that Hudson wanted to know where her thoughts were leading, Lanie offered, "Mr. Rinnas's house kinda looks like ours. They're both 'mid-century' designs. He was the first owner, but his house was already built when he moved in. Maybe he knows something about our house that he hasn't told us yet."

"I'm 100% sure of *that*," Hudson said.

Lanie cocked her head. "Why'd you say that? He's a nice guy."

"Yeah, I know. But he seems way too interested in the mine and you told me he's always asking your dad about the house—and what you guys are doing to the interior. If this place had a vault, people might be after it. *He* might be after it."

Hudson's memory was accurate. When they moved in, Mr. Speros had the garage floor resurfaced and modern sectional garage doors installed. Mr. Rinnas had come over, asking if her dad had done anything inside or behind the walls. Lanie remembered thinking they were weird questions to ask, but her dad told her it was because of the fragile older wiring and plumbing that the homes had.

"He's curious, but I'm not so sure about Mr. Rinnas's connection," Lanie said. "I'm wondering if he found something out about his *own* house though."

Without any other evidence to ponder, Lanie said, "Ah, whatever." She scooped up the lockbox and put it back into the drawer under the dinette. Hudson helped pull up the bunks, and the pair brushed their teeth in the kitchen sink together.

Chapter 7

# TOO MANY COINCIDENCES

By eight o'clock the following morning, heavy clouds had overtaken the woods and the breeze had turned into a stiff wind. Occasional thunder rumbled in the distance, and the sequoia trees were creaking and clacking in protest overhead. Hudson and Lanie had explored the grotto around the creek behind the motorhome after breakfast but were waiting to start their hike up toward the bluff that faced Yosemite.

Mr. Speros never came down the path with Isaiah, so the two friends headed back up to the campsite. When they emerged from the ferns that crowded the trailhead, Lanie and Hudson found Mr. Speros talking to the campground manager. Lanie surmised from the look on her dad's face that their hiking plans had changed. She was surprised to see the folding camp chairs and other items had been stacked in the Magna's outside storage bays. She'd only just unpacked the chairs a couple hours earlier.

"Good timing—you guys need to pitch in," Mr. Speros said. "The manager drove around to the sites letting everyone know that they need to clear the campground by noon; we need to get going soon."

"Why, what's going on?" Lanie's curiosity morphed into alarm.

"The highway department is closing the road between here and the town this afternoon. They're expecting the storm to bring freezing rain and hail that could make the road impassable," he said as he tucked Isaiah into his jacket. "We need to be outta here before the closure—or we'll be stuck."

Lanie and Hudson shared a concerned look, then she asked, "How long would we be stuck here? Could we go the other way?" She pointed northward.

"That road goes over the mountain summit. It's not a good road for large vehicles, especially in the rain," Mr. Speros replied. "They'll probably close that road later in the afternoon anyway." He pulled the bay doors down and locked up the coach door. "C'mon, we're going up to the office to get a couple things; I'll need both of you to help carry them."

Lanie couldn't imagine what they needed, but she and Hudson shrugged at each other and followed along with Isaiah. The wind pushed them around on the pavement, and Lanie tied her hair back with an elastic band as they climbed the narrow steps to the office door. Inside, the man and woman staffing the counter were preparing to close the shop.

The two-room office and shop combination was small. Rough plywood walls were lined with some typical items—campfire skewers, mosquito repellent, and freshwater hoses for RVs. Lanie also noticed they had snow chains, survival tools, and folding shovels. Mr. Speros requested some heavy bags of mixed salt and grit, used for breaking up ice on the road. One bag went to Lanie, the other to Hudson. Isaiah was handed a bag of freeze-dried fruit and other snacks.

Mr. Speros hoisted a large set of tire chains and cables over his shoulder. After they'd paid, the group stepped back out into the gathering storm. The clock over the door read 11:26 a.m. She and Hudson had remained quiet in the office; they assumed the time for questions would be later. But Lanie was unsettled by the materials her dad had purchased. She had seen semi-trucks and buses with tire chains battling the snow on one of the family's trips through Colorado. Piloting a large vehicle in those conditions looked treacherous.

The walk back to the coach was long, and Lanie pulled her hood over her head when the sprinkles turned into a drizzle. She watched the road's lumpy asphalt edge passing under her feet as her mind wandered over their trip itinerary for the next two days. Her thoughts were interrupted when she heard the bundle of chains hit the pavement ahead. Mr. Speros had dropped everything he held and was sprinting toward their campsite. Hudson gasped as he and Lanie both saw what was unfolding. There was a man leaning into an open storage bay on their motorhome. A second person was on the step, prying at the door with a screwdriver. The white Durango stood at the front of the motorhome, its two front doors open and headlights lit.

Lanie clamped her hand over her mouth and grabbed Isaiah by the shoulder. Tears of fear filled her eyes as she watched her dad charge toward the men at full stride. When they saw him approaching, the men stopped their assault of the Magna and ran for their SUV. Mr. Speros arrived as the Durango's doors slammed, and he yanked at the driver's door handle when they began speeding off. The window was open, and he reached in, grabbing the driver's shirt collar. But as the truck lurched away, Mr. Speros was knocked to the ground, narrowly missed by the spinning rear wheels. She'd just watched her father nearly get crushed, and Lanie was frozen with terror.

But when she saw her dad look up from the muddy puddle, Lanie became angry. Remembering her grandmother's words from the day before, she realized that she had a choice—she could be a helpless victim or she could be useful. Instantly, Lanie decided. Her dad needed help, and she was going to be useful.

Her eyes narrowed and her lips wrinkled in fury. She dropped her bag of salt and shoved Isaiah into Hudson's arms.

"GET BACK!" she barked.

Hudson bleated and stuttered, not knowing what Lanie was planning to do. He gripped Isaiah and backed away from the road. Lanie sprung forward and picked up a section of the heavy tire chain and started running straight at the SUV, which was speeding toward her. The driver steered the left wheels onto the grass, since Lanie wasn't giving up the road. As it passed, Lanie screamed in an animal-like roar at the windshield then swung the net of chain into a wide arc behind her head as though she intended to rope the SUV like a rodeo calf.

She slung the chain using every muscle in her body, engaging the back half of the Durango with a slap that sounded like the crack of a rifle shot. The rear-side window of the cargo area shattered when the chains whipped the bodywork. Flecks of white paint and red pieces of the tail-light lens fell to the ground with the chain. Her teeth were clenched as she watched the vehicle tear out of the parking lot and disappear. Mr. Speros stomped up, out of breath. He closed his arms around his daughter, and she began sobbing. A white bolt of lightning split the clouds overhead.

Hudson stood motionless with disbelief, and Isaiah didn't seem sure what to think, but he had tears in his eyes. Mr. Speros held up his left arm and Isaiah ran to him. The family embraced until their emotions stabilized. Lanie's dad waved again, motioning for Hudson to join them. When Hudson merged with the group, Lanie clamped her arm around him and pulled him close. Hudson's expression reflected his feeling of uselessness, and a steady, soaking rain began to fall.

The burly man from the camp store was running toward them, looking back at the main road. He shielded his eyes from the showering rain. "What was all that? Who was in that car that just sped out of here? Is anyone hurt?"

Mr. Speros looked up, then turned to look at the motorhome. They all ran back to the campsite, finding that the intruders had pulled items out of the open storage bays on both sides, scattering them about. The edge of the coach door was bent and scraped from the attempted break-in.

"I have never had this happen in all the years I've run this place," the burly man said. "I'm so sorry, folks—I hope there's no major damage. Do you know what they were looking for? Nobody's hurt, right?"

Realizing he'd said nothing yet, Mr. Speros finally answered, "No, we're ok." He surveyed the scene then looked at Lanie. His jaw was firm with resolve, but in his eyes, she saw concern. "This is ridiculous, I don't even know what to think." He turned next to the burly man. "I couldn't tell you what they were looking for, but we've seen the truck before—they may have followed us here."

"Jenny is calling the sheriff," the man said of his partner in the office. "But they're not going to come up here right now—not for this. The southern road's already closed; the storm is hitting the town below. But I'll bet we can get him up here in the morning."

"We're not staying until the morning," Mr. Speros said with conviction. "I have to get these kids home—we all need to get home."

The campground was empty except for a few long-term guests who were riding out the storm. "I really wouldn't advise going north toward Mammoth," the campsite host said. "You could hit black ice or snow as the storm comes through."

"How far is the drive to the summit?" Mr. Speros asked.

"About thirty-five minutes—it's not far. But the road is full of switch-backs and hairpin turns. The runoff will wash across the roads in some areas. If you're going to try it, take the chains and make sure your phone is charged. It will take a long time for crews to reach you if you have any problems."

Mr. Speros rushed the travelers into the coach, directing Hudson and Lanie to get dried off and prepare for departure. Isaiah had relaxed a bit and Lanie gave him his iPad so that he could start his animated shows. But Lanie wasn't relaxed. She stripped off her sweater and shoved it into the laundry machine to dry along with Hudson's coat, then looked up to see her friend staring at her.

"This is getting outta hand." Hudson's concern was obvious. "They were looking for the stuff we found in Seligman."

"I think so too," she said. "And I'm sure they followed us from there."

"What do they think we found?! I mean, it's just the microfiche and some old junk from the office!"

"I don't know," Lanie said. She also remembered the copper artifact from the junk yard. "They probably think we're on the road looking for something specific after we found that pit in our yard. But it doesn't make any sense, why follow us all the way here? And why would they know about the pit?"

Hudson's questions were the same, but neither he nor Lanie had any answers.

Isaiah took the opportunity to offer his theory. "They're looking for buried treasure," he said, as though it should be obvious. "The tow truck driver probably told them."

At first, Lanie dismissed Isaiah's comments, but then her expression changed. "Geez, what if he's right? Maybe the tow truck drivers are involved? What if those guys in the Durango think something's buried in the yard—something valuable from the mine?"

"I just said that last night. Weren't you listening?" Hudson said.

"Yeah, I know, sorry," Lanie admitted. "Our house might be the gateway to the mine tunnels." It felt weird to say it, but she didn't have any better theories.

Mr. Speros stomped in, slamming the door. He shook off his raincoat and left it lumped in the stairwell, directing everyone to get seated. He sat into the driver's seat and started the engine, revving it up to build air pressure quickly.

"Are you guys doing ok?" he asked Hudson and Lanie.

Feeling it would be more helpful to show confidence—not fear—she gave her dad a big thumbs-up.

"Let's ROLL," she said.

She was still scared, but her move appeared to relax and comfort Hudson. He also offered a thumbs-up, adding, "Let's roll."

"Lanie, aquarium. Then, get your belts on," Mr. Speros said.

Lanie moved Buster's aquarium to the sink, then rushed up front to fasten her seat belt. When they pulled out of the campground, the tree limbs flapped, waving them goodbye. Flashes of lightning were immediately followed by rolls of thunder, warning of the arriving storm's energy. The digital display on the dashboard indicated that the outside temperature had dropped to 46 degrees.

The low canopy of clouds had darkened the sky even more, as though the day had been reset to dawn. Ordinarily, Lanie enjoyed rowdy storms, sitting at home watching the rainwater blast from the gutter downspouts. But this storm wasn't like those rainy days at home—its convoluted, tumbling canopy carried destructive energy.

"I hope we don't hit any ice," Mr. Speros said as he navigated the sharp turns. The road was clear so far, but as they'd been warned, water could be seen welling up on the road's mountainside shoulder. In some areas, it was flowing across the pavement and into the creek.

After a few minutes on the road, Lanie's dad turned to her and said with a piercing look, "If you *ever* pull anything like that again, you will be grounded until you go to college, do you understand?"

She knew he was talking about her chain attack on the fleeing Dodge. Before she had a chance to respond, her dad's stretched lips transitioned to a smile.

"But... that was sure a heck of a sight," he said calmly. "The way you were slingin' that chain, I thought you were gonna take that whole truck out. You probably did three thousand bucks in damage to it."

Lanie's smile grew so wide, she thought her face might crack. The tears came back to her eyes, so she turned back toward the windshield. She felt very strong.

From the seat behind, Hudson grabbed her shoulder and spoke above the thunder. "Remind me never to tangle with *you* in a brawl."

The Magna pitched from side to side on its soft air springs as Mr. Speros navigated the tight turns. On the entry into a sharp left curve, Mr. Speros had to brake hard, and the motorhome leaned precariously to the right. Lanie stiffened her arms and grimaced, hoping they wouldn't tip over. Instead, a stack of dishes escaped from one of the overhead cabinets and crashed onto the floor, creating a storm of ceramic debris. Buster's aquarium tipped out of the sink and the whole assembly exploded in the stairwell, sending water and blue gravel everywhere.

Mr. Speros didn't look back, but said, "Sorry guys, my fault, too fast into that turn!"

Hudson jumped out of his chair and scrambled toward the door, sliding on the wet rubble. Lanie watched and Isaiah howled about the welfare of his fish. Hanging onto the door's handrail, Hudson stood back up, holding his hand high in triumph. Pinched between his fingers, he had Buster, who flopped frantically.

Stabilizing himself with one hand against the countertop, Hudson pulled a plastic cup down from the cabinet. He added water from the sink and flicked Buster in. Dropping to his knees on the carpet up front, he relayed the cup to Lanie. She stowed Buster's new home in the cupholder on the dashboard. Isaiah was satisfied and said, "Thanks, Hudson, good thinking!"

If the day's events hadn't included the incident with the snoopers at the campground, Lanie would have been frightened about the weather conditions—and the way her dad was driving. But she knew that they needed to get ahead of the storm, so she braced herself against the armrests, defying her fear.

"Slow down!" Isaiah yelled to his dad. He was struggling to keep the tablet on his lap.

As they rolled into the saddle between two ridges, Lanie could see water in the apex of a narrow turn ahead. There was a guardrail on the inside of the turn, protecting against a fifteen-foot drop to a wash below. Lanie's dad slowed as they approached. The water was flowing in a strong current across the road, then into the wash through the guardrail. The guardrail was bisected halfway through the turn by a jagged, spire-like boulder.

"I don't like the looks of this," Mr. Speros said. "The road under the water could be failing."

The flow didn't look threatening—maybe ankle deep, Lanie thought. Mr. Speros appeared to think the same because he started to creep through the water. As they entered the middle of the turn, Lanie felt stiff bumps when the motorhome's front wheels dropped into potholes.

Her dad applied more throttle and pushed ahead. As the rear wheels crossed the flowing water, the motorhome's tail hitched to the left, then the whole coach leaned toward the wash. Lanie screamed; she couldn't help it. Mr. Speros muttered some expletives, then he cranked on the steering wheel and accelerated. The coach's body shuddered and groaned as the tail was forced against the boulder by the water current. The worst thing to do would be to stop. Lanie's dad was aware of this, and he kept driving forward.

The Magna leaned so far that even Mr. Speros was uncomfortable. "Not good," he said as he watched the side mirror.

Hail was mixing with the rain, and it pecked at the roof and windshield. A blinding flash was accompanied by an immediate cannon-like slap of thunder overhead. Lanie felt the shockwave of the thunder as much as she heard it, and she ducked instinctively. A brilliant shower of sparks and embers fell, turning the gray rain silver. Then, something hit the roof of the motorhome. The flow of the water had pinned the coach against the tall rock. Water welled up around the back wheels and surged around the storage bays.

The roadway had buckled, having been undermined by the flow. With no shoulder remaining, the guardrail was also failing. Mr. Speros' eyes stayed focused on the mirrors, but he shook his head.

"The road's breaking up, hang on!" He looked briefly at Lanie and Hudson. "If we're pushed into the wash, your job is to get Isaiah, yourself, and Hudson to safety, do you understand? You do *not* assist me."

Lanie didn't say anything but nodded with wide eyes. She looked at the deep wash, then at the windows around her, suddenly aware that she might have to consider escape paths.

Stepping farther onto the throttle, her dad had to nose the Magna into the mountain on the opposite side of the road in order to escape the crumbling roadway. The fiberglass valance on the front fascia cracked and snapped as soil and rocks were pushed aside. A section of the roadway the size of a small car sank behind the motorhome, then rolled into the wash with an earth-shaking thud. Lanie's knuckles were white with tension, still clamped to her seat. The Magna's rear axle hopped and shimmied as the dual tires clawed at the road's receding edge.

Right then, the coach lurched forward, settling flat on the ground just before the guardrail succumbed to the current. Mr. Speros whistled in relief and cocked his head, then straightened the RV on the road. The Magna's Allison automatic transmission casually upshifted into second, then third gear as they accelerated up the mountain, leaving the new chasm behind.

There was no time for a damage assessment; swinging cabinet doors banged open and shut as they climbed higher toward the mountaintop. Mr. Speros was fighting patches of ice on the road and was too focused for any questions. The blacktop was covered in a layer of white hail that looked like snow, and the motorhome occasionally danced a dangerous sidestep as they crossed frozen stretches. Riding in a drifting car was entertaining to Lanie, but the same sensation in a motorhome felt unnatural and terrifying.

As they crested the summit, the storm's intensity flagged. The driving rain gave way to a drizzle and tracts of open sky started to appear overhead.

Despite its anger, the storm seemed hesitant to cross the top of the mountain, and it let the travelers go. Lanie unbuckled herself and sat into the sofa next to Hudson, sharing an uncomfortable glance.

"I hate to tell you this," Hudson said, "but I'm kinda ready for this trip to be over already." Lanie laughed out loud and leaned into his shoulder.

Mr. Speros pulled over in a long parking area on the side of the highway that semi-trucks used to check their brakes.

"I need to check this rig out," he said when he'd set the parking brake. "C'mon, let's take a breather."

The whole group took the opportunity to get out and blow off some steam. Outside on the tarmac, they could see the sprawling Nevada desert ahead of them on the horizon, with a broad lake visible in the distance. Lanie sighed, looking at the peacefulness of the open space ahead.

"Well, we made it," Hudson said, focusing on the distant horizon. "Man, I'm starving. We should make lunch."

Hudson apparently had not been traumatized enough to forget his appetite, and this made Lanie smile. "Yeah, good idea, let's put it together. I'll tell my dad." She walked around the motorhome, taking inventory of the damage. The body was coated in silt and mud up to its waistline, and the left side had gouges and scrapes starting about halfway back. The lower body panels behind the left rear wheels were gone, exposing the big radiator fans. The fans had leaves and mud packed between their blades, and Mr. Speros was digging it out.

"Oh man," she said, standing near him. "It's a little torn up, isn't it, Dad?"

"Yeah, the old girl took a couple hits today. She's running OK, though," he said over the clatter of the idling engine. He stood up and put his hands on Lanie's shoulders. "Been a tough day so far, but you've handled it like a pro. Thank, and thank you for managing Isaiah for me."

She downplayed her involvement. "You're the one who did the driving—nice work, Pops. We're gonna make lunch."

"OK, go ahead. You'll have to eat on the road—we have a lotta ground to cover today. And I'm not sure what we'll do about these clowns who've been causing us trouble." He cast away a big blob of pine needles and mud, then one of the electric fans resumed spinning. "But we'll figure it out, it's gonna be fine."

Lanie knew that parents were obligated to tell their children *"things would be fine."* She also knew that their troubles weren't over yet but worrying wouldn't help. She walked around the back of the Magna. Its rear fascia had been ripped loose by the guardrail, and cottony insulation flapped from a gash in the wall above the bedroom. *The tree hit by lightning fell on the roof!* Small branches hung off the roof's edge. When she got inside, she found Isaiah helping Hudson prepare microwave pizzas and chicken nuggets.

The day was slipping by fast. It was mid-afternoon and the sun was far behind them when the travelers set out again, into the valley beyond. Mr. Speros had decided to shorten their trip by a day, based on how things were going. Lanie knew they couldn't take their planned route to the beach through southern California anyway. "We're on the wrong side of the Sierra Nevada now," Mr. Speros said as the mountain range leveled off into the valley.

"Ugh, now what?" he added, then began slowing. There were flashing yellow lights ahead and Department of Transportation trucks were putting up road barricades at a junction. The crew was being escorted by a Highway Patrol officer who walked up to Mr. Speros's window as they stopped.

"Highway 395 is closed to the south," the officer reported. "Heavy snow falling near Mammoth—they won't even start plowing for a couple more hours."

Mr. Speros nodded, thanked the officer, and made the left turn onto a desolate section of highway heading northeast. Hudson and Lanie peered through the windshield at the nothingness ahead. Her dad squeezed his forehead. "Oh man," he said to the dashboard. "We're gonna have to go home through Las Vegas or Death Valley. Who knows where we're gonna stop tonight."

"Hey, we're gonna pass by Area 51 then!" Hudson said, attempting to lighten the mood.

Lanie had heard about Area 51's infamous reputation for secretive military aircraft testing, as well as supposed UFO sightings. "Oh yeah! Maybe we'll meet the aliens that dumped you with your parents twelve years ago," Lanie said, digging her knuckles into Hudson's shoulder.

"If we do, I'm gonna ask them for a ride home—before this thing leaves us stranded," he said, kicking away a broken cabinet door.

A sign came into view on the shoulder of the highway. Lanie's eyebrows arched when she read the destinations, and she nudged Hudson.

"Tonopah! Dad, we can stop there tonight!" She turned to Hudson and lowered her voice. "The other mine site was there—remember the cards in the box?"

Hudson nodded. "The way things are going, we might find another Myriad truck there too," he joked.

"Tonopah's as good a place as any," her dad conceded. "When we get some cell service, see if you can find an RV campground near town."

The crew drove late into the evening and the moon was creeping into the pink sky when the group arrived in Tonopah, Nevada. Mr. Speros parked at the curb outside a small Italian café along the highway. The old silver-strike mining town was quiet. A tall historic hotel stood nearby, and

Lanie could see the colorful lights of slot machines flashing behind the faceted glass of the lobby. Otherwise, most of the hotel's windows were dark. In fact, the café and a sketchy-looking bar across the street appeared to be the only other open establishments on the block.

The Speroses and Hudson were the only customers in the café, and the staff was happy to have the business. Largely devoid of decoration, the open dining room was brightly lit and clean. A chalkboard with daily specials was the only framed item on any of the walls. Their server was a friendly teenage girl with buck teeth; she brought flatware wrapped in paper napkins and ice water in ancient Coca-Cola-branded glasses. The tables were so old that the faux woodgrain had worn away from the surface on some of them. But all of this was just perfect, and Lanie was happy to be there.

The group split an assortment of pasta, buffalo wings, and fried mozzarella sticks while Lanie's dad listened to each traveler's own version of the day's tales. Isaiah's was the most humorous, as he considered all three of his companions to be crazy. "I dunno know why we stopped to see the road falling apart—somebody coulda been killed!" he lectured as segments of spaghetti sprinkled his lap.

When Hudson asked about the men who were trying to get into their RV, Isaiah told him, "Lanie taught 'em a lesson; she'll take care of 'em next time." This brought a roar of laughter from her dad. The environment was safe and comfortable, and Lanie was at peace. She was thankful the rough day was behind them, and they were able to finish the day with family time.

The RV campsite was only a quarter mile up the road, and it wasn't much more than a gravel parking lot with strategically placed RV connections. Hudson finally called his parents and let them know they were coming home early—and that their itinerary had changed. As he'd done the day before, he left out the day's most fretful details. Mr. Speros let Hudson know he didn't approve, adding that he planned to talk to the Newmans when he got home anyway.

"That's OK, we'll be *home* then," Hudson said with a smile. Hudson's mom would be a nervous wreck if she knew what had been happening.

Lanie swept the floor a second time, trying to collect any glass or ceramic debris before anyone walked around barefoot. Her face must have indicated she was plowing a field of thoughts in her mind, because Mr. Speros queried her.

"You look far away, are you OK?"

There were a million things cycling through Lanie's head. Clues and evidence were everywhere, but she'd had no time to piece anything together. "The guy I saw at the ATM in Tehachapi was the one driving the Durango today," Lanie said. She shivered with discomfort, knowing that he'd probably followed her into the country store.

"There were *three* today," Hudson interjected, surprising both Lanie and Mr. Speros. "There was a guy in the back seat; I think he was old. I didn't see his face very well, but he had a long gray moustache."

"Well, the *good* news is that they headed west toward Sacramento. With any luck, there are four hundred miles between them and us now," Mr. Speros said. "You guys get cleaned up and let's get to bed; I want us on the road early tomorrow. Isaiah's gonna sleep with me tonight."

With the lights out, the moonlit desert outside the windows had a bright, interstellar glow. As she sat in the dark combing out her hair in the reading chair, Lanie glanced up at the ridge behind the old hotel. There on the slope, the rusty iron headframe of a mine elevator stood among a yard of retired mining equipment. The iron tower looked nearly identical to the one in the canyon behind her house. A jolt of excitement rushed through Lanie's body when she saw a faded sign at the base of the headframe which displayed the Myriad Exploration logo.

"Hudson!" she rasped.

"What now?" He had been drifting off in his bunk but rolled over. He sat up right away when he saw what had excited Lanie, and promptly hit his head on the overhead bunk again.

"Oh wow, it's right here!" He rubbed the pain from his forehead, then pulled on his glasses and joined Lanie at the reading table window. The mine yard was fenced and appeared to be part of an outdoor museum. The whole compound was only a stone's throw from the old hotel. At the rear of the hotel, a black Tesla's nose protruded from the alley, parked in the shadows. By then, Lanie had become skeptical of coincidences—she would have bet money it was the same car she'd seen in Seligman.

"That car—I think I saw it on Route 66 our first day on the road," she said.

"It's a black Tesla, there are a million of them," Hudson said.

"In Tonopah, Nevada?!" Lanie tried to stifle her voice.

Staring at the fenced compound, Hudson said, "We gotta get over there in the morning."

"It's gonna have to be early; let's get up before my dad."

"Deal."

## Chapter 8

# THE INCIDENT AT AJH FORK

At dawn, Monday morning, Lanie emerged from a deep sleep to find her dad had already risen and begun preparing for departure. Leaning over the bunk, she looked down at Hudson. He was still out cold, lying face down in his pillow. *So much for our morning exploration plan*, Lanie thought.

The sun hadn't yet appeared over the eastern horizon when the Magna rolled out of Tonopah toward Las Vegas. Mr. Speros had declined Lanie and Hudson's request to stay until the mining museum opened, preferring to get them on the road early. Lanie wasn't awake enough to argue and sat slouched in the front seat. When he drove through the night—or early in the morning—her dad would listen to the music or radio shows of the 1940s on the satellite radio at low volume. The muted horns and strings of the big swing bands sounded ethereal, and Lanie would daydream that they were driving back through time to attend a glittering, ghostly ball.

She watched her dad's face as he drove. His facial features were exaggerated by the dawn light. Occasionally, he'd squint and bunch up his lips—a dead giveaway that he was focused on a stressful topic. It was too early to start a conversation, so Lanie guessed that he was thinking of the men who had interfered with their vacation.

Hudson leaned against the window, watching the passing desert in a morning daze. Isaiah had fallen back asleep sitting upright, clutching his blankie and a toy pirate ship. Lanie sprinkled a few fish food flakes for Buster in the cupholder.

Sometime around breakfast, the group meshed into morning rush hour in Las Vegas. Early sunlight lit the glamorous casino hotels along Las Vegas Boulevard as they inched along Interstate 15. The white columns on the towers of Caesar's Palace glowed in the reflection of the Mirage hotel's gold windows. Hudson was fully charged and ready for the day; he was scrolling on his mom's phone with a determined look on his face.

"What are you doing?" Lanie asked, noticing his furrowed brow.

"I'm reading about that mine in Tonopah—trying to see if there's any connection to the mine at home. The one in Tonopah is owned by the city now. It's closed, except for short tours of a couple tunnels."

"There might be no connection, other than that Myriad used to operate both," Mr. Speros interjected.

"The way things are going, I'm thinking both of these sites are not as abandoned as they look," Hudson said.

Mr. Speros seemed like he wanted to chime in but didn't have a chance—Sabine was calling. They'd played phone tag the night before, since the cell service was patchy in Tonopah. Lanie figured Sabine must have been freaked out because she was asking a lot of questions and pleading with Lanie's dad to get everyone home. He layered on assurances and briefed Sabine on their revised itinerary before he hung up.

Four more hours passed slowly, during which Lanie wrote out notes on the many pieces of their puzzle. As she listed their clues and events on the lined paper, it became even more apparent that the breach in their backyard was extremely important to at least a few people that they didn't know. Her notes also confirmed what she already knew—that their home on Constellation Way was hiding secrets. It was hiding a history that went deeper than the previous owners.

Just after lunch, Mr. Speros tapped the brakes and steered onto an exit ramp. Lanie glanced up, again seeing the sign indicating the exit for Seligman.

"We're going back to Seligman? Why, Dad?"

Hudson had been sprawled on the sofa but quickly sat up.

"I wanna stop and talk to this local yoyo that you met in the junk shop," Lanie's dad said. "I think he knows more than he was telling you about the Myriad stuff he had in his shop—and I think that's what got us into trouble. I wanna know what else he has. Paperwork, knick-knacks, anything."

Lanie wrinkled her nose and smiled, excited that her dad was embracing their case. She locked eyes with Hudson, who gave her a thumbs-up. As they coasted into the west end of Seligman, congestion and activity could be seen obstructing Route 66 ahead. The flashing red and blue lights of emergency vehicles sparkled in the wavy air that rose from the asphalt. When they drew near, Mr. Speros lifted his foot off the accelerator so that they coasted past at fifteen miles per hour. Fire trucks and sheriff's cruisers lined the block. Yellow caution tape stretched across the site of the antique store where Lanie and Hudson had bought their items.

The building was gone. Only a smoldering black and gray pile of rubble remained between the blackened brick walls. The roofs of the neighboring buildings on either side were perforated from the heat of the fire in between, and their windows were broken. Everything in the antique store—the roof, the furniture, the glass cases—was reduced to ash and cinder less than knee height.

Lanie's mouth hung as she pressed her forehead against the side window. She looked over her shoulder at Mr. Speros, who watched, but said nothing.

"Oh my gosh," whispered Hudson. He and Lanie exchanged flabbergasted expressions.

Firefighters picked and kicked at the wreckage in the center of the open space. Local onlookers stood near the yellow ribbon boundary. Mr. Speros didn't stop; he rolled past, then slowly accelerated away. He stared ahead in silence as he drove out of town.

Finally, he said, "Seat belts on please. Buckle back in; we're not stopping." As though he were speaking to the road ahead, he added, "I don't know what's going on here, but it's making me nervous."

After thinking a few moments, he continued, "The items you guys bought at that shop, keep them. Don't do anything with them; we're gonna lock everything up. We may have to get the police involved when we get home."

"Do you think somebody burned that shop down?" Lanie asked. "Those guys in the Durango?" She already knew the answer.

"It sure looks suspicious. That building was nearly one hundred years old; for it to burn to the ground only a couple days after we were there is one too many coincidences. But right now, that's what we have—a lot of coincidences and not a lot of solid evidence." Her dad didn't take his eyes from the road. "Not much we can do yet. But I don't think you should worry about this. We'll be safe, I'll see to that."

For the next hour, the travelers were quiet. Nobody felt like listening to music. Mr. Speros had veered onto the ramp near Ash Fork, heading south toward Phoenix. The highway between Ash Fork and Prescott was not heavily traveled; it was one of the reasons Mr. Speros liked to use it on his routes. Few drivers were in a hurry to pass the motorhome on the two-lane highway then, and he could drive at a leisurely speed. But that day, Lanie's dad drove faster. She knew he wanted to get them home, into the comfortable safety of their own house.

Lanie also figured that her dad felt responsible for having brought Hudson along on what turned out to be a dangerous journey. She turned to Hudson, who seemed to be content on the sofa, with the memories of their trip circulating in his head.

"You wanna sit up here?" she asked him. He nodded, so Lanie flopped herself on the sofa and Hudson buckled in up front. Isaiah was flipping through his dinosaur pop-up book in the chair near the door. The front of the coach bobbed and floated over some of the uneven road. Lanie stretched her neck to look over her dad's shoulder—their speed was seventy miles per hour.

Ten minutes later, they descended into a large, open mesa which allowed a view of the miles of straight road ahead. The highway divided on the mesa, creating a wide median between the opposing roadways. Lanie leafed through the pages of her notebook, reading the notes that Hudson had added. That's when she heard her dad curse in a low growl. She looked up to see him leaning forward, staring into the rearview mirror outside his window.

"Dad, what's wrong?" She pressed her cheek against the side window above the sofa, looking into the same mirror. Her skin grew cold. The white Dodge Durango was coming up behind them, moving fast. The driver would soon be attempting to pass them. Lanie shrieked, covering her mouth.

"What? What's going on?" Hudson asked, craning his neck, but he couldn't see.

"Alright, calm down," Mr. Speros said. "Is everyone's seat belt on? Snug them up."

Lanie tugged at hers, cinching it tighter around her waist as she twisted on the sofa to face forward. She didn't want her back to the window as the Durango passed. Lanie heard the familiar dial tone of 9-1-1 as Mr. Speros called for emergency service through his phone's hands-free connection. But the attempt only returned the *beep-beep-beep* of no service.

Hudson held onto the armrests rigidly, not knowing what to expect. In the mirror, Lanie watched with wide eyes as the Durango slid out from behind the Magna then began pulling alongside—and she thought her heart might climb into her throat.

"What's happening? What are they DOING?!" Hudson asked as he watched the SUV's white roof approaching through Lanie's window.

Mr. Speros began accelerating. They were moving fast—much faster than Lanie thought the Magna would go. Her dad had thrown his phone into the cupholder next to Buster, who was swimming idly.

The roof of the Durango was at Lanie's hip height, and she could see through its broken rear-side window. There were many items in the cargo area behind the back seat, including some of the Myriad Exploration artifacts she'd seen in the antique store, days earlier. The front passenger window of the SUV rolled down and the man with the white hair reached his arm out. He pointed a stiff, determined finger at Mr. Speros, then at the far roadside—he wanted them to pull over.

"DAD, DON'T *STOP!*" Lanie yelled, although she knew her dad had no intention of doing so. Mr. Speros focused on the road ahead, occasionally glancing at the man in the Durango. He gave the white-haired man no response, and they sped along side by side at over 85mph. The SUV's driver honked his horn and the white-haired man repeatedly stabbed his finger at Mr. Speros, demanding that he pull over. Lanie could see someone seated in the second row of seats, just as Hudson had told them.

Hudson had sunken in his chair and was keeping an eye on both the open road and Mr. Speros.

Isaiah asked "Dada, what's happening, why are you going so fast?" but he received no answer.

The two lanes narrowed as they entered a bridge over a wide dry basin. Guardrails lined either side of the highway. Lanie watched as the white-haired man leaned back into the SUV, then returned through the window, holding a small black gun. She screamed in horror, fearing that her dad might be shot. The man held the gun sideways, waving it at the ground in a final, threatening directive to pull over, then he pointed it at the front wheel of the motorhome.

Mr. Speros didn't wait for what was next; he yanked the steering wheel to the left. The coach heeled over and swerved into the Durango. Glasses and cups dumped onto the floor in a series of crashes behind Lanie. The Durango was swept sideways in a quaking slam against the motorhome's body, just outside of Lanie's window. Four times the Durango's weight, the Magna crushed the SUV against the guardrail on the left edge of the road, creating a screaming, squealing tail of orange sparks and dust.

Terrified at the proximity of the action, Lanie leaned away from the roof of the SUV, which was smashed against her window's lower edge. She was too aghast to scream, and her breaths were uncontrollably short. The white-haired man had dropped his gun and retreated inside the Durango, and he was yelling instructions at the driver. The force of the motorhome's impact had broken the glass out of the rear door and Lanie could see the old man in the back seat. He was holding onto the front seat headrests in panic.

Lanie's thoughts darted and flashed; seconds stretched as they raced along the guardrail. Sparks, pieces of broken trim, and silvery splinters of glass rained in the wake of the SUV. Mr. Speros didn't slow down. In fact, Lanie could hear the Cummins engine's turbocharger whistling in labor as he kept his foot planted on the accelerator. Lanie could see that the guardrail terminated only yards ahead, into a wide concrete pier that jutted out from the shoulder.

The Durango wouldn't fit through the gap—there would be a violent crash—and Lanie clenched her teeth and covered her ears, but she couldn't close her eyes. The Magna's twenty-thousand-pound weight was dragging the SUV toward the barrier as though it were a shopping cart. Hudson pushed his feet against the dash and covered his face with his forearms. Lanie's dad watched only the road ahead as though he were preparing to crash-land a plane. Then Lanie saw him do something shocking. As they approached the end of the bridge, he turned to the left and gave the men in the SUV one slow, confident wave.

The concrete anchorage ripped into the SUV's grille at chest height, forcing the vehicle upward in a thunderous, concussive blast. With nowhere to go, the Durango's hood and roof buckled, and the body shell collapsed like a tent whose poles had been ripped away. The windshield splintered, and a fog of smoke and white fabric appeared in all the windows of the SUV as its airbags deployed. The force of the impact punched the SUV into the Magna's flank, breaking the side glass and scattering wood and plastic debris through the interior.

The glass showered Lanie's back, and she hugged her knees tightly. A large trim panel was cast loose behind Mr. Speros's head and flew into the kitchen. A ripping, tearing, mangling cacophony of sounds echoed inside the motorhome as the Durango slid backward. Swerving back to the right, Mr. Speros peeled the Magna away from the SUV when it cleared the concrete barrier. Suddenly, it got quieter.

The airborne Durango seemed to glide in slow motion as it banked left, off the highway. Lanie couldn't see the men; the deflating airbags obscured the window openings. The truck began a nosedive into the median and Lanie saw that the vehicle had been mutilated—nearly beyond recognition. Its engine was exposed, spraying steam and liquid. The driver's door hung like a broken wing.

The white wreckage piled into the soft desert floor and began rolling through the brush. As it tumbled, a blooming plume of dust, glass, and plastic radiated in every direction. Items from the interior were flung high and far. After a few moments, the Durango disappeared behind a tall grove of sage bushes.

Only then did Mr. Speros lift his right foot, and the coach started slowing. But he didn't stop.

"Who's hurt? Is anyone hurt?!" he called out. Seeing that Hudson was intact, he spun his neck around. "Lanie, Isaiah, are you both OK? Answer me *loudly*!"

"OK!" Lanie said.

"OK!" Isaiah said through his tears. He was crying now, for the first time on the trip. Lanie unbuckled and ran to him, smothering him with a protective hug.

"It's OK buddy, it's OK. It's all over," she said and did her best to soothe him—though the panic hadn't evaporated from her own blood yet.

Mr. Speros slowed the motorhome to a school-zone pace and crept along the shoulder. He stopped at a turnout in the road three miles past the crash scene, dumping the air brake pressure. Untangling himself from the seatbelt, he ran back to his children and dropped to his knees, hugging them together.

"Are you both sure you're OK? Let me see. Dear God, Lanie, I forgot you were so close to the window." He searched her head and body and ran his hands through Isaiah's hair. "Hudson, come here."

When Hudson stumbled over, Mr. Speros searched him as well. Satisfied that the group seemed to be OK, he slumped onto the sofa. Lanie saw he was bleeding from his left cheek.

"You're hurt, Dad," she said, running to grab a paper towel from amongst the rubble of the kitchen. She dabbed a long cut on her dad's cheekbone.

"The trim behind the curtain hit me," Mr. Speros mumbled. "I'll be OK." He jumped up and grabbed his phone, looked at the screen, and dumped it back in the cupholder. Still no service.

"Hudson, check your mom's phone." He pointed at Hudson's pocket.

Likewise, no signal. Nobody spoke for what seemed like minutes, but only a few seconds had passed.

"Will they come after us?" Lanie asked, looking backward out the window.

"No. Those men are gonna need help. But they aren't getting it from us. We'll call for emergency service as soon as we see a call box or get a good cell signal."

A semi with a canvas-covered load rumbled past on the other side of the median.

"That driver will probably radio for help; our mission is getting us all home—and getting Hudson back to his parents. Those guys and their gun are on their own," he said, waving his hand toward the back of the coach. "I don't think they'll be a problem for us anymore."

Mr. Speros surveyed their situation inside. The interior was in shambles. The wall cabinets in the kitchen had fallen, unloading their remaining contents on the floor. The countertop and sink were separated from the wall and leaning. Broken glass and splintered wood covered the floor.

"I need to make sure this thing is safe to drive. Everyone outside for a few minutes, come on," Mr. Speros said.

On the outside, the situation was worse. Three of the four storage bay doors on the driver's side were gone, and the fourth was hanging by its hinge, dragging on the pavement in front of the rear wheels. A pool of water was forming under the coach, pouring from a shattered valve in the plumbing bay. The left rearview mirror swung on the front corner near the road, suspended by its wiring. Lanie knew the motorhome was ruined, but under the bedroom its engine idled with unfazed confidence. Green liquid dripped slowly from the rear corner under the exposed fans.

"It's leaking coolant," Mr. Speros said. "Something hit the radiator during the wreck. We need to get going."

With everyone back inside and belted in, Mr. Speros accelerated back up to highway speed. Wind noise roared through the broken windows now, but Lanie didn't care—they were moving, and moving quickly. She sat up front and Hudson sat with Isaiah at the reading table. She spun her chair sideways, facing her dad so she could see everyone.

"What are we gonna do now?" Lanie asked.

"We're gonna stop as soon as we can get any sort of mechanical service for this thing," Mr. Speros said. "I'll see if the Highway Patrol can meet us wherever we stop, and we can open a police report. And, I'm gonna call Hudson's parents," he said, looking at Hudson. "I don't know how that's gonna go, but you can bet they won't be thrilled."

Lanie looked at Hudson. "They're gonna *freak*."

"Yeah, they're gonna freak," Hudson echoed.

"There was stuff from the antique store in the back of the Durango," Lanie said. "I saw it when they were alongside. I'll bet they burned that store. I hope they didn't hurt Bud."

Mr. Speros didn't say anything, but his glance told Lanie he assumed the worst. Lanie had a terrible vision of Bud being pistol-whipped by the white-haired man while his accomplice lit a fire in the shop.

With the details of the event starting to coagulate in her head, Lanie recalled her dad's wave to the SUV driver. It occurred to her that her dad had a plan long before their encounter ended. The men in the Durango were *not* in control of their situation, and when they lost that control, they lost their focus. She also realized that her dad had a high capacity for dealing with emergencies without panic. She promised herself she'd follow his example in the future.

"You knew how that was gonna end as soon as they pulled up next to us, didn't you, Dad?"

Mr. Speros didn't take his eyes from the road. "You never know *exactly* how it's gonna go," he said. "But you can steer your odds by making good decisions fast—and early."

Lanie sat back in the seat, watching Hudson and Isaiah. Now that her head had stopped swimming, the events of the last hour were starting to seem less traumatic. This surprised Lanie. She thought she should feel scared—or want to cry—but she didn't. In fact, she felt... *pretty good*. The bright blue sky was reassuring, and long, tapered clouds pointed toward Phoenix. The danger and explosive action of the previous forty-eight hours had been an intense, new experience for her. She struggled to fit the new emotions and perceptions into the categories she already knew.

Lanie felt like she'd entered the next chapter of her life. It didn't feel wrong or right, it just felt... *new*. A smile grew on her face as her curls whipped about. She had no fear of what was next. She would welcome the adventures—and would be ready for them.

## Chapter 9

# WHY WE FIGHT

"There were parts of that truck scattered all over the highway and the median," Officer Rand said to Mr. Speros. "Whatever you tangled with, you wadded it up really well. But there's nothing else—the truck and whomever was in it are gone."

Mr. Speros was dumbfounded. "It's only been a couple hours! Those thugs must have at least been dazed, but more likely hurt—how could they be gone... and their truck be gone?"

"It would take a slick cleanup crew for sure. Especially considering that they picked up any pieces with the vehicle's identification number. They even picked up most of the pieces of your motorhome," the Arizona Highway Patrol officer said. "In all my years on these highways, I've never seen a crash disappear like that, but it supports your story that these people didn't want to be identified. I think a northbound truck driver stopped to assist, based on CB radio traffic. But nobody else called in the incident."

Mr. Speros rubbed the graying stubble on his chin. He and Officer Rand stood in front of Gemini Truck Service in the hills north of Prescott Valley, along with another officer who had responded in a separate cruiser. Lanie and Hudson sat nearby at a picnic table in front of the repair shop's slump-block office, listening to the conversation as best they could.

Looking dejected, Mr. Speros returned to the table carrying an envelope of paperwork.

"They can't do much, without the other vehicle involved," he complained. "I figured that might be the case."

After calling the highway patrol, Mr. Speros had called Hudson's parents, recommending that they drive up to Prescott to pick him up. It seemed silly to Lanie that the Newmans were driving up, only eighty miles from home. But Mr. Speros said it was the best thing to do.

Isaiah's metal Tonka dump truck toy survived the last leg of the trip, so he'd pulled it out and was playing in the dirt where Lanie and Hudson sat. She wondered if Isaiah understood what was going on. If he did, it wasn't concerning him. She'd heard that young children were more resilient in traumatic situations. *Hopefully that is true*, she thought. Staring down at her dirty shoes, many thoughts crossed her mind. It worried Lanie that there were more people involved in their pursuit than those they'd just run off the highway—they might all still be in danger.

"What do you think we should do when we get home? I mean about those guys who followed us," she asked.

Hudson had been tuned out, his eyes wandering the parking lot. "What... you mean like setting booby traps or something?"

Lanie thought about setting traps, then immediately had an image of her dad getting caught up in a falling net while doing yardwork, and she laughed. "Ahh, I don't know... doesn't sound very practical."

"Well, I'm open to ideas," Hudson said.

"Maybe we should get our parents to add more cameras that link to the ones we already have on our doorbell," she said. "The good thing for you is, these guys don't know who you are—or where you live. They know where *I* live though."

After thinking a moment, she added, "Maybe we should just leave the mine stuff out, so they can take it. Then they'll go away." Even as she spoke the words, Lanie knew it was a silly idea.

"They don't even know what we have," Hudson said. "They probably think we have some keys to a safe, or a map, or something. I don't think that would work."

Lanie smiled at Hudson. "We DO have keys and a map, stupid."

Hudson flashed a sheepish grin. "Oh yeah—I guess so. But that's *your* stuff. What if the punch cards and microfiche you found really *are* important? Why should we give those rats what we found?"

Lanie considered for a moment. "You're right, *we* found that stuff, and it's *our* neighborhood. None of it is theirs. We shouldn't give up *anything*." A determined look came over her face and her eyes narrowed. "We fight—and we win," she said, bumping Hudson's fist.

At first, she was proud of her motivational call to duty, then Lanie twisted her lips in discouragement. "We still don't know *how* we're going to fight and win yet though."

They both stared back out into the parking lot, then Lanie jerked her head back toward Hudson when she heard him cry out.

"Stupid idiot bird!" he yelled. A big black crow was leaving their airspace overhead.

Lanie saw that Hudson had a long, drippy white streak on his left arm. She immediately snorted out a hoarse laugh, then realized the bird poop had splattered on her own shirt as well. Looking disgusted, Lanie shook her head at Hudson. "Eighty more miles... we just gotta get eighty more miles, and this trip will be over."

Mr. Speros emerged from the garage carrying a cracked tray with sandwiches and chips. "Lunch!" he said as he came toward them. "*Late* lunch, anyway." When he saw what Lanie and Hudson were cleaning from their shirts, his smile slipped momentarily, then sprouted again. "At least our luck on this trip has been consistent!" he said through a laugh.

He spread out plates on the picnic table, which was shaded by a palo verde tree near the shop. Mr. Speros assigned menu items as the travelers sat for the final meal of their trip. He'd assembled roast beef sandwiches, along with a haphazard assortment of veggies, crackers, and hummus.

"I'm trying to use what's in the refrigerator, since it doesn't seem to be cooling anymore," he said.

"Dad, Hudson and I were talking," Lanie said as she rubbed hand sanitizer through her fingers.

"Uh oh." Mr. Speros smiled. "What did the two of you decide? I hope you don't have any other secret organizations you want to interfere with—the motorhome can't handle any more."

"We don't wanna give up," Hudson said. "If these people come back, we wanna fight—whatever we found is ours. And if this junk we found is important, we'll find out why."

Lanie nodded, signaling her agreement.

Mr. Speros appeared surprised. "Well, good for you guys," he said. "But you should know a couple things, first." He held up his index finger. "Number one—I've already let you both know that you do not ever, EVER engage anyone who approaches you regarding this situation. You run."

Extending another finger, he said, "Two—I'm in agreement. There was never any other option as far as I'm concerned. These guys messed with my family—and you, too, Hudson. They messed with our home and threatened our safety. When that happens, you fight." His eyes and expression were clear. "That fight is for *me* to lead—not you guys," he added. He pointed at the two friends. "Your safety—and Isaiah's safety—is my chief concern. When we get home, you both need to focus on school. I will figure out what our plan will be, and then you can help. Deal?"

"Deal," Hudson and Lanie responded together.

"DEAL!" Isaiah added.

Halfway through lunch, Hudson's parents arrived in Mr. Newman's gray Audi A8L. As they walked up to the table, Mr. Speros stood and shook hands with his neighbors. "Good to see you both. Thanks for driving all the way up here," he said as they all sat down.

Mrs. Newman squeezed Hudson in a bear hug, then held either side of his face with her hands as she looked into his eyes—presumably to see if his brain was still functioning correctly, Lanie thought. Spotting the smeared mess on Hudson's shirt, his mom quickly withdrew, wrinkling her lips. Mr. Speros was forthcoming with the Newmans, explaining that they weren't sure what their attackers were looking for but that they thought it was worth threatening the families.

Mr. Newman listened without interrupting, much like Hudson always did. Completely devoid of hair, Mr. Newman's scalp shined in the sunlight like an undecorated mannequin. His cool gray eyes monitored the expressions on Lanie's dad and the two friends as the details of the adventure were conveyed.

When the explaining was complete, Hudson's dad leaned away from the picnic bench. "Well, these fools messed with the wrong group. If they pop up at home, I'll be ready," he said with military-grade resolve. "And I'll come over at the drop of a hat—day or night—if you need help," he said to Mr. Speros. "I'll have your back just like my own family."

"Likewise," Mr. Speros replied. "Day or night."

Mrs. Newman, who had been quiet, said to Lanie, "Hudson tells us you are one tough cookie." Turning to Mr. Speros, she added, "She's got the soul of a warrior."

Lanie felt her ears getting hot. Her dad replied on her behalf, "Don't I know it, Pauline. We probably should have named her Athena!" He said, referring to the mythical Greek goddess of wisdom and battle strategy. "Tuesday, I'll call you over and we'll kick around the ideas you mentioned on the phone," he said to Hudson's dad.

119

The group was almost done with lunch when one of the technicians backed the Magna out of the shop. It didn't look any better but was at least mechanically safe. As they climbed into their Audi, the Newmans stopped at the sight of the battered RV. Hudson waved before he disappeared into the back seat. Lanie sighed—she was dismayed to see her partner whisked away.

# Chapter 10

# THE CORRIDOR

Just after dark, Mr. Speros swung the motorhome's nose into their neighborhood at the bottom of the hill. The familiar double-bump of the gutter at the crosswalk roused Lanie from her snooze. The headlights lit the brick mailboxes and desert landscaping of their neighbors' houses as the Magna entered the cul-de-sac of Constellation Way. Mr. Rinnas's house was first, with its saguaro cacti and kidney-shaped lawn.

Their own house next door was a welcome sight. Sabine's white BMW X3 was parked on the circular drive; Lanie figured her dad had called her as they neared Phoenix. When the front of the motorhome started crunching the gravel drive's pebbles under its tires, Lanie sighed with relief. Mr. Speros inched the coach through the side gate and parked adjacent to the back patio. The final whoosh of the air brakes was a relief to Lanie, and she stood to stretch.

The scent of the historic house was comforting as Lanie slid through the back door with her duffel bag. Everything seemed to be in its place, just as they had left it. Sabine was working on her laptop at the kitchen table and stood up as Lanie entered.

They'd met Sabine only a couple weeks after moving to Fountain Hills; she was a friend of their real estate agent. Over the past months, she and Lanie's dad had grown very close—close enough for Mr. Speros to be comfortable with her having a key to their house.

"Hey! You guys made it!" she said, offering a light hug. She leaned to one side to align her eyes with Lanie's. "Sorry it didn't go as planned, but I'm glad you're home safe."

"Yeah, it was a heck of a trip," Lanie wheezed, aware of how much of an understatement it was. "I'm glad we're home. Dad's coming in soon... Isaiah fell asleep before we got into the Valley."

Sabine's flawless sepia skin glowed under the warm light at the kitchen table. Her light brown eyes and perfectly puffed lips lent an exotic beauty that Lanie couldn't fault her dad for falling for. She didn't know Sabine's ethnicity, or anything about her family's roots—other than that she'd mentioned her father was from Brazil. Just the same, Lanie knew Mr. Speros wasn't looking for vanity; his relationship with Sabine had developed more out of their love of hiking and good food. The beauty was there for sure, but Lanie didn't discount Sabine's personality. She was kind and patient with Lanie and Isaiah—and didn't try to be a replacement for their mother.

It did, however, bother Lanie that some people assumed Sabine was Lanie's mom when they were all out together. She and Sabine both had curled, dark hair—but Sabine had to style her hair to get it to look that way. That's where the physical similarities ended. And Sabine was too young to be Lanie's mom anyway. Lanie bristled at the thought of Sabine being compared to her own beautiful mother, but she knew she was being a little unfair. In the three years since her mom died, Lanie had found her own way to deal with the grief, and she consciously kept that part of her life from affecting her relationship with Sabine. She secretly wished her dad would give her props for that, though.

Sabine went out to greet the other travelers, so Lanie set off to her room, flipping on light switches as she went. Her bed and stone-walled reading niche were inviting her to hole up for the night, but she knew she'd be expected to help unload. When she returned to the patio, Sabine and her dad had already formed a stack of items to be moved inside. The patio chairs were still in place around the pit where Mr. Speros had placed them. As she reached up the motorhome's steps to intercept a plastic tub, her dad asked, "Whatcha think, Lanie, let's order pizza?"

Lanie perked up. "Yesss!"

Her dad was never in the mood to cook after a long day on the road. He handed over his phone so Lanie could order online. She propped her back against the Magna's cracked nose and scrolled through their local pizza shop's menu. As she waited for the order confirmation from Atomic Pizza's app, Lanie realized that twenty-five feet ahead, she could see into the pit in the yard. The plywood had been shifted, exposing the edge of the hole. Under the plywood, in the blackness of the hole, Lanie saw a red light.

Her skin prickled in alarm and she stood straight, flattening herself against the front of the coach. Lanie's mind had spooked her into thinking the light was a lit cigarette, smoldering in the dark, then she felt foolish.

"Dummy," she murmured to herself, then crouched to get a better view.

It appeared to be an indicator light—like what might be on a TV when it was turned off. The light was far away from the hole, so she could only see it by peering into the opening at a shallow angle. This explained why nobody had seen it the night they found the pit. Lanie's sleepy mood was quickly washed over with excitement, but she also wondered who had moved the plywood. She wanted to show her dad right away but figured it would be best to wait until they had unloaded the motorhome; he was always anxious until the unpacking was done. Standing on the edge of the flagstone patio, Lanie watched her dad lock up the coach door.

"Did you get dinner ordered?"

"Yeah," she said. "Medium pepperoni, medium pesto, and a large Caesar salad, no anchovy," she recited from memory. It was their usual order.

Despite her tidy figure, Sabine had a weak spot for pub food. She whispered, "Ooh, pizza," in approval of the menu selection, then returned to collect another tub. Turning back to her dad after Sabine went into the house, Lanie said, "There's something you oughta see."

Mr. Speros glanced nervously at her as he walked toward the patio. "What's the problem now?" he said, looking around.

"It's fine, Dad, but look, here." She got down on her knees in the crushed granite and put her head close to the ground, pointing into the pit.

Lanie's dad did the same, opposite her. "Hmm... Interesting." was all he said.

Sitting on the gravel with her legs crossed, she waved a moth away from her glasses. "We gotta see what that light is; it might be a machine or something."

"Heh—not tonight, we're not," Mr. Speros said as he shook his head. "We came home a day early so that we could deal with this situation, and that's what we're gonna do. Bright and early tomorrow, we're getting started—and you're gonna help."

That plan sounded great, so Lanie turned to head inside when her dad gestured toward the house. Before she walked through the door, he held up a finger in front of his lips. "Keep this on the down-low. I don't want to tangle Sabine up in this if we can avoid it." Lanie nodded, then squeezed past.

Late that night, Lanie sat on the cushioned window seat in the bathroom that she and Isaiah shared, squeezing her hair dry. She was glad they'd come home early, despite missing out on a third of their vacation destinations. Her grandparents were driving up from Tucson the next day, and that made her happy. They would be staying in the spare bedroom for a couple of days to visit, then Isaiah would go home with them for a week. That plan was her dad's idea. With their pursuers at large—and the danger of the pit outside—Mr. Speros felt it would be best to give Isaiah some time with his grandparents.

After pulling the comforter and sheet down on her bed, Lanie sat and looked at the stone walls within her desk niche. The small workstation was a step up from her bedroom floor, with a built-in desktop and mesquite shelving. The stonework was the same native rock as the rest of the house, but not the glimmering pyrite-laced stones of the fireplace. A light recessed in the rockwork overhead gave the little study space a cozy, private feel. She thought it looked like the place she would be expected to stand if she were beamed up—like in an episode of *Star Trek*. She had already positioned the mementos from their trip on the shelving and cork board within the niche. The junk yard key ring hung on a hook above one of her most prized items—a shadow box commemorating the trip she'd taken with her mom in the Cadillac. It held a third set of keys to the car, which Mrs. Speros had given to Lanie in anticipation of her becoming a licensed driver on her sixteenth birthday. The shadow box was also the last thing that she'd given Lanie before she died.

After their dramatic day on the road, Lanie feared she'd have nightmares. But that night she drifted off quickly into in a long, dreamless sleep. Late that night, she was awakened by the sound of slapping, banging metal. The noise had come from near her desk and was over only a moment after it started. She sat bolt upright in her bed, her heart racing. The moonlight from the tall, narrow window next to her reading niche revealed that no one was in the room with her. At first, Lanie wondered if the sound had come from outside, but she saw nothing when she peered out into the peaceful yard. She slid off her bed and looked both directions down the hallway outside her room. Nobody else was up; she could hear Isaiah's deep sleeping breaths from his room next door.

Turning back to her bed, Lanie saw a sliver of red light on her desktop. Drawing near, she found the light coming from inside the cubby at the back of her desk. She snapped on the overhead light and opened the compartment. As soon as she'd slid the door open, the red light within the cubby went out. The little space was empty. Her Swingline stapler, old calculator, and other items were gone. At first, Lanie was alarmed, wondering who had taken her things. But she quickly calmed, figuring Isaiah had been rummaging in her desk. Pressing her cheek onto the desktop, Lanie saw the source of the red light—a small square lens flush with the inside roof of the cubby.

The exhaustion of the long day overcame Lanie's curiosity, so she resolved to investigate the little bin the following day. She let the cubby door slide closed and returned to bed.

Breakfast was a full-menu affair the next morning. When Lanie got to the kitchen she found Isaiah was already awake, sitting on the stool at the counter. Cool fall air was flowing in from the patio windows and she could smell bacon, sausage, and scrambled eggs. Pulling up a stool next to Isaiah, she tucked her flannel pajamas into the seat. She whispered, "Good morning, buddy," and rubbed his brown hair.

"Good morning, Lay-Lay," he said, nuzzling his face in her side.

"Well, hello!" Mr. Speros's voice echoed when he appeared from behind the stove. He slid a plate of eggs and berries across the counter to Lanie.

"Hi, Dad," she said. "What's with the big breakfast?"

"We gotta use all this food from the trip—it won't keep. Did you sleep good?" he asked.

"Yeah, I don't think I moved all night." She flashed a weak thumbs-up. "Dad... uhh... did you take anything from the bin in my desk? You know, the storage compartment just like the one in the desk in your room?"

"Why would I do that?" he said, then looked at Isaiah.

"I didn't touch ANYTHING," Isaiah said defensively.

They both looked back to Lanie. "All the stuff in that cubby is gone. My stapler, everything. I heard a bang last night, and there was red a light on in the cubby afterward."

Mr. Speros looked curiously at Lanie, then he glanced toward her room. "Show me after breakfast."

The Speroses' kitchen was a big, open space that was designed to accommodate professional caterers as well as routine home cooking. Skylights in the vaulted, wood-beamed ceiling made the room bright and welcoming during the morning. The breakfast counter was on the den side of the V-shaped kitchen, while a long counter backed with a frosted glass wall faced the dining room on the other side. The kitchen's original light blue General Electric wall ovens and stove range stood at the point of the V, against the end of the broad fireplace stack. Lanie loved the original kitchen—it was a showpiece of technology when the house was built, and everything still worked.

The long countertop near the dining room was supposed to be a prep area for plating dinners, but her dad used it for his big Italian espresso machine. The machine had been Mr. Speros's birthday present to himself in June. It was an industrial, flashy unit like those Lanie had seen in their favorite coffee shops. There were shiny chrome nozzles and levers along with polished copper carafes. It matched the design of the kitchen wonderfully, which was another reason Mr. Speros had bought such an extravagant appliance.

Lanie added some creamer to her cup of coffee as her dad sat on the stool next to her. She felt rebooted—the harrowing road trip was now a memory. While she picked at her breakfast, her dad stared through the windows at the mountains beyond the backyard. "Ready for some digging and climbing today?"

"Yes!" Lanie responded, jumping up from her stool. Her fork chinked on the floor.

"Whoa, easy," her dad said, lifting his espresso cup to sip. "We need to go buy a good ladder first. Help me clean up the breakfast dishes, then we'll go. I need to be back here before noon." She finished stowing the leftovers while her dad washed, then called Hudson right away.

"We're going into the pit—you gotta come over today. We're gonna go get a ladder, but we'll be back in an hour." Without giving Hudson a chance to respond, Lanie asked, "Oh, how'd it go last night... on the trip home?"

"My mom was freaked out, just like we expected," Hudson said. "Well, she still is. I'm not allowed to be over at your house unless your dad is there. At least for a while."

That condition seemed fair, and it was a less severe measure than Lanie was expecting. "So... you can come over today when we go into the pit?"

"If I tell my mom what you're doing, I'm sure the answer will be no."

"Well then don't tell her," said Lanie as though the solution were obvious. "Don't you think this is important? We might find out what all this mess is about." Realizing that she'd asked her best friend to lie to his parents, Lanie backed off. "Maybe just explain that you aren't gonna go down in the hole—you're just gonna watch." She knew his mom would never buy that. The other end of the phone line was silent. "Hudson?"

"I'm here. Lemmee talk to her; maybe I can work a deal. I can be *verrry* persuasive when I need to be," Hudson said, in his most confident tone. "My dad's at work until noon, so at worst I can come over with him after he gets home, and we can help."

The metallic blue paint on the Speroses' Jeep Wagoneer sparkled as Lanie's dad backed out of the garage, into the morning sun. It was a cool, breezy day, so Mr. Speros lowered all four windows. Lanie sat back into the caramel-colored seat and let the sun warm her face. As though he'd been waiting for the Speroses' garage door to open, Mr. Rinnas trotted across his lawn as fast as a man of his age could manage. Lanie's dad knew he was obliged to stop and shifted the Jeep into *park* near the foot of the driveway.

"Good morning!" Mr. Speros called as his neighbor approached Lanie's window.

"Top of the morning," Mr. Rinnas replied in his crackly voice. Lanie noticed that his natural hair was correctly highlighted to match his toupee that morning. Mrs. Rinnas stood near her rose garden with pruning shears and raised a white-gloved hand in her usual royal wave. Her beehive hairdo was as tidy as her embroidered sweater and floral skirt. She was more appropriately dressed to attend a church coffee social than to deadhead roses.

"So happy to see you're all home safe," he said, patting Lanie's arm on the window edge. He leaned against the faux woodgrain on the Jeep's exterior as though he were expecting the conversation to take a while. "Was everything in order when you got home?"

"Oh yes, everything's fine. Thank you so much for keeping an eye on the place."

"It was no trouble, of course. What are you gonna do about that hole?" Mr. Rinnas asked with intensity in his eyes.

"I'll probably have it backfilled with dirt," Mr. Speros said. "We'll shore it up and make a better cover this afternoon."

Lanie glanced over at her dad, surprised that he had withheld their plans to go into the pit.

"Ah, I see. Well, let me know if I can help. I can come by later. Whatever you need," Mr. Rinnas said.

"You bet, thanks again, Larry." Mr. Speros shifted back into reverse and Mr. Rinnas shuffled across his lawn. As they drove past his house, Lanie could see Mr. Rinnas sitting at his workbench. He claimed to use it for woodworking, though she never saw any finished projects. Lanie just figured he sat there watching traffic come in and out of the cul-de-sac most of the day so that Mrs. Rinnas couldn't assign him additional work.

"Why didn't you want Mr. Rinnas to know what we're doing this morning?" Lanie asked while they waited at the traffic signal near the bottom of the hill.

"The fewer people that know what we're doing, the better. Hudson's family is already involved; we don't need to make trouble for the Rinnases as well." Lanie kept looking at him, smiling, until he added, "Yes, yes, and also because if he knew what we were doing, he'd be in our yard all day looking over my shoulder."

When the Speroses returned, Lanie helped her dad unload, then walked Isaiah inside to get him a snack.

"I wanna play in my sandbox today," he told Lanie.

"Sounds good buddy; I'll open it up for you. You need your boots from your closet to play out back. Go get 'em; I'll wait." While she waited in the living room near the hallway, she leaned against the wall facing the fireplace. The late morning sun through the windows above the garage lit the stonework around the firepit. The roof windows were positioned to direct sunlight onto some part of the fireplace all day long. Lanie had to dip her head to one side because a sparkling beam of light was reflecting into her eyes from above the center of the firepit. She shifted out of the beam to see the source of the glare, as nothing above the mantle had caught her eye before.

Just out of reach, Lanie saw a small, glistening stone set into the mortar with the larger rocks of the structure. Standing back in the hallway, she could see that it wasn't a stone at all, but a polished quartz-like crystal. It was set over the top of a copper medallion, about three inches in diameter. From the floor near the hearth, it looked like a piece of jagged translucent quartz. But when Lanie returned to the hallway, she could see the medallion behind it. She pulled up a chair and stood on her toes to look closely at the stone. Bumping her glasses up closer to her eyes with her knuckle, she could see the copper disc had a black Omega character engraved on its face. Below that were small numbers:

$$\Omega$$

$$1959$$

Lanie's eyes widened. "Holy cow," she whispered.

Isaiah stood near the chair and said, "Whatcha lookin' at, Lay-Lay?" He was standing on his toes like his big sister. "Can I get up there?"

Lanie tripped and fell over the top of him as she ran toward the back patio. "DAD, DAD!" she called as she flung the sliding door wide. Mr. Speros was wadding up the yellow caution ribbon from around the hole and jumped in surprise when Lanie called out.

"Good Lord, what is the *problem*?!" he said, annoyed.

"Come inside, quick, you need to see this!"

Now more curious than alarmed, Mr. Speros tossed down the ball of ribbon and followed Lanie into the house. She'd run back to the hallway entrance and was motioning for her dad to move quickly, but he had stopped to kick off his dusty shoes. "Just hold on, I'm coming!"

When he stood next to Lanie and saw the quartz crystal, however, his tone changed. "Well... *that* is interesting," he said with his typical understated amazement. "How did you spot that?" he asked Lanie from his position on the chair near the mantle.

"The sun was hitting it through the roof window."

Examining Lanie's find closer, her dad remarked, "I think it's solid copper. I'm sure it was set there when the house was built." Stepping down, he lifted Isaiah up to let him see.

"Well, I'd say that confirms what we kinda already knew. This house is related to the mine—and that pit back there is the way in. I'm not sure what to do about that yet."

"Maybe this house was owned by Myriad Exploration?" Lanie offered.

"Maybe," Mr. Speros said, pushing the chair back to its position. "More likely though, it belonged to a company executive. The timing checks out," he said, referring to the age of the house in relation to the mine and the items from Seligman. "This house was built around the time the mine was decommissioned; I don't know how that fits in."

"But," he continued, pointing to the backyard, "that pit back there will probably clarify a lot. Let's go."

In the backyard, Isaiah headed toward his sandbox while Lanie and her dad stood near the hole. Mr. Speros had brushed aside the dirt on the sloped section, exposing a concrete slab with a jagged, broken edge. Bent iron rebar protruded from the edge. The cold, dry air continued to flow out of the opening.

Her dad had staged some wooden posts and his work light near the edge of the hole. "Alright, well let's get it done." He lowered the wide end of the ladder into the opening, seating it firmly on the floor below.

"Don't follow me until I say it's OK. The air coming up seems to be safe, but I don't know what the conditions are down in the room. Sometimes toxic gases accumulate in closed spaces—if I don't respond when you call, do NOT come in after me... call 9-1-1, do you understand?"

"Yes," Lanie said, nodding. Her dad disappeared into the hole.

"I'm OK so far," his voice echoed up. "This isn't a room, it's a *hallway*."

She grew more excited and began pacing around the hole. "Can I come down yet?"

"No—hand me my work light." Returning up the ladder, he added, "It seems safe, but we can't both be down there—not with Isaiah up there alone. When your grandparents get here in a couple hours, you can come down."

Lanie sighed. "Ahhhh!" She waved her hands at her side. "I gotta see what's down there; it's killing me!"

"Soon enough, just hang on," he said. "There's a cinder-block wall in the hallway over here," Mr. Speros said, pointing to the edge of the flag-stone patio. "It looks like the wall was added later to seal off this tunnel from the house."

Lanie swirled her hands. "OK, well what else?"

"The floor is concrete. At the other end of the hall," he said, pointing toward the back of the property, "about fifty feet back, there's a big steel door. There's a red light on the wall next to it—that's the light you saw last night."

Her curiosity was peaking. "Geez, Dad, that means this goes under the house," she said, then turned back to the mountain. "And the other end past the door leads out beyond our yard!"

"I think you're right. And that's a big deal," Mr. Speros said, scratching his ear. "The fact that there's something under this house is concerning— we don't know what it is, what's in it, or anything." Thinking a moment, he continued, "But there must be some sort of passage or hidden doorway inside the house to access this tunnel—or maybe a door that's been sealed and covered."

A giddy smile was spread on Lanie's face, but she didn't care. Images of every room in the house flipped through her mind, and her eyes scanned the air as she considered every blank wall space.

"Wowww, Dad this is *huge*, our house has a hidden passage inside somewhere—we have to find it!"

Her dad smiled back, but cautioned, "Yeah you're right, it's very cool. But it's walled off under here for a reason—and we don't know why. It's also safe to say this tunnel is related to what those guys in the Durango were after." The smile left her dad's face, replaced by a serious set in his brow. "That door at the other end looks like a vault door. What they think is on this property might be behind that door."

That possibility had occurred to Lanie as well. "Does it have a combination lock or any handles on it? Are there any signs?"

"No signs, no locks. It has a big steel handle, but I didn't try to open it."

"You didn't try?!" Lanie was shocked and pointed into the hole. "Well holy cow, Dad, go back down and try to open it!"

Mr. Speros laughed at her anxious directive. "Just wait, I wanted to make sure it was safe; we'll do—" He was interrupted and looked up to see Hudson sprint around the corner near the motorhome, scattering gravel in his wake. Mr. Newman wasn't far behind.

"What'd you find, what's down there?!" Hudson said, without wasting time on a greeting.

"Hello, Hudson; hi Wallace," Lanie's dad said.

"Ari, how are ya?" Mr. Newman offered his hand as he approached Lanie's dad. Her dad's name was Aristotle, but only Lanie's grandparents called him that—everyone else knew him as Ari.

Lanie's dad spent a few moments briefing Mr. Newman on their findings, then went down into the tunnel with him. Lanie rolled her eyes. "Oh man, I'm never gonna get down in that hole," she said to Hudson as they watched their fathers disappear.

Her feet fidgeted as she stared at the ladder, then she realized she hadn't shown Hudson the medallion on the fireplace. "Oh, come inside, I need to show you something."

Only a few moments later, Lanie had pulled the chair back over to the fireplace mantle for Hudson to ascend.

"That is crazy," Hudson whispered. "We knew it, and we were right!" he said, then bumped Lanie's forearm. "We knew your house had something to do with all this. And—there's a passage into that tunnel somewhere in here. That's AWESOME!" He stepped into the hallway, looking either direction.

"Yeah, I don't know where it would be. There would have to be some kinda dead space in the house between the walls or something—I can't think of one," Lanie said.

Facing the back patio, Lanie used pointed fingers to extend imaginary lines on the floor between the living room and the corridor under the yard. Lowering her hands down toward the carpet, she saw only the couch and end tables. Standing by the couch, she and Hudson scanned the room.

"Well, I guess there could be a hatch under the carpet or something?" Hudson said, trying to shift the sofa.

"I doubt it," Lanie said. "Why would a huge hallway like that pop up in a small hatch? I'll bet there are steps up into the house somewhere."

"What's behind that rockwork by the kitchen table?" Hudson asked, pointing to the wall to the left of the back door.

"That's my dad's bedroom."

"What about that huge boulder that makes up the back of the dining room? Maybe it's hollow?"

Lanie gave Hudson an exasperated look. "It's solid rock, are you serious?" Lanie turned to the front of the house. "I think it's gonna be in this end of the house—there are more walls and rooms."

Hudson ran into the entryway beyond the bar. The wide front door was the entryway's largest feature. The circular space also had four smaller doors that opened into other rooms. In the domed ceiling, a group of windows set in a circle had their own small roof. Mr. Speros called it a clerestory. It let sunlight onto the colorful compass points on the terrazzo floor. The entry hall for her dad's bedroom was here, as well as a door to the spare bedroom. Crouching to inspect the elaborate floor details, Hudson said, "Maybe it's under here!"

Salmon-colored terrazzo made up the compass points. They were divided from the rest of the ivory flooring by polished copper strips. Overlapping the compass, a series of copper ellipses and jade stones was arranged to trace the light's pattern through the roof windows at seasonal intervals. The whole array had been artistically laid to combine modern design with an ancient astronomical theme. Mr. Speros had recognized the celestial patterns on the floor when they first toured the house with their real estate agent.

"I don't think it's under here. How would this floor open—it's pretty much seamless?" Lanie asked, though her question was more of a statement. She stomped her foot on the sky-blue stone at the center of the compass. "Feels pretty solid."

"I dunno, but the floor in this area has always kinda weirded me out," Hudson said. "I'll bet it has something to do with what's under the house. What are all these arcs and stones that are built in?"

"My dad says it's a lunar calendar for—for watching stars and planets. It's... uhh... a *stereographic projection.*" Lanie smiled, proud to have been able to recall the obscure term. "Like this month—during the fall—the moon follows this line in the floor at night," she said, dragging her foot along one of the copper strips in the terrazzo. "One of the reasons he fell in love with this house was this entry," Lanie added. "See all the Greek characters around the outside of the circle?"

"What do they spell?" Hudson asked, scanning the perimeter of the room as he rotated slowly on his heel.

"Some sort of tribute to an ancient woman named Hypatia. She taught mathematics and philosophy."

Hudson had moved on, estimating wall thickness in the rooms off the entryway, but was discouraged. "You're right—doesn't seem to be any rooms that have space between their walls," he said when Lanie emerged from her dad's bedroom.

"Let's check the front bedroom—there's a closet in there," Lanie replied.

The spare bedroom used to be a study and was where the Speroses' guests stayed—usually Lanie's grandparents. The entire left wall in the room was made of the familiar stonework, and it stretched from the entryway into the front yard. A floor-to-ceiling window bisected the wall, separating the indoor space from the atrium outside. On the opposite wall, knotty mesquite bookcases spanned from one end of the room to the other. Lanie's dad had a lot of books on engineering and auto maintenance, but they only filled half of the bookcase. The rest of the shelves had knick-knacks and framed photos that didn't fit elsewhere in the house.

Hudson went from one section of the bookcase to the next, pushing on the shelving. He pulled out random books, expecting sections of the case to slide open. Lanie rolled her eyes.

"Those cases aren't gonna slide open like the movies, and anyway those are *our* books, dork. Why would they open a bookcase passage?"

"I'm just ruling things out," he said, glaring. "I don't see you knockin' on any walls; you're standin' there like a lump of meat."

Offended, Lanie turned and walked back into the entryway. Lanie shoved jackets and sweaters aside as she knocked on the walls within the coat closet near the front door. Nothing.

Between the master bedroom and guest room entries was the guest bathroom. It was long and narrow with an enclosed shower at the far end. An opaque window in the shower looked out into the same atrium as the front bedroom. Lanie didn't like the window; it always seemed to cast unnatural, ghostly light on the floor of the shower. She attributed the effect to the hammered-looking texture of the glass.

Returning to the entryway, she was going to suggest they look closer at the bathroom window but suddenly remembered the cubby in her desk.

"Oh, Hudson!" She grabbed his forearm. "I forgot to show you what I found last night—come to my room!"

Lanie stood over Hudson while he examined the cubby with his face pushed into Lanie's desktop. He stood upright with a smirk growing across his cheeks.

"What is it, a fancy trash compactor?" he quipped.

"Beats me," Lanie replied. "There's one like it in my dad's room too."

"I think that little red light in the top is a button," Hudson said, flashing a mischievous grin.

With their other unsolved mysteries swirling in her head, Lanie decided that pushing the red button couldn't possibly expose her to any more danger than she'd already experienced, so she slipped past Hudson, reached in, and pressed the little hidden red square. The light within the button began flashing, but nothing else happened. She withdrew her hand and let the cubby door spring shut. The two friends looked at each other and shrugged.

But before Lanie turned away, the sound of slapping metal reoccurred. The obnoxious bang reminded her of the noise made by the flapping metal door of a theme park's trash can. She quickly slid the cubby door open and was astonished to see the space filled with a boxy metal pod about the size of a loaf of sandwich bread. Hudson gasped and crowded up behind Lanie to get a better view. The pod's scratched orange paint indicated that it had seen many years of abuse. A clear acrylic hatch wrapped from the pod's top down toward its midsection, and it had flipped up when Lanie slid the cubby open. There was nothing within the little vehicle's interior. She tugged at its body, but it refused to leave the cubby.

From the bookshelf over her desk, Lanie snatched one of her unrestored Matchbox toy cars—a haggard gold Ford Cortina—and placed it in the pod. She lowered the little hatch and let the cubby door close. Unsurprisingly, the metal banging repeated, and the cubby was bare when Lanie reopened it.

"Uhh" was all Hudson could manage at first. "I hope that wasn't one of your favorite Matchboxes," he said.

"It's fine," Lanie said. "I'm more curious about where it went."

"Let's go look out back behind your room," Hudson suggested.

Lanie and Hudson saw their fathers sitting at the table on the patio talking. They found the two men were discussing the block wall in the buried corridor. Mr. Speros broke the conversation when Lanie walked up. "Your grandparents will be here in about fifteen minutes—can you please receive them when they arrive?"

"Yeah, sure," Lanie said. "Are you leaving?"

"No. But Mr. Newman and I are going to clean up that hole so we can take more tools down there. I ordered some materials from the construction supply and they'll be delivering about the same time." Sensing her anxiety, her dad added, "Just let us get the broken concrete stabilized, then you both can go down."

Hudson's head jerked toward Mr. Speros when he heard this, then he looked to his own dad.

"Yes, you can go down too—don't worry, Sport," Mr. Newman said to Hudson. Hudson hated when his dad called him *Sport*, so Lanie pretended not to notice.

"Get me the keys to the motorhome," Lanie's dad directed. "I need to make room for the delivery. Did you guys find anything inside that looked like a potential entry point?"

"No," Lanie said. "But we haven't finished looking."

"We'll look later; there's time," he told her.

When Lanie emerged from the house with the keys, she could hear the beeping of a truck backing up their gravel drive—for the second time in a week. This time it was the flatbed truck from the construction supply. It had three pallets strapped to its deck. Each pallet was stacked high with a variety of items, including concrete mix, gray cinder blocks, and bags of sand. While the driver unloaded the pallets, Lanie's grandparents walked through the open side gate, since she had not been inside to hear them ringing the doorbell.

"Hielloo!" said Lanie's grandmother in her unmistakable accent.

She threw her arms around Lanie, then blew a kiss to Mr. Speros. Her Grandpa Dimitri was close behind. He never moved as fast as Lanie's grandma, even when they were younger. Her grandma was wearing high-heeled black leather boots and a matching black skirt. Her maroon leather blazer finished the perfect look of mid-eighties adult fashion. Lanie loved

139

her grandma's sporty, dated wardrobe. Her grandpa, on the other hand, seemed to have quit shopping for clothing after 1977. He wore plaid slacks that matched his pastel-blue shirt.

"You have to tell me ALL about this crazy trip you had, koúkla," her grandma said. "Tonight, I make you a *real* dinner. Not the easy dinners you dad makes." She shot Lanie's dad a familiar, judgmental look. "Also, we celebrate you are home safely. We will do it nice, yes? Where is you little brother?"

"Sounds good, Gram—I'll help. Isaiah's on the edge of the yard, playing."

Her grandma moved on to say hi to her son and Mr. Newman, leaving Lanie to her grandpa.

"Hi, Gramps," she said as they embraced.

"Long time no see, eh missy?" he told her. He didn't have a Greek accent—or at least he hid it. "You are growing into such a beautiful young woman, you have to watch out for these boys now," he said, motioning to Hudson. Lanie was mortified but thankful that Hudson was too far away to hear. Not much for idle conversation, her grandpa moved on, addressing the adults. "Ohh-kayy, what are you men doing here?"

While Mr. Speros made the introductions, Lanie and Hudson stood at the hole opening.

"Dad says they're gonna jack up the broken slab first, then build block columns underneath to hold it up. After that, they'll fix the concrete on top and cover it all back up," Hudson said.

"How are we gonna get in or out then? Are they gonna break down that block wall in there?"

"Sounds like it," Hudson said, hitching a thumb at the large sledge-hammer leaning against the patio post.

Lanie smiled. "Oooh, I love me some demolition," she said to Hudson. "If we bust through that wall, we can probably follow the corridor under the house and see where it comes up."

"I think that's the idea," he said.

Lanie had been wearing her own flashlight for an hour, waiting to go down. By the time her dad gave her permission, she already was three rungs into the hole. She had a heavy black tactical flashlight of the same type as her father's. "Good enough for law enforcement, good enough for us," he'd told her.

As she descended into the opening of the hole, Lanie could smell the same aged, institutional scent that she recognized from inside their house. It reminded her more of a clean civic building or library than a residential home. With her feet on the floor of the corridor, Lanie saw that the walls on both sides were indeed of the same stacked stone as the house. Under the dust and dirt on the floor, the concrete was coated in taupe-colored epoxy. The corridor was larger than she had expected—about ten feet in width and height.

On the intact ceiling slabs, Lanie saw rows of unlit fluorescent light tubes along the top of the walls. Then she felt a tap on her shoulder and turned to see Hudson.

"Hey, welcome!" she said. "Whatcha think?"

"Creepy" was his only opinion as he looked around.

As Mr. Speros had described, the floor of the tunnel ramped down a couple feet at the threshold of the steel door. The door itself was about eight feet wide. To the right of the door was a robust-looking set of bronze louvers, through which a constant strong draft was flowing. This was the source of the air venting from the tunnel, Lanie assumed.

On the left side of the door was a sheer metal panel. It was unadorned, except for a brushed copper plate about the size of a sheet of paper. Mounted about elbow height, the plate stood an inch thick off the face of the panel. The small red indicator light at the top left corner was its only feature.

Lanie poked at the copper pad's hard face. "It feels like solid metal," she said. Thumping her knuckles on the anodized steel door, she added, "This is rock-solid too; it's not hollow."

"This setup was definitely designed to keep people in or out," Hudson said.

"Do you think this copper thing covers some kinda keypad or lock-box? Lanie said.

Hudson shrugged. "No keyhole or anything. But look at the door handle," he said, gripping the large vertical chrome pull. It was mounted on the edge of the door near the copper pad. He yanked a couple times, but it didn't budge.

"It looks like the handle from a walk-in refrigerator," Lanie said. "Except bigger." She shined her light on the door. It was less like a refrigerator door than the type used on a bank safe. Its hinges were concealed, as were its fasteners and welds. In the very center of the door, a large Omega character was stamped into the sheathing.

They both turned to see their fathers coming down the ladder. Mr. Speros carried the sledgehammer.

"Are you gonna break that wall down now?" Lanie asked.

Mr. Speros nodded. "The wall doesn't go all the way to the ceiling— there's a gap at the top," he said, pointing to a slot above the blocks. "That's why we're getting strange drafts in the house, I think."

"Ohhhh," Lanie said, nodding her head at Hudson. She had told him of the occasional phantom-like howling from the furnace ductwork and fireplace flue.

"The wall isn't holding the ceiling up—it can come down. Let's do it," Mr. Newman said, punching his fist into his palm. He pulled a pair of safety glasses off the collar of his tee shirt, where they had been stowed.

Mr. Speros put on his own safety glasses and pulled on a pair of heavy mechanics' gloves. "Everybody, gimme some room to swing please."

His first stroke landed the head of the sledgehammer in the center of the wall with a loud *THOCK* sound. A small hole formed in one side of the hollow block. After another strike, the block crumbled from the wall and cracks in the mortar joints formed in surrounding tiers.

"OK," Mr. Speros said, "the blocks aren't filled with concrete. Once I get going it will fall quickly—so stay back."

With another hit, more blocks fell. Lanie and Hudson stood high on their toes, peering into the darkness beyond the gap. Lanie shined her flashlight through the hole as her dad kept striking, but the dusty air prevented her from seeing anything beyond. On the next strike however, the center of the wall came down in a cascade of dust and masonry fragments.

The whole group shined their flashlights through the breached wall, and they could make out a turn in the corridor ahead. Mr. Speros stepped through, followed by Mr. Newman. Lanie and Hudson stayed close behind. Twenty feet past the block barrier, the corridor bent to the left.

On the right wall just after the bend was another door. It looked very much like the steel door at the other end of the corridor, though half as wide. "There are other rooms under the house!" she whispered to Hudson, thumping the door. Like the other, it was locked, so the group continued slowly, following the beams of their flashlights.

"I think we're under the den," Mr. Speros said.

Ahead, the hallway narrowed to about eight feet wide and the ceiling height had graduated as well. At the end of the corridor, the stone wall curved and continued up into a narrow stair passage on the left. Lanie's flashlight beam swept the wall, and it sparkled—reflecting flecks of gold back at her.

"Hey, look!" she yelled, waving her flashlight on the rock facade. "The pyrite stones from the fireplace!"

Mr. Speros scratched at one of the rocks in the wall. "Wow, yeah you're right, this is probably the footing of the fireplace above."

At the top of the stairs was another steel door, but this one had a different handle. A vertical chrome paddle the size of a smartphone protruded from the door's center. The group of four explorers clustered at the top of the stairs. They were so close, Lanie could smell Mr. Newman's antiperspirant.

Hudson's dad grabbed the edge of the paddle and pulled hard to the right. Lanie recognized the sound of an electric relay clicking over her left ear, then a larger *clack-thunk* noise sounded as the door latch released itself. The door began sliding to the right—into the stone wall. Light streamed into the dark staircase, then the group heard a surprised yell and commotion on the other side of the door. When the panel finished sliding open, Lanie's grandma stood before them all holding a raw pot roast with a look of shock frozen on her face. Speechless, the two older men stepped through the doorway and into the Speroses' kitchen.

Lanie's grandma backed up against the dishwasher and dropped the roast on the countertop.

"WHAT is happening here! What kind of parlor trick is this?!" she yelled, now more irritated than shocked.

Lanie turned and looked at the doorway. The kitchen's two ovens and the stove range had slid sideways with the door, disappearing into the cabinet against the dining room wall. The fireplace's width between the dining room and den concealed the stairwell.

"I knew it!" Lanie said. "I knew there was *somethin'* weird about this fireplace!"

Hudson snuffled. "*Shoot.* If you suspected the fireplace, we shoulda been over here checkin' this out earlier."

Lanie's grandpa and Isaiah had joined the group in the kitchen and everyone was talking over the top of one another in a jumble of excitement and theory. Isaiah started down the steps, but Lanie quickly grabbed his collar and hauled him back up.

"Not yet, Isaiah, you need to wait for us," she said.

Realizing it was pitch black down the stairs, Isaiah didn't protest.

"Simply amazing," Mr. Speros muttered.

"I wonder how you open it from out here?" Mr. Newman asked, and not a moment too soon because the passage started closing on its own. The entire group cried out together, waving hands, not knowing how to stop the closure.

Lanie inserted her foot into the gap as the stove approached the adjacent cabinet. Mr. Speros lunged forward, yanking her back by her upper arm, but the door had already stopped and reversed.

"Are you *bonkers*?! What were you doing? That may have crushed your foot like a grape!" he exclaimed.

"It works on an elevator—why wouldn't it work here?" she said.

Mr. Speros's furious expression then shifted to a neutral stare and he turned back to the stove.

Sure enough, on the concealed edge of the stove was a vertical rubber strip. When Mr. Speros pressed it, the group could hear the door relay click.

"Well, I'll be danged," he said. "You're right again." He shined his flashlight up into the gap between the oven and the stairwell door where the pulleys and crank arms of an ordinary elevator door mechanism were visible.

Lanie's grandma slapped the back of Mr. Speros's head. "Apologize to the young lady!"

"Indeed, apologies where they're due—sorry, sweetie," he said, nudging Lanie's shoulder.

"Even if we can't find the switch to open the door in here, we can put our own switch into the door control circuit," Hudson added.

"You're correct," Mr. Newman said, and he reached his hand up into the gap above the door. "There's a wiring bundle up here—I'm sure it won't be hard to do a little reverse-engineering. Do you want to prop it open for now?" he said, looking at Lanie's dad.

Suddenly, Mr. Newman yanked his hand back down, grinding his teeth.

A huge brown wolf spider dropped from the overhead mechanism and bolted across the floor. Isaiah promptly dispatched it with a *STOMP* of his boot.

"Did it bite you?" Mr. Speros asked.

"Nah, but it didn't like me rooting around its burrow," Mr. Newman said, smiling.

Turning to the door, Mr. Speros said, "Yeah, let's block it open, I wanna get the supplies down into the tunnel so we can close that hole up today."

Armed with flashlights, Lanie and Hudson covered every corner of the underground space while their fathers hauled in the cinderblocks and bags of mortar. The smaller door at the bend was not marked, though it did have a copper pad and an indicator light like the large door.

"There are no light switches," Hudson said, pointing to the rows of lamps along the ceiling. "I wonder how we turn these on?" He followed the metal conduit that linked the light fixtures together and disappeared around the corner.

Lanie stood at the smaller door. Based on its relative position to the fireplace, she figured the door was below the bar in the living room, and that it probably opened into a room under the entryway. Feeling around the sharp corners of the copper panel, she noticed there weren't even any screws or welds.

"You must pop out, or something," Lanie murmured to herself as she tugged on the plate's edges. It did budge a little, as though it were held to the panel by a latch or hinge.

With no good ideas, she went to the far end of the corridor to meet Hudson. Isaiah was there with him.

"What'd you find?" she asked.

"Nothin' amazing. But I think these little indicator lights are part of the door lock system. They probably get their power from whatever is behind this door—not your house." Then he raised his eyebrows at Lanie for dramatic effect. "There's something big behind this door, it's not just a small room—I'm sure of it."

He and Lanie both stared at the door, pondering what was beyond.

"It's a treasure room," Isaiah said. "There's probably gold coins, and diamonds and rubies in there. We'll be rich."

"Maybe, buddy. What would you buy then?"

"I'd buy an island with dinosaurs on it!" he said pointedly, as though Lanie should have known the answer.

The smell of the roast was in the air when the group came up the staircase into the kitchen. Without use of the oven, Lanie's grandma was cooking in the air fryer and an old Crock-Pot.

"I don't know how I supposed to *cook* if there is bricks and cement coming through the kitchen," she complained, waving a pair of tongs as they passed. "And *look* what you are tracking through!" she said of the fine gray dust on the floor.

The sliding door to the patio was closed, and it didn't take long to figure out why. Lanie could see her dad standing near the open hole, talking with Mr. Rinnas. His wife stood nearby, chatting with Lanie's grandpa. *They're probably comparing wardrobe notes*, Lanie thought, smiling to herself. After a few minutes of conversation, the Rinnases disappeared around the side of the house with Mr. Speros. A few moments later her dad returned and slid the door open.

"He's asking a lot of questions about what's down there, and he has theories," he said to Lanie. "But I still think it's best that we keep this quiet. If he asks you any questions, just tell him to speak to me, OK?"

Lanie nodded in agreement.

Around dinner time, Hudson's mom came over with Helen to see what was keeping her men. When she realized her husband would be busy late into the evening, she accepted the invitation to stay for dinner. To Lanie's surprise, during their dinner around the dining room table, Mrs. Newman was quite social and entertaining. She had a prickly, dry sense of humor that made Lanie's cheeks hurt from giggling. It became apparent that Helen's saucy, outgoing persona had come from her mom.

Lanie's initial impression of Mrs. Newman (when they'd met in June) was that she tended to stay in the background while her husband did all the talking, but the assessment was incorrect. Lanie learned that Hudson's mom had been a pilot and officer in the U.S. Air Force and was an accomplished aerospace engineer. She'd resigned her position with a local helicopter company when Hudson and Helen were born.

Helen was impatient to see the corridor after dinner, but Mr. Speros told the group that they needed to help clean up the kitchen first. As Lanie loaded the dishwasher, her grandma stood at the sink, handing her dishes.

"Hudson's mom is a smart lady, like you," she said, having watched Lanie at the dinner table. "You didn't know much about her, did you? You opinion of her has changed?"

Lanie was taken aback by her grandmother's assertion. "Well, yeah, I was kinda surprised. I never really talk to her much."

"I tell you dad this, and you grandpa *all the time*—because they are Greek and they have an opinion about *everybody*," she said. "But you need to know too. Be slow to make assumptions about people—or put them in a category—it is dangerous. If you don't know much about a person—you talk to them. Don't wait for them to say something to you. Look how many months you have known Hudson—how many times have you asked his mom about herself?" She nodded toward Mrs. Newman, who was entertaining Isaiah on the sofa.

"It goes both ways, too," her grandma said, pulling the drain plug from the sink. "You may start the conversation and find that you don't care for somebody. That's OK. But don't assume anything."

It was almost 10 p.m. when Lanie's and Hudson's fathers finished building new support columns under the corridor's damaged roof section. Mr. Newman worked above, shoveling sand and dirt onto the concrete patch, while Lanie's dad spread mortar on the gaps below, by the light of a single work lamp. Lanie stood next to him as he worked up on the ladder.

"So, you're back to school tomorrow," her dad said as he wiped grout from the last joint.

Lanie slumped, thinking of getting back into the school grind the next day.

"You need to get cleaned up—we'll wrap this up soon." Looking down at her from the ladder, he continued, "I'll be back to work too, and Isaiah is leaving in the morning. You'll be on your own for about an hour before I get home—do you want to hang out at Hudson's until then?"

Lanie shrugged. "Maybe. I'm sure I'll be fine at home though."

"I don't want you down here until I get home, clear?" he said, pointing a trowel at Lanie.

Lanie nodded, even though she knew that the space under the house was probably the safest on the property. Climbing the stairs, she found Hudson sitting on a bucket at the top of the passageway opening, high above the countertop. He had a bundle of wiring pulled down and was tracing the different colors of each strand that disappeared into the wall above the cabinets.

"What are you doing?" she asked. "Don't get yourself fried; we have to cook our meals on that counter."

"I'm trying to find the switch that opens this from the inside." He held a red wire with a yellow stripe and was following it with his hand, high inside the door gap.

"Yuck, there are webs all over in here," he said, wrinkling his lips. "This wire goes into the cabinet above the stove; I'm sure it's the one that triggers the door relay to open. But I can't... quite... reach the end. I need to close the passage to reach it."

Just then Lanie's dad came up, carrying a bucket of tools that needed washing up. "I'm done; let's call it a night. You too, Hudson."

Hudson stayed focused on his wiring. "Can we close this? I think I can figure out how to open it again."

Mr. Newman had come inside and was standing with the group.

"Yeah, it can't hurt. Worst case is we force it open later," Mr. Speros said.

Hudson jumped down and pulled the cinderblock away from the rubber bumper. The steel passage door immediately closed itself, and the stove and oven assembly followed. When the stove seated against the cabinet, Hudson climbed onto the bucket in front of the oven.

As Lanie and the two fathers looked on, Hudson reached into the cabinet and began handing down dusty cookbooks and old coffee mugs to Lanie.

"AH-HAAA!" Hudson cheered, shoulder-deep in the cabinet. Lanie heard the *click-snap* repeat itself and the oven slid sideways. Hudson stepped down, looking proud.

"Now *THAT'S* my Hudson," Mr. Newman said, beaming. He slapped Hudson between his shoulder blades.

"There's a little bracket up there that looks like it holds the cabinet to the wall—but it doesn't," Hudson said. "It's a rocker switch, you just have to press down on the bracket."

Lanie bumped Hudson's fist. "Teamwork," she said, closing the cabinet door. "So now we just gotta figure out what these passages and corridors are for."

## Chapter 11

# EMERGENCY KITS

Lanie ordinarily didn't mind sitting in class during the school day. She made a conscious effort to stay focused on the lesson but often allowed her mind time to think about things far away from the classroom. Whether or not she was listening to her teacher, she also did a lot of sketching and drawing. Mostly cars, of course. She daydreamed about being an auto styling executive at a big car company—and about the warehouse she'd buy to keep the classic vehicles she'd collect. She'd group the cars in rows categorized by the legendary stylists who had penned them, and lead tours for young designers and students. She'd even have an online video channel to showcase obscure cars that shouldn't be forgotten.

But that day, Lanie was anxious. She wanted to get home. During second period—the only class that she shared with Hudson—they had passed notes back and forth about how they might open the two locked doors in the corridor. She'd spent the morning sketching floor layouts of their house in blue ink, overlaid with the underground spaces in red ink to estimate the position and function of the mysterious rooms.

At lunch time, the two friends sat with their trays on the terrace in the school's triangular courtyard. The bouncing of balls on the crowded basketball courts was a constant beat in the background. Halloween was on Friday night, and the two friends debated whether they were even going to bother dressing up. They had also been discussing ideas for protection at home.

"Well, I still think we need to have a plan for when those guys come back," Lanie said. "They *are* gonna come back."

Hudson agreed. "I'm not completely ready, but I've been working with some ideas on the workbench at home. I still need to make some parts, but I'll be ready soon. I need your help 3D-printing some of the pieces I need."

"That's fine, we can work on the designs this week on my dad's laptop," Lanie replied. "We'll also need a way to communicate, since we don't have cell phones. You have your smartwatch; if I can get one too, we can send email and maybe do video calls—if we have internet access."

"I had no signal under the house yesterday," Hudson said. "I still think booby-traps are the best insurance."

"You keep saying that, but you need to give me some ideas. We could hurt Isaiah... or a delivery driver if we're not careful.

"What about my idea of alarms around the perimeter of the yard?"

"I think it blows," Lanie said. "Every time a coyote comes into the yard it would wake up the neighborhood. Plus, too expensive. And we already have the camera system out front anyway." Lanie furrowed her brow and thought of Hudson's booby trap idea. "I guess we could work on the traps. But they'd have to be things we can set up at a moment's notice."

"Yeah, I guess you're right," he said. "Stuff that's staged and ready to deploy. Maybe we could put emergency kits around our houses? You know, like things that could help us out of a jam. We could stash them in safe places, like hiding places or meeting points."

"You mean like flashlights and first aid kits?"

"Not quite. Flashlights yes, but also tool kits—and maybe things like plastic zip ties and tape."

Lanie was starting to understand his concept. "OHH, I got it. You mean like breakdown kits." Lanie's dad had put her in charge of those kits, which they hauled in their vehicles on trips. They contained the most useful items they might need if they were stranded. "With hardware, wiring, sealing tape, that kinda stuff?"

"YES!" Hudson said. "We probably wouldn't need to buy much. Both of our dads have tons of stuff lying around."

"Your dad has white outlines painted for everything in your garage—even your bike," Lanie said, raising her left eyebrow above her glasses. "He would know if even one screwdriver were missing."

"I'll figure something out. If we can put a kit in our front yards, and one in back—plus one inside—I think we'd be good."

Lanie was thinking of where she might stash them when Helen sat down, holding her lunch and a stack of fliers. She was wearing a baggy lemon-yellow blouse with ripped jeans. Her strawberry hair was pulled into a ponytail. Helen always looked and dressed cute; she didn't have the dense eyebrows and stringy hair that her twin brother was stuck with.

"What's all that?" Lanie asked.

"Fliers for the Harvest Formal," she said. "I'm on the committee for the dance this year."

"You *would* be," Lanie said, smirking. Helen and Hudson were usually required by their mom to participate in at least two or three committees or programs during the year.

"I gotta start posting these, and you two slackers are gonna help," Helen said, paring off parts of the stack for them.

"And," she said, looking squarely at Lanie, "you're gonna go to this formal, and you're gonna dress for it."

Lanie bit the side of her lower lip. The formal was only two weeks away. She scowled at Helen, pulling her hair back behind her ears. "I can look nice when I *need* to. I dunno why you think I can't pull off dressing for a school dance."

"Show me your hands," Helen said, flopping her own on the table, palms up.

Lanie reluctantly put her palms onto Helen's, then Helen leaned over to examine Lanie's fingers like a forensic scientist. Suddenly, Lanie was ashamed of her chipped blue nail polish and weathered fingertips.

"You can't go like this," Helen said, curling her lips. "I'll make a deal with you?"

Lanie and Hudson looked at each other. "Uhh, what kinda deal?" Lanie said and bumped her glasses up on her nose.

"Let me pick your wardrobe for the formal—and we're gonna get you a manicure, and get your toes done too."

Lanie's eyes widened; nobody ever saw her feet except her dad and Isaiah. "I don't even *own* any open-toe shoes!" she said, feeling self-conscious.

"Yeah, I *know*," Helen said. "And that's a problem. Let me do what I want. In return I'll help you clean up that creepy morgue under your house."

"I guess so," Lanie mumbled. "It needs to be mopped—do you know how big it is?"

"Don't worry about that," Helen said over the ringing of the bell. "OK, see you after school."

On the walk home after the twins had peeled off at their own house, Lanie surveyed the other homes on her street. The zippers on her backpack jingled in time with her steps. Most of the houses in her small neighborhood had natural desert landscaping that looked like the surrounding mountain preserve... only more manicured. A few houses had a green lawn; Mr. Rinnas's was one of them. He spent a lot of time on it, and he was out front sweeping up grass clippings as Lanie passed.

"Hello, young lady!" he called.

"Hi, Mr. Rinnas," she said with a wave from her waist.

"You all were busy pretty late last night, eh?" It was an inquiry more than an observation.

"Yeah, Dad was fixing the hole; we just helped cleanup," she said, being intentionally vague.

"Get it all fixed up, did ya?"

"Yeah, the hole is covered. It looks like it was never there," she said, which was the truth.

"Ah, so it's all sealed up now, huh? No way in?"

"Well, yeah, I guess so," she answered, which was *not* the truth. "Dad said he's going to look at the house plans at city hall to see if the pit is in any drawings."

"That won't be on the plans," Mr. Rinnas said, waving his hand toward the backyard. "What you got there is a clue—a clue to something much bigger. It'd be a shame if you don't explore it—you know, see what it was built for."

Lanie was getting uncomfortable—she didn't know what her father had told Mr. Rinnas. "Maybe we will. He just wanted to seal it up for now, since we had so many problems with those guys on our trip."

Mr. Rinnas's eyes narrowed. "Those guys have an idea of what that room is for, and they may come *back*. You need to be on your toes—and be ready. You might have to deal with a serious situation." His tone had changed. It was the first time he'd spoken to her as an adult. Even though she was concerned, Lanie appreciated it.

"We'll be ready," she promised with a determined edge in her voice. "We took care of those guys once, and we'll do it again."

Mrs. Rinnas appeared in the garage doorway. "Good afternoon to you, Lanie!" she said in the chirpy, aristocratic tone that she reserved for public appearance.

"Hi, Mrs. Rinnas, how are you? How's the Lincoln?"

"I'm just fine, dear." Mrs. Rinnas disapproved of her husband's participation in the maintenance he and Lanie performed on their vehicles. She considered Lanie's automotive hobby as unbecoming as if she were hanging around the boys' locker room. "It's running nicely, dear, thank you for fixing my window motor." She said this quietly, as though she didn't want the neighbors to hear.

"Anytime, happy to work on a classic!" Lanie said, secretly delighted to push Mrs. Rinnas's comfort zone. She excused herself after promising to help Mr. Rinnas change his brake pads the week following Halloween, then continued up the driveway.

Lanie's grandparents had left earlier with Isaiah and the house was quiet. On the kitchen table she found that her grandma had left her a note on top of a plate of Greek cookies, neatly covered in plastic wrap:

*Behave, koúkla, do not disappear into any caves please. Love, Yiayia*

Yiayia was Greek for grandmother. Lanie snuck a twisted, biscotti-like cookie out from under the wrap and headed to her room. "Koulourakia, yum!" she whispered. She giggled to herself, remembering how annoyed her grandmother would get when she and Isaiah called them "dog turd cookies." It was Isaiah's term, but Lanie didn't disagree that the curled cookies shared a resemblance.

She powered through her homework and was startled from her textbook reading when she heard the garage door motor start. Her room was near the garage, so she could always hear when her dad was coming or going. The wheezy sound of the Rambler's six-cylinder engine came next. Mr. Speros typically commuted and ran errands with the Rambler, which was relatively fuel efficient compared to the rest of their fleet.

Meeting her dad at the door into the garage, she gave him a hug, then heard the roar of a large truck approaching. Her dad turned around and Lanie looked past him in the doorway. She saw a Peterbilt semi-tractor pass their driveway towing a long, low flatbed trailer. It crept into the cul-de-sac and around the landscaped island in the center. The truck stopped on the other side of the street, then Lanie heard the whoosh of its air brakes. She turned back and found her dad watching her with an apologetic expression. She knew right away what was happening. Lanie felt her face flush with emotion, and she bit her lip.

"I'm sorry, sweetie, the insurance company closed the book on the old girl," he said, referring to their motorhome. Lanie knew it was coming; she'd seen the family photo from the Magna's bedroom propped on the fireplace mantle the night before.

Seeing that Lanie was wrapped up in memories of their motorhome trips, Mr. Speros said, "It'll be fine, Lanie, we'll get a different one—and we'll make new memories with it. It's just a vehicle. Steel, fiberglass, wood, iron. It might not last forever, but the memories will, right?" He pressed the key ring into Lanie's hand. "C'mon, you can make the last drive."

After he pulled the side yard gates open, Mr. Speros stood aside as Lanie backed the motorhome down the gravel drive. Without the left outside mirror, navigating was tougher, but she was still able to guide the coach down to the street in one attempt. Once on the street, she lined the front bumper up with the back of the flatbed. The truck's driver had just finished laying the ramps on the trailer's tail and was shocked to see Lanie piloting the coach. Relinquishing the driver's seat to the truck driver, she took a last look at the scrambled and broken interior before stepping out. In its condition, the Magna wasn't home for her family anymore.

Standing by Mr. Speros's side, she watched in silence until the driver finished chaining the coach to the deck of the trailer. They both stayed at the curb as the rig crept off down the street past Hudson's house, then the Magna disappeared forever when the traffic signal turned green.

Lanie stared quietly down the street, even after the truck was out of sight. Her dad watched her from the corner of his eye. "C'mon, let's go inside, I have something for you."

She glumly followed him into the house, where he pulled a white sack from his leather work bag. Handing it to Lanie, her dad said, "You deserve this. Please enjoy *responsibly*." He emphasized the last word, even though he was smiling.

From the sack, Lanie pulled a rectangular white box, and she recognized the label on the lid right away—it was a new iPhone.

"WHOA," Lanie said, forcing the breath from her chest. She hugged Mr. Speros, then flopped on the living room sofa to unbox the phone and its accessories.

"With everything going on right now, it makes sense for you to have one," he said. "But I'm sure you've heard the rules that your friends have with their phones—ours will be the same. Not in class, not in church, no shady apps, blah-blah-blah. Do I need to go into any more detail?"

"Nope," Lanie said, beaming. "Thanks a lot Dad, this is awesome."

"OK, good, have fun with it. I think the Newmans are probably getting Hudson and Helen phones too. I'm thankful I had to buy only *one*."

Mr. Speros started shuffling around in the kitchen, trying to figure out what they'd eat. "How was your day? Everything OK at school?"

Lanie briefed him on Helen's plans for the Harvest Formal.

"Ohhh, I forgot about the formal," he said. "Is it a date kinda dance, or more like a party?"

Her dad knew Lanie was uncomfortable with the "boys" topic, so she was thankful he treaded lightly. "It's just a party, mostly for the kids to listen to music and eat. I'm not going with a date," she said, making her dad's work a little easier. "Helen's gonna help me get ready. Can you drive us all in mom's Caddy?"

"Of course, we'll get it shined up. What will you wear? Do you need to shop?"

"Helen and I are gonna go to the mall with her mom on Sunday after church."

Her dad looked relieved; Lanie knew he hated shopping for her clothes. "What do you guys want to do for Halloween? Maybe you and Hudson can staff the front door here so I can take Isaiah trick-or-treating?"

"Sure, I don't think we wanna wear costumes this year anyway. I kinda feel too old to beg for candy." Lanie spun and headed for the front door when the chimes over the bar sounded. She swung the door open to find Hudson standing with an old Radio Flyer wagon behind him and she laughed spontaneously.

"What's with the wagon? Are you selling cookies?"

Hudson gave her an annoyed scowl and pushed past with the wagon in tow. In the entryway, he pulled off an old towel that covered the wagon's contents. It was loaded with a mix of tools, materials, wire, and other random items.

"Oh geez, you're really serious about this kit thing," she said.

"That guy had a gun," Hudson reminded Lanie. His voice was firm, and he suddenly sounded just like his dad. "We don't have a gun, but we have brains," he said, pointing at his forehead.

He was right, and Lanie nodded in agreement. They headed to the garage, where Hudson spread his items on Mr. Speros's workbench. Lanie's 3D printer was busy working on one half of a device she'd designed, and Hudson stopped to watch the printer's extruder sliding back and forth.

"Shoot, I wish I knew how to design stuff for this printer," he said, watching the nozzle add a layer. "It would take me *hours* instead of *days* to build some of the stuff I make."

"Yeah, I know, but you need to be able to use design software. I told you, I can help you learn it."

"Yeah, maybe during December when we're outta school. What's this thing working on anyway? You're always printing car parts—this looks like a flare gun. What are you up to?" he said to Lanie with a curious smile.

"Well, I got to thinking about your self-defense idea—I figured I'd try out a design of my own," she said.

"Heh, well show me what it does when you're done," Hudson said, refocusing on their task. He lined up five small plastic boxes with hinged lids. "We'll put a group of tools and supplies into each of these and stash them in places where people wouldn't think to look."

Picking up a small multi-tool, Lanie turned it over in her hand and pulled out a screwdriver, knife blade, and other common implements. There were several of the combination tools, along with boxes of matches, knotted sections of rope, and small fireworks. He had also bundled small groups of zip ties and steel wire. "Where did you get all this stuff?"

"I spent my whole allowance ordering things online."

Examining the assortment, Lanie realized it was probably a significant investment. "I can pitch in," she offered.

"Don't worry about it; you can buy whatever else we need. Help me load these boxes."

"OH! I almost forgot to tell you—I got a phone!" she said as she sorted the items.

"Yeah, me too," Hudson said in a droll tone.

"What's the matter? You wanted one?!"

"I have to share it with Helen... we had a fight about what the schedule would be." He was digging through the lockbox Lanie had bought in Seligman and changed the subject. "I have an idea about this thing," he said, pushing the box toward Lanie. "Let's fill it with junk paper and other bits, then lock it—we should leave it in a place where it's easy to spot. If they saw us leaving the shop with it in Seligman, it's what they'll be looking for if they break in."

"Yikes," Lanie said, "That's a terrible thought; I hope they don't break in!"

"Well duhhh, me either," he said. "But you're the one who said we need to be smarter—and one step ahead. This is an easy way to do it. Where's the stuff that was inside?"

"It's in my bedroom." Lanie grabbed a pair of plastic sprinkler pipe fittings from a box high on the shelf and jammed them into the lockbox with some loose nuts and bolts. "I'll put it in the bookcase in the study—you can see into that room from the front yard," she said.

They'd only worked an hour when Hudson was called home for dinner, and he headed off with the wagon and his boxed emergency kits. Mr. Speros was ready for dinner as well, but Lanie had just enough time to plant her own emergency kits around the property before sunset.

# Chapter 12

# REVELATION AT THE RED ROCKS

On Sunday, Lanie wore her favorite royal blue dress to church. With short sleeves and a thin collar, it was gathered at her waist and stopped just short of her knees. Helen had told Lanie the dress made her look like a guest star from the '80s TV show *Saved by the Bell*, but Lanie didn't care; she liked the way the dress fit. She knew the dress was outdated anyway because the old ladies in the church choir complimented her whenever she wore it. Besides, she heard the way they would murmur about the tight, revealing fashions that teenage girls wore to church—and Lanie didn't want to be the subject of any gossip.

The Divine Liturgy service at St. John the Baptist Greek Orthodox Church typically ran about two hours on Sunday mornings—depending on how intense Father Apostolides's sermon was. Two hours was just long enough to exceed Lanie's attention span, and this was one of the reasons she loved singing in the choir. Participating in the service was much more fun than sitting idle in the pews. She didn't like the sound of her own voice, but when it was merged with the other voices in the choir, she felt comfortable with her intonation.

That Sunday, Fr. Apostolides had to cut his Gospel discussion of the rich man and Lazarus short due to a baptism that was to take place after the services. This worked out great for Lanie because Mr. Speros offered to drive her and Helen to her favorite coffee shop with the extra time. They were all supposed to meet at the nearby mall at 12:30 anyway. As they headed to the car under the blazing sunlight, Lanie pulled her phone out of her dress pocket to call Helen.

"Hey!" Lanie said when Helen answered. "We're gonna come and pick you up to go to Red Rocks—be ready in ten minutes. We'll meet your mom at the mall later."

"Yay!" Helen yelled into Lanie's ear. "Are you ready to do some shopping today? I have a vision for you."

Lanie closed her eyes. She knew Helen was planning to make her a project that afternoon. "If I drink some coffee first, maybe. See you in a few."

The grayish-green paint on the Cadillac's vast hood looked like a Mediterranean tidal pool under the bright sun. Lanie kept the clear coat finish waxed so well that the chrome hood ornament and passing street signs reflected in it.

She loved all the dramatic chrome and broad surfaces of the Fleetwood. When her dad had surprised Mrs. Speros with the car, she told Lanie, "Look honey, it's big, bold and full of curves, just like your mama." She'd smacked her hip as she leaned on the rear fender, smiling. It was a vivid and lasting memory—one that made Lanie's heart hurt.

Lanie's earliest mental images of her beautiful, energetic mom had been permanently dampened by the final memory she had: Leaving her mom's bedside at the hospital the night she died. She'd heard the doctor tell her dad that the chemo and treatments just weren't enough. Unconscious, pale, and connected to tubes and wires, Mrs. Speros's last night was the most painful and lasting vision Lanie had of her mom. When Lanie left the hospital room with her grandma late that night, she had looked back from the doorway. Her dad didn't notice Lanie leave; he sat at her mom's bedside, unmoving. He kept his forehead down, pressed to Mrs. Speros's hand at her side. Lanie knew—even then—that it would be the last time she'd see the emaciated woman who was struggling to breath.

Lanie tried not to dwell on memories of her mom because it could suck away her happy mood even on the nicest of days. The memory of her mother was always standing by as though Mrs. Speros were waiting to step in to fill any gaps in Lanie's thoughts. It was a fine line Lanie felt like she had to walk; she had to move on, enjoying life's happy moments—but almost every happy moment reminded her that she didn't have her mom there to share the experience.

The Cadillac, however, was a part of Mrs. Speros's departed personality and spirit that was still physically tangible. She'd driven with Lanie to Hollywood and the beaches of California, sitting in the same gray leather seats. They'd eaten cheeseburgers in it at a car hop in Burbank and scorched the interstate between Phoenix and Los Angeles listening to the music they liked. They snickered to themselves after a highway patrol officer had let them off with a warning when Mrs. Speros got pulled over for speeding. More than her mom's reading chair, or the clothes she used to wear, Mrs. Speros's car was the closest material connection Lanie had.

Memories with the car—and infinite others—rolled and tumbled in her mind like a sea that had to be kept behind a locked door. If she opened the door even a crack, the memories would push through in a surge. Then the wave might overcome her, and she'd spontaneously break down in tears—even in the middle of a restaurant. This used to happen often, and the episodes were heartbreaking for her dad. So Lanie did her best to keep the memories locked in the back of her mind. This was rarely easy to do.

Lanie even noticed that Mrs. Speros lived on in Isaiah, who exhibited their mom's mannerisms—even though Isaiah was too small to remember her. As Mr. Speros drove, Lanie brushed some windblown locks of hair behind her ear, and her eyes wandered to the shift lever on the steering column. Isaiah's hospital ID bracelet from the day of his birth—along with Lanie's—hung from a braided maroon prayer rope there. "These are reminders that I should slow down—you both need me to be home for you at the end of the day," her mom had told her.

Helen was sitting on the low garden wall near the Newmans' front door when the Cadillac pulled up. She hopped down, trotting toward the car in a camisole top with cutoff denim shorts and strappy sandals. Lanie felt cold just looking at her, then thought of Helen's critique of her own footwear.

"Do you have any shoes that *cover* your toes?" she asked as Helen lifted the door handle.

"Ha-ha, you're hilarious," Helen said, plunking into the seat. "We're gonna dress Lanie really girly today, Mr. Speros."

Knowing it was better for him if he didn't get involved, he simply said, "Hi, Helen, I'm sure you'll both look amazing next weekend."

Red Rocks Reading Room was at the corner of the mall's parking lot in a building it shared with the golf pro shop of the neighboring country club. Despite its name, Red Rocks was primarily a neighborhood coffee shop. But there was a wide room to the right of the shop which had floor-to-ceiling bookshelves and worn high-back reading chairs. Floppy, tired books filled the bookcases. If customers left a book, they could take a book. There were also some new titles offered for purchase, but they only tended to be the current bestselling dramas.

The scattered, mismatched shelves, overgrown potted plants, and reading chairs also damped the noise of the coffee house. This made the reading room a great place to not only sit with a book but also talk serious business... or just think. Hudson liked to sit near the glass and watch the amateur golfers make divots in the tee box on the seventh hole.

The reading room's floor was split between two levels. On the lowest level were tall windows looking over the golf course and its lake. Themed like the northern Arizona town of Sedona, the reading room's interior was decorated in earth-tone pastel colors with acres of whitewashed oak, red sandstone, and traditional Yavapai tribal artwork. The environment was stuck in the nineties but was clean, cheerful, and comfy.

Lanie and Helen pulled together a couple shabby reading chairs under a skylight and sipped their icy coffee while they caught up on current events. Lanie didn't pretend to be interested in the social goings-on at school but was entertained by Helen's reports on other students' fashion violations.

"Are we gonna read today or just hang out?" she asked Helen.

"Well, I kinda wanted to talk about the formal," Helen said. There was apprehension in her tone.

"What's the matter?" Lanie inquired. She let her Mary Jane wedges drop to the carpet and tucked her right foot up under her thigh.

"Nothin' really, it's not *bad*."

"Well, geez, get on with it then," Lanie said.

Helen pushed the words out in a quick string. "Lance Davis asked if I'd be his date."

Lanie's back stiffened. This was not comfortable territory. Helen usually discussed crushes and boy business with her friend Stephanie.

"Uhh... well, what did you say?" Lanie didn't know what else to ask.

"I said *maybe*—but I thought it might be good if we did a double-date thing."

Lanie's eyes widened. "Oh no way, noo waay," she said, waving her hand.

"Aww, c'mon, Lanie, it would be a good way for you to meet new friends other than me and Hudson! Besides, it's not like a *date* kinda date—like high school. We're just gonna hang out at the formal and take pictures," Helen said.

"Yeah, I *know* that, but I don't even *want* to be somebody's date. And anyway, you have to *like* somebody to be their date, right?" Lanie said, suddenly unsure if that was accurate.

"Well, I guess—but just going as friends is fine too," Helen replied.

"I just thought I was gonna hang out with you and Hudson at the formal," Lanie said.

"That's the point! We *will* hang out; you'll meet other kids—I think it's time for you to do that. My other friends ask me why you don't hang out with us. They all think you're kind of a loner."

"I don't mind hanging out, I'll say hi and talk to whoever you want, but I don't really want to be anyone's date... not just *because*." Lanie was uncomfortable with the whole thing, but asked, "Well, is there somebody you already had in mind for me? 'Cause it sounds like there is."

"Well, I know that Danny Austin kinda likes you," Helen finally dropped the name that she'd been holding back.

Lanie stared off into the distance. "Danny? That guy who needs a haircut? How do you know he likes me?"

"He told Lance—they're friends."

"So wait," Lanie frowned, "Lance's buddy needs a date, so you're hooking me up? Is that the reason you want me to do this?"

Helen was quiet for a moment; she knew the discussion was teetering precariously. "Look, here's the deal," she said. "Lance was hoping to have a date, and Danny is shy—he's never gonna approach you. And you have no date, so it's just a harmless way to take some cool group photos and meet new people. Isn't that OK? Nobody said you had to spend the whole night with Danny. You've lived here a few months—you should know more people than you do."

Lanie's face softened; she knew Helen's logic was solid. "OK," she said. She'd been staring at her iced coffee, then caught Helen's eyes. "I'm OK with it—if we're just gonna do a group photo and talk a little, that's fine."

She pushed her glasses up and pointed at Helen. "He needs to toughen up and ask me though. I'm not just gonna show up and be his date."

Helen slumped in her chair in relief. "I'll take care of that. Thanks, Lanie, you're the bestest."

Lanie looked out at the golf course. Having a date just complicated the night; now it didn't sound fun at all. She was almost hoping she'd catch a cold—or have *any* reason not to go. But then she remembered what her grandma told her about friendship. "It goes both ways—your friends are not put on this earth to be a friend to you; you are put together to be friends to each other."

In that moment, she realized she'd been rotten to Helen. She glanced back at Helen's pale blue eyes, which were scanning a book jacket, and Lanie felt ashamed.

"Sorry, Helen," she said quietly.

Helen looked up from her book, surprised. "For what?"

"This date thing means a lot to you, and I was only worried about me. I'm sorry, that was uncool."

Helen smiled and sprung over to Lanie's chair to hug her. "We're cool, it's OK. Thanks though. It's gonna be fun; you'll see."

The acoustic guitar music that the Red Rocks played in the background felt just right for the environment, and it helped Lanie relax. The dance was a week away, so she chose to brush it from her mind. Feeling better about herself, and her friendship with Helen, she shifted her thoughts to the corridor at home—it was a more comforting topic than wondering how to be somebody's date. Her eyes wandered as she turned over Omega clues in her head.

Outside the windows, Lanie noticed a young man at the pro shop next door, unloading a large box from a van. Fumbling on his belt while juggling the box, he grabbed his employee ID tag and swiped it against the reader next to the door and let himself in. Lanie gasped and leapt out of her seat. "THAT'S *IT*!"

Startled, Helen flinched her leg and her sandal flew across the aisle. "*O-M-G*, what is wrong with you?!"

Standing with her coffee cup, Lanie became aware that other customers were looking at her, and she slowly sat down, her eyes blazing.

"I know how to get into those rooms. It's the cards—I'm sure of it!" she whispered. "Does Hudson have your phone? Does he?"

"No, no, I have it here!" Helen said.

"Ah, shoot—I'll talk to him later." Her mind raced; she wished she was home straight away—but knew she'd be stuck at the mall all afternoon.

Mrs. Newman walked into the coffee shop and pushed her sunglasses up into her hair, scanning the room for the two girls. Lanie saw her come in and waved. "C'mon," she said, bumping Helen's knee. "Your mom's here."

The mall adventure took forever. Lanie's mind paced and darted like a cat in a bathtub as she and Helen milled through the department stores and shops looking at dresses. In general, Lanie only shopped for clothing because she *had* to; picking outfits was no more entertaining than buying school supplies.

Conversely, Helen reveled in the experience, considering every ensemble that she passed. Lanie could only imagine it was how she'd shop for her first car. She had tried on at least five dresses that she thought were just right, but Helen was having her hold out for "the special one." They'd even bought shoes already, which Lanie thought was bizarre, since she'd heard that shoe selection was supposed to be based on the dress.

"Don't worry, these shoes look too good on you; we'll find a dress that goes with them," Helen had said.

In their fifth store, Helen pulled out a slender cream-colored evening gown. "Yessss! Try this one!" she said, handing it to Lanie.

"Uhh, I don't know if I'm gonna fit into that," Lanie said, turning it on the hanger as though it were missing some parts.

"You'll fill that up *gooood*," Helen replied, pushing the fabric against Lanie's shoulders. She shoved Lanie the box of neutral-colored shoes they'd picked out earlier. "Let's see the whole thing."

When Lanie came out of the dressing room, she found that Helen had rounded up her mom, and both were waiting to see the result.

"*THAT* is the dress," Helen said, pointing at Lanie. She was bouncing on her toes with delight.

"I'd have to agree," Mrs. Newman said with a smile. "Your dad might not like it much, but that's an awesome look." Lanie turned to view herself in the mirror. The hemline of the dress was tapered up above her ankle at the front but nearly touched the floor behind her. The silky material stayed close to her skin, but not too tight. A pronounced "V" seam in the waistline matched a similar cut in the neckline. She knew she looked good and shrugged at the Newman ladies.

"You two know what you're doing, I'll admit it." Lanie spun once more, gauging how much of her skin was showing from different angles. "I don't know if I can do a whole night in these shoes though," she said, pointing to the ankle-strapped corset heels that Helen had picked.

"Amateur," Helen said to her mom, hooking a thumb at Lanie. She looked back at Lanie and added, "We'll break them in before the dance... Now get changed and let's get outta here."

When they pulled into the driveway at the Newmans' house, Lanie flung her door open before Mrs. Newman had even shut the engine off. Hudson heard their arrival and was coming into the garage when Lanie slammed the car door.

"Hudson, I gotta show you something. C'mon, can you come with me? It's important!" Lanie motioned for him to follow as she trotted down the driveway.

Hudson objected to the hustle. "Wait, what did you find? I have work that my dad wants me to finish!"

"You—we—you can come back soon! C'mon, you're gonna want to see this!" Lanie yelled as she ran awkwardly up the sidewalk in her church clothes. She paused momentarily to watch a dusty black Chevrolet Suburban with United States Government license plates pass by. It had come down from the cul-de-sac and was being followed by a Chevy Silverado Z71 pickup with a U.S. Department of the Interior decal on its front door.

Mr. Speros wasn't home when Lanie and Hudson burst in. She ran to her room and scooped up the two plastic punch cards from her desk drawer, then grabbed Hudson's hand and towed him to the kitchen. Reaching back into the cabinet over the stove, Lanie opened the stairwell passage and ran down the steps, then stopped. It was still pitch dark.

"Grab the flashlights from the table," she called back up to Hudson, who hadn't started down yet. With the kitchen passage open, the draft from the tunnel took the easiest path out and Lanie squinted as the current of air tried to push her back up the steps.

At Mr. Speros's request, Hudson had added a *"hold open"* switch on the passage door so that when it was activated, the metal door and cabinets would remain retracted. Lanie had 3D-printed a small switchbox that they screwed to the inside of the adjacent cabinet, so that both switches were less likely to be hit by a stray pot or probing hand. She'd hand-painted fake woodgrain on the box to camouflage it—something her dad laughed at her for doing, but Hudson loved it.

Lanie ran to the small door near the bend in the corridor and pulled one of the two cards out of her pocket. She held it up to Hudson, displaying it as though she were about to perform a magic trick. She pressed it against the copper pad next to the door. Nothing happened, so she slid it around a bit. Still nothing.

She jammed it into her dress pocket and pulled out the other while looking at Hudson apprehensively. Lanie slapped the card against the copper plate, and the red light turned green. They both drew in a gasp of air when the bottom of the plate swung away from the wall about an inch. A small black tray extended from the edge underneath the copper plate.

On the inset portion of the tray was the white outline of a card, with an arrow pointing upward. Lanie laid the punch card on top of the outline and the tray withdrew halfway, then stopped. This was followed by a *KA-CHINK* sound and the door popped ajar. The card tray slid back out for Lanie to retrieve it. The two friends glanced at each other wide-eyed, and Lanie pulled the door open.

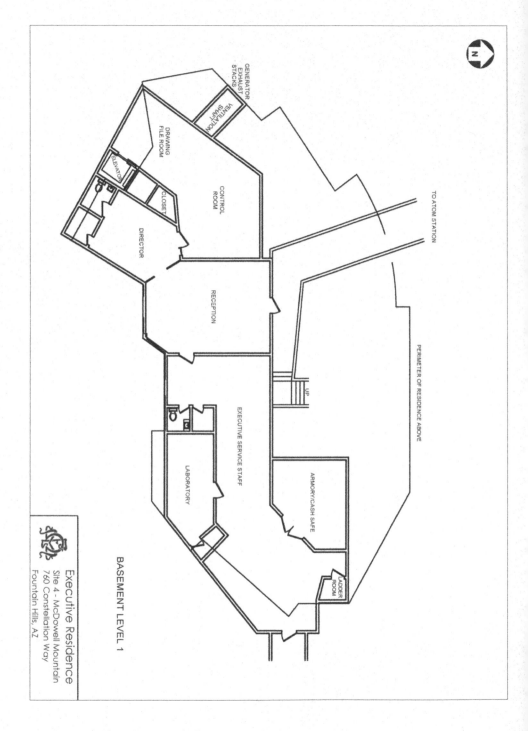

N

GENERATOR
EXHAUST
STACKS

VENTILATION SHAFT

DRAWING
FILE ROOM

ELEVATOR

CONTROL
ROOM

CLOSET

DIRECTOR

RECEPTION

TO ATOM STATION

PERIMETER OF RESIDENCE ABOVE

UP

EXECUTIVE SERVICE STAFF

LABORATORY

ARMORY/CASH SAFE

LADDER
ROOM

BASEMENT LEVEL 1

Executive Residence
Site 4 - McDowell Mountain
760 Constellation Way
Fountain Hills, AZ

# Chapter 13

# THE EXECUTIVE SUITE

The room was predictably dark inside. Warmer air swirled from the doorway and Lanie recognized the smell of leather—old leather. A faint overhead light cast shadows over some furnishings in the room. She shined her flashlight in at the floor, illuminating textured lime-green carpeting. As soon as she stepped up into the doorway, a motion sensor clicked and the whole room filled with light.

Lanie and Hudson shielded their eyes as their pupils adjusted. They were in a large office suite of what looked like two rooms. Straight ahead was a reception desk made of maple-stained teak wood. The walls were paneled in similar teak, and framed geological maps were hung throughout the space. Behind the reception desk was a credenza that stood on narrow copper legs just like the desk. Above that, a large Omega symbol was set into the wall, cut from gold-flecked white marble. To the right of the desk was a row of square, low-back armchairs covered in coarse green fabric.

"This is beyond nuts," Hudson said, his eyes still wide. Lanie was speechless.

The ceiling above the reception area was made up of polished copper beams arranged like spokes in a wheel. Light from overhead shined through the translucent ceiling above.

"Check that out!" Lanie said, pointing up. "It's the compass from the floor in the entryway! Light from the skylight comes through it."

The wall panels behind the reception chairs were glass, made up of two layers. Between the two layers, tiny pieces of copper, turquoise, and quartz were suspended, giving the glass wall the look of a cosmic starfield. The office behind the glass wall had a much larger teak desk, arranged in a U shape. A series of small television monitors shrouded in white plastic binnacles were built into the desk's right flank. Writing pens lay on a leather blotter and looked to have just been set out for use, frozen in time. Lanie walked into the large office, soaking up the smells and the ambiance. Both offices were spotless as though they'd been dusted weekly.

A brown leather executive chair was pushed in behind the larger desk. Glass display cases lined the left end of the big office, which Lanie presumed was under the front bedroom. The cases were full of various lumps of crystalline rocks on stands, as well as an assortment of mechanical instruments that Lanie couldn't identify. Large bookcases filled the adjacent wall, its shelves packed with volumes on engineering, geology, and metallurgy.

A portrait of an older man with a huge forehead and wide mouth hung on the wall near the display case. "Maybe that's the boss, back in the day?" Hudson said.

"That's President Eisenhower, dork," Lanie said, pointing at the brass plate below the portrait, which read "Commander in Chief."

"So, wait a minute," Hudson said as he poked through the reception desk drawers. "Is this mine a business or was it run by the government?"

"I don't know, but this doesn't seem like what a mining executive's office would look like." Lanie motioned for Hudson. "Oh wow, come check this out."

The right wall of the executive office was also glass. Beyond the glass wall was a small room with a pair of metal control consoles. Lanie pushed the glass door open and went in; like the office, the lights automatically switched on. A bank of bronze file cabinets stood along the far wall. The butter-yellow consoles faced each other in the center of the room and were divided by a frameless sheet of glass that extended to the ceiling. An array of buttons littered each console. Lanie noticed some were labeled, others were not, but all were made of what looked to be polished crystal. In the center of each console was a circular plate, through which the top of a brushed copper ball protruded.

"These look like some kinda crazy old video games," Hudson said, sitting down at a console. "Look, they have roller balls... to control something." He swirled his palm over the copper sphere.

Lanie stood next to him, scanning the other buttons and levers. "I don't see a 'power' button, or any monitor or display—I wonder what these are for?"

"I don't know, but this row of buttons on top has labels that look like locations."

Each of the glass block buttons in the row had print captured within it.

| GEOTHERMAL | BIODOME | RESIDENTIAL | COMMONS | GARAGE | MECHANICAL | INFIRMARY | ENTRY TERMINAL |
|---|---|---|---|---|---|---|---|

Below was a second row of unmarked glass buttons along with a flexible public address microphone. Lanie noticed that the glass partition was tinted such that it appeared clear unless you were seated at the console, then it became opaque gray. There was also a metal slot with a glass plate below it.

"There, look, I'll bet you can view those micro-fiche things we found into that slot!" she said.

"Probably. This glass looks like a screen. We'll have to figure out how to power it up," Hudson said.

"Just start punching buttons," Lanie said, poking the console.

"Hey, hey!" Hudson grabbed Lanie's hand. "Don't start pushing buttons if you don't know what they do. You could launch a missile or something."

Lanie's eyebrows flattened. "I'm sure you can't launch a missile attack from here, double-oh-seven."

Hudson wasn't entirely convinced. "We should still be careful. What's a biodome? And isn't geothermal something to do with the earth's hot core?"

"I think so. I think a biodome is a place where plants grow indoors to make air. But let's keep looking around—my dad's gonna be home soon."

"Dang, that's right. Are we gonna tell him about this? Or my parents?" Hudson asked.

"I don't know. I think we might wanna keep this to ourselves—at least for a couple days."

Hudson seemed uneasy. "OK, but the *secrets* thing just sounds like trouble."

"I'm not saying we keep a secret—I'm just thinking it'll be more fun to explore this place for a couple days without anyone telling us *don't touch this*, or *don't look in there*."

"Yeah, you're probably right—let's give it a couple days." He stood up and walked to the back of the room where there was a narrow metal door. "Hey, this isn't locked!" he said, pulling up on the handle.

They both peered into the small closet and saw an aluminum spiral staircase, with perforated steps leading both up and down. A beam of sunlight filtered down the staircase from above.

"Wow, there's something below too?!" Hudson said, looking into Lanie's surprised face.

"Let's go up first," Lanie proposed. "Wait! Go in and close the door, then come back out so we know we aren't gonna get locked in there."

"Good thinking."

Convinced they wouldn't be trapped in the dark shaft, Lanie headed up the staircase first. She could see the sun coming through a small glass dome in the rooftop above. The walls and ceiling were painted black and at the top of the stairs was a small landing, but there were no doors. Cobwebs dragged across Lanie's face as she ascended. The sunlight coming through the dome was being focused on a curved mirror on the wall, which in turn reflected the light onto an opaque glass window.

"THAT'S weird," Lanie said, waving her hand through the intense beam of light. "Well, we're back at ground level—we must be inside the house somewhere."

Hudson was probing the walls, shining his flashlight around. "No door handle. Oh wait I see." His foot had bumped a small metal pedal at the base of the wall. With pressure from his toe, the pedal dropped, and a section of wall released and swung outward.

Lanie and Hudson walked through the opening, and into the front guest bedroom. They'd emerged from a section of the bookcase that had opened. Lanie grimaced because she knew what was coming.

"HA! What did I *tell* you!" Hudson said, opening his arms toward the shelving. "Maybe you should watch more movies—it's ALWAYS the bookcase!" He proudly poked Lanie's shoulder.

"OK, ok, yes, you were right. It was a good hunch," Lanie conceded. "How do we open it from in here?" she said, examining the edges of the open casework.

Inside the passage, Hudson tugged on a flexible metal conduit in the corner near the hinge. "It must be electric, otherwise anybody could get in if they found it by accident. Look for a button or switch."

Scrambling all the books, photo frames, and knick-knacks around again, they saw nothing.

"To get into the office we needed the card," he said, pointing at Lanie's hip pocket. "We probably need to use it up here too. Wave it around the face of the bookcase."

Lanie pulled out the two cards. The one without the red stripe had opened the door in the corridor below. She waved it past the shelf edges, but nothing happened. Along the whole width of the bookcases at waist level was a brushed copper decorative strip. "There," Hudson said. "Wave it along the metal." When she slid it along the surface of the copper near the door's edge, an electric latch snapped, and a little punch card tray slid from inside the cabinetwork—just like the door in the reception office.

"That's it," Hudson said. "Let the bookcase close."

Lanie gave Hudson a smile. "You know your stuff; good call," she said, bumping his fist.

"Lanie, is that you in there?" Her dad called from the kitchen. Lanie and Hudson jumped in surprise, then Lanie quickly slammed the bookcase shut.

"Umm, yeah! Hi, Dad! We're in here!"

Mr. Speros appeared in the doorway. "What are you guys up to in here?" He eyed them suspiciously while chewing on a slice of French bread.

"We, uhh... we put the empty lockbox on the bookcase in here," Lanie grabbed the box from the shelf near her shoulder. "That way if those dirtbags come back, they find it quickly and leave."

"That's both a good idea and very disconcerting," her dad said with a concerned stare. "I sure hope they don't try to break in. But I have some plans in place to deal with that, just in case." Without elaborating, he turned back to the kitchen. Speaking back over his shoulder, he added, "I didn't hear you guys come in. Hudson, you can stay for dinner if you want. Lanie, come set us a table."

Hudson and Lanie shared a look of silent relief and headed into the kitchen. After dinner, Lanie retreated to her room, trailed by Hudson.

"My dad's gonna leave to meet a friend in a few minutes," she said in a low voice. "After he's gone, I wanna show you something else."

"OK, but I'm gonna have to go home in about half an hour," Hudson warned. "We didn't even try to open the wide door at the far end of the corridor."

"Ugh!" Lanie grabbed Hudson's wrist in disappointment. "How could we have forgotten to check that door! I don't think we can do it tonight—not now. We also didn't get to see where the spiral staircase leads down to."

"Shoot." Hudson said. They shared the same deflated expression.

"That reminds me," Lanie said. "Did you see that dark-tinted Chevy Suburban with government plates coming down from the cul-de-sac earlier? And the truck that was with it?"

"Yeah, government black-tops stick out like a sore thumb. It may as well have been a parade float. Do you think they were up by your house?"

"Don't know," Lanie responded. "The trucks were dirty. Maybe they'd just come off the fire road through the Ranger's gate by the Mindehanis' house."

Mr. Speros stuck his head through Lanie's bedroom doorway on his way to the garage. "I'm going to meet Brian. Call me if you need me."

Lanie waved and pushed up her glasses. "Bye, Dad."

When they heard the Jeep start in the garage, Lanie jumped up and motioned to Hudson to follow. They walked to the guest bathroom off the entryway. Lanie leaned against the sink, pointing at the shower.

"That window in the shower *looks* like the one in the front yard atrium," she said, enunciating like a TV news anchor. "But it's not—the one out front is a dummy! The sun gets bounced into this fake window from the glass dome in that little stair passage."

Hudson tilted his head back. "Ahh, pretty smart." Stepping into the shower, he peered into the opaque glass. "So that stairwell is behind the shower. I wonder what else this house is hiding."

Lanie led as they both returned to the offices downstairs through the bookcase, but Hudson was called home before they'd even entered the room, and the two friends had to suspend further exploration.

Lanie slouched into her desk chair, trying to motivate herself to finish up homework that she'd neglected all afternoon. She considered going back underneath the house but knew that if her grades slipped, her dad would cut off her access to the new spaces they'd found... and probably her new phone too. She also knew Hudson would be offended if she went exploring without him. Looking through her bedroom window, Lanie could see a nearly full moon rising over the mountain peaks. *Night visibility would be excellent*, she thought and smiled to herself. She pulled on a sweater and headed out to the barn to get her binoculars from her Polaris.

She stayed up on the hilltop surveying the mine through the binocular lenses until she saw the lights of the Jeep turning up their driveway. Inside the house, Lanie said goodnight to her dad when they met in the kitchen, then she headed to the darkness of her room. She stopped when her feet reached her bedroom doorway—the light in her desk cubby was flashing again. Flipping on her bedroom light, Lanie rushed to her desk and slid the little wooden door open. Inside, a different pod was standing. Light blue in color, this one's condition was no better than the orange one she'd seen previously. The angular pod's hatch was open, and inside Lanie found a surprise.

Sitting atop a small ivory envelope within the pod was a rare sea-green Matchbox Opel Diplomat toy car in its original yellow cardboard box. Both the car and its box were in exceptional condition. Lanie carefully lifted it from the pod along with the note below. The envelope had Lanie's name fastidiously printed in handwritten text. Inside was an ivory card with a gold omega character on its face. Within the card, more tidy handwriting read,

**Looking forward to meeting you soon.**

—

The next day at school, Hudson ran to meet Lanie at lunch, since they hadn't had time to talk beforehand. "I've been sending texts—didn't you see them?"

"I told you, I'm not supposed to power my phone up at school unless it's an emergency; my dad can monitor my usage."

"Oh yeah, I forgot. But check this out, I have something to show you!" He pulled a small cobbled electronic device out of his pocket and was about to demonstrate its function to Lanie when Helen appeared, grinning.

"What's up, dungeon dwellers?"

"I hope you're keeping up your end of the deal," Hudson said to his sister. "Nobody should know anything about Lanie's house or what's under it."

"Chill, little brother," she waved her hand at Hudson. Actually, she was only older by nine minutes. "I haven't said anything to anybody. But you heard Mom and Dad—you'd better not be down there messing around if Lanie's dad's not around."

Hudson was looking away, pretending not to hear, so Helen turned to Lanie. "The formal's this weekend!" she sang through a brilliant smile of braces.

With all the excitement at home, the school formal was farthest from Lanie's mind. "I didn't forget; I'll be ready." She responded with the same enthusiasm she'd show for a scheduled medical procedure.

Helen's own enthusiasm wasn't dampened. "I know you're not super excited, but I'm sure you'll have a blast. I'll come over and help you with makeup; it'll be fun. After I help Hudson get ready, that is."

"I can tie my own necktie just fine," Hudson said in defense.

"Yeah, but you can't be trusted to style your own hair. At my aunt's wedding in May, he looked like he'd combed his hair with flypaper," she said to Lanie.

"Did you also get *Hudson* a date?" Lanie didn't mask her sarcasm.

"He can find his own girl," Helen said while she tossed Lanie's curls. "I wanted *us* to have dates to our first dance together."

As she packed up her lunch remainders, Lanie reminded Helen that she wouldn't be doing any dancing.

"Fine, so don't dance—just be nice to your date."

"I'll be nice to Danny, don't worry. He finally asked me, by the way," Lanie said.

"OH! How'd that go? How'd he do it?!" Helen asked.

"He caught her in the hallway this morning when we were going into second hour," Hudson said through a chuckle. "He was so nervous that I thought he was gonna pass out."

"He's nice enough," Lanie said. "I just hope he gets his hair cut before this weekend."

"Yeah, he's chill, you'll see—there are a lot of nice folks around you. Maybe you should spend less time with that printer in your garage, and more time getting involved at school."

Lanie didn't answer—she didn't like Helen's tone and the remark stung. But she didn't want to argue.

Helen jumped up and trotted across the courtyard to meet an approaching friend and waved goodbye to Lanie. "Gotta talk to Amy, see ya!"

Lunch was nearly over, so Hudson returned his device to his backpack. It looked like a modified remote for a car's keyless entry system. "I'll show you this later... not enough time now," he said. "You know, I'm only going to that dance 'cause you're going."

"I know, and I'm glad," Lanie responded. "We'll do it together, just like everything else."

## Chapter 14

# ENOUGH IS ENOUGH

Lanie, Hudson, and Helen walked home together that afternoon. Their conversation topics were related to the upcoming formal, since Lanie and Hudson had started limiting their discussion of the Omega discoveries to themselves.

The garage was open at the Newmans' house when the three walked up the driveway. Mrs. Newman was backing her Honda out and waved at Helen to get in. "C'mon, Helen, we gotta go," she said, leaning through the window.

"Picking up some of the decorations for the formal, I'll see ya later," Helen said as she disappeared around the back of the SUV.

As they drove off, Hudson turned to Lanie. "Lemme show you what I made—finished it late last night."

"I thought we were gonna go down the spiral stairs today!" she said, looking at her watch.

"Just gimme a minute. You'll like this stuff." He led Lanie to the third garage bay, which Mr. Newman used as a workshop. This was where Hudson was required to do his tinkering with inventions, after he'd burned a hole in his bedroom carpet with the soldering iron.

"I went up to the hilltop last night after you left," Lanie said casually. "The fence around the old mine is fixed."

"No way," Hudson whispered. "Those trucks we saw!"

"Yep," Lanie nodded.

"But the Fed? Why? Why not the usual County crews?"

"Who knows," Lanie said. "I'm more curious about why they had to have people in an unmarked Suburban up there supervising the work."

"Yeah, I was thinking the same thing. Do you think there's a hidden entrance up there? I mean, other than the covered-up shaft?"

Lanie shrugged, then pointed to Hudson's workbench. "OK, whatcha got?" She saw a variety of electronic devices scattered around. Some were disassembled, while others looked to be half built, with wiring and circuit boards hanging out. She laid her backpack down on a bin of Hanukkah decorations and pulled out her water bottle.

"I'm making things that we can use to stop intruders," he said. He had a pair of industrial cable retractor reels taken apart, as well as something with springs and serrated teeth that looked like an animal trap. "I've got stuff that we can set up right away in an emergency, but also some stuff we can hide or bury."

He held up the animal trap. It had a battery box and a bundle of wiring neatly tied alongside. "This has actuators from a car's door locks, watch." He pulled a car's key fob from his pocket and pressed the lock button, and the jaws of the trap slammed shut, crushing a piece of white plastic pipe that Hudson had laid across the teeth. "I can set it off with this remote, or from my phone app. I wrote a special Arduino program that we can use for anything I build, so we'll be able to set off traps or activate lighting from our phones when I'm done."

"Ahh! So that's why you wanted door parts from an old Toyota at the wrecking yard!" Lanie was impressed, examining the custom linkages he'd fabricated.

Hudson looked proud. "Yep, Camry door lock motors don't need much power to actuate—I can use smaller batteries."

Lanie frowned at the shattered section of pipe. "I'm not sure I want this thing hidden in my yard just yet." A dismantled yellow plastic gun shell was nearby. "Was that a taser?" she asked.

"Yeah, I was gonna show you that next," he said with a devious smile. "That one's my favorite."

From the corner of her eye, Lanie saw a blue crew-cab Ram pickup truck pass outside. She was about to ask Hudson about the corridor's magnetic punch cards but did a double-take at the truck. Sucking air in through clenched teeth, Lanie grabbed Hudson's arm.

"Oww, what the—what are...." Hudson first drew his arm away, then stopped speaking when he saw what Lanie had seen.

The driver of the truck was the white-haired man from the Dodge Durango. Hudson dropped what he was working on and the two ran to the edge of the garage to watch the truck. It circled through the cul-de-sac and stopped across the street from the Speroses' driveway. A second man was in the passenger seat, but neither Lanie nor Hudson recognized him.

Her breathing was shallow, and Lanie could feel her heart pulsing in her neck. The white-haired man stepped out of the truck, revealing a cast on his right arm. He also had a knee brace on the same side. The two men surveyed their surroundings as if to see if anyone was watching. Because of the curve in the road, landscaping obscured their view of the passenger, but Lanie saw he had a beard when he came around the front bumper. The two men crossed the street together and headed up the path toward the Speroses' front door.

Lanie's fists clenched. "Those lousy dirtbags," she said under her breath. Tears wanted to fill her eyes, but she squinted to keep them back. She'd have already been inside the house when they broke in—if she hadn't stopped at the Newmans'.

Hudson had pulled out his phone and was preparing to dial 9-1-1.

"Hold on a second," Lanie said, surprising Hudson. Her face was calm but intense.

"Those morons couldn't even manage a roadside heist with an unarmed family in a motorhome. I'm thinking they're completely incompetent... they're stupid," Lanie said with absolute confidence. "I don't think they could even rob a hot dog stand correctly, and I'm tired of 'em." Lanie punched her fist into her backpack. They're jamming us up. I think we need to get rid of 'em—for good."

Hudson was shocked by Lanie's fearlessness. "What? I mean... how?" He wasn't sure where to start but managed to blurt out, "OK, what's your idea?"

"Get your stuff together," she said, pointing to his workbench inventions. "And give me those big wire cutters."

Hudson handed her a pair of red-handled side cutters, and she walked over to Hudson's mountain bike.

"Here's the plan," Lanie said. "I'm gonna take care of their truck—it will only take a minute. While I do that, you get hidden in the bushes near the side of my house. Then we'll call the police. When we know they're on the way, we're gonna lure those idiots out, so they chase me down the block in their truck. I wanna cause them some pain, so they know who they're messing with."

Lanie saw confidence growing in Hudson's expression. "If they break in, they'll connect both our families," he said. "They could hurt Helen or my parents...." His eyebrows dipped, and he lowered his voice. "I think this is crazy, but let's get 'em."

Lanie grabbed Hudson's hand and locked eyes with him. "Can we do this smart?" she asked.

"Yes."

"Then let's do it."

Hudson stretched what appeared to be a thick silicone oven mitt over his left hand. Lanie didn't have time to ask what it was. He grabbed his bag and ran across the street.

"Call me—now," he said to Lanie and put a hands-free ear bud into his ear. Lanie did the same, then called him so that they had an open communication channel while they were apart.

"I hear you," Lanie heard in her ear as she watched Hudson trotting behind the neighbors' hedge.

Lanie tucked her hair into her hoodie and pushed the bike through landscaping to stay out of view. She couldn't see the men as she crouched in front of the blue pickup. The Speroses' front door was ajar, and it made Lanie furious that they were inside her family's home. She lay on the sidewalk and rolled into the shade underneath the truck.

At each front wheel she used the wire cutters to sever the brake hose, then slid along the curb to the back of the truck, where she did the same at each rear wheel. Brake fluid dribbled onto her hands, then the asphalt. The truck's hot muffler burned the back of her forearm, but she remained silent.

"Call 9-1-1 *now*. I'm coming over," she said to the bottom of the truck. Lanie hung up once Hudson had confirmed. From under the truck, she could see Hudson had strung his steel trip wire mechanism across the walkway by her front door. The spring-loaded wire retractor he'd devised was hidden behind a rosemary bush. He had crouched into the shrubs near the false bathroom window, out of sight.

Rolling out from under the truck, Lanie stood up and pushed the bike across the road. She left it on the path near the garage, then joined Hudson against the house. He was already on the call with the 9-1-1 dispatcher. He recited Lanie's address and provided a description of the men along with their truck's license number. Lanie had recovered her emergency kit from behind the gas meter, and from the box she pulled out the snub-nosed weapon she'd printed.

"What does that thing do?!" Hudson whispered, covering the phone with his hand.

Lanie straightened her glasses. "You'll see. If it works, it's gonna be very painful for one of these guys. But I only have one shot; I gotta be close range." On her own phone she pulled up the security system app and found detected motion in both the master bedroom and her own room. She let out a squeak of fury, then stifled herself.

Hudson hung up his phone, though Lanie still heard the dispatcher talking to him. "Alright, what next?" he asked. His voice was anxious, but he was focused. He was wrapping a legwarmer around the wrist end of the silicone glove.

"Here's the tough part," she said, standing up. "Be ready to run—but stay here to back me up. I want them to speed down the street after me, so I'm gonna draw them out toward the truck, then ride down the block. I'll meet you in your garage."

"What if he has his gun?"

"He's not gonna start firing shots in the middle of the neighborhood in broad daylight. I don't think they're *that* stupid," Lanie said.

On her phone, she again pulled up the home security app and pressed the *PANIC* button. Inside the house the alarm sounded, and her phone began vibrating. Now her dad would be notified as well. She knew they were past the point of no return. She mounted the bicycle in the center of the pathway, then watched the front door, ready to ride off.

Before anyone appeared at the front door, she was grabbed from behind. The second intruder—a tall, younger man with a scratchy red beard—wrapped his arm around Lanie's torso and began dragging her toward the house. Panic coursed through her body, and she screamed like a banshee, kicking at her assailant. Lanie had been foolish to wait so close to the garage, but it was too late for regret. She wrenched her arm free, then fired her weapon straight into the side of her bearded attacker's face. A small faceted black ball studded with fishhooks shot into his cheek and

190

immediately drew blood. The man yelped but didn't slow. He yanked the plastic gun from Lanie's hand and tossed it, yelling obscenities as the hooks' barbs tore at his cheek and fingers.

With the fishhooks' barbs hopelessly entangled in his skin and beard, the man continued toward the front door. Lanie ripped at his bare arm and flailed her legs. Digging between his left pinky and ring fingers, Lanie violently tore them different directions as though she were peeling a banana. She heard and felt his pinky snap, and the bearded thug howled in pain, then punched Lanie in the back of the head.

He held Lanie tight against his side, crushing the breath out of her lungs; she couldn't reach around to defend herself. She growled and screeched, wondering what they'd do to her when she was inside the house. Her glasses were knocked off her face as the front door approached. If he got her inside, it was over.

From the corner of her eye she saw Hudson stand up and start charging toward her but also noticed they were approaching the trip wire. The milliseconds passed slowly; Lanie felt like she was wasting time. Panic was going to get her killed if she didn't get herself together. In those split seconds, Lanie realized that she wasn't thinking clearly—or smartly. She forced aside thoughts of what the men *might* do to her and focused instead on what *she* could do to save herself. She focused on the thin wire. Lanie arched her legs over it, planting her feet on the other side.

The gray wire looked like a joint in the concrete, and her bearded assailant strode straight into it. He triggered the retractor's spring, and the wire viciously yanked against his ankles. As though he'd been standing on ice, both feet were swept behind him and he fell forward. He had to let go of Lanie to break his fall, and she seized the opportunity, spinning around. With a two-stepped lunge, she used all her thigh muscles to boot the downed thug as though his head were a kickball. His face took the brunt of the hit, and he let out an angry, pained yell—then Lanie stomped hard on his tattooed neck. She dropped her full weight on her foot, crushing his cheek into the concrete. The man was much stronger, though, and tossed Lanie against the garage wall among a row of rose trees.

By now, Hudson had descended on the bearded man. Lanie watched as her friend clamped the criminal's forearm with his gloved hand. Instantly, the man stiffened and began to convulse. He yelled in stunted blasts.

Lanie stood frozen—she had no idea what was happening at first. But when her attacker collapsed to the ground in a twitching seizure, Hudson maintained his grip as though he were holding the leash of an unruly dog. While the man shuddered on the ground, Hudson pulled three large zip ties from his back pocket. Nodding toward the door, he yelled, "Heads-up!"

Behind her, the front door slammed against the wall and the white-haired intruder emerged, coming toward her. He was reaching under his coat with his left hand, and Lanie saw the glint of his gun. Lanie's fists clenched, and she grabbed the first thing that looked useful—a heavy wooden post that supported one of the rose trees. Ripping it angrily from the ground, she positioned it over her shoulder like an oversize baseball bat. He wasn't left-handed and the white-haired man fumbled with his gun. Lanie burst toward him in a sprint, screaming at the top of her lungs.

Surprised that she was charging at him, the man stopped in his tracks and, at that moment, Lanie detected fear in his eyes. In those fractions of a second, as her retinas burned into his, she knew that she had the upper hand, and her courage tripled. Confidence and determination surged into her muscles, and she whipped the five-foot post toward the intruder's head. He raised his injured arm to block her swing. The descending stick smashed his cast in a direct hit, forcing it into his face with a hollow crash. He dropped the stolen lockbox he had been carrying with his right hand. Still screaming, Lanie swung again, landing a crushing blow across his ribs. He staggered forward and fell to his knees, wincing in pain.

The gun bounced on the path and slid into the ivy. Lanie was about to swing again when she stumbled over the tripwire herself, landing on the white-haired man's back. Her falling mass pushed him back into the pathway and she felt his tenderized ribs snap. He cried out in breathless agony but shoved Lanie aside. She fell into the roses... again. Regaining his footing, the white-haired man ran past Hudson, ignoring his partner.

When she reemerged from the rose tree hedge, Lanie saw that Hudson had zip-tied the bearded attacker's hands behind his back. Likewise, his ankles were strapped together and he flopped like a disoriented fish, with the barbed ball still hanging from his cheek. Lanie recovered her wooden post and tore after the fleeing white-haired man. Moving at twice his speed, Lanie growled and repositioned the post, intending to inflict maximum damage. Clutching his ribs with his debilitated right hand, he yanked the truck's door open with the other. Lanie could hear approaching sirens in the distance when she reached the truck.

She arched the stick over her head like a pickaxe and swung it so hard her feet nearly left the pavement. The post impacted the injured man's shoulder with a dense *thunk*. He tumbled forward into the driver's seat and the stick bounced off the roof of the truck. When it recoiled, the post split, throwing Lanie backward. The top of the post rocketed across the roof of the truck, narrowly missing Mr. Mindehani, who'd run out of his house to investigate. Starting the engine while he pulled the door closed, the white-haired man leaned over the steering wheel, struggling to suck in air.

Hudson then appeared on Lanie's left and he pitched a metal canister through the driver's window glass. He'd thrown it with so much force that it bounced off the passenger door and into the back seat. White smoke poured from around the back tires as the criminal sped off down the block with the Hemi V8 at full throttle. He'd abandoned his accomplice. Within a few yards of Hudson's house, a misty explosion occurred inside the cab of the pickup.

"Are you OK?!" Hudson asked.

"Watch," Lanie said. She kept her eyes on the receding truck. "I'm OK—are you alright?" Her voice was cracked and hoarse.

"I'm good."

The truck raced past Hudson's house then started to jerk from side to side when the brake lights came on. The truck didn't slow but continued to pick up speed. It careened down the curved road without any brakes. Mr. Rinnas was coming up the street toward his house and was forced to steer his red Chrysler into Hudson's yard as the pickup barreled past, but not before its front bumper caught the rear corner of the Chrysler. The impact kicked Mr. Rinnas's car into a spin through the Newmans' yard, and the rear bumper fascia flew into the alcove by their front door.

Two Fountain Hills police cruisers tore into the neighborhood down by the traffic light just as the truck reached the intersection. Unable to make the turn at high speed, the Ram plowed off the road and into the landscaped parkway. Crashing first through a low block wall, it slammed headlong into a giant ficus tree. The force of the impact smashed the truck's hood all the way up into the windshield. The two friends watched the truck flip then come to rest in the pond at the entrance to the neighborhood.

One of the Ford Crown Victoria Police Interceptors stopped at the pond, while the other raced toward Lanie and Hudson, it's engine roaring and strobes flashing. To her right, Lanie found that Mrs. Mindehani had joined her husband in the driveway, but was no more helpful. Both stared at Lanie and Hudson with eyes wide and jaws hanging.

Standing in the middle of the road, she and Hudson watched as the responding officers jumped out, looking around. One officer asked her to drop the remainder of her post. Lanie complied, then collapsed into a sitting position on the warm asphalt with her head in her hands. Hudson dropped to his knees and wrapped his arms around her.

By now, other neighbors had come out of their houses to see what was going on. Mr. Rinnas was simultaneously shocked and confused and he milled around amongst the responding officers, hoping to get information. One officer stayed with Lanie, while the other had run into the Speroses' house to assess any remaining danger. He came back to the patrol car with the bearded man, who was restrained in conventional handcuffs.

Lanie was in control of her emotions by then and pulled her disheveled hair back into a ponytail. Hudson returned from the driveway holding her glasses and helped her up. Deep scratches on her arms and cheeks were swelling up, a result of her tangles with the roses. She squinted into the afternoon sun as the officer confirmed her version of the events. Returning her dusty glasses to their position, she saw that the neighbors had assembled across the road and were busy speculating about what had happened.

Hudson was surprisingly composed as the second policeman took his statement. He pulled off his electrified glove in a bundle, handing it to the officer. About this time there was another searing squeal of tires down at the intersection. Lanie turned to see her dad's gold and white Rambler dive onto Constellation Way, casting off a front hubcap. Mr. Speros sped up the block, dodging pedestrian traffic, and skidded to a stop on the sidewalk in front of their house.

Emotion started to well back up in Lanie's eyes when she saw her dad jump out of the car, his face fraught with panic. He ran past the officers who were approaching him and threw his arms around Lanie. They embraced for what felt like an hour, then Lanie spoke up.

"I'm fine, Dad... we took care of those guys. I don't think they'll be back." Her face was still flushed but her voice was firm.

Mr. and Mrs. Newman had already arrived and were with Hudson in the Speroses' open garage. Mrs. Newman's cheeks were stained with tears, and her husband sat on the Wagoneer's tailgate with his arm around Hudson. Lanie's dad was so shocked about the scene that she couldn't tell what he was thinking. She didn't know if he was mad, scared, thankful, or a combination of the three. Lanie was happy that Hudson and his family were there because it seemed to be keeping everyone's sentiments in check.

By 5 p.m., a detective from the police department was inside, collecting fingerprints and other evidence, and two officers remained to take measurements from the street and pond. The families were left to themselves in the garage.

195

"They'd been casing your house," Mr. Newman said, showing Lanie's dad footage from their own doorbell camera on his phone. It showed the blue truck coming and going from the street during the workday at least a few times throughout the week.

"Did anyone say anything about the underground rooms?" Hudson asked the group. They all shook their heads.

"I think we *should* have," Mrs. Newman said. "I think this has gone far enough." Lanie sensed that her comments were directed at Mr. Speros.

"I don't disagree," Mr. Speros said, running his hand through his hair. "But now I'm concerned that it would only make things worse. It could generate media coverage and exposure—and cause us more trouble."

"He's right," Mr. Newman said. "We don't know the whole story yet. By flushing out whatever's going on under the house, we make the Speroses' home a target. And potentially ours too, Pauline," he said, turning to his wife. "I think it's best that we continue to keep it quiet."

"I'm just glad everyone's safe... well, mostly," Mr. Newman added, noting the scratches on Lanie's arms.

"Can we all please agree then that the children will not be doing any more detective work? Or apprehension of criminals?!" Mrs. Newman said, her lower lip trembling.

"We can all *certainly* agree on that," Mr. Speros said, glaring at Lanie and Hudson.

An officer came into the garage; the shield on his chest said "Bennett." "Detective Garcia would like to know if you would pull up the footage from the home's security cameras for review?" he asked.

Lanie and Hudson glanced at each other. Their parents were about to watch a complete replay of their whole operation. Slowly, Hudson slid off the tailgate and the group went into the Speroses' den.

"Lanie, you're the tech expert. Pull the footage up on the TV please," said Mr. Speros, extending a hand at the large screen on the stone wall.

Lanie obliged, cuing up the doorbell camera video on her phone so it could be streamed to the TV. She started with the intruders' initial entry into the house, showing how they'd forced the front door open. The detective asked why this hadn't set off the alarm.

"It wasn't armed," Mr. Speros said. He looked at the floor, disgusted with himself.

The detective jotted notes then directed Lanie to move ahead. As the motion unfolded during the six minutes of action in the front yard, Lanie thought Hudson's mom might faint. She was pale, covering her mouth with both hands. Hudson's dad, on the other hand, was glowing with pride and working hard to hide his emotion as he watched Hudson yank the zip ties tight around the bearded man's ankles.

Lanie's dad stood near the monitor, watching every detail. He took an anxious step back when Lanie ripped the post out of the ground and charged toward the camera. Watching her unleash a fury on the wounded attacker, Mr. Speros's lips pursed, and his cheeks puffed up, as though he wasn't sure how to react.

Detective Garcia and Officer Bennett watched without expression. When the truck sped off the screen, Lanie paused the video and she and Hudson scanned the other faces in the room.

"Well, I gotta say...," the detective said, looking impressed, "If that doesn't...," she stopped, appearing to reconsider her words. Instead, she addressed the two friends directly, "I'll tell ya what, the Special Forces need more recruits like *you two*." The comment drew a spontaneous snorty chuckle from Mr. Newman. He quickly shielded his eyes and pinched his lips, knowing he'd be in hot water with Hudson's mom.

Officer Bennett walked up to Lanie and placed his hand on her shoulder. "Young woman, you are as fierce as a mountain lion; I hope my own daughter develops the courage you have." Lanie's expression said thanks, but she remained silent.

To Hudson, the officer said, "What did you throw into the truck that exploded? The suspect and truck interior were coated with a gel that irritated the responding officer's eyes."

Hudson glanced at his dad, then back at the officer. "Umm, well, it was habanero chili powder mixed with Vaseline—propelled by a $CO_2$ charge. I set it off by remote."

Officer Bennett's eyebrows raised, and he cocked his head. "Well, it was very efficient. I hope I see your future work on tactical equipment; you're an impressive builder. But I'm afraid we're keeping your taser glove as part of the investigation. And, please, don't build any more of them." He winked at Mr. Newman as he turned to the door.

"Go ahead and download those video files for us, please; upload them to the link on my card," Detective Garcia said to Lanie and her dad. She handed him her card and a copy of their response report. "I'm glad you both are safe—we'll call you with any leads or developments." Turning back, she added, "Both of you, leave the heavy lifting for us next time, alright? That truck could have killed somebody down at the intersection— or in the crosswalk." Her expression indicated that she was both serious and concerned, and Lanie nodded in confirmation.

When he'd closed the door, Mr. Speros returned and sat down with the others in the den. It was quiet for a few long moments.

"I think," Mr. Newman started, then paused, "I think, what we really need is for the two of you to understand that this mine situation is a big deal. There was big money involved originally, and there still could be now. It could get you guys killed. Or your siblings." His gaze was stern. "We need you to step back and follow our lead. You should've simply stood aside and called the police today—and that's what you *will* do going forward. Do you both understand? Ari, do you agree?" he said, turning to Mr. Speros.

"One-hundred percent," Lanie's dad replied. "You both did some astonishing work today, but some of it was luck. It was a risk you shouldn't have taken."

Mr. Speros paused, staring at the floor. Lanie figured this was for disciplinary effect, then he continued, "I don"t suppose either of you thought about failure when you made your plan. What if those men had restrained you and gotten you both inside the house?" He looked at Lanie. "What was on their minds? What would they have done to you?" He closed his eyes and rubbed his forehead, which is what he did when the words he wanted weren't coming to him. He sat down next to Lanie, looking at the TV screen. It was paused on the image of she and Hudson huddled on the street saturated in yellow afternoon light, with long shadows behind them.

Focusing on the same image, Lanie couldn't help but think it was the one she'd pick if her story were ever put on a magazine cover.

"Foolishness," Mrs. Newman said. "You were both being foolish— your logic was flawed. You should never have approached those men."

It became uncomfortably quiet again, then Mr. Newman broke the tension. "Alright, I know you guys are feeling the pain; we made our points." He stood up and offered a hand to his wife. "I think these two probably need a few minutes to sync up," he said to Hudson's mom. The look on his face said to her, "Give them a break."

Lanie's dad agreed. "Catch up a little bit, then Hudson can head home. I have other plans for us tonight," he said to Lanie. She glanced up at him, but her dad added nothing, only a soft smile.

The three parents went out to the atrium beyond the front door to talk, and Lanie could see Hudson's dad pulling up the steel stake and trip wire Hudson had installed. The sun was nearly set, and the orange glow lit the remnants of the Ram's broken glass in the cul-de-sac. The neighbors had dispersed.

"We did it," Hudson said, smiling. He plopped onto the sofa next to her.

Lanie smiled weakly but felt exhausted. "Yeah. I thought I'd feel different right now. I thought I'd feel... I dunno... charged up."

"It's all the excitement and adrenaline. You'll probably feel better in the morning." He patted her forearm.

Lanie winced and sucked in a breath through her teeth.

"Oh geez, sorry," Hudson apologized, withdrawing his hand from her red skin. "We can meet up tomorrow at lunch. With those guys out of the way, I think it will be a lot more fun to explore the rooms now."

Walking Hudson to the door, she nodded. "Yeah, I think my attitude will be better in the morning." Her voice was still hoarse. "But we did the right thing, I mean, made the right decision, even if we got busted... and we did it together. That didn't go exactly like I expected, but still a success." She offered her fist to Hudson.

Hudson smiled, bumping Lanie's knuckles. "We owned it, and you killed it. You kinda scared me with your psycho stick attack—that was nuts. No wonder that guy ran off."

"Thanks, I'm glad you were here with me." She gave Hudson a hug, then watched him walk down the driveway with his parents.

Mr. Speros pulled some broken wood shards away from the damaged deadbolt on the front door jamb as he passed through.

"Why don't you go shower, sweetie? Put on some nice jeans; I'm taking you out tonight. We're doing a date night."

In the shower, Lanie let the warm water fall on her face—the flow helped to wash the distress from her mind—but the water stung her lacerations. She pulled on some jeans and a pearly white V-neck sweater that felt good on her skin. When she returned to the living room, her dad was waiting on the sofa. He smiled and stood, then reached for her hand. "You look much more comfortable," he said.

They drove down Constellation Way in the Cadillac, and Lanie noticed the Newmans' house was dark. *They must have gone out as well,* she thought. Mr. Rinnas's poor Chrysler had been hauled away. Yellow caution ribbon surrounded the broken wall down by the traffic light. The flatbed tow truck and its crew were still dragging the mangled pickup out of the pond, much to the irritation of the resident ducks. A couple curious bystanders were watching the process. Mr. Speros said nothing but drove on when the light turned green.

"So... where are we going?" Lanie asked.

"The Biltmore—you'll like it. I was gonna take you there for your sixteenth birthday, but I'm adjusting my plan."

The short drive was quiet; neither Lanie nor her dad felt like small talk was necessary. The smooth roads and broad parkways of Scottsdale were free of traffic that evening. After a few more minutes, Mr. Speros turned onto a narrow driveway that led across a canal bridge. On the other side, among beautiful gardens, the Arizona Biltmore Resort came into view. The grand old hotel looked to Lanie like an elaborate Mayan castle, made of thousands of stacked cubes of tan concrete. The blocks had been cast with an intricate pattern, giving the building a texture that somehow appeared both ancient and extraterrestrial. Warm lighting lit the many columns and overhangs.

A uniformed attendant opened Lanie's door when her dad stopped the Fleetwood at the valet. Another attendant whisked the car away, and Mr. Speros offered Lanie his arm. "Shall we?" he said, smiling.

"This was where your mom and I would go on date nights during college," her dad said as they walked through the vast lobby. "It used to take me a week's work wrenching at the Chevy dealer's service department to pay for those dinners, but it was worth it," he added.

They were escorted to a private table against the window, with a view of the garden and city lights in the distance. Lanie arranged her silverware on the white linen while her dad looked at the menu. It was Lanie's first candlelight dinner, and the environment was lovely. There were crisp, fresh carnations in a vase next to the window. The low hum of dinner chatter mixed with peaceful piano music was very comforting, and Lanie could feel her anxiety sliding away.

As they enjoyed their dinner, father and daughter talked about the upcoming school formal and other current events. While they waited for the table to be cleared, Mr. Speros addressed their looming topic.

"I thought tonight was the right night to do this because it would reframe the day for you," he said. He put down his napkin and focused on Lanie. "Today was a little traumatic—at least for me. You've had so much to process over the last couple weeks, between our disaster road trip and these issues at home. I've been meaning to set aside some one-on-one time for us, so tonight seemed right."

He raised his glass of water in a toast, and Lanie picked hers up as well. "Here's to my little girl in the household, who's suddenly turned into a woman."

Lanie felt herself blushing a little as she clinked her glass against her dad's. "I'm still the same," she said. "I'm just learning to be useful."

"*Useful*," her dad repeated and squinted at her with a crooked smile. "Yeah, you've given me quite a few surprises over the last couple weeks. You've tapped some of the fiery temperament that your mom gave you. When I watched that video today, I was very scared at first." His look of concern shifted to a proud smile. "Then, you yanked that post out of the ground like a superhero, and I felt like I was watching your mom. You move like her, and your fearsome battle cry even sounded like her." Mr. Speros chuckled and looked down at his plate, waiting for his emotions to taper.

"Your mom enjoyed a fight, and she fought to win. Even if it was just a disagreement about how to rearrange the furniture," he said. Her dad forced a serious expression on his face and continued.

"I realized, watching that video, that I didn't need to worry about you as much as I thought. You're not *little Lanie* anymore, and that's OK. I *do* think you have a lot to learn about taking risks and what it means to lose." He focused on Lanie's eyes. "But... the Lanie I saw today isn't going to lose very often."

202

He reached over the table and took Lanie's hand. Holding her fingers, he kissed the scraped skin on top of her knuckles. "Ms. Speros, you are meant for amazing things, and I will help you achieve them—not hold you back—I promise."

Lanie realized that her dad was releasing his image of her as the little girl on the training-wheeled bike with a helmet. He was welcoming who was next—the Lanie of the future, with her own abilities and identity. She knew the moment had to be a big deal for her dad, and she smiled warmly to convey her thanks.

The remainder of their father—daughter date passed without any dramatic discussion, and Lanie let the day's memories find their position in the file folders of her mind.

Dessert was wonderful, and Lanie sampled everything in the assortment that the chef had sent out with his compliments. She still felt tired, but she also felt relaxed, strong, and empowered. And, she was proud of her dad's new faith in her. Lanie also knew that she needed to protect it. She thought of Isaiah, far away at her grandparents' house. She would help keep not only the household safe but also her little brother. It's what her mom would have asked her to do.

Chapter 15

# THE OMEGA DIRECTOR

First period was usually slow to kick off, since Mr. Aarons meandered through roll call each morning as though it were the first time he was seeing his students' names. Looking over the top of his reading glasses, he didn't say anything as Lanie straggled in but noted the tardiness. She'd overslept, and her dad hustled her to school on his way to work. Slipping quietly into the classroom, she tucked herself into her desk, happy that her bangs were shielding her face. She held her eyes wide, hoping to force the droopiness from them.

Her late arrival seemed to draw a lot more attention from the other students than it normally would have, so Lanie looked down at her shoes to make sure she hadn't accidentally worn two different color socks, or made some other wardrobe mistake. Mr. Speros had offered to let her take a sick day and stay home, but she'd declined.

Her mind was elsewhere when Lanie heard whispering that included her name from over her shoulder. Reeling her thoughts back to the classroom, she twisted her head to see Helen's friend Amy gossiping in the ear of another girl. Lanie didn't know Amy very well, but the limited interactions they'd had were cordial. When the girls saw Lanie look over, they stopped their gossip and faced forward. Helen had probably relayed the previous day's tale to her network of friends. Lanie closed her eyes in weariness, wondering how many people knew.

By the time the lunch bell sounded, Lanie had regained some of her spirit and rushed to meet Hudson at their usual table in the shade near the auditorium.

"My sister flapped her mouth to her friends about yesterday," was Hudson's first statement. "It's getting around school... even Coach Martinez knew about it."

Lanie sighed. Coach Martinez was their boisterous P.E. instructor, and he loved a good motivational story. He often told his students sanitized tales of his wartime experiences serving in the Desert Storm military campaign.

"I heard a couple girls talking about it this morning in homeroom," Lanie said. "It doesn't matter; it's not like we got caught doing something stupid."

"My mom says that's *exactly* what we were doing," Hudson snickered.

"Yeah well... she'll get over it. Sounds like your dad has your back though."

"Are you kidding? I thought my dad was gonna cry last night; I haven't ever seen him so proud." Hudson ripped open his bag of barbecue chips and they scattered on the table. "He said if I have any other ideas on things to build, he'll set aside some money to buy the parts and help me work on them."

Lanie was both shocked and relieved. Hudson often complained that he and his dad couldn't find a way to connect. "Well, now you know what it takes to impress your dad, and that's a good offer. We'll probably have to take him up on it." She brushed the chips back toward Hudson. "I'm assuming he's not gonna let you build any more weapons though?"

"He didn't say anything about that, but he wants to approve my designs before I make anything that can get me killed or hurt. Speaking of which, I want you to show me that barb blaster you made. That thing is awesome!"

"Thanks," Lanie said. "But I'm leaving the weapons biz to you; it's not my bag. The discharge spring split the gun body when I fired it. I threw the whole thing away."

"I may steal and improve your design," Hudson said. "What did you and your dad do last night?"

"We went to the Arizona Biltmore and had a fancy dinner. He told me he's OK with us doing what we need to do for this old Myriad mine stuff."

"Sounds like a nice night. I'm surprised he's OK with you staying involved. My mom is not cool with it at all, but my dad's working on her."

"Yesterday shocked him into realizing that we're teenagers, and we don't need to be protected from everything anymore," Lanie said. "We freaked my dad out pretty good."

"*You're* a teenager. I'm not thirteen until next month," Hudson lamented. His gaze focused past Lanie as he finished his statement. "Amy's coming."

Lanie scrunched her lips and stared down at her sandwich. She didn't feel like explaining what happened to anybody.

"Umm... Lanie?" Amy was by herself, holding her backpack in front of her knees.

"Hi, Amy."

Obviously uncomfortable, Amy stumbled over her purpose for being there. "Uh, Helen told me about what happened yesterday, and I just wanted to say I hope your family and your house are OK." She tucked her thin blonde hair behind her ear.

Lanie's expression softened. "Oh! Well thanks. Yeah, we're OK. Just a couple repairs—and some healing," she said, waving her scratched arm.

"Helen also told us about how you took out the two robbers. I, uh, just wanted to say that you... you kinda rock." Amy blushed, and gave Lanie a *hang loose* gesture with her left pinkie and thumb. "I'll see you at the dance Saturday, right?"

Lanie flashed a reassuring grin. "Thanks, Hudson and I did it together. He's a good partner. But, yeah, I'll be there Saturday; it'll be fun."

When Amy had walked off to join her larger group of friends, Hudson scowled after her. "You'd think I wasn't even there yesterday. She didn't even look at me."

"Amy probably didn't get the whole story from Helen... like how you saved me from that bearded jerk." She leaned across the table to connect her eyes with Hudson's. "Amy might not know that part, but I know, and I owe ya one. Thank you. Your inventions are what *really* saved us."

"Thanks a lot," Hudson said, offering half of his oatmeal cookie. "But you'd have done alright without me."

Lanie slumped after checking the time. "Three hours left of school. I just wanna hang out under the house and see what's in all those drawers and cabinets. That's our space now; we gotta move in! Maybe we can have pizza delivered there," she chuckled.

"You keep forgetting about the other door!" Hudson reminded her. "I'll bet you a million bucks that the tunnel continues past that door, and it leads toward the mine."

Lanie had thought about that possibility earlier in the week. The mine entrance was over a quarter mile from their back patio. "If it does, that's a loooong tunnel," she said, chewing on a blackberry.

After school, Helen stayed to prepare the gymnasium for the coming formal, so Hudson and Lanie trotted nearly the whole mile home. Hudson stopped to check in with his mom, who presented a list of new requirements before she'd let him accompany Lanie home. He promised to check in every hour and that he'd be home before dark. He rolled his eyes at Lanie as he reentered the garage, then grabbed his bag of gadgets on the way out. On their remaining trek up the street, Mr. Rinnas caught them near his driveway.

"I heard you two warriors put those punks in the slammer yesterday," he said, leaning on his lawn mower's handle. "Quite the display of team-work; good for you guys."

"We don't think there will be any more of them," Hudson confided.

"Let's hope not," Mr. Rinnas said. "Did they find anything in the house?" he said, sounding curious.

Lanie quickly took over the conversation, blurting out, "No, they only tossed the stuff out of the drawers in my room. They were looking... I mean, we're not really sure what they were looking for. One of 'em was the guy who caused us trouble on our trip." She turned to see Mrs. Rinnas pulling into the driveway in her big Lincoln, wearing a lavender hat whose brim was crowded with fake flowers. She waved imperially at Lanie as she inched the car into the garage.

"Well, I'm a semi-retired old guy and I'm usually here all day. If you guys find anything, or if you need any help, I will come right over, got it?"

"Got it," Lanie said. Hudson nodded.

Lanie craned her neck to see the vacant spot adjacent to the Lincoln. "Where's your Concorde?"

"Well, the insurance company wants to total it... but I think I'm gonna have it fixed," Mr. Rinnas said, winking. "The car has too many sto-ries to tell now. I couldn't let it go to the crusher."

"Larry, I'm sure the neighbors have been watching you standing over the lawn mower like hired help," Mrs. Rinnas said, emerging from the garage. She glanced up and down the block. "I do hope yesterday's fra-cas isn't going to become a routine in this neighborhood," she said to the friends. "But I'm glad to see you're both safe."

"I'm considering hiring them as my personal security detail," Mr. Rinnas said, pushing his wife's buttons.

"Yes, well, the only thing you need protection from is your own hands in the garage," she replied. "Please help me unload the car, would you?" Mrs. Rinnas said, aiming to pull her husband from the curb.

Mr. Rinnas gave the two friends a thumbs-up and followed his wife up the driveway. Lanie and Hudson went their own way, sharing a relieved sigh. The white rose tree that Lanie assaulted a day earlier was lying across the sidewalk, with nothing to prop it up.

"My dad's gonna take all these rose trees out," Lanie said, stepping over it.

Locked inside the house, Lanie grabbed a snack with Hudson and they both stuffed a couple bottles of water in their back pockets. Using the bookcase passage, the two friends resumed their self-guided tour from earlier in the week. This time, Hudson spotted a light switch as they passed into the black bookcase stairwell. When he flipped it, a flood of fluorescent light filled the space. The light tubes were in the corner of the stairwell and went down—way down. Lanie could see, in looking over the handrail that the stairs descended at least four levels, maybe further. A couple of the fluorescent tubes had gone bad, and others buzzed, but there was plenty of light in the vertical concrete shaft.

"Whew," Lanie said. "Who knows what's down there!"

"Only one way to find out," Hudson replied and started down the staircase.

"We still haven't been to the door in the tunnel yet. Maybe we should do that now while we have some time?" Lanie queried.

Hudson turned around. "Good call. Let's do the door."

Stepping into the control room of the executive suite, Lanie almost felt like she was home. The mid-century modern design of the rooms felt comfortable and logical, making the space a natural extension of the house above.

When she rounded the corner toward the large office, Lanie stopped and jumped sideways when she saw someone move. Her fists clenched, and she braced for another fight. When Hudson saw Lanie jump, he bolted around the corner, ready to attack.

Seated in the leather chair at the executive desk, an elderly woman was watching them. She was dressed in a jet-black blazer and black skirt, with matching black nylons and highly polished shoes. Her hair was also black—in a bun atop her head—and her plump face carried a comforting smile. Lanie's panic started to fade because the woman emitted a friendly aura. Hudson dropped his hands and they both stared at their visitor without a word.

"Lanie, Hudson, I am happy to finally meet you both." The woman stood slowly, leaning forward to shake their hands. "My name is Esther. We're about to become very close friends."

They both accepted Esther's hand. "How do you know our names?" Lanie said.

"Well," Esther said, settling back into the chair, "I know a lot about you both suddenly. If anyone had told me a month ago that we'd be meeting this way, I wouldn't have believed them. I just assumed my time with this place was going to end, and the flame would go out."

Realizing that Lanie and Hudson were confused, Esther went on. "Take a seat, please." She motioned toward the aqua blue chairs in front of the desk.

"We will need hours and hours for me to explain the situation. All things will be told in time. Since your visit to Seligman, I've been watching your activities."

The two friends exchanged a concerned glance.

"For years... many years, my job has been to lead the team protecting the Omega Contingency." Esther reclined and crossed her legs. "The whole program was conceived in 1955, when the Cold War was just getting started. Back then, I was working on my engineering degree at UCLA, but we'll get to all that later." Their mysterious host waved off the past.

"The Omega Contingency's purpose was...." She raised a bejeweled finger and corrected herself. "...*Is* to provide a way for mankind to survive its own disastrous end." Esther looked around, pointing at the different areas. "These rooms are the director's office suite—or rather, they were. Years ago, the director and executive engineer worked out of this complex under your house, managing the construction and commissioning of the entire facility." Esther leaned forward for emphasis. "But the main Omega site is much larger. You'll see it all—soon. Ms. Speros, your home is a gateway, and it holds many secrets."

"I don't understand. What do you mean? It's like a fallout shelter?" Hudson asked.

"In concept," Esther said. "I see you know a little history. The Omega Contingency provides a place for people to go when the earth above is either threatened or will no longer support life on the surface. And there is more than one location, obviously—the United States is a large, populous place." Esther briefly checked her watch, then continued, "The Omega project was a top-secret program, originally built and operated by the Department of Defense. Engineers and architects like me were recruited and given unique security clearance, and we became a core group, traveling to develop these sites." Esther's eyes glazed for a moment as she undoubtedly recalled scores of memories.

"Funding for the program was easy at first," she said. "Money poured in from government agencies, grants from trusts, and from wealthy donors. Every Omega site had benefactors. But as the Cold War became a household word, and as the threat seemed to decrease, interest in the program tapered off. Politicians had come and gone; they didn't know much about our work, and the budget was pulled away. Local governments couldn't continue to invest, and neither could Congress. The core teams who had classified knowledge of the program were sworn to secrecy and reassigned to other projects. Are you following me so far?" Esther said, searching the eyes of the two friends.

"Yes," Lanie and Hudson said together. "What happened after that?" Lanie pressed.

"A small team of classified engineers was selected by the board of directors to oversee the completed sites, since they were to be decommissioned." Esther shook her head in disappointment. "Decommissioned before even being completely tested." The irony seemed painful to her.

"Anyway, the original top-secret program needed a shell organization, to avoid media interest or exposure, as well as to protect the investments. The mining conglomerate Myriad Exploration Group owned two of the sites that the Department of Defense was looking at. The company was insolvent due to the mining partners' embezzlement, so the DoD took over the company and used it as a cover for the operations that would be converting the mine sites into Omega bioshelters."

"What's a bioshelter?" Lanie interrupted. "Is it out behind our house?"

"I'm getting there. I've been waiting forty years to make this speech; cut me some slack," Esther said with a chuckle. She took a small bottle of water from her black handbag and sipped.

"Our bioshelters are a self-sufficient subterranean colony. Each Omega site was designed to accommodate ten thousand people and had the capacity to grow and process its own food, filter its own water, and treat its own air and waste. The sites generate their own power and were set up to provide medical treatment to residents and staff."

The size and scope of the organization was becoming more apparent, and it gave Lanie a nervous feeling. She was starting to realize why people were willing to kill and commit crimes to gain access. "So, these guys who've chased us around and invaded our home, what do they want?"

"You're talking about Michael Donahue," Esther curled her lips in disgust. "Like me, Michael was one of the original engineers. He was assigned to life sustainment systems, and this is the site he and I worked on most. This is the only site to have a geothermal power plant, and he was involved in the geological engineering necessary to make it run. He was a brilliant man."

"Was?" Lanie asked, locking her fingers in her lap.

"He didn't survive your crash up near Ash Fork," Esther said.

Lanie immediately knew who the old man was in the back seat of the Durango. "Ohh," Lanie said, looking down at her hands.

"Anyway, when the Omega program was terminated, the directive of the Sustainment Unit was to protect the three completed sites. Sixteen people were sworn into executive duties, and funding was guaranteed for minimum upkeep of each site. This was my site," Esther said. Her pride was apparent in her smile.

"It was Mike's site too, but at some point, he decided that cashing out suited him better, and he attempted to steal some of the assets. We stripped him of his credentials, and he's been looking to find a way in ever since. If you know where to look, this site will make you wealthy." Esther looked dismayed. "He knew where to look. He tried to use your family as his way in."

Esther straightened her blazer and resumed. "He hooked his son, Ethan, on the idea of returning for the site's assets. Ethan is the man you battered with your stick yesterday," Esther said with a bent smile on her face. "That's why I'm here. I knew that you both had been entering the complex with an original keycard, but when I saw what happened yesterday, I knew it was time to visit."

Lanie's phone buzzed, and she checked the screen in her lap. "Thank God, my dad's running a little late," she said.

Hudson, who'd been silent—shifted in his chair. He looked anxious and likely had a thousand questions queued up.

"I have a dinner engagement tonight; I can't stay. Walk me to my car, won't you?" Esther stood up, heading toward the control room.

"I don't go up that spiral staircase anymore, my hips won't do it," Esther said, pointing to the back of the room. She pulled out a weathered punch card of her own and waved it against the side of the console, and the crystal-like buttons began to glow a pale blue. She pressed one of the buttons next to the copper sphere, then Lanie heard and felt a muffled *CLACK* from the room below.

"She just closed some sort of big electrical contactor," Hudson whispered into Lanie's ear. "She powered something up."

"You're a smart young man, and you're right," Esther said, turning and placing her hand on Hudson's shoulder. "That's why I'm here. Follow me."

They walked through the reception office door and into the corridor, which was now filled with bright light.

"I'll come back tomorrow, and I'll show you amazing things. I'll need you for the whole evening, so you need to make arrangements with your parents to be available."

Stopping at the foot of the stairway to the kitchen, she turned to the two friends with a firm, cool expression. "The two of you are blessed with some amazing talent, and your skills become even more impressive when you're working together. This was apparent to us even before you both got tangled up with the Omega history. But since then, we've watched you two courageously fight armed intruders barehanded, and we've seen you use your gifts of brains and technical prowess to get you into a facility that's been dormant for over fifty years."

She paused to prepare the two friends, then continued. "You two are the people we want to carry the torch of Omega for the future. This will be your site... *if* you can handle the training."

Lanie's pulse thumped in her ears. She didn't even know anything about the site, or what *managing* it involved, but it sounded like a full-time job. And it sounded dangerous. From the corner of her eye, Lanie could see Hudson smirking as though he'd just been kissed.

"You don't have to agree to do it yet, and it's too early for you to make that decision anyway," Esther said. "But if you decide to participate, you won't need to worry about the livelihood of you and your families for the rest of your lives—you will live well. When I show you what I know, you'll make the decision to take the role."

"Why us? We're only thirteen," Lanie said, stating the obvious.

Esther turned and started up the stairs. Without looking back, she said, "Only thirteen? If you think your age is a handicap, you'll only achieve the things a thirteen-year-old is expected to do." Lanie and Hudson followed close behind, and Lanie caught the peaceful fragrance of rose-scented perfume.

At the top of the stairs, Esther turned back. "It seems to me, neither of you *think* like thirteen-year-olds. When your age isn't constraining you, your mind will enable you to achieve amazing things that most adults could never hope to accomplish." She looked Lanie in the eyes. "I designed the transportation system for this site at age nineteen, and I've seen some of your drafting work. I'll bet you could already fix shortcomings in my original design. Do you want your first job to involve counting change at a cash register in a couple years? Or would you rather work on a seven-hundred-volt underground vehicle system next month?"

Lanie's mind swirled, and she wondered if her path for the rest of her life were changing. Proceeding through the kitchen, Esther looked the house over. "Coming in from the *other* direction takes much too long; tomorrow I'll come through the front door here," she said to the two recruits. "I haven't been up into this house for years. This was a beautiful home in 1959—and it hasn't changed much since."

Esther saw the questions behind Lanie's eyes. "I'll tell you about the house, and everything else, don't worry. There's a lot more to this house and its basements than what you've seen so far. The house itself has a very complicated layout whose purpose is to mask the building's mission."

"Is that why all the rooms are such strange shapes?" Lanie asked.

"Yes, I'm sure you've noticed that there are relatively few right angles in this house. That was done because the human mind is not as effective at gauging the depth of a space when a room doesn't have square corners. This design approach helps conceal hidden spaces and compartments."

Pulling the front door open, she added, "You two, take care of each other. I'll see you around half-past three tomorrow. I'm assuming I don't need to tell you both that you—and your parents—must protect the site's secrecy?" She stared at the two friends but didn't wait for their affirmation. "I turned on the primary lighting circuits for the whole site so that neither of you get killed falling down a shaft in the dark, but I strongly advise that you don't do any further exploring until I get here tomorrow."

Esther patted Lanie's upper arm then smiled at the two friends. She turned and walked down the entry path, stepping carefully over the rose tree. A black Tesla Model S with tinted windows sat at the curb. As she approached the car, a driver clad in a navy blue suit stepped out and opened the rear door. It was the car Lanie had seen in Seligman.

When Esther was seated, the driver closed the door and walked up the path toward Lanie and Hudson. From the inside pocket of his coat he pulled out a pair of thin, brushed-copper metal plates the size of standard business cards. Handing one each to the friends, he bowed, then smiled without a word and returned to the car.

Lanie saw the Jeep pulling into the driveway as the Tesla vanished down the street. She flipped the metal card over in her hand. Aside from a large Omega emblem printed in glossy black, the front was blank. On the back, there was an email address made up of a cryptic mix of letters and numbers, along with a toll-free number that was noted in small print for "emergency use only."

Lanie's dad came around the corner from the garage, looking over his shoulder at the receding Tesla. "Now who was *that*?!" He was apprehensive and stared into the faces of the two explorers. Lanie and Hudson glanced at each other, smiling. "Dad, you probably better come inside so we can show you something."

# Chapter 16

# WHAT'S NEXT?

Mr. Speros sunk into the aqua desk chair Lanie had sat in only thirty minutes earlier, and the creases on his face had smoothed with amazement. He looked around, speechless. Lanie sat in the big executive chair, and Hudson stood near the console, examining the lit buttons.

"This is just beyond belief," Mr. Speros said. "And she asked you what? To be the caretakers of this place?"

"Not just *this* place, Dad," Lanie said, pointing to the floor, "the entire site."

"Whaddaya mean, *'the entire site?'*"

"She's coming back tomorrow. There's a huge underground complex in the mountains behind the house—it can support thousands of people in a catastrophe. It has its own power plant, hospital, everything."

Mr. Speros appeared flustered, and he ran his hand over the afternoon stubble on his chin. "She's going to put two thirteen-year-olds in charge of a giant underground complex? Like, when? During your school lunch breaks and before dinner? I don't understand, did she leave you a phone number? This sure seems like something the parents ought to be involved in." Mr. Speros had started to grow agitated, but then caught himself and took a deep breath, remembering his discussion with Lanie at the restaurant the night before.

"OK, well, I'll meet her when she comes. But I don't understand," he said again.

Lanie thought his response was reasonable, considering their circumstances. But she also knew he didn't need to worry; they were being presented with an amazing opportunity, and Lanie was ready to accept the mission.

"Check this out," Hudson said, from the seat at the console.

Mr. Speros followed Lanie in, looking around at the furnishings of the room.

"This copper ball is like a mouse. You use it to make selections from menus on the screen," he said, pointing to the glass partition.

Lanie was amazed to see that the tinted glass had a grayscale image on it. Looking up, she could see the projection emitting from a black notch in the ceiling above Hudson.

"This is basically a primitive computer," Hudson said. "The projection is only a set display of options—like a complicated slide projector. But it also doubles as a microfiche reader. This drawing is of the ventilation tunnel network—it's from the box you got in Seligman."

He swirled the ball around again, and more buttons lit on the console. "This is super cool, watch. This console is a control panel for the power distribution throughout the whole complex. I can remotely switch power off and on at all the locations from here. I think you can also control the central door locking systems from here."

"Awesome," Lanie said. "So each of these rows of buttons lights up based on what menu you're on?"

"Yep," Hudson replied. "It's old tech... gonna take some getting used to. It's not like Microsoft Windows, that's for sure."

Now that the initial shock of the site's size had abated a little, Mr. Speros began to relax and started asking questions. He'd seen the spiral staircase passage but pointed to another door in the back corner of the executive office.

"What's in there?"

"It's a little bathroom," Lanie said.

"What's in all these big file cabinets?" Mr. Speros asked of the units lined up along the wall.

"They're blueprints of the whole complex," Hudson said as he continued fiddling with the console. The buttons lit his face grayish blue. "I haven't had any time to look at them," he said, turning to Lanie's dad. "But there are layers and layers of mechanical, structural and electrical drawings; it looks like they're broken down by ward."

"Ward?" Lanie asked.

"The wards are the different zones of the complex," Hudson said, pointing at the row of buttons across the top of the console. "I noticed there's nothing referencing where we are—it's almost like this place and your house above were designed to be isolated and separate."

"What's down below here?" Mr. Speros asked, motioning toward the spiral staircase door. "The stairwell goes down much farther."

"There's an electrical room with a huge Detroit Diesel backup generator one floor down," Lanie said.

"Ahhh, a generator!" Mr. Speros smiled as he nodded his head. "That explains a lot—such as the huge stainless-steel exhaust port next to the fireplace outlet at the top of my bedroom chimney."

"Yeah, there are high-voltage transformers down there," Hudson said. "And the generator is big enough to run our whole neighborhood—I'm gonna have to bring my dad over here to check that room out."

"We haven't been below the electrical room," Lanie said. "We didn't have time. Hudson and I were going to try to open the big door under the yard. That's when we met Esther."

Mr. Speros turned from the stairway and looked toward the reception room. "That's right—the big door! Well, that's obviously the entrance to the rest of the complex. Let's go!"

Lanie giggled at her dad's youthful urge to explore. "Esther told us that we probably ought to wait to go in there until she's with us," Lanie admitted. "But it wouldn't hurt to peek in, would it?"

Hudson jumped up and followed behind as they headed into the corridor. When they reached the door, Lanie pulled out the punch card. Mr. Speros appeared to be stifling his impatience as she slid the card into the extended tray. The light turned green and a series of six loud clanks sounded as the door's deadbolts retracted. Mr. Speros gave the handle a mighty pull, expecting the door to be heavy, but it didn't budge. Instead, it started swinging open on its own. Looking impressed, he stood aside. "Ha! It's motorized."

Not knowing what to expect, all three explorers held their breath as the space beyond was revealed. The first thing Lanie saw were two strange vehicles. The concrete corridor continued past the door in a wide arc to the right, with the walkway disappearing out of sight over a quarter mile ahead. Along the right edge of the walkway was a handrail, beyond which was a recessed roadway.

The road area and adjacent wall were painted black. Immediately at Lanie's right, two small carriages sat on the roadway where it ended. About the size of a compact minivan, each carriage had three rows of gray seats and a glass canopy with a white roof. The wheels were hidden by a long finned skirt that ran along the side of the body. The skirting of the forward carriage was aqua blue, and the other a vibrant gold. A treaded ramp led down to the platform where the vehicles were parked. There was otherwise very little in the long space.

Lanie almost felt deflated—her imagination had prepared her to expect a vast underground world just beyond the door. She knew this was silly though; the site was in the mountains behind their neighborhood—not under her backyard.

"Oh man," Mr. Speros whispered, looking to the end of the curve. "I'm sure this will take us to the core of the facility. We can't do this walk tonight; we need to get some stuff together before we try to go way down there. I don't want to be a hundred yards down this hall if the lights go out."

Lanie imagined having to walk back in the darkness, with only a cell phone light, and the idea was chilling. Turning to the little vehicles, she stepped down the rubber-studded ramp. Hudson had already opened the sliding door of the blue vehicle and was sitting at the console in the front seat. The console had no steering wheel, nor were there any pedals on the floor, but the console had a joystick, as well as a small cluster of buttons. She sat down next to Hudson, who slid over to make space.

"It looks kinda like the little trams at an airport terminal," she said to Hudson as she inspected the gray fabric and carpet. "Except it doesn't smell like old shoes and sweat," she chuckled.

"I'm sure it probably works about the same way," Hudson replied. "It just follows the roadway, and it looks like you pick a direction at junctions with this joystick. I think you have to tell it where to stop when it prompts you, but I can't tell without powering it up."

"Can you see how to turn it on?" Mr. Speros said. He was leaning over the door opening with his forearms on the roof.

Remembering Esther's earlier access to the system controls in the office, Lanie slid her hand along the side of the little operator's console. There were scuffs in the pale blue paint where key cards had been rubbed previously, so she placed hers over the spot. The console lit up, and a *tik-tok* sound like a car's turn signal accompanied the flashing of two blue arrows. One pointed ahead, the other behind.

Hudson smiled. "It's asking you whether we wanna go forward or backward," he said.

"Don't touch anything," Mr. Speros said to Lanie. We'll mess with this thing later, after I get to talk with the mystery woman you met today. Let's go back to the house for now; I want to think about this and make a plan."

Lanie and Hudson begrudgingly followed as Mr. Speros led their way back through the kitchen passage. Her dad disappeared into the master bedroom to change clothes. Lanie and Hudson went to her room, where she flopped onto the bed, staring up at her ceiling fan.

"We don't need a plan... we just need time to be in there and explore—this is killing me! There's too much to see, and we're sitting right on top of it!"

While he was similarly frustrated, Hudson's style was more reserved. He sat down at Lanie's desk. "I don't think he wants to be left out."

Lanie sat up and pushed her back against the wall. "Yeah, I know, he thinks this is just as cool as we do. I know my dad; he's still our age inside. He's just gonna freak out about safety though."

"Yeah, well yesterday's circus in front of the house has our parents a little *on edge* about our safety; I'm lucky I was even allowed to come over here today."

"Ugghhh, and I forgot about that stupid formal, too," Lanie straightened her arms, pushing her fists into the mattress. "We could be exploring the whole complex Saturday! But instead we're both gonna be dressed up, sitting at a table watching other kids dance."

Hudson swiveled back and forth in the chair, chewing his thumb nail. He had been pressured to attend the dance, just like Lanie, but he offered some optimism anyway. "I know. But it'll be a good break; we've been kinda stressed. Besides, we'll get some time inside with Esther tomorrow; it's only Thursday."

The explorers had more questions than answers after their strange evening, so they agreed to call it a night. Lanie had homework to do anyway; she knew she was going to be up late... again.

Friday was a whirlwind of school activities and passed quickly. The students and faculty were scattered, attending events and special assemblies in preparation for the next day's formal. Helen caught up with Lanie before she'd left her fourth-hour classroom. She was hustling, carrying a cluster of bedazzled navy-blue paper bags. If they had contained miniature diecast car models, Lanie would have loved to receive one of them, but she already knew what hid inside.

"Lanie!" Helen said with a broad grin as she swung the bags behind Lanie's back in a crushing hug.

"Hiii," Lanie replied with an uncomfortable smile, thinking, *Be nice, Helen's worked very hard.*

"OK, here's your Expression Bag," Helen said, peeling off one of the sparkling sacks for Lanie. "You gotta do the stuff in here tonight, so you're ready when we go tomorrow."

"I know, you told me already. I picked up my dress," Lanie said, averting the bag topic.

"OH! How's it look? I'll bet it's even hotter around the curves than when we bought it, right?"

As she was thinking of her own image in the mirror late the night before, Lanie's eyes glassed over. "Umm... yeah, it's definitely more *fitted.* My dad is probably gonna be nervous." Lanie raised an eyebrow at Helen. "I can't believe your mom lets you wear dresses like the one you picked for me."

"I *can't* wear dresses like you—my mom says I won't have those kinda curves until I'm fifteen." Helen laughed out loud, then conjured up a jealous scowl as she scanned Lanie's figure from head to toe.

"Don't look at me like that, you perv!" Lanie could feel her cheeks getting hot, but she had to laugh at Helen.

Hudson had walked up, and Lanie's eyes got wide. She swiped her hand across her neck, warning Helen to drop the dress discussion.

"What's up?" he said to Lanie, brushing off his sister.

"Helen has a surprise for you." Lanie pointed to the cluster of stuffed bags.

"I already *have* mine." The way he and Helen looked at each other, it was apparent they'd already fought on the topic.

"I'm gonna keep handing these out; see you in the morning for manicures," Helen reminded Lanie as she backed away.

Lanie turned to Hudson with a defeated expression. "Did you ask anybody to go to this thing with you... like... a date?"

"Nah. I don't need a date. None of the girls know my name anyway. I'm just going for the food."

"And to hang out with me, you punk."

"Yeah, and to hang out with my friend Lanie... who's afraid of social events." His sarcasm was mild.

"I'm not afraid; it's just not my kinda event."

"With me there, it will be!" Hudson assured her.

## Chapter 17

# THE SITE

When the flood of students drained from the school's brick-paved court-yard at 3:10 that Friday, Hudson and Lanie found the black Tesla waiting at the curb. It looked delightfully out of place amongst the hulking yellow buses. Happy to be picked up like celebrities, the two friends changed their course and headed to greet the driver. He stepped out as they walked up.

"Ms. Speros, Mr. Newman, good to see you," he said, nodding a per-fectly coiffed crest of hair.

Lanie figured he was in his mid-thirties. His face was chiseled and handsome, and his broad shoulders and biceps filled his well-tailored suit. He pulled open the rear door for Lanie first, then let Hudson into the front seat. Esther was waiting in the back, looking relaxed and cheerful. Lanie settled into the white leather seat and buckled herself in. She saw some classmates near the buses staring as she pushed her backpack to the floor between her feet.

Without moving, Esther greeted them both with her sharp dark eyes. "Good afternoon, you two."

Lanie wasn't sure how to interact with their polished host, but she felt comfortable. Esther's hair was in the same bun, and Lanie assumed that she must get it colored its unnaturally black shade. She had green emeralds in each earlobe which matched one of the two large rings she wore. Lanie imagined Esther standing in the Omega executive suite in 1960, wearing a black pencil skirt with her then silky hair in a similar bun.

"Did the two of you talk to your parents—are we a *go* for this afternoon's trip?"

Lanie glanced at Hudson; neither wanted to admit that their parents were hesitant. Speaking up, Lanie said, "I gotta be honest, Mrs... *er...* Esther, my dad really wants to meet you."

Hudson watched Esther for a reaction, as his parents had made the same request.

"Perfectly fair." Esther patted Lanie's knee. "If I were your parents, I imagine that's the least I would demand," she said with a low, smoky chuckle. "Hudson, have either your mom or dad come over to the Speroses' home this afternoon. I want one point of contact from each household. I'll meet with them before we set off."

By car, the trip from school was only a couple minutes. As the Tesla coasted along in silence, Esther said nothing. When the driver made the right turn onto Constellation Way, she looked out the window at the pond. The landscaping team was repairing the block wall and damaged shrubbery.

"Donahue's son is in rough shape," she said finally. "He'd already spent a few days in the hospital after the Ash Fork wreck before he crashed here. I'm told he almost didn't survive, since he wasn't wearing his seatbelt when the truck wrapped around that tree—and one of his lungs had already collapsed before that, thanks to Ms. Speros. You both won't see him again... he's out of the picture for good, I think. There are federal agents guarding him because we got the charges amended to include attempted child abduction and armed assault in two different states. That will put him away for a long time." She smiled at her own efficiency.

"Who was the other guy?" Lanie asked of her driveway attacker.

227

"Robert Dunn—a convicted felon out on parole that the younger Donahue hired. He's back in prison already; it will be years before he gets out again. Donahue's other partner—the driver of the SUV from Ash Fork—he was a long-time associate of the Donahues. He's still in the hospital in Flagstaff, but it's likely he'll never walk again."

The Tesla was stopped in front of Lanie's house. Lanie stared out, thinking of all the troubled men. She *almost* felt pity for them.

"It would appear they picked the wrong families to mess with." Esther's dark eyes glittered, as did her white smile. "Come on, let's head inside."

Lanie wondered how Esther knew all the details but figured she still had a strong government association. Lanie was also still concerned there would be others.

Esther must have read her face, because as they walked toward the front door, she said, "There will always be some sort of threat to the Omega sites and those who protect them. The group of men you both eliminated were the most imminent threat that I know of. I think you shouldn't worry about them anymore."

"Somebody cleaned up that wreck in Ash Fork and rescued the men— they must have help?" Lanie countered, closing the door behind them.

"*I* had that scene cleaned up," Esther said. "The last thing this organization needs is an investigation by local authorities; we couldn't take the risk. The only reason this site and its sister sites are still intact is because they've been forgotten by a government that has moved on. For now, it needs to stay that way." She extended her arm toward the living room. "We'll wait here for your parents."

Esther walked into the semi-circular bar and shuffled a couple items around, then the low shelf against the frosted glass wall started to raise, along with the bottles and glassware on it. Two more mirrored shelves appeared from underneath, exposing a vast selection of liquors and bottled sodas. Some looked very old—as old as the house.

Lanie watched the mechanical motion with her mouth hanging open.

"Like I said, the house has a lot of surprises," Esther said. Her face then grew serious. "You both need to be aware that there is a larger threat to our organization, though... a group that is a very real—and lethal—risk to our team. You'll be briefed on that history soon. But for now, just understand it's another one of the reasons that the Omega Contingency's secrecy—and the secrecy of your association with it—is paramount in everything you do."

Esther's revelation worried Lanie, but she knew she probably wouldn't be able to get details out of Esther that day.

Hudson began unloading his many questions on Esther as she poured herself a drink. "We saw the electrical room below the offices. Where is the high-voltage power under this house coming in from? What is that huge diesel generator a backup for? Does it power this house too? Do we need to worry about losing power while we're deep underground? How can a site like this even be forgotten, anyway? Who is maintaining all the equipment?" He ran out of breath before he ran out of questions.

Esther sunk into the corner of the sofa and glanced at Lanie. "Is he always this inquisitive?"

Lanie was seated cross-legged on the fireplace hearth. "The only reason he doesn't ask *me* so many questions is 'cause I can't usually answer them."

"We'll get your questions answered, don't worry, Hudson. Some of them will be answered on our trip today." Esther cleared her throat and surveyed the room. "Nobody ever lived in this residence in an official capacity. We expected that the sustaining director would live here. Back then this was miles from Phoenix; there were only small ranches in the vicinity. The owner you bought the house from had no idea what this place was for."

Lanie hadn't met the original owners; her dad had bought the house from the family's estate when the wife passed away.

"Mr. and Mrs. Walker kept this house beautifully," Esther said. "When the program was defunded, we knew the house would draw too much attention if it remained vacant, so I listed the house through a federal real estate agent, and the Walker family bought it. I managed the transaction."

After a sip from her drink, Esther continued. "We negotiated with the Walkers contractually so they couldn't make changes to the house—for fear of finding the site access. Just to be safe, we walled off the basement corridor anyway. We told the buyers that the house was a prototype home with unique construction qualities that required it to remain unchanged. Nowadays you'd never be able to do that, but it worked back then."

Looking at Hudson, Esther added, "But to answer your question, no, this house gets its power from the local utility, just like every house in the neighborhood. What you saw below was a local power distribution room fed by the Omega energy plant. The security features, door locks, and other basement equipment are powered by that plant. The generator backs up this complex and the command center, half a mile away."

"Are you an electrical engineer?" Hudson asked.

"My goodness, no," Esther said, chuckling. "I'm a mechanical engineer." A sentimental softness crept over the deep creases of her face. "Our chief electrical engineer was one of the other principals—Martin Leistra. Marty was a genius electrician and a good man. I miss him very much; he passed away in 1989—the first of us to move on from this earth." Pulling a tiny glass container from her handbag, Esther scooped a fingertip of lotion and began rubbing her thick hands together.

"Michael Donahue was the third principal, and the fourth was an amazing horticultural PhD named Wanda James. Wanda disappeared in the mid '70s; I've not heard from her since. I suspect she fell in love and married—she may have left the country. I don't fault her for that—I often wonder what life would have been like if I'd married and had a family of my own," Esther said with a touch of emotion. "But Wanda beat me to it." Her eyes wandered as she gazed into the past. "We were all *so* young—the board of directors wanted a young staff that didn't understand the word *impossible*. I was only eighteen when I got recruited from college in 1957. But by 1975, with Michael ejected from the team, only Marty and I were left. It's a lot of work to keep this place going. There really does need to be a complete team of four principals to run it."

Lanie heard the garage door rolling up, accompanied by the sound of the Rambler's engine. Two car doors slammed, after which her dad came through the doorway with Mr. Newman. They were both still dressed for work and stood in the afternoon rays of sun near the fireplace, staring at Esther. *They look like two students who've arrived at the principal's office*, Lanie thought to herself. She arrested a smile from her face as Esther stood to greet them.

"Mr. Speros, Mr. Newman, I'm pleased to meet you." She offered her hand to the men as they stepped forward. "My name is Esther Andersen. I've come to answer many of your questions; but I also have much we must speak candidly about. Can we step downstairs for a while?"

The two men reintroduced themselves with their first names, and Lanie's dad said, "We were expecting you. Thanks for your time." Then he stopped in surprise when he saw the expanded bar. "I'd offer you a drink," he said, "but I'm glad to see you're all set!"

Mr. Speros kissed Lanie's forehead as he passed. "See you in a bit," he whispered.

While the oven and stove slid aside, Esther looked at the two young friends.

"I won't be long with your fathers, but we need some privacy in the office. You both can take a look around the lower levels."

His entry into the executive suite was Mr. Newman's first visit, and both Lanie and Hudson enjoyed the vicarious experience of seeing his shock and delight when he stepped into the preserved environment. Lanie and Hudson passed into the control room, while the three adults stayed in the executive office. Esther pulled the glass door of the control room closed, stopping short. "Don't start any equipment, but *do* check out the lounge on LL3," she said, then clicked the door shut.

Hudson glanced at Lanie. "Lounge?"

Lanie shrugged, then they both headed to the staircase. They passed the humming transformers of the electrical room on LL2 and wound down to the metal door at LL3. It opened into a gold-carpeted foyer, which was lined with the same types of comfortable square chairs from the executive suite. Like the suite above, there were more ashtrays in the foyer. The walls were paneled in dark mahogany. Modern abstract paintings of the period hung above the chairs.

"Geez, did *everybody* smoke in the 1950s?" Lanie asked, nudging an ashtray base with her shoe.

Hudson had gone ahead to the doorway at the end of the foyer. There were opaque tangerine-colored glass doors with raised wooden panels floating in the center. Pushing through, Hudson looked back at Lanie in excitement. "I think I just found our new headquarters," he said.

Lanie slid past him, curious to see. More mahogany paneling lined the broad lounge. Brown leather chairs were grouped in pairs between bronze wall sconces, and each pair shared a table with a jade-shaded lamp.

A curved cocktail bar near the back of the room had stools for ten people. It was a larger variation of the one in the house above, with a high frosted-glass wall that was lit from behind with amber bulbs. The bottles and condiments on the shelf looked ancient and untouched. Framed images hung throughout the room, and most appeared to be photos of the site construction and the project teams. A sparkling Wurlitzer jukebox stood in the shadows near the bar. The arched ceiling was also trimmed in mahogany but had hidden lighting in soffits that washed the whole room with a warm glow.

The hearth of a monstrous fireplace occupied the wall nearest the bar, above whose mantle was a glass case containing a scale replica of the little vehicles they had seen in the corridor. A group of high backed leather chairs were clustered around a small coffee table near the hearth, as though four people were expected that evening.

The most impressive part of the room, however, was at the end opposite the bar. The floor dropped away beyond an intricate banister to a level below. A curved staircase against the left and right walls led down to the lower level, which had intimate booths with more tables and lamps.

The whole area was focused on the distant high wall, which was made of glass panels arranged in an arc. Beyond the glass was a lush tropical garden, with hairy ferns and dense shrubbery. There were prehistoric-looking rubber and philodendron trees with drooping green leaves as big as elephant ears. Moisture dripped from the foliage and a mist seemed to hang in the air beyond the glass. A large red-and-white tropical bird stood on a tree branch near the corner of the window, staring at Lanie.

"Whoa... how is this even possible?" Lanie said as she stood before the glass. A phantom-like dim light filled the space outside the window, as though clouded sunlight was penetrating the seventy-five feet of earth above. A long, padded window seat followed the curve of the glass.

"That bird wants to know how we got in here, I think," Hudson snickered. "These plants are real! Who's been taking care of them?!"

"I don't know, but this is amazing—it's an alternate world underneath my backyard," Lanie said as she descended the steps to the lower level. "My brain doesn't even know how to grip all this. What a killer place to have a party, though." Staring back at the bird, she added, "I'm wondering what other animals are out there. That bird can't be living alone?"

"Another question for Esther. I gotta start writing this stuff down," Hudson said. He went to either end of the windowed wall, looking for a door into the atrium, but found none.

Lanie sat into an oversize chair near the glass. "Talk about a great place to do homework, or, pretty much anything," she said.

"Yeah, this is definitely gonna be our hangout," he replied, leaning against one of the booths. "Too bad we can't show it to anybody else." Then his lip twisted, and he looked down at the carpet.

"What's wrong?" Lanie asked.

"I was thinkin' about something last night. Even in the 1960s, there were way more than ten thousand people living in the valley. If there had been a war or emergency, who decided which people got to use this site?"

It was a good question, and Lanie was sure the answer was complicated. "We should ask Esther. I'll bet they had a plan."

"I'll bet they *still* have a plan," Hudson said. "I wouldn't want that job."

There were more doors behind the bar, so Lanie walked back, with Hudson close behind. She yanked open a small door near the back of the bar, then opened her eyes wide.

Standing nearby, Hudson craned his neck in curiosity. "What? What's in there!?"

She dropped her jaw, dragging out the suspense. Hudson sucked in a breath. Suddenly, she cracked a crooked smile and pulled a vintage vacuum cleaner from behind the door.

"It's a closet," she said, wrinkling her nose.

"Ugghh, you dork." Hudson rolled his eyes, then turned away.

The hallway next to the bar led to a small prep kitchen with a yellow tiled floor. Various familiar but antique kitchen appliances sat on the countertop and a streamline Frigidaire stood in the corner. More surprisingly, Lanie also found a set of elevator doors. "Hudson!" she called.

Hudson had pulled the refrigerator door open, but finding nothing to snack on, joined Lanie. "Heh!" he said, poking the call button. "I figured there had to be an elevator in here somewhere. We gotta see where this goes."

The doors opened, revealing a little elevator car whose walls were made of the same frosted glass as the bar. Esther was also in the elevator and startled the two friends. She stepped out, smiling as she passed. Lanie and Hudson followed her back into the lounge, where she stood looking fondly at the framed photos.

"Many a fun night were spent in this room with our team of engineers and supervisors," she said, running her hand along the top of the jukebox. "As you both bond with this site and its history, this room will be just as important to you as it was for us. Feel free to move in and make it your own." She squinted, peering toward the glass wall at the distant end of the room. "You need to be briefed on the site's botanical needs sooner than later; we'll do that next week. Keeping this place filled with breathable air is priority one, and it's a big part of the job. We've got a long way to go—let's get moving."

Esther shuffled back to the elevator and pressed the call button. "There are some places here I just can't go anymore—too many steps. But the most important ones can be reached by elevator—or on the Atom."

"Atom?" Hudson asked as they crowded into the narrow elevator.

"The Atom is the Automated Motorway through the site."

"Oh, the tram from in the tunnel above!" Lanie said.

"Trams are for Disneyland's parking lot," Esther said, stepping out into the control room two levels up. "The Atom is much more specialized. It can either pick a destination for you, or you can give it one; you'll learn how to use it today. Though, to be fair, my concept was inspired by the genius Imagineer who designed some of Disneyland's early ride systems. I'm rather proud of it—the Atom has been one of the more reliable systems at the sites."

Lanie turned to see the elevator opening as she stepped out. She hadn't even seen the flush-mounted door in the wall earlier. Moving briskly, Esther led the group down the corridor to the large tunnel entry. Using her own punch card, she started the huge door's powered opener.

"Always keep two vehicles up here—just in case," Esther said as she climbed through the open door of the carriage. She motioned for Lanie to sit in the driver's seat and slid across to the far side. Hudson sat in the second row and pulled the door closed.

Without being prompted, Lanie powered up the console.

"Looks like somebody's been doing their homework!" Esther said with a twinkling eye. "OK, hit the forward arrow."

Lanie obeyed, and the carriage accelerated away from the station. Other lights on the console lit as they departed. Suddenly, excitement blossomed in Lanie's chest. The site they'd heard so much about lay unseen before them, and the Atom carriage seemed like a perfect vessel to use for the introductory journey.

"The console wants to know where we're going," Esther said, pointing to the blinking arrow. "Follow the flashing lights," she told the two friends. "On all the consoles you'll find, following the flashing lights is generally what you should do. The first flashing light is asking for a destination, and the second will show you route alternatives—if there *are* any. The third will prompt you to select a speed. You need to have a destination picked before we reach the elevator," Esther said as the carriage slowed. They were approaching a broad metal door in the roadway.

"Hit *COMMONS*," she directed Lanie.

From the row of flashing buttons at the top of the console, Lanie pushed the corresponding location. As they waited for the elevator door to slide open, Lanie spotted a glass door beyond the handrail on the adjacent walking path. The door provided access to what looked like a phone booth, which was embedded in the concrete wall. A strange key lock protruded from above the door handle.

"What's that room?" Lanie asked.

"It's an emergency service shaft... a critical one. You'll see that a different day," Esther replied.

The carriage rolled itself into a dark room. Almost before the door closed behind them, the floor dropped into the darkness. The lighting on the console was the only illumination and it cast a ghostly glow over the occupants. They were descending far below the surface; Lanie's ears popped after a few moments.

"How far down are we going?" she asked. The elevator platform wasn't slowing yet.

"We're stopping around a thousand feet down," their host said. "It's not the lowest point in the site. I don't really want you both any lower yet—you must be with me for your first visit to some locations; there are dangerous places down here. If you were killed or injured, you might never be found."

Lanie didn't look at Hudson in the seat behind her but assumed he considered himself warned, as she did.

Finally, the platform stopped, and the black door ahead rolled up. The carriage crept into a small room with steel doors on either end, and the door ahead didn't open until the one behind them had closed. Their little vehicle accelerated into a dimly lit, unremarkable corridor lined with blue tile. Lanie had nearly given up on seeing any epic parts of the site, but then her jaw dropped as they emerged from the corridor and onto a towering concrete bridge.

The arched bridgeway spanned an enormous open space that Lanie estimated was over twenty stories high, and their roadway on the bridge's spine was at least ten levels up from the cavern floor. The cavern's open space was so large, the boundaries were hidden in the shadowy distance. Above, the ceiling was a mix of natural cave and carved rock, supported by both stone columns and man-made structures.

The size of the space eclipsed what Lanie had imagined, and she suddenly felt very small. What little light there was in the space was projected upward from tall light towers. The warm light lit the cavern's ceiling, which then returned soft, diffused lighting to the floor below. Very few of the thousands of light towers were lit, but Lanie could make out the windows and terraces of buildings on the rocky ledges of the cavern's walls. The buildings were linked by meandering pathways that snaked up and down amongst the natural rock formations. Lanie realized that exploring the perimeter of the cavern alone would probably take weeks. She even saw a colossal waterfall at the farthest corner and wished they could stop.

"Hudson, did you see...?" She had turned to draw Hudson's attention to the waterfall, but he was already focused on it.

"Yeah, we gotta come back here—as soon as we can."

Their bridge crossed the cavern near its center and shared the space with a massive vertical cylindrical structure which had rows of balconies around its exterior. Behind the balconies' mesh handrails, hundreds of doors were lined up alongside each other. There were no handrails on either side of the bridge, and this amplified the reality of how high up they were on the narrow roadway. The track passed through the tower's center and the two friends watched in awe as the looming structure approached.

"We're above the Commons, and this building is the Residential Tower," Esther said above the hum of the Atom's hub motors. "You can explore this on your own—it's pretty safe. There is a large garden and park on the floor below... well... what's left of it anyway. The Commons are around the cavern's outside edge, and there are lots of little shops and service centers. There are also automated snack shops and sundries vending machines down there." She turned to look at both Lanie and Hudson together. "This site has been idle for sixty years—don't eat anything out of the vending machines," she warned. "Not even the Twinkies... forget what you may have heard."

The Atom entered the cylindrical building and the group whizzed past what looked like the front desk of an optimistic jet-age hotel. A circular series of glass partitions at the reception desk matched the radial arrays of furniture and walls. The curious décor was mechanically familiar, and Lanie realized that the hotel's shape and architectural details all appeared to be inspired by a jet turbine. After gliding through the seating area of the lobby, the Atom passed out of the other side, into the open cavern. Lanie marveled at the scale of the whole space and imagined the feats of engineering that were involved in its construction.

Near the end of the bridge, the roadway split, with each track leading into a separate tunnel. Seeming to know the ideal speed for its route, the Atom carriage slowed for the track switch. It then coasted into a banked turn that descended toward a station closer to the cavern floor. The *tik-tok* of the flashing arrow on the console advised that their stop was approaching. They arrived at a paddock where several other Atoms sat in parking slots.

"We'll stop here. You both can take a quick look around," Esther said.

The Commons station was more like a wide, semi-circular veranda. The open deck afforded an elevated view of the park-like cavern floor beyond. Multiple stairways led from the veranda down into the shopping and dining areas, most of which were shrouded by tall evergreen trees. With so few of the light towers lit, the whole cavern seemed to be stuck permanently in a nighttime state. The Commons looked to be only a small portion of the vast network of buildings around the outside of the cavern. On the floor of the mall below, a long, twisting creek snaked through the courtyard of planters. Water babbled over polished stones and blocks of brightly colored glass.

Esther pointed to the water feature. "You'll see creeks like this throughout the site—they have an important life support function, and they must remain flowing. The domestic water for this facility comes from the underground springs and lake, and it's filtered through these rocky channels. The running water also helps with air exchange in the caverns, which is critical for plant and animal life down here."

The many shops around the station were unlit, except for a couple exit path lights in each. Lanie could see the entrance to a vast dining hall, and a grove of fruit trees separated it from a small coffee shop. A fully stocked bookstore and newsstand sat on a rocky ledge overlooking the mall, surrounded by neatly organized tables and chairs.

It occurred to Lanie that with the flowerbeds blooming, and with coffee brewing and people milling around, the little square must have been a peaceful place to socialize. Lanie picked up a magazine from the rack nearest the coffee shop's entrance, finding it to be a mid-August 1959 issue of *Vogue* magazine. The strawberry blonde woman wearing a silvery-blue silk blouse on the cover could have been considered fashionable today, Lanie thought. Other magazines nearby were of the same vintage.

"Are all these books from 1959?" Lanie asked, looking through the dark shop.

"Nearly all of the merchandise you'll find in this cavern was stocked that year, yes," Esther said. "Vendors and suppliers who sponsored the site staged each store as though the site would be used within the year. It was mostly done for a walk-through to demonstrate the completed site to top government brass. It is quite the time capsule, isn't it?"

"So... none of these hundreds of shops are used?" Hudson asked.

"Oh, some are." Esther said. "You'll find that some of the store windows have some fairly modern items. I'll let you both discover those."

Turning to look at Hudson, Lanie saw he had begun taking notes. "Good call, you should write down some of these places so we can remember how to get back."

"I'm mostly making notes on the systems. I think it's amazing this place is in as good of shape as it is."

"We've had our problems over the years," Esther chuckled. "Flooding, structural failures, other such things. But the power plant and the water circulation plant are the biggest deal. Without those, the whole site is just a big, useless pocket in the earth's crust. That's why the role that the four principals play is so critical. Each is responsible for their own group of wards—but none can survive without the others. The principals need to share a relationship that is more durable than even the ties to their own families."

She checked her small jeweled watch. "Goodness, we have to move on. It's easy to lose track of time down here. Come along. You can explore these places on your own."

As Lanie turned away from the balustrade on the edge of the platform, a shadow moving in the park below caught her eye. She spun back, but the figure was gone. "There's somebody down there! I just saw someone moving through those bushes near the creek!"

Esther looked briefly, then waved her hand. "It may have been a draft, dear. There wouldn't be anyone working in here today."

Lanie turned toward the Atom but watched the park over her shoulder, not entirely convinced.

Esther directed Hudson to take the controls when they boarded the Atom. "I almost forgot; I have these for you." She dug in her purse and produced a pair of clean, new key cards for Lanie and Hudson. The plastic was engraved with their respective names and the punch card patterns were unique.

"You can keep the one you have as a spare. Just make sure it doesn't fall into the wrong hands."

"We actually have two," Lanie said. "There's one with a red stripe on it; we haven't figured out what it opens yet."

Esther looked both surprised and concerned. "Oh dear," she said, shaking her head. "That card is extremely important; store it in a safe place. It holds an enormous value."

Lanie pulled it from her back pocket and offered it, but Esther waved, declining.

"It's as safe with you as anywhere else at this point. I'll show you what it's for on a different day. There's some training you need to go through

241

first." Nudging Hudson's arm with her forefinger, she added, "OK, Mr. Newman, get us rolling. Select *TRANSPORTATION*—speed setting 3."

The Atom gathered speed much faster, departing the Commons to plunge into an unlit tunnel.

"Why were valuable punch cards and drawings for the Omega site sitting in a junk store?" Lanie inquired, thinking of the other items she'd seen in Seligman.

Esther chuffed with displeasure. "The items you found were stolen, Ms. Speros. The unfinished Omega 3 site near the Grand Canyon was raided by a group of the construction workers when the project was terminated. Marty was at the site that week in November of 1963 to close things up, and the crew took his whole truck and everything in it. Until you bumped into them through pure luck, we had no idea whose hands those items had landed in."

"Omega 3? Then which site is this?" Hudson asked.

"Omega 4," Esther responded.

Expecting the answer to be more detailed, Lanie asked, "And—where are the others?"

"For the moment, that's on a need-to-know basis, dear," Esther replied. "You both have been exposed to enough danger already—I don't need the problems from other sites finding you as well."

Lanie thought that Esther's statement was concerning and wondered if it had to do with the threat to the sites she'd mentioned earlier.

In the darkness of the tunnel, the occasional red light would zip past. Pointing one out, Esther advised, "If, for any reason, you become stranded on the Atom in a tunnel, find the red exit light; there is a stairway that will take you to a service corridor so you can walk back. You should never walk the motorway—*ever*. The high-voltage bus bars on the track would kill you instantly if you accidentally bumped them. But it's more likely you'd be hit by another Atom."

Lanie was wondering how that could happen, if there was nobody but the three of them traversing the motorway. She wrinkled her eyebrows.

"Surely you don't think we're the only people who work in here?" Esther cackled, having seen Lanie's face.

"I haven't seen anybody else," Hudson said. "How are we gonna know if we see people—whether they are intruders—or just staff when we find them?"

"There won't be any intruders down here... well, alive, anyway. The facility is too secure and remote," Esther said. "Don't worry, I'll introduce you to the crew. The crews are grouped by their craft and live on site in the crew dormitory. Their days are full; you'll rarely see them unless you're at the biodome, energy plant, or mechanical facilities."

The Atom had stopped to enter another elevator shaft, where their carriage was lifted to a different level. When the doors ahead cracked open, Lanie's ears popped and a gust of air shook the carriage. Esther started to explain about the facilities crew shifts and how their employment worked, but the Atom had emerged into a partially lit, enormous cavern that was paved with concrete. An enclosed section of the cavern had high glass windows reaching to the stone ceiling, separating the main room from a large parking compound.

Lanie grew excited and pressed her hands against the window. Behind the glass walls were rows and rows of vehicles. Cars, trucks, and buses all sat in the semi-darkened room, lined up in tidy rows. Lanie's eyes frantically scanned the fleet as they rode past; she didn't see any vehicles newer than about 1960 model year. "We gotta stop—can we stop?" she urged, looking anxiously at Esther.

"What's the problem—do you need a restroom?" Esther asked.

"She's car-crazy... she wants to see the cars," Hudson said, hitching his thumb toward the garage.

"Oh yes, how could I forget," Esther said, grinning. "Well, you'll be in car heaven in the motor pool garage." She reached back to pat Lanie's knee. "Ms. Speros, your advanced driver training will start in that garage next month. There are some important vehicles in there too—one in particular; we'll go back, but not today. I need you to see the other end of the transportation ward."

Just beyond the garages, the Atom stopped at a platform in the center of a vast paved area, on which rows of lanes and arrows were painted. It looked like a theme park's empty parking garage.

"This is an extremely important cavern to remember," Esther said after she'd stepped out. Her voice echoed off the distant stone walls.

"This room is the only other documented way in and out of this Omega site aside from the executive residence. All materials and staff come in and out through this Intake Center. In the event of a site activation, this is where the refugees would be received."

Lanie noticed Esther's driver standing beside the black Tesla; he was parked along a row of Atom carriages that were lined up on a convergence of motorways. She searched the perimeter of the cavern for the place he would have driven in. At the distant end—200 yards away in the shadows—she saw a set of giant sliding doors, like those of an airplane hangar.

"This is the most vulnerable point of the complex, because if anybody knew how to get to those doors, it would be relatively easy to gain access." Pointing up, Esther continued, "We're still deep under the mountainside, but this is not an environmentally protected part of the site. There's a road and tunnel beyond those doors. It's accessible by a road we share with an adjacent military facility. We'll see the base in a day or two." Esther smoothed her black skirt. "Our time is up this evening; I promised your fathers you'd be back by 8:30. I'll leave you here... you'll find your own way home."

Hudson and Lanie shot each other an apprehensive look.

"I trust you can figure it out," Esther said, then walked down the stairs to the floor of the intake terminal. The two friends stood on the loading platform looking as though they were being left on Mars.

Standing at her open car door, Esther turned back. "OH! One more thing." Her voice boomed through the open space. "The conversation with your parents went well—very well. I expect they will trust you to spend more time down here on your own going forward. I'll contact you both and advise of our plans for Monday; I know you have your school event this weekend."

With a nod of her head, Esther added, "Goodnight, my new friends. Welcome to a new phase of your life." She sat in and pulled her door closed, and the car slipped off toward the door.

## Chapter 18

# A NEW FACE

Suddenly feeling isolated and uneasy, Lanie turned and surveyed the site's vast entrance cavern. She figured they were *at least* three miles from the basement under her house.

"We need to figure out how to get back," she said, motioning toward the Atom carriage they'd arrived in.

"All we gotta do is sit and press the button... we can be back to your house in twenty minutes," Hudson said.

"Yeah, well, I kinda wanted to stop on the way."

"Oh, that's right... you wanna stop at the garage. Let's do it; I kinda wanna see it too." Hudson trailed Lanie along the station platform. The Motor Pool office they'd passed on their way through the station was only a few yards back. There, mint-green tiled walls were hung with pencil-sketched renderings of rocket-propelled cars and monorail trains. Chrome-framed chairs covered in avocado-green vinyl furnished the waiting area near the service window. Lanie imagined men in crisp white shirts with skinny black ties sitting in the glossy seats, waiting for their pool vehicle to be brought up.

Near the service counter, an archway in the cavern wall opened onto steps which led down to the garage floor. Lanie was striding toward it so quickly, Hudson had to trot to keep up. Four lanes of concrete roadway passed the curb at the foot of the stairs, leading to the garage. In the other direction, the lanes passed under the Atom motorway and into a tunnel toward the entry terminal.

"When you take a vehicle out, you probably go this way," Lanie told Hudson, who was still descending the stairs.

"Let's go see what they've got," he said.

Lanie mouthed a silent "yeah!" and pulled her wrists up to her chest in a display of bubbling excitement. They walked across the roadway and into the sea of vehicles. The rows of parking stalls extended far into the corners of the partially lit cavern. Lanie walked past a row of early-sixties silver Chevrolet service trucks, all of them with the same door logo they'd seen on the junk yard truck. There were boom trucks for utility service and four-wheel-drive trucks for off-road work. But the rows that interested Lanie the most were just past these.

The scowling chrome faces of a fleet of 1960 Plymouth Fury sedans made up the first of three rows of pool cars. Most of the sedans were either turquoise or a sandy pink color. Like everywhere else they'd been, the vehicles they came upon were dust-free. Some of the Furys had flat tires, but otherwise looked as though they'd just been parked a few hours prior. Beyond the Furys was a group of 1959 Mercury Park Lane coupes and sedans in the same condition.

Hudson could tell from Lanie's silence that she was having an automotive overload. "I hope you're not gonna blow a gasket or something. We need to get home before I get grounded."

"This... is... the best day of my life. Bar none," Lanie whispered. She threw her arms around the winged rear corner of a rose-colored Mercury coupe as though she was embracing a new puppy.

Hudson sighed and shook his head. "Yeah, you're gonna blow a gasket."

"I'm gonna get every one of these cars started and running... eventually," she said, pointing a chipped blue fingernail at Hudson.

"Well, you're not starting any tonight; let's look around more. I wanna see those trucks at the back before we go," he said as he continued up the row.

Lanie grumbled but moved on, knowing they did need to watch their time. Farther down the row, she passed a group of silver Chevrolet Impalas, and at the end of the row sat two 1959 Cadillac Sedan de Villes, both in black. Their proud bullet-tipped tail fins were visible from yards away. Lanie broke into a sprint ahead of Hudson when she saw them. They were parked next to a pair of black Lincoln Continental sedans, whose slab sides and massive bumpers almost made the Cadillacs look small.

"These must have been for the executive team?" Lanie wondered out loud.

"I'm sure they weren't for the plumbing technicians," Hudson snarked. "I don't know why you like these huge land yachts." He pointed at the Lincoln's profile. "There's enough steel in this car to make *six* R34 Skylines," he said, referring to his favorite Nissan sports car.

"That's what makes them so cool," Lanie said, looking offended. "This car rolls with style; it *commands* respect wherever it goes!" She gave her best impression of an auto show model, sweeping her hands along the glossy fender.

"It commands a lot of gas," Hudson chuckled to himself. He pointed to the open concrete pad near the cavern's back wall, where some large vehicles stood in the shadows. "That's what I wanna see." A tall semitruck-like vehicle was covered with acres of tan muslin fabric. Only it's huge age-cracked whitewall tires were visible under the cover's edges. Lanie hadn't seen it earlier, but she gasped when Hudson pointed it out. Lanie would have assumed the vehicle was a freight locomotive, based on its huge profile. But the series of tires at the base of the cover gave away its tractor-trailer configuration.

"Geez, whatever this is, it's gigantic!" Lanie said. "Those are the biggest whitewalls I've ever seen!" She pulled up the corner of the cover, revealing an expensive-looking finned alloy truck wheel behind a tall chrome bumper. Lanie quickly dropped the cover and stood upright because they both heard a thump noise from behind them. Lanie turned to see their Atom driving off, unmanned.

Hudson started to run toward the station. He stopped himself after only a few steps, realizing his effort would be wasted; the Atom was gone.

"*That's* not good," he said through his fingers as Lanie walked up behind.

"OK, let's not panic," she said, trying to sound calm. "We'll try to call another one from the console at the station; it'll be fine."

They were short on time and had to leave, but Lanie glanced back at the shrouded truck as they both began walking toward the station platform. Something about the vehicle was creeping her out—she was sure it was hiding a story of its own. That's when a louder slamming noise surprised them from inside the service garage.

Lanie ducked down in the shadows at the front of one of the Lincolns and peered around the bumper. "That was a door closing!" she whispered, pulling on Hudson's wrist. "Get down!" Hudson ducked down next to the car with Lanie and they watched the dark workshop.

"Why are we whispering? It's OK if we're in here." Hudson kept his voice low anyway.

Lanie caught a glimpse of a thin figure walking between the hoists and workstations. When the stranger passed under one of the overhead lights, Lanie saw that it was a girl. At least she thought it was a girl—about her own age. She wore black cargo pants and a gray sweater. Her wavy blonde hair was short and bobbed, and she had barrettes holding back her bangs above either ear. Rounding the corner of the garage onto the motor pool drive, she walked into the darkness of the road's underpass. *Who was this girl? Why was she down here?*

Feeling comfortable with their distance, Lanie and Hudson stood up to see where the girl was going, but she didn't emerge into the light on the other side of the underpass. The two friends shared a puzzled look. Lanie set off in the direction of the underpass but stopped near the end of the row of cars. Her eyes searched the shadows, but the girl had vanished.

"I think she's gone. I also don't think we should sneak up on her," Hudson said.

"She kinda looked like she knew where she was going, huh?" Lanie responded.

"Yeah. C'mon, let's go see if we can say hi."

Approaching the four-lane underpass, Lanie slowed her walk. She was apprehensive about walking into the dark area, even though she could see the roadway on the other side.

"There must be a door under the motorway," Hudson said. "I don't see her—she just disappeared."

Against her better judgement, Lanie walked into the shadows. The supports for the motorway were solid concrete, and she didn't see a door on either side of the road. About halfway through the underpass, the road was at its lowest and Lanie came upon a drinking fountain cove in the concrete. Then she heard a soft, echoing voice that seemed to come from all around.

"Hi."

Lanie squealed and jumped out into the roadway, assuming her best defensive position. Hudson turned to run and tripped on his own shoes, falling into the road next to Lanie.

"It's cool; I'm not gonna cause trouble." The blonde girl stepped out from the dark cove and offered Hudson a smile and a hand as she kept her eyes on Lanie.

"Do you study karate too?" the girl asked Lanie.

Lanie blushed, realizing she was holding her hands upright, with her feet spread. "Uh, no... I don't. I mean... hi, I'm Lanie." Embarrassed, she waved from her hip and stood up straight.

Hudson accepted the girl's offer for help and locked wrists with her to get back on his feet. She shook Lanie's hand next.

"I'm Amanda. How did you guys get in here? Why were you following me?" Despite her questions, Amanda seemed excited to see them.

"Well, uh... we weren't sure who you were, or are...," Lanie stammered, realizing Hudson had been right. "We shoulda just said hi when we saw you, sorry."

"We're friends of Esther," Hudson offered. "We live in the neighborhood nearby."

"Oh! OK. Yeah, Esther's kinda like my auntie," Amanda said cheerily. "I live here. Well...," she pointed behind her, "I don't live *here*—in the *garage*—but I live in the crew quarters. My dad works here."

The two friends looked at each other in amazement.

"You live here—underground?" Lanie asked, bumping her glasses up to her face. "Are there any other kids?"

"No, just me. Most of the facilities crew is pretty old. My dad is the only one young enough to have kids." Amanda was taller than Hudson, but almost as skinny.

Hudson couldn't wrap his head around Amanda's situation, and he surveyed her appearance. "You seem... uhh... kinda normal."

The same thing occurred to Lanie, but she rolled her eyes at Hudson's lack of diplomacy. "He means you don't *look* like you live alone down here."

Amanda giggled. "I don't live *alone* down here. It's just my home, really. I go to school in North Scottsdale."

"Oh!" Lanie cocked her head. "Way on the *other* side of the mountain?"

Smiling through thin lips, Amanda corrected her. "You're actually closer to Scottdale than Fountain Hills where we're at. You're the one who lives in the executive residence, right?"

Lanie wasn't sure if that was good or bad—but answered honestly. "Yeah, we moved in a few months ago."

"I haven't been in the house or the executive complex, but my dad says it's wonderful."

"Yep, it's a nice house for sure—very retro. Kinda like everything down here." Lanie rolled her head and pointed every direction."

"I live a few houses down from Lanie," Hudson added when he saw Amanda's curious glance.

"I was wondering about that. You guys don't look like you're related."

Lanie had a growing list of questions for their new friend but recalled their time constraint. "Aww, Hudson, we are way late."

Hudson slumped as he consulted his watch. "8:40," he said in disappointment. "Can we meet up with you again this weekend? Do you have a phone?"

"Yeah, I have an iPhone, but there's no signal down here. You can email me though." Amanda pulled a wrinkled brown napkin from her back pocket.

Lanie recognized the napkin's print right away. "Hey, Red Rocks! That's my favorite hangout."

Amanda was writing her email address and phone number on the napkin against the concrete wall but looked up excitedly. "Hey, yeah! I love their smoothies. It's pretty far from the north gate, but my dad takes me sometimes."

Hudson took the napkin and promised to write that evening. "Maybe we can meet up on Sunday?"

"Yeah, let's do it! I can show you guys some cool stuff." After a pause, she added, "There are some places I'm not allowed to go, but I know my way around pretty well."

"Oh shoot, our Atom left us; we've got no ride." Lanie glanced up at the motorway.

"No way... you guys have Atom cards?!" Amanda said. "That *rocks*! I can't go anywhere with those. I have to walk *everywhere* in here."

"If we call one from the station, will another one show up?" Lanie asked.

"Yeah, you just can't park more than two at any end-of-line station. So if there are two at the Executive station, you'll have to wait for one of those to get here."

In thinking of the key cards, Lanie suddenly remembered the copper artifact from the junk yard truck, then dug in her pocket. "Oh man, I totally forgot to ask Esther about the little copper blade we found." She slipped it out of its box and offered it to Amanda for inspection. "Do you know what this thing is?"

"Oooh, that's pretty," Amanda said, holding it up to the light. "Uhh, nah, I've never seen—" her voice trailed off, then she looked back at Lanie with wide eyes. "Wait! Yes! I think this is a key. I think I know where this goes!" She led the group up to the Atom platform. "I gotta get back home. But on Sunday, I'll take you where I saw one of these locks," she said, handing the blade back. "See you on Sunday. It was nice to meet you both!"

The meeting seemed too short, and Lanie felt disappointed as she watched Amanda disappear into a passage near the end of the station. "I wish we could've talked to her a little longer," she said, turning to the station control panel. She powered up the console and selected *EXECUTIVE* from the row of destinations. In less than five minutes, a coral-pink carriage glided into the station from the tunnel. When they stepped into the cabin, the destination was already lit, and the door closed itself.

Hudson had been quiet since they'd gotten underway, and Lanie looked over to see him half-smiling, lost in his own thoughts. When he sensed he was being observed, Hudson jerked in surprise, as though he'd been caught daydreaming.

"Oh my gosh," Lanie's jaw dropped and her eyes widened. "You think Amanda is cute."

Realizing his face gave him away, Hudson wrung his hands. His cheeks flushed with embarrassment.

Not wanting to ruin the moment, Lanie changed her tone. "She seems really nice; it'll be cool to hang out with her on Sunday."

"Yeah" was all Hudson responded, then he looked out the window. Lanie smiled to herself and watched the motorway ahead.

They were traveling a different route back to the house. The motorway forked just past the Infirmary station they'd seen earlier, and the Atom slowed before its tires *thump-thumped* over the track switch joints. On their new route, the carriage sped through long stretches of dark tunnel.

They passed only one station, whose sign indicated "COMMAND CENTER." The terminal had striking glossy black tilework from floor to ceiling. All the fixtures and furniture were black with chrome framing. Light seemed to be draining into the black surfaces, and it gave Lanie the chills. A turnout in the station accommodated several Atoms, and two black units with chrome stripes sat idle there. As the station disappeared behind them, Lanie and Hudson glanced at each other.

"Geez, that place looked really severe," Lanie said.

"Yeah... I think that's the place I wanna see next," Hudson said, peering back over his shoulder.

By 8:55, the friends had made the long elevator trip up in the Atom and parked at Lanie's stop. Feeling exhausted, she bumped fists with Hudson at her front door.

"See ya tomorrow morning. It's gonna be a long day."

"For you it will be. I get to sleep in!" he replied, then disappeared around the corner of the garage.

Lanie's appointment to get hair and nails done was at nine o'clock the next morning, and she was to meet Helen and her mom for the ride over. When she locked up the front door, Lanie turned around to find her dad standing in the doorway to his bedroom. He was brushing his teeth, looking annoyed.

"Hi, Dad. Sorry we're late. It wasn't Esther's fault."

Mr. Speros walked back to rinse, then returned with a hand towel. "I figured it would be a longer night. Just don't make a habit of it; remember our agreement—family and schoolwork first."

"Yep, agreed. I thought Gram and Gramps were coming home with Isaiah tonight?" Lanie missed her little brother.

"Tomorrow," her dad said. "How was your evening down there?" He put his hands on her shoulders. "I'm itching to get a grand tour when you've mastered the new territory."

"It was awesome, but we saw very little—just sped past most of it. There's a city-sized cavern with a waterfall. You'll be blown away. Oh, and they have a million historic cars parked down there. All of them are pretty much brand new, like they were stuck in a time warp or something. You would go crazy. I can't wait to take you in there." She looked at her dad over the corner of her glasses. "What did you guys talk about with Esther, anyway?"

"Well...." Her dad sat into a living room chair and motioned her over. "I'm not supposed to discuss all of our conversation with you, at least not right now. But, what I can say is that you and Hudson have made a very big impression on her. She gave us her assurances that the time you spend with her won't have a negative impact on your family, education, or your ability to grow up 'normally.'" Her dad held up air quotes with his fingers for that statement.

255

"The issue, obviously, is that you can't grow up *completely* normally when you are learning how to adopt a city-size bomb shelter."

Lanie didn't know how that was supposed to work either, but then she thought of Amanda. She was going to bring up their new friend, but Mr. Speros continued.

"To be honest, the job she's talking about sounds like a lot of work, even for an adult. I'm wondering why either of you would want to sign up for this kind of thing. Don't you just wanna be kids? You've got your adult lives ahead to build careers and work hard."

Lanie gave her dad a disapproving scowl. "So you think I should join a band, or play video games or team sports or something? You want me to be an average teenager? C'mon, you know that's not me—I don't like to do any of those things." Lanie straightened up and grabbed her dad's hand. "It's not that we're signing up to be employees—we're signing up to be part of something epic," she said.

"Down there it's a whole different world from ours; I wanna be part of preserving it. You know me, Dad. I was never gonna be the girl who grows up to get an average job in an average company. I learned that your career can be your hobby—from you."

"I guess I can't argue with that logic," her dad said, grinning. "Wow, your mother would be so proud of you. I'm amazed at your confidence. I wish I was as strong as you." He paused for a moment, filtering his thoughts. "Anyway, I think Esther's plan is workable, and I believe she's trustworthy. So, if you want to be part of this, I'm good with it. It sounds like you and Hudson would have months—maybe years—of training, including self-defense and geology classes. Even some intense engineering training."

Lanie didn't think she needed to state her answer, but for her dad's assurance, she replied, "I wanna do it."

Mr. Speros nodded, then after a moment said, "I just need you to stay honest with me. If you feel too much stress or anxiety, or you get tired of it—any part of it—I need to know."

"Got it, Dad."

Her dad stood up and headed toward the kitchen. "OK, head to bed, you have a dance tomorrow. I demand that you get me a sappy Harvest Formal photo before you become a secret agent."

# Chapter 19

# THE HARVEST FORMAL

Sunlight streamed through the tall window in Lanie's bedroom that Saturday morning, and it warmed her blue comforter. She sat upright against her headboard, letting the sun wash the sleep from her face. She didn't feel beautiful, and the idea of trying to *get* beautiful by 5 p.m. sounded lousy. But she *did* feel comfortable, so she lay over on her side, piling the warm pillows over her head. Before she'd decided to move on her own, she heard her dad's footsteps on the carpet outside her room.

"You're up! Nice... I'm spared having to throw you out of bed. Let's go, I made breakfast."

"Unngghhh," she whispered under the pillows, then sat back up. Flipping the covers off her legs, she twisted her upper body in the sunlight, releasing clicks and snaps from her joints. It was a lonely breakfast without Isaiah chattering beside her. Even though she was the one who cleaned up the soggy Cheerios from under his stool, Lanie was glad he'd be home that afternoon. His little black mop of hair and cheery brown eyes made the morning much more complete.

"You look much more approachable now," Mr. Speros said as she sat at the counter. He had energy in his step and enthusiasm in his voice.

*He's already had his two espressos*, Lanie thought, looking at the carafe near the steamer.

"Shall I brew you a cup?" he offered as he dried his hands.

"No, I'll probably get a coffee with the Newmans after we get our nails done." Lanie slouched back into the stool.

"You'll have fun. Don't go into tonight thinking about the parts you won't like." Mr. Speros swept Lanie's bangs aside to see her hidden eyes. "Think about the cool things that *might* happen. It's an open house and your friends will be there with you—it shouldn't be stressful.

"Besides, nobody said you had to act like a princess." He winked at her, then pulled away her half-eaten pancakes. "You just have to *dress* like one!" Cracking himself up with his own dad humor, he shoved the dish into the washer and then started clearing the grounds from the espresso machine's brewer.

Once he felt his comic moment had steeped long enough, he turned back to Lanie and said, "I'm actually just waiting for you to get outta here so I can go down into the Omega site with Hudson's dad. We wanna explore without you bosses around, and I wanna see these cars you were talking about."

"Don't worry, I'll leave you my key." Lanie grinned, assuming her dad's voice. "Don't fall in any open pits."

She pushed in her stool and headed toward her bedroom as her dad was mentioning something about her being a *big shot*. Lanie shed her pajamas and pulled on her favorite ripped-knee jeans and drawstring sweatshirt. Helen's orders were to wear flipflops to the manicurist and Lanie didn't want any trouble, so she dug her old pair out of the closet.

The prickly desert environment around her house was hazardous to exposed feet—so Lanie rarely wore anything but sneakers or boots outdoors. Staring down as she sat on her bed, Lanie observed that the skin on her feet was two shades lighter than on her ankles, but it was too late to do anything about that. She started the walk to Hudson's, noting that the weather was gorgeous. The temperature was barely 70 degrees, and Lanie wished she was going to be outside all day instead of mixing with the crowds at the shopping center.

Down the block at Hudson's house, the whole family was outside. Hudson had been drafted to trim the thorny bougainvillea bushes against the Newmans' living room wall, while his dad was attempting some sort of garage cleaning. Helen had loaded the last of the items for the night's formal into the back of her mom's Honda Pilot, and watched Lanie approach. Lanie greeted her with their traditional finger hook, then she threw her mini backpack and her pair of Ariat cowgirl boots into the back seat.

"What's all that?" Helen asked, peering through the window.

"I brought boots and socks, just in case. And some hair bands."

"Umm, yeah... you won't be able to use any of that. Once we get your hair and nails done, they gotta stay untouched 'til game time." Helen tilted her head and raised an eyebrow. "Have you seriously never done a glam day like this?"

"I've never really *needed* to," Lanie said, pulling the car door closed.

Helen's mom had settled into the driver's seat and interrupted. "Lanie's got great skin and hair, Helen; she doesn't need much help to look classy." She winked at Lanie. "But we do need to get your nails done once in a while. I wouldn't expect your dad to sit around a salon while you do that."

It had been at least three years since Lanie sat for any sort of spa experience, but she was relieved when it wasn't as uncomfortable as she remembered. By noon she had gleaming dark red nails, and Lanie had to admit that they looked great. She held up her fingers by the fountain in the plaza and texted a photo to her dad. Like most adults with undeveloped smartphone etiquette, he responded with a series of emojis: *Surprised, shocked, happy,* and *hearts.*

After a quick lunch, she had to sit with the hair stylist, which was much less pleasant. Lanie was sure the stylist was trying to rip her hair out—one strand at a time. Helen was long finished by the time Lanie rejoined her at the coffee stand nearby. She sank into a shady chair next to Mrs. Newman, who was talking on the phone to one of the other event moms. The scent of baking bread, vanilla, and cinnamon was flowing out of the café, and Lanie drew in a deep breath of the crisp fall air.

"You... look... perfect!" Helen said, her face glowing. Lanie looked up at her own tamed curls, which were parted off-center and pinned up over her ears on both sides.

Mrs. Newman also gave a double thumbs-up while she negotiated on the phone over who would staff which room at the school. Helen's strawberry blonde hair was gathered on the back of her head in a whimsical mix of wide curls and thin braids. The style was perfect for Helen's sleeveless, pale-pink gown. Lanie wouldn't expect anything less than perfection from her fashion adviser.

"Thanks, you look cute, too. I like your mini braids," Lanie said.

"We're going, c'mon," Helen said. "I'll get unloaded then help you with your makeup."

Lanie slid out of the Newmans' Honda in front of her house at four o'clock, which left her barely enough time to dress and freshen up before her dad drove them all to the event. The garage was open, and the Jeep was absent. Lanie was relieved that her dad wasn't home—it would be easier to show off her whole look when she was ready to go. Her grandpa's old Mercedes 300D was parked on the right edge of the driveway, which was his prescribed spot, since its engine leaked nasty black oil.

Sabine's BMW was parked in front as well. Lanie figured there would be a big family dinner that evening, and it sounded like more fun than her own plans. She found her grandma reading a paperback forensic mystery novel on the back patio. Lanie collected hugs and compliments, then promised she'd sit down with her grandma after the dance to catch up. There was nobody else in the house; the rest of the group was with her dad.

Half an hour later she stood in front of the mirror in her bedroom, looking herself over. Her dress was the warm tone of vanilla bean ice cream, and the Newman ladies' fitter had made some alterations that wrapped the dress even closer to Lanie's own shape. The satin fabric gathered around her waist with just the right amount of tension and was slit up her left leg a couple inches above her knee. Lanie didn't like showing any skin at all, so she was happy that the tiny sleeves covered her shoulders. But she knew she looked as good in her new dress as the day she tried it on, especially with her heels strapped around her ankles. They showed off her pedicure without revealing too much of her farmer's tan.

It had only taken Helen twenty minutes to do Lanie's makeup, but it felt like an hour. Lanie didn't complain though; she knew Helen would bring out her features without putting on layers of product. Helen and her mom wore very little makeup, preferring to let their freckled skin glow. Lanie thought it was ironic how Helen's freckles gave her a striking, mature look—while the same freckles made Hudson appear younger than he was. After Helen left, Lanie examined her own olive skin in the bathroom mirror and smiled at her dark cherry lipstick. *Helen has a definite talent for color selection,* she thought.

When Lanie walked out of her bedroom, she found her dad had returned, and he stopped mid-sentence where he stood in the living room. He had been arguing with her grandpa about who made the best pneumatic garage tools, but now his attention was only on his daughter. A broad smile spread on his face when he connected with Lanie's greenish-gray eyes.

"My dear, you look stunning." He walked over and kissed her cheek as she stood before the whole family. "Here, now, is my daughter—in the likeness of her mother as a young woman," he whispered in her ear.

Saying nothing, her grandma beamed from where she sat at the corner of the bar and gave Lanie an "O-K" symbol and wink, raising her glass of Ouzo in a silent toast. Isaiah—who was both impressed and happy to see Lanie—ran toward her with cupcake frosting on his hands and face. Mr. Speros intercepted him before he smeared himself onto Lanie.

Lifting Isaiah up mid-stride, he said, "Not right now, little dude— she'll give you hugs later tonight."

"Lay-Lay, you look beautiful. Are ya going on a date?"

"Yeah, buddy, I'm going to a dance tonight." She kissed his forehead. "I missed you. I'll cuddle you up when I get home."

The elder Mr. Speros said, "Oh-oh, this young vixen is going to be out terrorizing Fountain Hills dressed like a super-model tonight?"

"Hi, Grampa," Lanie said, getting another kiss on the check.

"Your mama would approve," he said to her. "I'm speechless. You will take their breath away tonight." He turned to Lanie's dad and said, "Get this beautiful young lady to her dance—she didn't dress up to hang out with two old farts and the Cookie Monster!"

"What about me?" Sabine objected. She stood behind the bar, smiling at Lanie and her grandpa. "I'm no old fart, but I agree, you look wonderful." She tugged at the silver chain she always wore around her neck and bent over the bar to see Lanie's shoes. "Nice... I knew you could pull off some spicy heels if you needed to," she said to Lanie.

Thankful that her grandparents didn't mention the cut of her dress, Lanie grabbed the matching satin handbag from the hall table and headed toward the garage. Her dad opened the front door of the Cadillac and let her slip in. As he shut the door, Lanie wondered how she'd get through the night in the suede heels, but for now they were comfortable enough.

As they coasted up in front of the Newmans' house, Mr. Speros glanced over at Lanie. "I want to hear about the reaction you get from your classmates," he said as he shifted into *park*. "Some of them are probably gonna be blown away by your new look."

Lanie was aware she'd draw more attention than she usually did but figured that was OK. She knew plenty of girls who felt bullied or pressured to conform to a fashion code by their peers, but in her new school Lanie felt completely fashion-neutral; nobody seemed to notice her—and she was OK with that. Though, since the story of her episode with the criminals got around campus, she noticed that students seemed to step out of her way as she walked the halls.

Helen was coming toward the car, motioning with both hands for Lanie to step out.

"C'mon, let's see it. You can't make me wait until we get there," she said, grinning from ear to ear. Mr. Speros had gotten out to open Helen's door and let Lanie out.

"Oh YEAAHH!" Helen said in a scandalous voice. "Now THAT'S what I'm talkin' about! Did you know those curves were hiding under the cargo pants she wears?" she asked Lanie's dad. She didn't wait for an answer but hugged her friend daintily—to avoid any hair interference.

"You look lovely, Ms. Newman," he said as he showed Helen to her seat.

Hudson wasn't far behind and walked up to Lanie with a sheepish and uncomfortable expression.

"Wow, you look... pretty darn good," he said, bumping her fist.

"Lookin' good yourself," Lanie replied, sizing him up in his pinstriped brown suit. His hair was styled with precision that evening, and it looked so nice that Lanie wondered why he never made the effort on school days. His light-colored tie matched his eyes; she knew Helen must have been involved in the color coordination.

The Harvest Formal at Superstition Canyon Junior High was originally a social event to introduce students to the dance formals they'd experience in high school. Over the years, however, the meddling of parents who wanted to be part of their kids' debut ended up turning the event into more of an open house. What was once a series of catered tables in the gymnasium had morphed into a heavily decorated themed evening that spread into other areas of the school. Two of the teachers' lounges were used as gathering spots for the parents and chaperones, which thankfully kept them out of the gymnasium for most of the evening.

The theme was "Over the Moon," and Lanie knew that the Newman ladies had been instrumental in selecting decorations and materials. Mr. Speros piloted the Fleetwood into the school's driveway, mixing in with the flotilla of anonymous SUVs that were unloading other students.

As they waited for a space near the curb, Helen reached over Lanie's seatback and asked, "Did you remember the stuff from your Expression Bag?"

"It's in here," Lanie said, holding up her little clutch bag. The faculty believed that nametags were instrumental in icebreaking at social events, so some sort of name tag interpretation figured into every occasion. There were game and gift raffle coupons in Lanie's expression bag, which she'd stuffed into her clutch as well. But the silver plastic tiara with stars and moons she'd left at home.

"It didn't fit in my bag," she told Helen, hoping the excuse would fly.

"Ahh... it's OK, I don't think I'm gonna wear mine either," Helen said. "Those were my mom's idea anyway."

Mr. Speros nosed the Cadillac into a gap at the curb and went to open the ladies' doors. When he disappeared with the car a few moments later, Lanie felt exposed, as though a curtain had been raised. Turning around, she saw the same bustling activity and faces of a routine school day, except everyone was well-dressed and generally more behaved. Lanie detected that the eyes of other students were following her, but she tried not to think about it.

The group of three walked toward the school's courtyard together. As they approached the iron gates, Lanie's anxiety stepped up a level when she saw her date, Danny. He was nervous, waiting near a column in the breezeway. He looked classy in his black suit. He'd caught Lanie after school on Friday to ask what color her dress was, and she figured he planned to coordinate colors. Danny had done so... and had done it well. He wore an ivory dress shirt and cufflinks under his suit jacket, with a deep red silk tie that matched Lanie's nails.

Most noticeably, though, he'd changed his hair style. His classic men's cut was high off his collar with a neatly parted wave in front. Lanie was both impressed and relieved that her date had gone to so much trouble. Shifting on his feet, he seemed anxious as Lanie walked up. But he was smiling, and his eyes were focused on hers.

"Hi, Lanie," he stammered, offering his hand for a shake. "You are... I mean, your dress... you look awesome."

Figuring it was appropriate, Lanie ignored his hand, hugging him instead. "Thanks, Danny, you look really nice too. I like your haircut and your tie," she said, straightening it for him.

"What's up, Danny?" Hudson said from a few feet back. Danny smiled and waved.

Helen had connected with her own date and had rejoined the group. "Let's go!" she said to the whole crew. "I wanna show you how it looks inside."

The gymnasium was as decked out as Helen had promised. Silver and black bunting was stretched overhead from each corner of the ceiling to the center court. Two starfield projection machines in opposite corners created a slow-moving galaxy over the entire room. Silvery chrome moon-and-star cutouts swirled above each of the many tables.

Helen had assumed the role of emissary for her group, and she selected a table on the edge of the dance floor. Lanie was happy just to fol-low along. She felt like she had to focus on her posture—and every step—in the tall heels. The black tablecloths were scattered with chrome-like star confetti, and a couple circular star charts with a spinning face lay on either side of the centerpiece. Lanie appreciated the centerpieces, which were gray-painted foam balls the size of basketballs which had been carved to look like planets with craters. They were lit from below by tiny electric tealights. The planet on Lanie's table looked more like the Death Star, but she was cool with that.

Sitting as far from the dance floor as she could, Lanie flipped her handbag on the table and her eyes swept the room. Most of the other students were congregating at tables in their usual pods of friends, and a few brave girls were dancing independently in the center of the gym. She picked up one of the star charts, finding it was an adjustable guide to the constellations—typical of what would be used to identify star formations for an astronomy class. As she spun the face, different arrangements of stars were revealed through the opening—and Lanie immediately realized the significance of the skylight in the entryway at home. She wished she was home to investigate her discovery.

The music was loud and frantic. A disc jockey sat behind a table in the corner with a laptop, blasting mixes of the current tracks from the Top 40. Wearing his earphones and dancing as he shuffled the laptop's mouse, the DJ seemed to be having a lot more fun than anyone else in the room. Danny sat next to Lanie but didn't offer any conversation starters. With her heels, Lanie was taller than Danny (as well as most of the other students), so she was glad they were seated for the moment. At some point, she knew she'd be pressured to dance but chose not to think about it.

A long group of tables covered in various finger foods was set up along the retracted gym seating, and Lanie could see Mr. Aarons moderating the flow of students with their plastic plates. Lanie expected events like the formal to have a big punch bowl and rows of clear plastic cups, but she saw none. Instead, a tub of ice was stuffed with bottled water and Lanie stood to go grab one.

"I'll get it!" Danny said, following her line of sight. "Don't worry, I'll get you one." In a flash he was over and back clutching four bottles, which he distributed to the table.

"Thanks, Danny!" Lanie yelled over the music.

From across the table, Helen broadcast her voice. "COOL, HUH?!" She pointed around the room at the decorations.

Lanie nodded and replied with a thumbs-up, then held up the astrological chart. "Very cool!"

After they snacked, Helen twisted Lance's arm into dancing and the pair merged into the still-small group on the open floor. As Lanie picked at a section of chicken wrap, she watched Lance and Helen navigate around each other on the dance floor, twisting and swaying. It didn't look very natural—and Lance didn't look comfortable. Even Helen seemed to be a little uncertain of how to maneuver with the music, and Lanie decided right then that she wouldn't be doing any dancing that night.

Danny was leaning forward with his arms folded on the table. He was watching Lance and Helen as well. With his clean haircut, Lanie could see Danny's ears, and the proportions of his face seemed more masculine and mature.

"I don't really wanna dance, I'm sorry," she said in Danny's ear. Her tone was apologetic.

With Lanie's face that close to his cheek, Danny's back straightened, and he drew in a fast breath before responding. "It's OK, I don't want to either—I would probably smash your toes." He stared down at his buffed shoes.

Lanie didn't pull her phone out to check the time but figured she'd only been there twenty minutes, and she sighed. *The night might be very long and awkward*, she thought. Looking back up at the students clustered around the tables, Lanie concluded that the environment in the gym was about what she'd expected. It was too dark and too loud, and she was uncomfortable on the hard seat of the folding chair.

Watching the flashing lights reflect in her glossy fingernails, Lanie wondered if there was something wrong with her attitude. She wondered if she was supposed to *pretend* to have fun—and whether other students thought the same thing. She searched the room for Hudson—*surely, he'd have an opinion on the topic.* But she didn't see him anywhere. *How come it was so easy to be part of a dangerous, epic underground world but so hard to hang out at a dance?*

From the dance floor, Helen was motioning and pointing for Lanie to come out with Danny. Instant anxiety. Lanie didn't *want* to pretend to have fun, and she didn't want anyone else to pretend with her, so instead she pretended not to notice Helen.

"Do you wanna walk outside?" Lanie motioned toward the open doors at the end of the gym.

Relieved, Danny welcomed the idea and stood right away, offering a path to Lanie. He'd been coached on proper etiquette, she noticed. Her grandpa often told her what behaviors to expect from a gentleman, though Lanie figured that some of the traditions were so historic that her generation might not even recognize the efforts. But Lanie did, and she respected Danny for doing his homework. Stepping ahead, he held the side door of the gym open as she passed through.

Outside the gym, the long breezeway connecting the walkway to the classroom quads was lined with more decorations, along with a couple booths which were set up for photographs. Lanie walked side by side with Danny and peeked into the booths. Kids were wearing different props as they posed for pictures in front of a green screen. They wore wigs, oversize glasses, feather boas, and hats while an attendant was positioning their photos over a variety of backdrops on a monitor outside. Lanie smiled to herself, wondering if they had any cool backdrops of wrecking yards or half-built space stations.

Catching her smile, Danny asked, "Do you wanna do one of those pictures?"

"I think we're supposed to wait and do them with Helen and Lance later," she said. "But we can do one with just the two of us too—I'd like that."

269

Satisfied with the plan, Danny walked on with her. Part of the open house format of the Harvest Formal was to give students an alternative to the dance floor, which Lanie thought was brilliant. The art room, music room, and library were all open and staffed with chaperones. As they passed the music room, Lanie saw Hudson's friend Mark holding a steady, complicated rhythm on a drum set while a red-headed girl plucked different chords on a tired guitar. Other students sat and watched.

Since Danny didn't offer any ideas, Lanie steered them toward the open library doors. The library was her favorite room on campus. Not necessarily because it held the types of books she liked but because of the environment. The school's block columns were exposed in the library, holding up a high ceiling. A mezzanine framed the whole triangular space; it was like a miniature version of the courtyard outside, but lined with bookcases. A large planter in the center had niches and booths for reading. The planters were stacked and staggered, rising into the center of the room like an Inca pyramid.

House plants reached toward the skylights from each of the brown brick planters, and Lanie was familiar with each segment; she was part of the school's greenhouse club that took care of them. Her favorite spot to study or make plans with Hudson was a small booth built into the brickwork, a few steps up from the main floor. The little booth for two was relatively private, with hanging ivy on either side.

"Wanna sit and talk for a few minutes?" Lanie asked, heading for the niche. Danny nodded, looking more comfortable. "This is my favorite place in the whole school," she told him as he slid into the seat. Realizing she'd never seen him in the library, she added, "What are you into? I haven't seen you on any of the sports teams."

Thankful to have the ice broken, Danny responded with confidence. "There's a group of us who do gaming," he said, motioning toward the courtyard. "We hang out under the patio at the auditorium at lunch. But I'm also in the school band."

Lanie didn't even own a video game system and couldn't think of where to go with that topic. "Oh wow, I didn't know you were in the band—what do you play?"

"Alto sax," he said. "I've been playing since I was ten."

She liked the saxophone and was going to ask if she could sit in on one of his practice sessions, but Danny switched topics.

"I heard about what happened at your house last week. I'm glad you're OK."

"Yeah, I'm glad it's all over with," she said, forcing a sigh. "Hudson and I were tired of those idiots; they ruined our vacation. We decided to deal with 'em ourselves."

Danny appeared taken aback by her confidence in dispatching two adult criminals. "I heard parts of the story. Word is, you guys gave them a beat-down and had them all tied up before the cops even got there."

"It wasn't *quite* like that," Lanie said, glancing at the neatly folded handkerchief in Danny's breast pocket. "But yeah, Hudson did tie one of the guys up. The other one crashed his truck trying to run off like a big chicken."

Danny was laughing, engrossed as Lanie gave him a more accurate version of the story. His eyes were focused on Lanie's. "Did they get into your house? What did they want? My mom said I shouldn't ask you about this stuff, but you're kinda famous at school."

Before Lanie had to shift the topic away from the Omega history, she was saved by Hudson, who called from the library doorway. "I *thought* I might find you in here!"

Lanie smiled and waved as he headed up the steps. Sitting on the planter across from the booth, Hudson looked at the couple. "Had enough of the dance?"

"It wasn't really our scene," Danny said. "We were just talking instead."

"Helen's been looking for you. It won't take her long to catch up with us in here," Hudson said, pointing his thumb over his shoulder.

"Did any of the girls compliment you on your suit?" Lanie asked Hudson.

"Nah. But Amy asked me to dance," he said as though he were not surprised to be in demand.

"Didn't Amy come with a *different* guy?" Lanie asked, flashing Hudson a scandalous expression.

"Yeah, she came with Oliver, but I guess he won't leave his chair at the table," Hudson snickered. "Besides, she wanted to ask about our crazy day at your house."

The disappointing cloud over Lanie's evening began to lift, and she felt comfortable—and she was starting to have fun. The trio talked about the other couples in the gym and laughed about some debatable fashion choices.

"Oh, I forgot to tell you... the kid from my science lab...." Hudson paused, staring at Lanie, trying to recall a name. "Ah... I don't know who he is. But he asked me if *you* came with a date. He thinks you're hot."

Lanie caught Danny's brown eyes and smiled. "That's cool, but I have my date."

Danny blushed and looked back to Hudson. Just then, Helen appeared in the doorway, towing Lance by his hand.

"Lanie Speros, why are you in the library? We spent three days decorating the gym, not the library!"

"We're getting to know each other," Lanie said, nodding to Danny. "It's too loud in the gym. Besides, the library is pretty cool."

Helen looked around as though it were the first time she'd been in the room. "Yeah, I know, I hang out in here with you, too. You're not gonna dance?"

Lanie paused. She didn't want to offend Helen, but Danny spoke up just in time. "Neither of us really wanted to dance, but we'll go back to get some snacks in a while."

Helen dragged over a padded bench from the adjacent booth and sat down with Lance. "I guess I can't blame you much. After the first half hour, my arches started hurting anyway," she said, pulling off one of her heels. "My mom hasn't come out of the lounge yet. I think Mrs. Kelderman smuggled some wine in, and they've been sipping since about four o'clock. My dad's gonna have to come and drive her home."

The whole group laughed, then Hudson stood up. "Wait, I'll get some snacks for us!" He slid down the handrail toward the library doors. A few minutes later he returned with bottles of water and little cellophane bags tied with black ribbon. He'd also returned with Amy.

"Oh hey, he brought us water too—good call, brother!" Helen said. Noticing Amy, Helen's eyebrows arched. "Did you ditch your date, Amy?!"

Amy looked guilty and ducked her head a little as she followed Hudson up the steps. "He's busy... found something more fun to do I think," she said, and didn't appear to be disappointed.

Hudson spread the snack bags on the bench, and they all made their pick. Some bags had chocolates while others had pretzels or cookies. The bags were out of reach for Lanie and Danny, so Hudson tossed them across the aisle. Danny intercepted his, but Lanie spastically grabbed at the air as hers sailed past. She averted her eyes in embarrassment, feeling like the whole group noticed her ineptitude.

"It's OK, I'll get it," Danny said, reaching over Lanie's head to retrieve the sack from the tangle of ivy in the planter. They talked a while longer about teachers, hobbies, and viral dance videos. Lanie was excited, as though she'd had a shot of espresso. It was the first time since moving from Tucson that she felt like part of a big pool of friends.

"I wish they would play some older stuff in the gym, like Frank Sinatra or Ella Fitzgerald," Lanie said. Revealing her unconventional taste in music was a risky move, but she was already tired of worrying about what people thought of her. "I think it's easier to dance to that kinda music."

"You mean like this?" Danny held up his phone, and "Summer Wind" began playing.

"Yeahhh," Lanie whispered. "I would dance to this."

As if on cue, Danny stood and extended his hand in an invitation. This time, Lanie had no apprehension and stepped into the aisle. Slipping her free hand behind Danny's back, they began a slow, waltzy dance between the planters.

Helen was beside herself with pleasure and yanked Lance up from the bench to join them. The two dancing couples released Hudson's inhibition, so he turned to Amy and drew her into the small dance party.

The song that Lanie had lingered on so many times in the past suddenly seemed short. She watched Danny's eyes, then glanced down at her feet as they stepped naturally around Danny's shoes. It was the first time that she'd enjoyed a dance—with a partner who wasn't her dad or grandfather. *Now this feels right*, she thought to herself.

When the song ended, the group laughed at the irony of their own private formal in the library, then sat back down, talking in overlapping conversations. Lanie promised Helen she'd try to dance to a more modern song in the gym, and Hudson was incorrectly demonstrating how to do the electric slide when they heard the muffled drone of announcements from outside. Helen turned to listen, then checked the time on her phone. "Oh... they're gonna start the raffles soon; let's go see if we won anything. We bought some cool prizes they're gonna give away."

As the group made their way off the island of reading nooks, Helen turned to Lanie. "This was a pretty good idea... the library was a good break." She hooked pointer fingers with Lanie, then glanced up past Lanie's head toward the mezzanine and froze. Her eyes widened, and a great smile pushed up her cheeks.

"OOHHH! Yesss!"

The whole group stopped. "What?" Lance said. "What did you see?"

"I have a killer idea," Helen said, pointing up to the mezzanine. "We gotta do our picture in *here*. My mom is always telling me about this awesome '80s movie about some kids who are stuck in a library during detention. We should recreate the pic!"

Lanie knew of the movie too; her dad had The Breakfast Club DVD in their collection, but she hadn't seen it. She knew the cover art well, though, and smiled. "I know what she wants to do," Lanie said to the group, wrinkling her nose at Helen. "Everybody upstairs!"

While the others headed up the staircase, Helen kicked off both heels and climbed up the terraced planter to the highest point—a place that was off limits, if any faculty had been around. She propped her phone against a bamboo plant and aimed it across at the mezzanine.

The rest of the group had assembled along the wood-capped handrail in front of the juvenile fiction stacks. Lanie elevated her right heel on one of the reading ottomans, and Danny stood next to her with his forearm hanging off her shoulder. Hudson leaned over the handrail near Amy and let his tie hang in the open space. After sliding back into her own heels at the top of the stairs, Helen joined the group, leaning into Lance's chest. She triggered the phone's camera from her smartwatch and captured an image—the photo that Lanie was sure would be the definitive image of her junior high school years.

As the group walked through the library's doorway, Lanie stopped when she caught motion in the corner of her eye. Looking left she saw their principal, Mrs. Weaver, sitting in the librarian's alcove, sipping coffee. Lanie was surprised; she didn't know anyone had been in the room with them.

When she saw that she'd been spotted, Mrs. Weaver stood up. "That's going to be a timeless portrait," Principal Weaver said. "You're a good-looking group tonight. Good for you guys." She smiled at Lanie and put her coffee down. "By the way, I met a wonderful woman yesterday—her name is Esther Andersen. We had a pretty amazing discussion. She's going to make some advanced government-sponsored programs available to our school, specifically to accommodate the skills that she sees in you and Hudson. I think you and I should catch up next week." She winked, then nodded to the door. "Better catch up with them." The uncertainty on Lanie's face melted into appreciation, and she waved as she left the room. Lanie's spirit was soaring, and she wished she could run home and tell her mom all about the new feelings.

An hour later, the group of friends assembled again near the gates of the courtyard. Lanie's dad was near, to take the group home. It had turned out to be a great night. Lanie was happy with all the new memories circulating in her head. The air was unseasonably warm—just nice enough not to need a coat. Danny had won a cellophane-wrapped gift basket crammed with candy, gift cards, and a stuffed beagle in the raffle drawing, and he gave the puppy to Lanie. The rest of the basket he offered to the others, who dug through, looking for anything sweet.

"I have an idea," Lanie offered. "Lance and Danny, can you guys call your parents and tell them *we'll* bring you home?"

The two boys looked at each other, then nodded their heads. "Probably," Danny said. "Whatcha thinking of doing?"

She handed Danny her phone to call home. "We can see if my dad will take us to the Pink Cow."

"Oooooh," Helen said, looking to Lance. "Yeah, that sounds awesome."

The Pink Cow was an ice creamery that made their own flavors in the store, but they also made their own waffle cones and cookies, and even roasted their own coffee. Lanie loved the cinnamon swirl waffle cones, but because the coffee was awesome, she knew it wouldn't be hard to talk her dad into stopping with the group.

When she saw the Cadillac pull up, Lanie leaned in the passenger window and pitched the idea to Mr. Speros.

"I'm in—that's a good plan," he said with a thumbs-up. "How many people you got there? That's more than we came with?!"

"There's room," Lanie said, pulling open the door. She hiked up her dress to her knees and slid across the leather into the middle of the front seat, and Danny sat next to her. The three others piled into the back seat. They all rolled down their windows as Mr. Speros pulled out of the parking lot.

Cruising down the boulevard near the mall, the full Cadillac's tail sat low to the ground as the car wafted along under the streetlamps. The boulevard was popular with cruisers on Saturday nights, and Lanie's guests hung their arms out in the warm air, watching the cars and people. The wind coming through the windows scrambled Lanie's hairdo, but it felt just right. She cranked up the radio as they rolled along the strip next to a classic Mustang convertible full of women.

Lanie twisted around and smiled at her carload of friends. In the back seat, even Helen had let her hair go. The braids that had been gathered neatly on top of her head were fluttering against the seatback as she held her face to the open window.

"Thanks, Dad," Lanie whispered to her driver as they sailed past the lit shops and pedestrians. Glowing from how awesome the night was, Lanie thought of how her dad had told her to look forward to the good things that *could* happen. *What did happen was even better*, she thought.

## Chapter 20

# DANGEROUS EXPLORATION

Leaning on her music stand in the choir loft at church Sunday morning, Lanie felt slow. She was alert enough—but looked forward to relaxing for a couple hours later in the day. The idea of sitting in the executive lounge under her house, reading a book by the improbable tropical paradise sounded wonderful. She even looked forward to seeing the curious red bird, whom she'd named Bob. Though tired, she was happy, thinking of the new friends and experiences from the night before. She was also excited about going back into the caverns to meet Amanda with Hudson that afternoon to do some exploring. She'd made more friends in the last five days than the last five years.

The late morning sun was filtering through the stained glass above the church's altar, washing the congregation with a kaleidoscope of light. Lanie could see her grandparents with Isaiah and felt very much at peace—and at home—for the first time in months. When the services finished, she hung her choir robe in the practice room, then collected the rest of her usual hugs and kisses from the older members of the choir. Hustling down the stairs to the main doors, she spotted her family on their way out. Most of the older Greeks in the parish tended to congregate right outside the doors after the services and Lanie had to thread her way through the gossiping herd to catch her group. When she found her grandparents, Isaiah was with them, but Sabine and her dad were gone.

"They're going to have lunch on their own today, koúkla," her grandma said as Lanie watched the Wagoneer turn from the parking lot. She was surprised her dad had made plans separate from the rest of the family.

"C'mon, we take you to get some coffee at you favorite Red Rocks place, then Grandpa wants to watch his game." Her grandma hooked Lanie around both shoulders and pulled her close. "Besides, you didn't finish telling me about you boyfriend; I want to hear more."

Lanie's eye twitched and she glared at her grandma. "I told you, Danny's not my boyfriend, Gram. He was just my date to the dance—we're just friends."

"Yes, yes, *friend* who is a *boy*, I know," she showed her palm to Lanie, playing down her incorrect choice of words.

Back in her room at home, Lanie peeled her black cotton blazer off her skin and flapped her arms around to cool off. The air-conditioning in her grandpa's old diesel Mercedes worked, but he didn't use it, and that annoyed Lanie. Through text messages, she'd confirmed that Hudson would come over around 2 p.m. so they could travel to meet Amanda. She wasn't sure how she was going to slip away from her grandparents, since they didn't know about the Omega site.

Pulling on a pair of khaki cargo pants, Lanie picked out a long-sleeve jersey tee in preparation for the day's exploration. Nearly every place in the Omega site was 68 degrees and some areas were drafty. Her choice of wardrobe would raise questions with her grandparents because Lanie needed a utility belt and good walking shoes in the caverns. In the living room, Lanie's grandpa had found his football game on TV and was oblivious to his surroundings. Isaiah was plowing building blocks around the room with his bulldozer, and her grandma was following behind, picking up after him. Hudson rang the doorbell on the strike of two o'clock and the two headed into the garage without any greetings.

"My dad's not home yet. I dunno know where he went, but I was hoping he'd be back by now. My grandparents are gonna want to know where we're going."

"Tell 'em we're going back to my house," Hudson said with a careless shrug.

Lanie slipped her flashlight into the leather loop on her belt. "That doesn't sound like a good idea."

"Well, you can't go back into the house looking like Indiana Jones." Hudson pointed at the accessories that hung from her belt.

Lanie knew he was right, but then assessed his outfit and said, "You don't even have a flashlight?"

"It's all in my backpack at the door. I dunno why *you* don't use a backpack. It would be easier than rigging yourself up like that."

"You're one to talk, Inspector Gadget," she said. "Your backpack weighs almost as much as you. I'm surprised you could fit through the door."

Their debate was interrupted by the growl of the garage door motor. Sunlight cracked under the door, and Lanie stepped aside as her dad drove the Jeep in. Mr. Speros was looking at her suspiciously through the windshield.

"I hope you're not going back into the house dressed like that," he said, stepping out of the Wagoneer.

Lanie rolled her eyes and started pulling the items off her belt. "Where's Sabine?" she asked as she bunched her flashlight and multitool into a plastic bag.

"She had some errands to run—she'll come over for dinner after your grandparents head out." Mr. Speros turned back to the two friends and pulled the hallway door open. "She was hoping to have some one-on-one time with you tonight, so don't be gone all afternoon; be back here by seven."

The idea of time alone with Sabine made Lanie uncomfortable. Sabine was easy to get along with, but they never talked much and didn't share any hobbies. She was concerned that Sabine wanted to talk about her growing relationship with her dad. That was the last thing Lanie wanted to be part of, but she didn't want to hurt her dad's feelings, so she kept any expression from her face.

"OK, I'll be here for dinner." Lanie pointed to the living room. "Can you let Gram know I'm leaving?"

"I will. You two be careful. Just look around; don't mess with any equipment, not until Esther spends more time with you down there."

"Yeah, Dad." She scooped her hand at Hudson, and they followed Mr. Speros into the house.

The guest bedroom was just out of view of the living room, so Lanie and Hudson used the bookcase passage to get downstairs. Lanie had stocked the pantry in the lounge's kitchen with miscellaneous snacks, and she grabbed a bag of cheese-flavored crackers for the ride. Not wanting to be late for their rendezvous with Amanda, Hudson had already powered up the Atom when Lanie jumped in. He picked the COMMONS stop and the two sat back for the trip. As she ground a mouthful of crackers, Lanie noticed that Hudson had combed his hair in preparation for the day's meeting. She smiled but didn't say anything.

It wasn't quite 3:30 when their gold Atom coasted into the Commons station. When they descended the carved stone steps of the station veranda, they found Amanda sitting at one of the picnic tables near a brook. Though her hair was still pulled back behind barrettes, she was dressed less homely than their last meeting. Wearing denim shorts with a fitted pink sweatshirt, she waved enthusiastically as the two friends approached.

"I'm glad you guys could come today," she said. "This place will be tons more fun if we can all hang out down here together."

Lanie didn't think they'd be doing too much *hanging out*, based on what Esther's plans were, but she agreed. "Yeah, I was super excited to get outta church today so we could come down."

"I'll bet you really know your way around this place," Hudson said. "We wanna know how to get around without the Atoms, just in case we get stuck somewhere."

"I can definitely help with that," Amanda said. "At least, in most places I can. There are a lot of passages and tunnels that connect the different wards. Some are original mine tunnels—those don't have very good lighting." She itched the top of her nose, then her whole body wriggled as though she'd felt a chilly draft.

"Are you OK?" Lanie asked.

"Yeah, sorry, I shiver sometimes, but I'm not cold. My dad says it's called a transient tic." Amanda smiled, drawing away any concern. "It throws people off, but it's harmless. It'll probably go away before I'm eighteen."

"Did you tell your dad about us? Does he know we're here?" Hudson inquired.

"Yeah, he knows. He runs the control room for the energy plant, and the console there tells him when any of the site perimeter doors are opened."

Lanie and Hudson exchanged glances, unaware that anybody but Esther knew they were coming and going. Before they could ask for details, Amanda added, "He said you guys are kind of a big deal." Her expression didn't give away her own opinion.

"What does *that* mean?" Hudson asked.

"Esther meets with my dad and the crew once a month, and she told them that you two were starting training to be the next generation of principals. Principals have access to the entire site," Amanda said. "You guys will be able to go anywhere, even into the command center. My dad and the crew can't even go in there."

"What's the command center for?" Lanie asked.

"The executives and chief engineers can run the whole site from there," Amanda replied. "The main security office is there, along with the treasury. Also, life support system controls."

Like Hudson, Lanie was now very interested in the command center, but knew they'd have to wait for Esther to make that trip.

"Let's walk; I wanna show you guys around the grotto," Amanda said, pointing toward the waterfall in the distance.

"That's exactly where I wanted to go," Lanie said, grinning. She'd been to Central Park in Manhattan, and the lamp-lit paths and clusters of trees in the cavern were like an indoor version. A wide creek split the cavern, and several arched bridges crossed it at different points.

"Did you bring your copper key thing?" Amanda asked as they began their walk.

"Yeah, I've got it," Lanie replied, slapping the pocket of her cargo shorts.

"Kinda crazy... it's a real park," Hudson said, dragging his hand across the top of a leafy shrub. "Except it's night all the time."

"Almost," Amanda replied. "There are big flood lights that come on in here every few hours—the plants need it. But they don't run them for long. My dad says they use too much energy. That's why there aren't as many plants in here as there should be."

The park was larger than it looked, and it took the group half an hour to reach the far end. The roar of the waterfall grew louder as they approached. Other tributaries merged with the widening creek as they neared. Despite the park's beauty, some unusual features caught Lanie's eye. Unlike a natural river, the creek's banks were cut from stone, with definite edges that followed a deliberate path through the park. Likewise, the planters and garden foliage were arranged in a logical and patterned fashion that appeared to have a specific purpose, though Lanie didn't know what it might be.

They'd also come closer to the many little shops and offices on the ledges of the cavern wall. Through the trees and hedges, Lanie saw small paths which led away from the park's main walkway. They allowed access to the hundreds of ramps and stair sections which connected the buildings in the cavern's granite faces. Aside from the modern windows and façades, the shops and offices reminded Lanie of the ancient cliffside dwellings that Native Americans had built. The display windows in some shops were lit up, as though the locations were still in use. Lanie spotted a larger shop near the corner of a rock outcropping that appeared to stock modern industrial clothing and boots. Still, other retail shops displayed ancient toys or housewares that clearly hadn't been touched in sixty years.

A large lagoon was the source of the creek they'd been following. The same lagoon was also the basin of the waterfall. Lamp posts and benches dotted the shore, and, like the dormitory tower, Lanie felt like the area had only recently been vacated. Amanda led her two new friends through an overgrown hedge to the end of the lagoon, where the mist of the waterfall hid a passage in the rockwork. She used her own key card to unlock an obscure rust-coated steel door at the end of the tunnel. It opened into a narrow passage whose walls were unfinished, jagged rock.

'C'mon," she said, motioning her guests into the darkness.

As they stepped through, a chilled blast of air swirled around Lanie, forcing an involuntary shiver. Their motion switched on a series of floor-mounted electric lanterns, exposing sharp turns in the passage, hiding what was ahead. The unpaved floor of the tunnel was lined with fine red dirt.

"This is one of the main galleries from the original mine," Amanda said. "You gotta be careful because some of the mine's vertical shafts and passages still open into these galleries, and they don't usually have handrails. If you fall into one of those, you're dead meat—nobody will ever recover your mangled skeleton."

At first, Amanda's statement seemed comical to Lanie, but after rounding a few corners, they walked within inches of a crack-like opening on the tunnel floor. Looking over the edge, Lanie saw a distant shelf of stone several yards down, beyond which was black nothingness. She backed away from the edge and jumped when Amanda started speaking again.

"This is one of the first vertical cuts in the mine," Amanda said. "The shaft goes down another three hundred feet and the only access is with these ladders." She nudged a rickety, rotted wooden assembly near the edge. "The gallery we're in is at the mid-level, where most of the original mine cuts are. There are a few on the lower levels that I haven't been in 'cause they're flooded." Amanda kinked her mouth sideways. "These galleries are the only way to get between some of the wards if you don't use the motorway. It's a lot of walking, and it's kinda dangerous."

"Kinda?!" Lanie spluttered. "Your dad lets you cruise around these old mine passages alone, and he's cool with it?!"

"I grew up here, and I do professional rock climbing; he knows I'm pretty safe." She kicked up her left foot, displaying a dusty shoe to her friends. It looked like a ballet slipper, with a heavier rubber sole.

"Ahh! Climbing shoes," Hudson pointed, smiling because he hadn't noticed before.

"I compete nationally," Amanda said. "I win a lot of trophies. He doesn't need to worry about me in here."

Impressed, Lanie nodded her head and smiled. "So, you've had training to do climbing? Like in rock gyms?"

Amanda laughed. "Nah, my training has all been on natural rock formations and mountains. That's the only place you can really learn how to do the rope access work I do."

"How in the world did you learn your way around? Just by exploring?" Lanie asked in disbelief.

"Partly." Amanda lowered her head as if to share a secret. "You gotta study the drawings. If you don't know how to read blueprints, you gotta learn. Otherwise, you could be lost for days. You can't count on the Atom to get you everywhere."

"The file room," Hudson said, looking at Lanie.

"Yeah. We'll pull the drawings out. I know how to read them, and Hudson can read electrical drawings too," she said to Amanda.

Amanda motioned to follow. "C'mon, I wanted to show you guys something *way* cool down here." The tunnel narrowed again, and small light bulbs strung on a common wire were anchored overhead. The hot bulbs hung so low that some grazed Lanie's hair. Many were burned out, so Lanie and Hudson stumbled as they stepped. They came upon a rusty iron folding gate with a tattered sign that read "NO ADMITTANCE." Both looked to be over a hundred years old, but the gate had been forced open at some point and lay ajar. There were no lights beyond.

Amanda looked back at her guests as she stood in the narrow opening, and in an ominous tone said, "Either of you afraid of heights or confined spaces?"

"Uhh, are you kidding?" Lanie asked.

"I'm fine," Hudson said without hesitation.

Not wanting to appear hesitant, Lanie added, "Let's go," and she wagged a finger toward the darkness.

Amanda pulled a small flashlight from her hip pocket and shined it up under her chin. "Turn on your lights," she said. Her smile seemed unsinkable, Lanie thought. Their new friend was wonderfully interesting.

A few paces ahead, Amanda navigated the passage with fluid, yoga-like motions, as though her body were flowing with the shape of the rocks. Lanie, on the other hand, was scraping her shoulders and knees like a moose in a broom closet as she passed through the niches. The passage was pitch black ahead and behind them, and the isolation was extreme; Lanie felt that she was as far from humanity as she could ever be.

"Ouch! Dang it!" she muttered after her ear brushed a rock. Hudson was behind, ducking and bending with fewer scrapes.

Lanie wasn't sure how far they'd traveled, but she felt like they'd gone over fifty yards in the blackness. Then the passage opened into a cavern the size of Lanie's living room. A musty breeze swirled in the chamber, and she could hear trickling water. Shining her light around, she saw dramatic milk-white stalactites hanging from the ceiling, but did not see Amanda. There were small pools around the cavern's perimeter, but near the center was a bowl-like pit. Its smooth sides funneled to a hole in the middle, into which a steady stream of water was draining. Ancient iron candleholders protruded from hand-drilled holes in a few places around the cavern. Standing still, Lanie reached behind to confirm Hudson was still with her, and he grabbed her hand.

"I'm here... where's Amanda?" he said in a whisper.

"Amanda?" Lanie said.

Amanda's light switched on at the far end of the room. She stood leaning against the wall and struck a match. She lit some old stumpy candles on the iron hangers. The air smelled damp, but the thick dust on the floor was like a cushion of sifted red flour. Hudson had inched up to the edge of the hole in the middle of the room. "Oh WOW," he said. "Lanie, come see!"

Looking across at Amanda, then Hudson, Lanie crept forward and craned her neck over the dished edge where Hudson stood. More than one hundred feet down the vertical shaft, the reflection of Lanie's flashlight bounced back with a shimmer.

"Water?" she said, looking up.

"Yep," Amanda said. "It's a hidden bay—it connects to the underground lake."

A striped climbing rope hung over the edge. The rope's top end was knotted to a metal spike in the wall nearby. "You've been down there?!" Lanie asked.

"Yeah, it's not as far down as it looks. We'll go after you guys can handle the rope climb. It's a neat room. But that's not what we're here for."

Lanie shined her flashlight around the room; there were no other openings or passages. The water that was draining into the smooth bowl on the floor was dripping from a crevasse in the ceiling. A modern rope ladder was hanging down from one edge. Amanda shook the ladder. "This is what we're here for—We're going up."

"Oh, HELL no!" Lanie said, stepping back from the dripping stalactites near the ladder. Her knees suddenly felt rubbery.

Even Hudson looked uncomfortable. "I don't know, uhh... I haven't... I mean—."

Amanda interrupted, "It's OK, I put the anchors and ladder in. I know they're good for at least six hundred pounds."

"Nope," Lanie said. "Maybe we should try this a different day. I can practice somewhere else first... how high up does this go?"

Unaffected by Lanie's resistance, Amanda smiled back, remaining pleasant. "The opening goes up over two hundred feet, but we're not going that far. The ladder's safe. Please?"

"I'm not worried about the ladder," Lanie cried. "I'm worried about falling off of it!"

Hudson shot a tentative look at Lanie. "She knows what she's doing; I trust her. If I do it, will you do it?"

Lanie tried to wrangle the fear out of her own eyes as she stared at Hudson. She looked over at Amanda's reassuring face next. Amanda nodded, and her eyes twinkled in the dim light on the other side of the ladder. "You can do it. It's no biggie."

Amanda and Hudson watched her, hoping for a response. "OK, I'll do it," Lanie said. She wasn't sure she could make her muscles comply, but she would watch and learn.

Amanda bent down and picked up a bundle of climbing rope from behind a rock near the wall. "We're only going up about eighty feet, but you have to be careful where we're getting off. If you misstep, you could fall back down the shaft. Don't use the ladder to step off—use the loop I anchored on the rock when you get there. Always maintain three points of contact. You should never have more than one hand or foot off the ladder at any time."

"It's pitch dark up there. How will we know where to get off?" Hudson asked.

Amanda had shed her small backpack and stowed some items on her belt. "I'm going up first. I'll light the lanterns and call when you can come up."

Lanie bit her lower lip. She wasn't reassured at all, but watched, saying nothing.

Amanda started up the ladder, then called back down when she was almost out of sight. "Oh yeah, you might get a little wet, so watch your grip."

Lanie could think of ten good reasons not to climb the rope ladder, and she imagined what her dad would say if he knew what she was about to do. Hudson was two rungs up the ladder, watching her face.

"This is just one of a million times that you're gonna have to get outside your safety zone," he said. "You can do this as easy as I can. Be the fearless Lanie from your driveway last week; forget about the scary part, just focus on the destination."

Lanie was surprised by Hudson's motivational speech, and she laughed, momentarily forgetting her fear. "You're funny, Jedi Master." Her face firmed as she looked at Hudson. Lanie knew she couldn't spend the rest of her life wondering what her dad would think whenever she did something. "Yeah, I know, I gotta get used to doing this kinda thing. Let's do it."

Amanda called from above, and her voice bounced around the vertical shaft before it reached them. "Come on up!" A glow of light was visible from the same direction as her voice, though the falling drops of water made it hard to look up. "Slow and steady, focus on your grip and foot position," Amanda called down.

Hudson disappeared up the ladder, and Lanie steadied the bottom as it wagged during his climb. When he'd reached the destination, Lanie felt the ladder calm—it was her turn. "OK, come up Lanie!" Hudson yelled down.

Thankful that the low light masked the height, Lanie started climbing. One rung at a time, she inched closer to the ceiling of the cavern. Once she was a few feet above the ceiling, Lanie realized that the ascent was easier than she expected. Focusing on the rungs, she didn't worry about the accumulating height below. She started to feel empowered and quickened her climbing pace. The face of the shaft where Amanda had anchored the ladder was out of the path of the falling water, up until the point where Lanie saw the light above. As Lanie neared, the rungs became wet, and she felt her grip soften. An occasional droplet would poke her hair from above, then Lanie looked down. Immediately she became filled with terror. The distance to the dimly lit cavern below might as well have been a mile. Her breathing became shallow, and she froze.

Without panic in her voice, Amanda said, "You're almost here—just come up a few more rungs."

Lanie looked through the ladder ahead of her and saw that the shaft wall had tapered away, revealing a sloped ledge. Amanda crouched on a rock, holding out a loop of rope whose end was anchored to the wall. "Reach around and grab this and pull yourself toward me."

It took a few moments of concentration, but Lanie forced her right hand to leave the ladder. She extended her arm and grabbed the loop, drawing it in slowly. She noticed that Amanda didn't pull or help. "You got it. Now steady yourself with the loop and step onto the ledge," she said to Lanie.

When Lanie had her right foot planted near Amanda, she leaned forward and slumped toward a stalagmite, letting the ladder return to the shaft behind her. Amanda didn't say anything but patiently waited for Lanie to stand.

"OK, it wasn't so bad," Lanie said, her voice quivering. "I could do that again—better next time." Offering a hand to Amanda, she added, "Thanks, you're a good coach, and thanks for letting me do it on my own."

Skipping the handshake, Amanda hugged her, chuckling. "I knew you could do this, girl. You did good."

"So what the heck did we come up here for? I hope it was worth it," Lanie said as she straightened her glasses and pulled back her hair. Hudson sat nearby on a boulder and gave her a thumbs-up.

"It's worth it, I promise!" Amanda climbed up the narrow path between the stalagmites on the sloped ledge and disappeared around a corner. Lanie and Hudson followed and ducked under a low rock into a crawl space.

When Lanie emerged on the other side of the rock, she heard more rushing water and the distant roar of the waterfall. She had to climb out of a rough hole, then stood up in a shadowy room where the cavern ceiling was high overhead. They'd surfaced on a relatively smooth, solid granite surface, into which a wide waterway had been carved. To Lanie's left, water was percolating up from the solid rock in a turbulent, splashing bath. The water then calmed as it channeled into the fifty-foot waterway. To the right, the water was accumulating in a small pond. Lanie offered Hudson a hand and pulled him up from the hole.

Suspended in the middle of the waterway was what looked like the deck of a small ship, only a few feet above the water. It was as long as the waterway and originated against the back wall, above where the spring was flowing up from the rock. At the other end—in the little pond—the platform widened into a circular deck, in the middle of which was a round, glassed-in room that looked like a futuristic gazebo.

Amanda stood near the pond, looking proud. "I found this access," she said of the hole they'd emerged from. "There are only two ways to get up here, and the other way is from that locked door on the far end of the platform. But that's not the cool part—come look!" She waved them over.

"Take your shoes and socks off," Amanda said as Hudson and Lanie approached the water's edge. "Follow me in; it's only a few inches deep over here."

Lanie rolled up her pant legs and stepped in with her eyes pinched shut, expecting the water to be ice cold. Instead, it was more like bath water. "Whoa, this is really warm!" she said, smiling at Amanda. "I could stay up here all night!" She waded over to a sandstone ridge, where Amanda was perched. The ridge was only knee-height, and when Lanie approached, she stopped short. The pond's water was cascading over the rocks to her left, into the lagoon, far below. She had a bird's-eye view of the entire residential cavern and commons, which stretched out of sight ahead of her. The dormitory tower in the distance was small from their viewpoint, and vapor hung in the air near the top of the cavern. It was one of the most beautiful and otherworldly visions she'd ever had, and she had no words to describe her awe.

Similarly dumbfounded, Hudson stood next to Lanie, looking out at the vista. "Nowhere else on earth could you get a view like this," he whispered.

"I know, right?" Amanda said, sitting on a boulder near the ledge. "You mentioned the hill behind your house is your thoughtful spot?" she said to Lanie. "This one is mine."

Without taking her eyes from the view, Lanie smiled and said, "Yours is better."

"I brought you here because it's cool, but it's also important." Amanda turned to face her new friends. "Let's go up onto the platform; I'll show you why."

Amanda led the group back onto the dry granite, then to the back of the cave near the tumbling, splashing flow of water. She pointed to the deck's handrail, which terminated in the wall near two large doors. "We gotta inch out at the water's edge and duck under the handrail. C'mon," she yelled over the gurgling water.

The ledge was narrow, and Lanie was apprehensive. "What if I fall in?" she said, looking at the churning whirlpool.

Amanda smiled. "Then you get wet!" Seeing Hudson was similarly concerned, Amanda added, "Don't worry, you can't fall down the spring; the water will push you out. Then, you'd get washed downstream into the channel and it's easy to climb out."

Sliding under the stainless-steel handrail, Amanda extended a hand, pulling Lanie through. Lanie then pulled Hudson through and the three walked down the narrow deck toward the waterfall.

"So, this structure floats up here above the water?" Hudson asked, stomping his foot on the metal decking.

"Nah, it's anchored to the rock underwater," Amanda said. But you can't get on here—through that door back there—without a red-striped principal or regent badge."

"What's a Regent?" Hudson asked.

"They're the people who get selected to be the leaders when the site is full of refugees," Amanda replied. "They're different than the principals— my dad said new regents get selected every ten years or so."

The group had arrived at the round portion of the deck and Lanie found that it had the same bird's-eye view of the cavern, a few feet back from the waterfall's edge. Lanie could see that the glass room was empty inside, except for a circular handrail around the top of a spiral staircase, leading down. Surrounding the room, the decking was coated in stone tiles in the same pattern as the entryway at the Speroses' house. Near the door of the round glass pergola, a little console was anchored to the deck.

"Here," Amanda said, motioning to Lanie, "get your key out."

The console had five key slots under a chrome-plated metal brow. The slot in the middle had a copper bezel around it, and it took Lanie a moment to realize why it looked familiar—it was just like the lock she'd seen on the booth-like glass door in the Atom corridor near her house.

"Yours is the fancier copper key—it goes in the middle lock, I think," Amanda said.

Hudson watched as Lanie slipped the key out of its tin and into the lock cylinder. It fit perfectly, and when Lanie turned it, the key locked in its position and a beam of light projected into the key's crystal from the brow. The red beam cast a series of clear numbers on the console's face:

665 660 130 418

"Whoa, that light source filters out some of the numbers in that crystal!" Hudson said, bending to look under the brow. "What are they for?"

"For that keypad on the glass door!" Lanie said, pointing to a series of push buttons that had illuminated on a pad next to the door. Lanie relayed the numbers to Amanda, who dialed them in, but nothing happened.

"Still locked," Amanda said, pulling on the door.

"I think we need another key," Hudson said, pointing at the console. The four unoccupied key slots were flashing their light beams. "It must take more than one key to get in, like a group of people need to be here."

"Probably the regents," Amanda said. "Oh, well. I was kinda hoping to see what's down there. My dad doesn't know what's down that staircase, either."

"Ahh, shoot," Hudson said. "At least we know this is a key now."

"There are other places in the site that have those key slots. I'll show you some on a different day. Let's head back though," Amanda said. "It's gonna take us an hour just to get to get back to the Atom station."

"I wanna learn how to climb," Lanie said, looking into Amanda's eyes. "I want to come back here. Will you teach us?"

Amanda beamed and bumped her shoulder into Lanie's. "Of *course* I will."

As she slid back through the granite passage, Lanie tensed up. "Oh man, I gotta go back down that ladder of doom, don't I?"

Hudson smiled. "Should be easy this time, yeah?"

She twisted her lips to one side, staring toward the ladder hanging in the void. "Ugh...."

Amanda stood near the edge, waiting. "I'll go down last, so I can turn off the lanterns. Going down is a little tougher. You need to have both hands tight on the ladder before you step onto it. Gotta pull the ladder in to step onto it."

When she looked at the ladder hanging in the dark shaft, anxiety pulsed through Lanie's limbs. She couldn't make herself step out to the edge. "I don't think I can do it. Are you sure there's no other way out of here?"

"Well, we can't get through the doors on the platform, so you either jump off the waterfall or go this way," Amanda replied. "You can do it."

"Take a few minutes, get focused," Hudson said. "I'll go down first and steady the ladder for you."

"No... I'll just do it," Lanie said. Clenching her fists with resolve, she looked at the ladder, then the sloped ledge. Crouching low, she inched out to the ladder and hooked it with the toe of her shoe. Her palms were already clammy when she clamped the rungs. She watched Amanda with wide eyes as she stepped on with her left foot. Her brain kept reminding her of the distance below. *Eighty feet... Eighty feet...* The weight of the ladder began to draw her out into the void, and her right foot started slipping away from the ledge. Lanie sucked in a breath, and she felt her body go rigid.

"It's normal; that's what you want. Just get both feet on, and let the ladder slide out into the shaft," Amanda said.

Lanie stood stiffly on the rung, and the ladder rolled and swayed when it slid into the cavern. Then her weight shifted, and the ladder twisted toward the cavern wall, nearly throwing Lanie off. She squealed, hugging the ladder as it swung. She didn't look down, but instead waited for her fear to taper.

"OK, you're gonna have to use your foot to spin the ladder back around," Amanda said calmly. After some deliberation, Lanie pushed off the cavern wall with her shoe, and the ladder rotated. Lanie's shallow breathing could be heard by Amanda and Hudson, but she didn't care.

"You got it. You're good to go now," Amanda said.

One hand and one foot at a time, Lanie started down. She focused on each individual activity. "Release, move, grip, release, move, grip...." After a few feet of descent, the fear morphed into determination, and Lanie started to feel stronger. When her feet touched down on the cavern floor, she knew she wouldn't fear heights again.

She steadied the ladder as Hudson and Amanda descended, then the group began their return trip. After several quiet minutes during their hike through the passage, Lanie said to the others, "If I hadn't been so freaked out, I probably wouldn't have rolled the ladder around. I'd have been down in only a couple minutes—no drama."

"You're right," Amanda said without looking back. "Most people get a few scares before they figure out that fear makes the climb twice as dangerous, and some people *fall* before they figure it out."

"It would have taken Amanda and I only an hour to return with emergency help if you fell. No biggie," Hudson joked.

Lanie swatted his shoulder as he walked past. "You're hilarious, but-thead. Just keep walking."

When they reached the lagoon in the park, Amanda led them up onto the maze of pathways amongst the cliffside buildings. The narrow paths and stairways were lit by lampposts under a permanent night sky. Lanie passed a small stainless-steel-clad storefront that had small appliances and kitchen utensils lined up in its window. Another offered dated evening wear. Each storefront had a unique style, but all seemed to incorporate a modern, metallic architectural element that contrasted the carved stone on either side. There was almost no wood used, and Lanie realized the mixture of steel, glass, and rock was what an early settlement on another planet might look like.

The paths amongst the shops meandered through narrow stone channels and walls, but there were occasional wide spots and terraces that had benches or small tables.

"If people had to spend months or years down here, I imagine there would need to be tons of different places to hang out," Lanie observed, stopping at one of the tables. It overlooked a ball field in the park below.

"Yeah, my dad said that lots of studies were done to determine how to make people more comfortable, so that they didn't become anxious or unruly while they lived together down here."

"Geez, like ants in an ant farm?" Hudson considered.

"It doesn't seem like it would be *THAT* bad," Lanie said. "This is nicer than many people's neighborhoods. I might miss the sunlight, but I think I could get along down here for a while."

"Heh, we'll come through here when the floodlights are on next time. Yeah, you'll miss the sun. The floodlights are intense, but they don't feel natural," Amanda added. "It's just like being in a football stadium at night, that's all."

"Oh look, a little bakery shop!" Lanie said, pointing to a small glassed-in café. There were painted plaster cupcake and cookie figures along the ledge over the glass. The figures cast bizarre conflicting shadows down on the three explorers. Lanie wasn't sure if the little shop was comforting or creepy.

"This is one of Esther's favorite shops," Amanda said. "At Christmastime the shop gets stocked with tasty stuff, and Esther kinda runs it. That's one of the traditional things she does for the crew."

"She *bakes*?" Lanie couldn't imagine Esther in a baker's hat and apron standing at the counter.

"Ohhh yeaahh," Amanda said with a warm smile. "And she's good at it. Though I think she gets some help from one of the crew's commissary chefs."

The group continued up the paths, passing dormant clothiers, shoe shops, and even a hobby shop whose window was crowded with vintage toys and crafts.

Amanda led them through an arched passage to a steel door, which opened into a wide concrete tunnel. It was as though they'd stepped into a different dimension because the intimate, dark space they'd just exited was the opposite of the brightly lit corridor that stretched out of sight in either direction. The walls were lined with piping of various sizes and colors. The service corridor was coated in glossy gray paint and was big enough to drive a vehicle through.

"Whatcha think, a pretty different world down here, huh? Imagine being six years old, riding around down here in a golf cart with your dad."

They'd started walking and passed a fenced chamber with four huge gray pump motors standing on vertical pipes. The motors whirred in a low industrious hum that was accompanied by a slight tremble in the corridor's floor.

"What are those pumps for? Hudson asked.

"There are eight circulation stations around the site," Amanda said. "The water has to stay moving; it gets pumped from cavern to cavern to exchange air, and I think it stops bacteria growth." She twisted her lips, trying to remember if she had her facts straight. "This is a small station. There's a bigger pump station near the biodome."

"This place is berserk," Hudson said. "And we haven't even seen the most intense parts. I can't believe you grew up exploring these caverns."

"What I can't believe is how you've managed to keep it secret," Lanie said. "I mean, between friends and relatives, I don't know how you didn't slip up." In a sudden change of topic, Lanie asked, "Does your mom live here too?"

"I don't really know my mom," Amanda said, examining her dirty hands. "My parents split up when I was a baby and my dad moved here to take this job. They were both in the military together. My dad had special security clearance at the base where he worked, and he got recruited to be part of this place. Before I was born, he was stationed at a place called the Cheyenne Mountain Complex in Colorado." She looked up at Lanie and added, "I think I probably slipped up once or twice at first, but who's gonna believe a little kid if they say they live in a secret underground city?"

"Good point," Hudson said.

Amanda led the group into a small staging stockroom that had caged supply shelves and a loading dock for Atom transports. "You guys can catch the Atom back home from here. Maybe we can hook up later in the week?"

"I kinda have a better idea," Lanie said, smiling at Hudson, then turning to Amanda. "You wanna come for dinner tonight?"

Amanda looked both surprised and flattered. "Really?! That would be awesome! Oh wow, thanks, I'd sure like to." She hugged Lanie, then bounded up onto the Atom platform. Hudson and Lanie swapped a curious look, surprised that she'd turned away so quickly after the invite. Amanda opened a small metal box which was anchored to the station console. A bulky yellowish telephone handset was inside. It had a rotary dial on the microphone end. Amanda dialed in a short series of numbers, then smiled when she held it to her ear.

"Hi, Dad!" she said into the handset. "Yeah, I'm with them. We're at the logistics room on LL30." A brief shiver rattled her body as she listened to her dad on the other end of the line. "Yeah, I know, I did it already. That's why I called. Can I go to the executive residence for dinner? Lanie invited me."

Amanda's eyes wandered the room as she listened to directions over the phone, and a grin spread on her face. "I will. Thanks, Dad, see you tonight."

Lanie raised her eyebrows over her glasses and leaned toward Amanda, who was placing the phone back in its compartment. "So? He said yes, right?"

Amanda spun around and stomped her feet, wiggling with excitement. "Yes!"

Hudson looked excited too, though he seemed to be trying to play it cool. "You'll stay for dinner too then?" Lanie asked him.

"I'm sure it's fine; I'll call when we get back to your house."

Lanie made an eager churning motion with her hands. "It'll be a big group; we can use the dining room."

Hudson had summoned an Atom, which entered through an opening in the wall. "Can you come with us right now? Or do you need to go home first?" he asked Amanda.

Amanda looked down at her dusty socks and reached up to the barrettes in her wavy hair. Lanie guessed she was assessing her condition as best she could without a mirror.

"You look fine; you can clean up at my house," she said, throwing an arm around Amanda's shoulders.

In the wall near the desk that Amanda had just made her call from, a compartment with a metal sliding door caught Lanie's eye. It was nearly identical to the one at her desk. She tugged Amanda's shirt sleeve before stepping into the Atom.

"What is that little cubby in the wall? There's a couple like it up in my house."

"That's the IWIT system," Amanda replied.

"Eye-wit?" Hudson repeated.

"I-W-I-T. It means Inter Ward Item Transfer... at least I think that's right," Amanda said. "Basically, a little shuttle to send stuff all over the site. They get flung from one station to the next by some kinda magnetic slingshot."

"Well, THAT explains a lot," Lanie said, rolling her eyes at Hudson. As they whizzed through the tunnels and stations, Lanie turned and hooked her elbow over the seatback to address Amanda.

"How come you don't have a key card for the Atom? Your dad must have one?"

"He does, but he doesn't need to come this far from the plant often. He says that if he rides everywhere, he won't see things that are broken. So, he usually walks the corridors."

"That's probably smart," Lanie said, staring out the window. They were slowing to make the elevator trip up. "But I thought you said you can't get to some places without the Atom?"

"Only a few," Amanda's eyes darted around as she searched her memory. "Your house is isolated; the motorway is the only way to get in... at least I think so. Cmmand center is also isolated; it's in a group of caverns that are a half-mile from the main complex." She squinted her eyes. "My dad says there might be a foot passage that leads from the executive residence to the command center, but it's not on any drawings."

"We'll show you the lounge and offices under Lanie's house—they're awesome," Hudson bragged. "We're gonna make the lounge our home base."

In the corridor outside the reception office, the threesome bumped into Mr. Speros, who was just emerging from the office door. "Oh! There you are. I was looking for you both." He smiled when he saw their new guest. "I'm guessing this is Amanda?"

"Yeah, she's staying for dinner, if you're cool with it," Lanie said, not giving her dad much of an option to refuse.

"Sure. We'll do it up nice tonight," he replied. "You and your whole fam are also welcome, of course," Lanie's dad said, turning to Hudson.

"My parents are going out tonight, but I'll call Helen," Hudson said, then he cocked his head toward Amanda. "You finally get to meet my pushy sister," he said with a crooked smile.

"You're all helping with dinner tonight. Come up in about an hour," Mr. Speros told Lanie.

The three friends proceeded down to the lounge, where they sat in the oversize leather chairs. Hudson had powered up the Wurlitzer jukebox, and Lanie selected a pair of songs by Elvis Presley—one of the few artists on the playlist that she recognized.

While Hudson queried Amanda about her school and daily routine, Lanie stood and walked back to the bar, having spied a large color portrait of four people on the wall. She hadn't noticed it before. Right away, she knew the photo was of the site principals. A brass plate at the bottom of the frame read "1961." The photo had yellowed a bit, but still conveyed the enthusiasm in the faces of the four chief engineers. Lanie picked out Esther first, in a white knee skirt and black fuzzy sweater—just as she had imagined.

Where Esther's chubby jowls were now, Lanie saw soft dimples in the photo, but the smile was the same. Thinner in her early twenties, Esther stood next to a heavy man in a ubiquitous black pencil tie and black-rimmed glasses. Lanie figured this was Mike Donahue; she recognized his hairline—it had already begun receding in 1961.

The second man, who would have been Marty Leistra, was a dashing young example of 1950s style; he wore a Hawaiian-patterned shirt untucked, with a black-banded Panama hat and jet-black moustache. At the far left, Lanie saw a beautiful African American woman.

"Wanda," Lanie whispered.

Wanda had bowed lips, a button nose, and a piercing gaze that seemed to cross the time gap of the photo. Wanda looked more modern and familiar to Lanie, as though the elegant woman had traveled through time to be part of the photo. Lanie was imagining the group sitting at the bar where she stood, enjoying drinks, and comparing notes after a long day at the bustling site. Her thoughts were interrupted by the ringing of a bell. The ringing stopped, and then started again.

Lanie looked at Hudson, who was as perplexed as she was.

"That's a site phone," Amanda said, waving a finger around the room. "Find it... somebody's calling!"

Lanie followed the sound behind the bar. Hidden behind a row of neatly stacked cordial glasses was a black telephone. Its red light was flashing along with each ring.

"Hello?" she said, trying to sound natural.

On the other end of the line, she recognized her dad's voice. "Bring your crew up here. We need to start dinner and set the dining room."

Lanie's voice stiffened. "Where in the world are you calling from?"

Hudson watched her, looking for clues about the mystery call.

"There's a call box in the kitchen passageway next to the stove. Now come on up," Mr. Speros said, then the line went dead.

Lanie set the receiver back on its cradle. "We gotta get started on dinner; you guys are gonna help."

Amanda's eyes were wide as she walked into the house. She smiled when she saw the vista behind the yard, then spun around to see the period décor, geometric wallpaper patterns, and floating glass walls. "This is even cooler than I imagined in my mind," she said. "You have the most awesome house in the world."

"Thanks, I think it's pretty awesome too." She offered to show Amanda around. Isaiah was watching a show with puppets, who were demonstrating how to count by twos.

"This is my little brother, Isaiah," she said as they passed through the den. "He's a nice little guy, and I love him lots." Lanie wrapped her brother in her arms and cradled him back and forth on the couch.

He wriggled loose, trying to see the screen around Lanie's hair.

"Hi, Lay-Lay," he said. After a quick first glance at Amanda, Isaiah looked up again, intrigued by their guest. "Who are you?" he asked, smiling.

"I'm Amanda. Nice to meet you, Isaiah," she said, shaking his little hand.

"You're pretty!" he said, digging in his nose.

"Thank you very much," Amanda giggled.

After they'd toured the house, Lanie and Amanda started peeling and slicing carrots in the kitchen while Hudson set the white marble table in the dining room.

Sabine showed up half an hour later, after the girls had gotten the carrots into the pot. They were tearing leaves and cutting tomatoes for a salad when Sabine hauled a couple canvas shopping bags into the kitchen. She greeted Lanie with her usual hug and was surprised to see Amanda.

"Hi, there!" she said, offering a slender hand to Amanda. "Looks like there's another special guest tonight besides me!"

"This is Amanda. She's a new friend... from... school." Just then, Lanie wondered how long and how complicated it would be to hide the truth from people as she grew older.

"Nice to meet you! Well, we certainly have enough food," Sabine said, pulling a lump wrapped in white paper from one of the bags. "I have to season this tri tip roast before we stick it in the oven. It doesn't have to cook long."

Sabine began pulling open cabinet doors around the oven, and Lanie became concerned. "What are you looking for?" she asked.

"I need a roasting pan—just a little one."

Lanie slid over and pulled out the steel drawer under the stacked ovens, revealing the shallow pans.

"Ah... perfect, thanks!" Sabine arranged the roast, and then rummaged in the other bag. "Where's your pops, anyway?"

"I think he's in the garage."

"OK I'll go see him in a few," Sabine said. "Since he's not here, I'll just ask you myself. Can you and I do a ladies' night on Wednesday?" She winked a long-lashed eye at Lanie. "I heard your dad's taking Isaiah to his friend's birthday party. You and I can do our own thing. Whatcha think?"

"Sure, that'd be cool," Lanie said. She was being half honest. Her dad had tipped her off about the idea, so Lanie was expecting the invitation. It would be fine. Sabine was so outgoing, Lanie figured her own contributions to their conversations would be brief. She just hoped that Sabine wasn't going to use the evening to ask Lanie to adopt her into the family in a permanent, motherly role.

The group dinner was a success that night. Sabine's tri-tip was medium rare, just as Mr. Speros preferred, and nearly all the food disappeared as the group ate and talked. Because Sabine was present, very little of the discussion could focus on Amanda's home life. This made it tough for her to answer all but the most basic questions about herself. Beforehand, the three friends agreed that their story would be that Amanda lived in a neighborhood on the other side of town.

"Arcadia Heights?" Sabine said to Amanda with a thoughtful lip twist. "Hmm, I don't know that neighborhood. Ah well, I'm glad you all connected, 'cause it sure seems like it's working out well. You guys are a pretty tight team already."

The three friends looked at each other along their side of the table. "Yeah, it worked out awesome," Lanie said, elbowing Amanda with a smile. "I'm teaching Hudson how to drive the *right* way, and Amanda's going to show me how to rock climb."

"Great... not *another* hobby," Mr. Speros said as he cut Isaiah's meat. "Your hobbies already take up too much garage space! If you get into something else, I'm gonna have to put a car out."

Dinner wrapped up earlier than Lanie had anticipated, which was great because she'd have some time to spend with Hudson and Amanda on her own. Helen was at Amy's, so it would just be the three of them. Mr. Speros gave Lanie a pass on helping clean the kitchen, since she had guests, so she and her two visitors pretended to leave through the front door, then doubled back into the guest room. Amanda hadn't seen that passage yet and her face glowed with admiration. "This place is amazing!" she said as the bookcase swung closed behind them.

Back in the lounge, they found a neatly folded note on the bar top that read "check the refrigerator." In the lounge's small kitchen, Hudson pulled the old Frigidaire's door open with the girls looking over his shoulder. It had been stocked with cold snacks and a glass pitcher of pink liquid. On the top shelf, a plate of carefully frosted sugar cookies displayed a second note.

Lanie lifted the note, which read in tidy cursive: "Welcome to the Site 4 Team." It was signed by Esther and several others—whose names she and Hudson didn't recognize.

Amanda reached past Lanie and grabbed the pitcher. "Oooh, I know who made this," she said, smiling at the other two. "Grab some glasses," she said to Lanie.

"What is that?" Hudson asked, pointing to the pitcher.

"This is Radwood's Saguaro Cider," Amanda replied. "Simpson Radwood is the manager of horticulture. He's a crabby old geezer, but he knows lots of Pima tribal secrets. He's part of the Akimel O'odham tribe. He makes this cider from saguaro cactus blossoms, and it's amazing. Usually Mr. Radwood only makes it around holidays unless Esther asks him to make a special batch."

Lanie held up a glass to the light then sipped. "Oh, wow, this *is* awesome! Kinda like an apple and passionfruit juice mix!"

The threesome returned to the leather chairs near the dormant fireplace and settled in with cider and cookies. "Do you have friends from your school in Scottsdale?" Hudson asked.

"Yeah, I have a couple friends I hang out with when I'm on campus," Amanda replied. "But it's been tough because I can't invite anyone over. They probably think I live in a van or something. Whenever they ask to come over, I have to say no." She looked dejected. "We have to live at the site 'cause my dad is on-call 24/7. It's hard to have a best friend when you can't just walk down the block to be with them."

Lanie and Hudson both spoke up at the same time, talking over one another.

"Well, you've got best friends now," Lanie said. Hudson had said something similar. Lanie saw Amanda's eyes moisten, and she stared down at her napkin.

"You guys are never allowed to move," Amanda said, without looking up. She swiped her finger under her eye, trying to hide her emotion. "I hope your parents are cool with you never leaving the nest!"

"I'm not going *anywhere*," said Lanie.

"Ditto," Hudson said. "My dad's as excited about this place as we are—we won't be moving."

Lanie then brought up a topic that she thought might be sensitive. "Why didn't Esther ask you to do the same training that she's going to have us do?"

"I don't know," Amanda said. "I didn't know there *was* training until I met you guys. But I can tell you right now that my dad probably told her I couldn't be part of it."

"Why?" Disbelief cracked Hudson's voice. "You could even be helping to train *us*!"

"My dad is hoping I'll go to college and live a normal life after high school; he doesn't want me to spend my life down here like he is."

That made enough sense to Lanie. "Well, we're still gonna go to college too," she said. "But after being part of this growing up, I think a 'normal' life might be kinda boring for you."

Amanda didn't say anything but nodded. Lanie figured it was best not to dwell on the topic. She shot a glance to Hudson that said as much. "Anyway, we think we can learn a lot from you, and where we go, you'll go too."

Hudson nodded his head in agreement.

"I'll show you everything I know," Amanda said. "I promise!"

"Deal," Hudson said. "Lanie and I do things together, and so will the three of us now."

He held up a fist, and the three of them bumped together over the green glow of the lampshade in the center of the table.

# Chapter 21

# THE NORTH GATE

Hudson's mind wasn't with them as he and Lanie walked to school Monday morning. He was staring at the sidewalk in front of his feet and had spoken very little. A low fog was limiting visibility, but the sun was burning it off.

"Whatcha thinkin' about?" Lanie asked.

"Nothin."

That obviously wasn't true. He looked like he wanted advice, and Lanie wondered why he wouldn't ask her. Wasn't she his best friend? Yes— she was. It was clear he felt torn about *something*.

It didn't take long for Lanie to connect the dots in her mind. The only topics a guy would hesitate to discuss with his female best friend would be intimate. *He had a crush on Amanda.* It was so obvious, Lanie felt dense for not thinking of it right away. She followed Hudson's logic, and his predicament became apparent: their new three-way friendship was going to grow strong, but Lanie knew that mixing in a crush would *probably* make things weird.

Not probably... *definitely.*

She pursed her lips and focused on the dew-covered grass of the school fields ahead. *Maybe the crush will pass,* she thought. She'd had crushes on boys before, but after spending time with them in class—or at events—the feeling would fade. Either way, Lanie figured it was best to just give Hudson some time, so she didn't press for details.

"Well... just so you know, you can talk to me about anything, right?"

"Yeah, I know, thanks," Hudson replied.

"Where's Helen?"

"My mom drove her to school early," Hudson said. "They needed to meet with the yearbook crew to compile pics from the formal."

*The photo!* She'd nearly forgotten about the picture they'd taken in the library and looked forward to seeing a copy. When the bell rang for third hour, Lanie bolted to the science lab because it was the class she shared with Helen. Snaking a path into the room past the crowded lockers, Lanie spotted Helen coming in through the opposite door.

"Hey!" she yelled, waving above the crowd.

Helen cut across the room, bulldozing at least three other students from her path. "Oh man," she said to Lanie with an impish grin. "Wait 'til you see what I have."

They sat down at adjacent desks and Helen began rummaging in her oversized tote bag. She produced a haggard green file folder and handed it to Lanie as though it were a priceless historic document.

Lanie saw what she was expecting to see when she opened the folder, and it made her flush with pride. The large library photo from the Harvest Formal was better than Lanie had imagined in her mind's eye. She thought the group looked positively heroic. The comfortable smiles on their faces told the whole story of the successful evening, and the image was perfect.

Looking up at Helen, Lanie's expression said everything she felt.

"I know, right?" Helen said. "That picture will be hard to outdo—ever!"

"I'm getting this framed, like *this week*," Lanie said, sliding the photo back into the folder. There was so much going on in her life now, Lanie couldn't believe that only a month prior, a busy day for her would have been designing scale models or car parts to 3D-print in the garage.

When Lanie caught up with Hudson and Helen after school, the discussion topic for their walk home was the gossip from the previous weekend's formal. Lanie's fashion debut was a popular thread in Helen's social network, and she was itching to tell Lanie about it.

"I had a lot of kids today asking me who I was with at the dance, and they weren't talking about Lance," Helen said through a laugh. "I think Danny is gonna have some competition next time we have a formal."

Lanie was flattered but was honest with Helen. "That night was a one-time thing," Lanie said. "I'm not gonna try to keep up with you and Amy's wardrobes."

"Well, if you wanna dress like a hobo the rest of the year, that's *your* deal, but I'm sure glad we did it," Helen said.

"Yep. See, like I told you, I can look decent when I need to. Oh, and by the way, thank you for all your help." Lanie realized that she hadn't shown any appreciation for Helen's assistance. "I couldn't have looked as good without you. I'm buying at Red Rocks this week," she promised.

"I'm in for that!" Helen replied. "And don't worry, I didn't forget—I'll help you mop your dungeon this weekend."

"Uhh... it's OK," Lanie said. "I'll give you a pass; you don't need to clean it." She looked out of the side of her eye at Hudson.

As they passed the Newmans' house, Lanie could see the black Tesla's mouthless face watching them from the curb up the street. Hudson had seen it too, so they both waved goodbye to Helen and headed up the sidewalk together. The driver's name was Adam, and he stepped out as they approached, greeting them in his usual, formal fashion.

"Ms. Speros, Mr. Newman, good afternoon."

Lanie wondered what he did when he wasn't driving Esther around. She pictured him sitting on a scruffy couch in a sleeveless tee shirt, drinking beer, and she spontaneously snickered through her nose, nearly blowing snot on her forearm.

"Hi, Adam," Hudson said, offering his hand. This was a non-standard greeting, and Adam hesitated before accepting Hudson's gesture. He dispatched the handshake and resumed his posture next to the car, but he didn't open Esther's door. Instead, she rolled her window down.

"Hello, you two. Hop in."

When Lanie sat into the back seat, she found Esther wearing her usual black ensemble. She was also sporting a silver brooch with an emerald cluster in the shape of a wriggling lizard. The design was common in Native American art, but Lanie didn't know the significance.

"The gecko symbolizes rebirth," Esther said, catching Lanie's stare. "It reminds me of you two."

"Plus, I think it looks lovely," she added with a smile. "So, how was your school event?"

"It was really cool... much more fun than I was expecting," Lanie said. "Oh! That reminds me," she added, remembering the star charts on the table at the formal. "What's the deal with the entryway at my house? That big astrological layout on the floor is more than just decoration, isn't it?"

Esther smiled appreciatively. "Once I heard that you and your dad could read Greek, I figured that some of the floor's details might stand out."

"Yeah, I figured out that it's a kind of celestial clock, but I haven't told my dad," Lanie said.

"Very sharp observation. You're not that far off," Esther said. "The light that gets focused on the floor in that room provides seasonal information to the command center, and the layout of the floor and the windows above must remain unchanged. Without input from that room, after months or years underground, the site residents would likely lose track of dates and seasons. There's more to the entryway than that, but I'll let you investigate on your own for the rest," she said.

Adam guided the Tesla down to the traffic light, where they waited to turn. "We're not going into the site today?" Hudson asked.

"Oh, we are. We're going in through the north gate. You'll both need to know how to get there, and so will your parents." From a pouch within her bag, she produced two thin ID cards, which she handed to the two friends. Lanie saw an unflattering photo of herself in the left upper corner, to the right of which was her full name. Under her name there was additional text in a small, block font:

### LANIE MARION SPEROS
### SECURITY CLEARANCE 4 – PRINCIPAL

#### FORT MCDOWELL – BRAVO GATE
#### UNITED STATES DEPARTMENT OF THE INTERIOR

On the bottom corner was a small seal showing a buffalo standing before a setting sun, but next to that, a similarly sized Myriad Exploration Group logo was embossed. This logo was different than the others she'd seen. In the middle of the logo, a gold leaf "P4M" was laid in.

"What are these for?" Lanie asked, turning the badge over. There was a brown magnetic strip on the back.

"You must have these to enter the base to access the Omega site's north gate, and you need them to get out as well. Guard that badge like you would your passport, but keep it with you wherever you go. Oh, and I finally have these ready for you as well." She pulled two square boxes from her bag.

Lanie opened the glossy blue box and found a black device that looked like a smartphone which had been cut in half. She and Hudson pulled them out, examining them curiously. It looked more like a black glass coffee-table coaster than a phone. Lanie touched the screen, and an animated, shimmering Omega emblem appeared. Then she was prompted for a pass code.

"Last four of your Social Security number, last two of your house numbers," Esther advised. "They have apps just like a smartphone. Motorola made them for us, so they should be intuitive for you to use. Unlike your own phones, these com units will work in the Omega site. Keep them on your person at all times so I can reach you *directly* in an emergency."

"Even in school?" Hudson asked. He logged into his square device and went to work on it.

"*Especially* in school," Esther responded. "You both need to understand that when you start this training, your lives will be different. You'll be more like government agents than junior high students. It will require a reset of your priorities and behavior, especially after you start high school next year." She smiled to lighten the mood. "I'm not asking you to skip your early teen years and the important milestones they bring. But, you must be ready to switch into Omega representatives at any moment. I know you can do it; that's why we're all sitting in this car together."

"That reminds me," Lanie added. "Our principal at school called Hudson and I in today."

"Did she?" Esther said, smiling.

"Yeah, she says that you are partnering with the school district to offer special classes like drafting, metal working, and programming."

"The classes sounded pretty cool," Hudson said.

"Most junior high schools used to have vocational classes like those; it wasn't a stretch for me to pull that string," Esther said. "But the classes I'm working on for your high school district are tougher. Most of your advanced training will be done at Site 4 by the Omega staff, but there are some classes that you'd be better off taking with other students in a civilian setting."

Adam had driven into the desert north of town and Lanie noticed they'd entered the Fort McDowell Yavapai reservation. Remembering what she'd meant to ask earlier, Lanie spoke up. "Why didn't Amanda get picked like us, to learn to be a principal?" She realized then that she didn't know Amanda's last name.

Hudson glanced at Lanie, concerned that she may have broached a sensitive topic. But Esther's expression didn't flinch.

"I figured there was a chance you'd meet Amanda before I was able to introduce you. She's a wonderful girl. Fearless, and brave as a warrior—like you," Esther said.

"Ms. Reyes also has *your* calculated, laser-like focus under pressure," she said to Hudson, peering around the headrest into the front seat. "Unfortunately," she continued, "her dad has made it clear that he'd like his daughter to explore a more *conventional* career path and lifestyle, and I must respect that; I *want* to respect that."

She sighed and patted Lanie's hand on the seat. "Just the same, I hope you both will stay close with her, and use her as a resource. She can learn a lot from you as well. You can—and should—protect each other. Who knows, maybe someday her circumstances will change."

Thinking of Amanda, Lanie's eyes wandered through the landscape outside. Adam had slowed for a fork in the road, then accelerated down a narrow, empty highway. Only a couple miles up the road, he lifted his foot off the accelerator and began coasting. Lanie looked ahead and saw that a black Porsche Cayenne SUV was stopped along the roadside. A brunette woman in a ball cap stood near the Porsche on the shoulder, waving. Though he remained focused on the road, Adam reached his right hand into the center console and kept it there as they approached the woman and her SUV. Lanie looked at Esther and found her sitting erect, intently studying the stranded woman.

"Adam...," Esther said, in an urgent but low voice. Then she nudged his shoulder.

"Understood," Adam replied, then he stomped his foot on the accelerator.

Lanie's head was slapped into the headrest and her internal organs seemed to flatten against her spine under the force of the Tesla's dual motors. Even though the roadside situation looked suspicious to Lanie, she hadn't arrived at her own conclusion yet when Adam reacted.

Just as they overtook the SUV, a man emerged from the front door holding an automatic rifle and began firing at the side of the Tesla. Lanie screamed and lay over into Esther's lap as a series of cracks and pops echoed through the car. As soon as the shooting had started, it was over. The Tesla was moving at a phenomenal rate, and Lanie sat up, searching herself for bullet perforations.

"Hudson! Are you OK?!" she yelled.

"I'm OK, I'm OK!" he said, turning back with a look of horror.

Esther smiled thinly. "*Of course* you're OK... the car is armored."

Adam removed his hand from the center console, where Lanie saw the satin nickel grip of a large, semiautomatic handgun. He closed the arm-rest's lid and focused on the road ahead. They shot past an open gate in a fence. A big yellow warning sign was posted at the gate, but they passed it so quickly, Lanie couldn't read the print.

When Adam reached his desired cruising speed, the Tesla twitched and undulated as the highway was devoured underneath the car. Lanie stared at Esther, then checked their speed on the Tesla's center display. One hundred twenty-six miles per hour. In the rearview mirror she could see a fantail of dust being whipped from the roadside behind them—and farther back, the Porsche.

"We're gonna shake them," Esther said. "If you think this is exciting, try it in a '59 Impala!" Her eyes narrowed as she laughed from her belly.

Lanie couldn't comprehend the humor that Esther seemed to find in their situation. She looked back to Hudson, who wore the anxious expression of a person who'd unwittingly gotten into a vehicle with a group of escaping bank robbers.

At the speed they were traveling, the mountains ahead approached quickly. The Porsche had caught up, and its driver bumped the Tesla's rear, attempting to force the sedan off the road. Lanie heard the crackling sound of the car's rear fascia and taillights being broken, but she didn't turn back. She scrunched down into her seat, pushing her knees into Adam's seatback.

"It'll be fine; we'll be rid of them shortly," Esther said.

Before they reached the foothills, another high fence came into view. It extended to the horizon in both directions. Unlike the first fence they'd passed, this one had two rows of silvery barbed wire along the top. The electric sedan was not decelerating when they came upon a guarded opening in the boundary.

Esther held her phone up to her ear momentarily and said, "Sierra Tango, ten-thirty-two. Admit us—then stand by."

A small checkpoint booth stood near the road, so small it couldn't possibly accommodate more than one standing person. As they drew closer, Adam planted the accelerator again and they began to pull away from the Porsche. They thundered past the guard station at one hundred forty miles per hour, so fast that Lanie couldn't tell if the guard stationed at the kiosk was male or female. Only then did Lanie turn to look back.

Immediately after they cleared the gate, a steel plate lifted from the road, forming a wedge, with the vertical side facing the Porsche. Lanie's mouth dropped open, and she heard Hudson exhale in shock as they both watched the Porsche flatten into the face of the barrier. A gray mist of debris and smoke enveloped the whole checkpoint. The Porsche seemed to stop undramatically, but Lanie knew it was an illusion created by their distance—the checkpoint was probably a chaotic mess of smoke and wreckage.

She turned around, speechless, just in time to see a black Chevy Suburban race past them in the opposite direction. Red and blue lights flashed within its grille. Both Lanie and Hudson looked at Esther then.

"Our plans for today must change, unfortunately," she said. "We'll get you two home. But don't worry about this situation, it happens from time to time. It will be critically important that you are both ready to deal with the Detractor Group before you're old enough to drive."

"Were those people with the organization you were talking about?" Hudson asked.

"Yes."

Esther picked up her phone again after it vibrated, then addressed who was on the other end of the call. "We are ten-thirty-six... stick with the plan—we'll see you at the office."

"She's using standard radio communication codes," Hudson said to Lanie, who leaned toward the front seat to hear. "She just told someone we don't need any more help."

"You'll both need to learn the codes," Adam said, without taking his eyes from the road.

"What is 'Sierra Tango'?" Hudson asked.

"It's the Omega code for *surface threat*," Adam replied.

Adam slowed as they entered the base, and within a few minutes they'd crested a hill, which exposed an isolated valley below. As flat and devoid of life as an ancient lakebed, the valley contained a small group of vacant buildings, surrounded by a decrepit network of roads. A broad parking lot held groups of large military vehicles. The olive-drab trucks stood resolutely under the sun, saluting the Tesla as they entered the building area.

Tan brick structures with clusters of rectangular windows stood on either side of the road, facing each other in an endless stare, watching one another's painted trim peel. Their windows were hazed with years of inactivity, and generations of dried tumbleweeds blocked entryways. Wild jacaranda trees had sprouted in sidewalk gaps. Their purple flowers were the only cheerful color Lanie's eye found in the dystopic scene.

Adam didn't stop here; the group continued through the vacant town without slowing. The tired asphalt continued to the edge of the valley, where it abruptly widened into a newer three-lane ribbon of blacktop. The wider road disappeared into a tunnel at the foot of the mountainside.

When the Tesla passed under the concrete tunnel abutment, Lanie's vision went black. A few seconds passed before her eyes adjusted to the low light. The road within the tunnel was descending in a curve, which stopped daylight from reaching around the corner. Ahead, the hangar doors of the entry terminal came into view. Their enormous gray sliding panels began to open as the car approached.

Inside the cavern, Lanie was expecting they'd stop at the Atom dock near the transportation garage, but instead they drove into the shadows in an opposite corner. Hidden there by a rock outcropping was a large elevator door. Adam guided the car into the lift and reached through his window to a control box hanging from an overhead wire.

No one spoke while the car was lowered. When the doors ahead opened, Adam drove out onto a pitch-dark roadway with a guard rail along the left edge. The cavern was so dark, only the headlight-lit road ahead was visible.

"Where are we? What's in here?" Lanie asked, holding her hands up to the window.

"This is Black Lake," Esther said. "The water reservoir for the site."

Lanie couldn't even see a glimmer of still water—they may as well have been driving through outer space. The dark road forked, and Adam veered off into a narrow side tunnel. Within a quarter mile, the passage opened into a large round gallery with a high ceiling, braced by concrete arches arranged like the spokes of a wheel. The cavern was at least four hundred feet in diameter, and their road formed a circle near the perimeter. Between the road and the cavern wall were many parking spaces, and Lanie was surprised to see them occupied with modern vehicles. Most were Chevrolet trucks and SUVs, wearing U.S. Government license plates.

In the center of the circular roadway were wider parking bays that surrounded a circular office building which extended from the floor to the cavern's ceiling. The three-story building was the hub of the room and was about fifty feet in diameter. The office's exterior was paneled in dark red metal with bluish glass. A planter of dense tropical foliage surrounded the base of the office building, its greenery at odds with hard surfaces of the surrounding environment. Crisp-white illumination emitted from modern LED lighting on the concrete arches overhead.

Adam parked in one of the wide spaces near the main office door, where a stern-looking older man stood, waiting. The man had gray hair, with streaks of smoky black over his ears. He stood ramrod straight, with his hands at his side. His pale, striped shirt was tucked into equally drab slacks. He was handsome but unremarkable. His complete look appeared to have been taken from one of the elaborately drawn adult comic strips (which never seemed to be funny) in the Sunday newspaper. But more importantly, he was the man Lanie had seen at the mine through her binoculars a few weeks earlier. As Esther stood out of the car, the man's face softened, and the crow's feet around his eyes gave away his weathered, cowboy-like smile.

"Welcome, Ms. Andersen," he said. "The pleasure is mine, as always."

They kissed each other on the cheek, and Esther introduced him. "Friends, this is Arthur Stone, and he's a man you'll learn to love." She grabbed his shoulder, looking into his aged eyes. "Lord knows it took me *thirty years* to warm up to him; hopefully it won't take you that long."

His smile faded, but he was still cordial. "Art, you'll call me Art," he told them.

Lanie and Hudson introduced themselves, shaking Art's hand.

"Esther's briefed me on the two of you. This young woman and I have also seen each other from a distance," he said, smiling at Lanie. "So, these are our fearless new recruits, eh? I guess I was expecting you both to look more minacious."

"Art is the Chief Engineer at this site," Esther said. "Nobody knows more about the infrastructure and life support systems here than Art." She caught herself, raising a jeweled hand to Art's chest. "Well... nobody who's still alive, anyway." After a laugh at her own grim joke, Esther continued, "The crew all report directly to Art. His four subordinate engineers function as both officers and technicians, and each has a small crew reporting to them.

"Art is responsible for keeping this site ready to activate at a minimum level, which is to say the site could be put into use within forty-eight hours if it became necessary. His entire adult life has been spent with this same mission, and he takes his role seriously." Esther showed a steely face to the young friends. "Your job is to help him retire, not make more work for him—keep that in mind."

"Who are we kidding, death will come to me before retirement," Art said to Esther with a sentimental smile. "But she's right." He turned to Lanie and Hudson and his face solidified. "You need to learn. You'll open your ears and listen first. You'll watch with your eyes. You'll ask questions. You won't start any projects or make any changes to systems, not without my oversight, at least for now."

Lanie turned and looked at the Tesla, whose rear plastic bumper fascia was missing. Shiny inch-round divots of bare metal were scattered in the doors on the driver's side. Hudson stood nearby, and he shared a glance with Lanie. They both felt like the attempt on their lives merited a little more concern, but neither said anything.

Sensing the tension, Art put his hand on the two friends' shoulders. "I know this looks scary, but we'll show you how to deal with these types of situations," he said to them. "It is never boring here, but you need to stay vigilant."

"This is the site's administration office," Esther said. "When the site's not active, it's used as the main operations center. Come on in."

As Lanie followed Esther through the entry door, she saw Adam slip away in the damaged Tesla. Inside, the office reminded her of the interior of a science-fiction space station. The walls were paneled in glossy white metal, and the furniture and cabinetry were a shimmering metallic gray with brushed stainless-steel trim. Despite their frigid appearance, the open spaces were comfortable and smelled of coffee and donuts.

The group sat at a white conference table near a bank of elevators and Esther poured herself a cup of coffee. "Those two in the SUV were likely hired by the Detractors," Esther said of their earlier pursuers. She shook her head. "They're a highly organized but small group of people who want to see the Omega Contingency exposed and disbanded. They are our single most important security threat."

"The first generation of Detractors are our age," Art said, motioning to himself and Esther. "There used to be many more of them. But as they've died off, a new generation has continued the fight, though they're a much smaller organization now."

"What's their problem?" Lanie asked.

"Well," Esther said, sharing a cautioned glance with Art, "we'll get into that in a few minutes."

At the gap in the conversation, Hudson took the opportunity to pepper Art with questions. "So, umm, can you explain how the power system for the whole site works? Where's the biodome, and how did all these plants and soil get down here? Who drives all these vehicles? Why is it always the same temperature?" Hudson flipped open his notebook and touched the pen's tip to paper, ready to write.

"Hot dang, son, that's four hours of explanations you just asked for." Art then held up a hand to Hudson. "Don't worry, you don't need to take notes. Jay Reyes will take you down to the turbine hall and energy plant— you'll see it with your own eyes. That's as close to hell as you'll ever be during your life on earth." Art laughed, appearing to share an inside joke with Esther.

"Super-heated steam from fissures in the earth's crust is what spins the turbines," Art continued. We only have two of the six steam turbines running these days; two are down because they need repairs, and we don't have the crew to perform the work. The other two were never commissioned. That's why we can't power up all the wards together; the two turbines won't run it all. You'll learn about those systems during your utilities training."

Hudson was about to insert more questions when Art resumed his explanation. "The energy plant generates our electricity, but also steam to heat water for climate control and other domestic needs. The same system also circulates the air, so we need to import very little atmosphere from the surface."

"Is that why it's so clean in here?" Lanie asked. "There's no dust on anything."

"Bingo," Esther said, looking up from her phone. "We have our own microclimate down here. Convection and gravity naturally filter the air. Without residents stirring up dust, the air will naturally stay pretty clean anyway."

"I thought you said the site had financial savings," Hudson pointed out. "Why can't you hire staff to fix all of these things?"

Art chuckled. "The money's not the problem, son. Finding people who are trustworthy—and who can keep their mouth shut when they're outside the site—is our challenge."

"Does Amanda know about all these systems?" Hudson asked.

"Oh yes," Esther said. "She's seen most everything, but there are some places she shouldn't be, and this will be the same for you two; at least until you've been trained.

"Like the command center?" Lanie asked.

Esther's expression stiffened. "The command center is a different story; I'll train you on that operation myself. You'll meet the site executive when we go to the command center, but I need you to attend a security briefing first. The site executive is the most senior full-time member of the crew. That person is Art's leader and reports directly to me."

"Is the executive the person who manages the regents?" Lanie asked.

"My goodness, you two kids get around, don't you?" Esther said, narrowing her eyes. "I probably don't even want to know what dangerous places you've already explored in the site." She topped off her coffee cup then added, "No, the site executive doesn't manage the regents—but *does* help recruit them. I'm assuming you learned about the regents from Ms. Reyes?"

"Yeah," Hudson said. "Amanda told us they do a different job than the principals."

"They do indeed," Esther replied. "The regents are highly-educated, respected experts in the fields of medicine, science, history, and sociology. They are the people who effectively govern the refugee population if the site must be activated, and they work hand in hand with the principals. The principals are responsible for the site; the regents are responsible for the people who occupy it."

Esther sat back in her chair and looked at Art, then the two friends. "It's too early for you two to learn about these things. A site activation is a highly organized and potentially terrifying operation. The regents are part of mainstream society, and they know they could be called upon at any time, just like the principals. You will never meet them, unless the site is activated. The regents also have no physical knowledge of their assigned site; they only know that it exists and have basic information on how it functions.

"But you should know," Esther added, "that not everybody believes the Omega Contingency was developed with humanity's best interest in mind. Two of our first four regents had a falling-out with the others over a disagreement about which civilians would be admitted to the site in the event of a nuclear attack or natural disaster."

She took a sip from her cup, then continued. "You both need to understand that the sites were constructed—above all other priorities—to establish a place that would preserve human life on earth. The board of directors selected the regents to deal with the human factors. From a prag-matic standpoint, we—the principals—didn't care who occupied this place. We only designed and built it, then ensured it could be filled fast enough in an emergency. But the regents' job is tougher. Their disagreement was never settled."

"And for one regent and his supporters, that disagreement became a life-long crusade to end the Omega Contingency's charter," Art said. "Thankfully, their attempts to expose our operation have mostly gotten them labeled as conspiracy theorists and fanatics, a reputation that the Omega Contingency Board of Directors took as an advantage. Whenever they stage an attack, the Detractors typically hire mercenaries or contrac-tors. The Detractor membership is part of the mainstream population—they typically don't have the courage or skills to execute an attack themselves."

"Well, how much do these people know?" Lanie asked with a con-cerned expression. "Do they know Hudson and I are involved?"

"No," Esther said. "In their current membership, the Detractors are limited in their knowledge of the physical sites, especially this McDowell Mountain Site. They don't know about the executive residence—or about you two—and that's why we need to be diligent in our secrecy."

"As far as we can tell, the only risk to the executive residence would be the family or associates of previous principals—who are all presumed to be deceased, or incarcerated," Art said.

Esther stood and pushed the elevator call button. "I'll send you a debrief on today's incident once I've met with the site executive," she said to Lanie and Hudson. "You'll get debriefs going forward. I'll find you tomor-row to resume our training." Esther smiled as the elevator door closed.

"You both can head home from here," Art said. "We'll pick a different day to see the energy plant and biodome." He pushed the elevator's call button. "Take the elevator to the Atom station on level forty. I'll see you both again soon."

Before leaving them, Art suddenly turned back. "Oh, hang on, I almost forgot something!" He ducked behind the reception desk near the entry and pulled out a small, weathered cardboard box. Wearing a casual smile, he handed the box to Lanie. Inside, she found a mangled Swingline stapler and some fragments from her calculator. She looked back up at Art with one eyebrow raised.

"It took our technician quite a while to remove these remains from the IWIT accelerator near the command center," Art said through a coarse laugh. "The shuttle pushed them for a quarter mile before it finally gave up." His face then stiffened. "Esther will be looking to send notes and items up to the house using that system now, so don't store things in those portals anymore."

Lanie and Hudson watched Art disappear into the adjacent hallway. Lanie abandoned the junk in the adjacent wastebasket before they stepped into the elevator. "Today was freaky," Lanie said, selecting their floor after the doors had closed.

"I'll bet there's always something to deal with around here. I wonder if this is what it's gonna be like for us for the next twenty years?" Hudson said with a weathered expression.

"Twenty?!" Lanie said. "Esther has been doing this for almost sixty years! No wonder she never had a family." She looked at Hudson thoughtfully. "We are gonna need more help here when Esther and these other people are gone. I hope they've got more candidates in mind than just the two of us."

"Yeah, the gravity of this job is starting to sink in a little bit," Hudson said. "But I wouldn't trade it for another job."

"Me neither," Lanie confirmed. "We'll find our help."

The Atom station at level forty was no more than an elevator vestibule facing a small motorway stop. An Atom carriage was already waiting. "We should probably head back toward the house. Anywhere else you wanna stop?" Lanie asked, scanning at the rows of buttons on the Atom console. "I think we have time."

"I wanna go see this mechanical complex Esther mentioned. Maybe if we stop there we can find Amanda's dad?"

"Maybe," Lanie said, pushing the appropriate button.

Lanie and Hudson had barely gotten underway when a red light began flashing on the console's face, accompanied by a buzzing sound.

Hudson pressed the glass button marked *COM* next to it and stammered, "Huh-hello?" His face lit up as Amanda's voice filled the cabin.

"Hey guys, where are you at? Are you done with Esther?" said the voice over the speaker.

"Oh, hey! Yeah, we just finished. She had to run off to deal with an issue. We're on our way to the Mechanical ward," Lanie said.

"Yeah, my dad got the call to meet. I heard something happened on the base," Amanda said. Lanie and Hudson grinned at each other but didn't say anything about their incident.

"We've had some weird surface threat calls in the past couple years," Amanda said. "Sometimes a hiker finds a ventilation shaft and trips a motion detector. Once there was a group of alien abduction crazies trying to drive onto the base at the north gate in an old Volkswagen micro-bus," she added, and her laugh filled the Atom's cabin. "Do you guys wanna meet for a while? I have homework to do, but I figured we could at least say hi if you're down here."

Hudson and Lanie both nodded to each other. "Yes!" Hudson said. "We were gonna try to find your dad, but I guess we could do our homework together in the lounge. Where do you wanna meet?"

"I'll jump in with you at the Residential Tower stop."

The threesome spent the afternoon in the executive suite, looking at old photographs and microfiche. Lanie scanned drawings on the screen while Hudson and Amanda dug through the cabinets.

"Hey, guys, come look at this," Hudson said. "I found a layout for the executive complex. I'm not sure, but it seems like there are tunnels leading away from the house in a couple different directions. Maybe the Atom isn't the only way in and out of this complex!" The drawing had unlabeled rooms and was watermarked with a 'CONFIDENTIAL' stamp across the print.

"This drawing shows the main motorway elevator shaft too, where it connects to the corridor behind our yard," Lanie said, pointing to a box on the center of the diagram. Near the main shaft, the phone-booth-like room Lanie had seen near the elevator door was shown but was unlabeled. It was the room that Esther had called an "emergency service shaft" during their first trip into the site.

"I'll bet the construction team used the mine's original main shaft for the Atom's elevator, which means there might be a hidden access to the surface in that fenced compound," Lanie said, "where the old truck is."

"Oh wow, but look at this tunnel," Hudson said, pointing to an angled corridor that lay under the Speroses' dining room. "Where do you—" He was interrupted by Mr. Speros's entry, along with Mr. Newman.

"Dinner!" Mr. Speros boomed as he held up plastic bags of Chinese takeout. Hudson's appetite eclipsed his interest in the drawing, and the group headed down to the lounge to eat. Around seven o'clock, Mrs. Newman drew the line, and called her two men home. Disappointed at having to cut the evening short, Hudson and Lanie walked Amanda to the Atom terminal.

"Oh check THIS out," Amanda said as Hudson opened the carriage door. She waved a key card at her two friends. "My dad gave me a new card, so I can use the Atom now! Esther met with my dad; she must have softened him up a little."

"Awesome!" Lanie said. "Now you can come over here on your own."

Hudson slid the carriage door closed, and waved goodbye to Amanda.

As the Atom disappeared around the curve, it occurred to Lanie that their new friend was an exceptional, strong personality. Lanie's own confidence was elevated while she, Amanda and Hudson were all together. It was a strange feeling, but she liked it. She could tell that the three of them had started a friendship that would be both lifelong... and critically important.

# Chapter 22

# THE VAULT

Wednesday started out with an ominous monsoon squall, which began as Lanie walked to school. Blowing dust and lightning were common in the evenings during the autumn storm season, but rarely occurred in the morning. It was as though the day was warning her to stay home, Lanie thought. She'd awakened that morning feeling less youthful, as though the previous twenty-four hours had adjusted her perception of what to expect as an Omega Principal. She felt she'd been naïve to think that vast site would simply be a clubhouse for her and Hudson to maintain. Now, there was so much more to consider.

*The Detractors.* The name sounded unpleasant, and its members sounded unreasonable. She and Hudson would be starting self-defense, advanced driving, and weaponry classes soon—something Mr. Speros had been briefed on by Esther. These topics swirled in her mind, and they felt heavy—too heavy for that morning. So she decided to clear her thoughts and process the day hour by hour.

She pulled the hood of her wind breaker over her head as she passed the Rinnases' house. From the corner of her eye, she saw the outline of Mr. Rinnas standing in his front room window. She hadn't seen much of him lately; he'd become a little distant after Mr. Speros had covered the hole in the yard. Mr. Rinnas had been insistent about asking for details, and he knew Lanie and her dad were being cagey with their answers. He didn't wave as Lanie passed; Mr. Rinnas probably thought she couldn't see him.

The clouds were low, sliding overhead as Lanie walked on. The wind was stirring up the fallen leaves, creating eddies in driveways. Helen and Hudson joined her for the walk to school, but they didn't talk much, as the rumbling thunder and wind drowned out any topics that came up. Hudson and Lanie had received text messages from Esther to meet at the mechanical ward that afternoon, with instructions to bring their flashlights. Lanie was looking forward to the meeting, because they'd finally be introduced to Amanda's dad.

The storm stalled over the valley throughout the school day, intermittently splattering the classroom windows with rain. Lanie was preoccupied and restless as she sat in her classes. The obnoxious weather had put her in a weird mood, and she felt like something was off. She had tried to text Amanda a couple times and had no response. On their walk home, Hudson confirmed that he hadn't heard from her either.

"She might have a doctor's appointment, who knows?" Hudson said. "I don't think you need to worry about her."

"You should invite her to Red Rocks with us," Helen said. "You both talk non-stop about her; I wanna get to know her better."

Hudson seemed defensive. "I don't talk *THAT* much about her, come on."

"OK, Hudson, whatever," Helen said, looking at Lanie. Her eyes told Lanie that she knew of Hudson's crush.

The trio split up at the Newmans' house, and Hudson promised he'd be over at five o'clock for their meeting. As Lanie waved goodbye, she turned and spotted Sabine's BMW X3 parked further up the block.

"Shoot!" Lanie muttered to herself. She'd forgotten about the girls' night she'd promised Sabine. Lanie knew that if she called Esther, the night with Sabine would take priority. Esther had been very clear about family obligations. *She's not really family*, Lanie thought as she started up the driveway. *At least not yet.*

In their conversations, Esther hadn't brought up the topic of Lanie's family situation. In fact, Esther seemed to know quite a bit about Lanie's history without ever having asked. Lanie smiled to herself, figuring Esther probably had file folders on everyone in the neighborhood. She sat on the bench near her front door and pulled out her Omega communicator. Because of its bizarre shape, Lanie didn't hold it up to her ear—she used its speakerphone instead. As always, Esther answered before the line began to ring.

"Yes, Ms. Speros, is everything OK?"

"Hi, Esther, yes it's fine—uh, well, kinda. I forgot I'm supposed to have dinner with my dad's girlfriend tonight—"

Before Lanie could offer to cancel her dinner plans, Esther countered. "Oh no problem, dear, let's make it Thursday—same time and place. Have a fun night. I'll let Mr. Newman know."

Lanie was hoping that Esther would object and ask her to cancel. A twang of guilt vibrated through her; Sabine had surely gone out of her way to make it a nice night.

"Oh, Esther, wait!" Lanie said, raising the phone back up.

"Yes, dear?"

"Is everything OK?" Lanie asked. "After what happened on Monday?"

"Check your Omega email account—the situation is under control for now. The attack on Monday seems to have been a disorganized operation funded by the Detractors, and we're running down a lead, but nothing you need to worry about right now."

Lanie called Hudson next, but Esther had already texted him with an updated meeting time.

"It's fine," Hudson said on the phone. "My mom has been complaining that I've been gone every evening anyway. See you tomorrow; let me know how it goes with Sabine." Lanie could tell he was snickering when he hung up the phone.

Lanie found Sabine in the kitchen. She appeared to be looking for the right pots and pans for whatever recipe she'd picked. Some cabinet doors were open, and utensils were spread around the countertop. Two canvas grocery bags were piled on the counter as well.

"Hi, there!" Sabine said, standing up with a skillet. Dressed in jeans and a knitted purple top, she looked more comfortable than in the business attire she wore most days. Lanie wasn't clear on what Sabine's job involved, but knew she worked at a law firm in downtown Phoenix.

"Hi Sabine," Lanie said as she slid her backpack onto the kitchen table. She sat down on one of the stools facing the kitchen. "What are we making tonight?"

Sweat was beading on Sabine's forehead as she rooted through the bags. She caught Lanie's glance and dabbed her brow with her sleeve. "I forgot half of what I bought at home, so I had to run to the market here by your house," she said, exhaling. "We're gonna make tacos, then decorate our own cupcakes!" Holding up a bag of corn tortillas, she searched Lanie's face for approval.

"Sounds tasty," Lanie said, giving a thumbs-up. Seeing that Sabine was flustered after running all her errands, Lanie offered to help. "I can make the frosting—Dad says my buttercream is awesome."

"You're on!" Sabine said and laid a frying pan on the countertop.

Mr. Speros and Isaiah arrived next, and Isaiah was already buzzing with the excitement of a night at the pizza parlor for his friend Jeremy's birthday. The pizza parlor's notchy animatronic figure show was only marginally better than their cardboard-like pizza, and Lanie was thankful for her own plans. She greeted her dad and gave him his usual kiss on the cheek.

"Hi, Dad, was your day ok?"

"Hi Sweetie—it was fine, we've been prepping test vehicles for the winter testing in Minnesota. I've got a few long days coming up next week."

Sabine's face softened as she collected her kiss from Mr. Speros. They exchanged the tales of their day as Lanie watched their body language. Sabine sucked in her cheeks and raised her right eyebrow as Mr. Speros explained how he expected the birthday party to go. Lanie noticed a familiar contour in Sabine's expression—one of contentment that she'd seen in a different face. Sabine caught Lanie's stare and smiled back. The familiarity in Sabine's look was pushed from Lanie's mind, because Isaiah had stomped into the room looking for a greeting from his big sister.

"Oh hey, buddy! Don't worry—I didn't forget you!" Lanie dropped to one knee, crushing Isaiah with a bear hug.

"I'm gonna go to Jeremy's birthday party to eat *junk food* and watch him open presents," he informed his big sister. "I'm gonna try to win a Lego dinosaur kit with Skee-Ball tickets. Don't get inta any trouble while we're gone," he said.

"The house is safe with me," she said and shoved him toward the den.

Sabine's cell phone began vibrating on the countertop, and she looked pained. "I gotta take this; it's a work call," she said as she stepped onto the back patio. Mr. Speros was shepherding Isaiah toward the garage, holding the Jeep keys and a stuffed gift bag.

"You two have fun; don't talk about me too much while I'm gone," he said, then disappeared into the hallway. When the door to the garage slammed, Lanie turned to see Sabine smiling at her as she came through the sliding door.

"They left already?" she asked, leaning to see through the den.

"Yeah, it's an early party." Lanie rounded up her backpack. "I'm gonna wash up and get ready to cook, I'll be back in a minute.

"Ok, yeah, we've got time," Sabine said, waving Lanie off with a glance at her smartwatch.

Lanie changed into a more comfortable short-sleeve tee and closed herself into the bathroom to freshen up. She checked her phone again—still no response from Amanda. Her face felt streaked from the dust and rain, and she viewed herself in the mirror as she flushed warm water over her nose. Pulling her hair back with a fluffy elastic tie, she surveyed her own facial features in the mirror and gave herself a half-smile. In that instant, the synapsed circuitry of her brain connected the various facial features that were floating in her subconscious. She was hit by a wave of panic that made the inside of her chest flutter. She remembered exactly where she had seen Sabine's expression before.

Looking straight into her own wide eyes, Lanie recalled the large photo in the lounge—the photo of the Omega principals standing together in 1961. Wanda James had the same eyes, nose, linear eyebrows, and even the same bowed lips as Sabine. Lanie's mind began speeding and swirling, and she sat down. She tapped the toes of her shoes on the bathroom floor, wondering what the resemblance meant. *Was Sabine Wanda's daughter? If so, why hadn't she told us?*

Her hands trembled as she sat on the window seat, trying to calm herself. *Maybe they are just look-alikes*, Lanie thought. *It has to be a coincidence*, she reasoned. But the reasoning wasn't working. She thought of the timing—how Sabine and her dad had met only days after they moved to Fountain Hills. Lanie's mind knew the facts didn't look good, even though her heart was hoping she was being irrational. Either way, she had to get herself together. Standing up straight and drawing in several long, slow breaths, she looked at herself in the mirror. She sent a text to Hudson.

*Alone with dads gf. Do you think she looks like Wanda James? I'm scared*

Hudson didn't respond; Lanie would be on her own. She considered texting her dad but realized how ridiculous her hunch might sound. She gathered her thoughts and promised herself she'd stay calm. *So... what if Sabine was Wanda's daughter? Was that bad? If she was, why was Sabine keeping it secret? Just ask her some questions—and relax.* She pulled the bathroom door open and walked quietly to the hallway arch. Sabine wasn't in the kitchen. Lanie couldn't see or hear her anywhere.

The skin on Lanie's neck prickled. *This situation is very bad,* her intuition warned. *She's probably in the front bathroom—you need to chill,* her logical side reasoned. But Lanie felt sure her intuition was right—Sabine was Wanda's daughter. *Too many coincidences.*

The only sound was the electric ticking of the sunburst clock on the wall over the fireplace. Lanie debated whether she should bolt for the door, or call Sabine's name. Nearly deciding to bolt, Lanie thought it would be better to first grab her key card, then sneak down into the passage. She turned to her bedroom and immediately saw Sabine standing in the doorway. Lanie's heart leapt, and she sucked in a breath between her teeth.

Sabine held up a dark gray gun for Lanie to see, and she recognized it right away as her father's nine-millimeter Springfield—it was pointed right at her. The expression on Sabine's face was calm, and her eyebrows were stretched flat across her forehead. She focused on Lanie in a calculated, impatient stare.

"I kinda figured you had something goin' on in your head, and made the connection," Sabine said, tapping her temple with her middle finger. "Looks like I was right. What you need to do now is *NOT* be stupid." She waved Lanie toward her bedroom. "Come here. Don't try to be a hero or a mad dog, just come down here slowly."

Lanie complied, passing under the beams of the recessed lights. Her mind was rifling through potential options and escape scenarios, but they all ended in a gunshot.

"I'm not a pushover like your kid friends or those boneheads who broke in—your face is easy to read. Don't think, just follow my instructions." Sabine said. "Give me your phone, and lay face down on the floor."

336

"What are you gonna do to me?" Lanie stammered.

"Right now? I'm not gonna do *anything* to you," Sabine advised. Her diction was crisp. "Unless you become stupid. If you get stupid, I'll start putting holes in you—and I don't wanna do that."

As Lanie got to her knees, she saw that Sabine was wearing jogging shoes and a utility belt. Attached to the belt were a small flashlight and a set of handcuffs. When Lanie was flat on her stomach, Sabine placed a foot in the center of her back and pushed the breath out of her chest. She flung Lanie's iPhone into Isaiah's room, where it thudded against the wall. Pulling the handcuffs from her hip, she locked Lanie's hands behind her back. When she was sure the cuffs were inescapable, Sabine yanked up on Lanie's arm.

"Get up," Sabine ordered. "Get into your room."

Sabine had been rooting through the drawers, and Lanie was irritated almost as much as she was scared. Another person had violated her private space.

"Get the key cards—all that you have." Sabine shoved Lanie across the room, against her reading niche wall. "I want the red-striped card and the copper key."

"I can't reach them," Lanie said, wiggling her wrists behind her back. "They're underneath my drawer, pull it out."

Sabine kept the gun trained on Lanie's chest, and yanked the desk drawer out, scattering notes and scrap book items. She reached into the opening and pulled out all three key cards. "Where's the key!?"

"What key?" Lanie replied.

"Don't act stupid—the principal key with the crystal!"

Lanie reluctantly nodded to an antique tin Tonka van that sat on her bookshelf. "It's in the back of the van."

Sabine pulled out the key and tossed the toy on the floor.

"I'm going to explain this once, so don't test me—and don't cause any delays." Grabbing Lanie's forearm, Sabine pulled her into the hallway. The grip from her thin fingers was painful. "You're going to open the passage into the caverns, and you're going to take me to the vault. We're going to open the vault, and I'm going to take as much as we can carry, then we're coming back up here."

Slinging Lanie into the kitchen, Sabine growled, "Show me—now."

Lanie guided her to the release button in the cabinet over the stove, realizing that Sabine had probably been looking for it since the first time she'd been invited over,and that angered Lanie more. Stumbling because she was being pushed from behind, Lanie made her way down the steps, hoping her dad would check on her from the party.

"It took me way too long to get this far... months of putting up with you, your little rat of a brother, and your incompetent dad." Sabine shook her head. "Six months of my life wasted, while you've been exploring this place like some sort of dumb, starry-eyed puppy." Sabine huffed at Lanie in contempt.

After the main entry door powered open, Sabine demanded instructions on how to start the Atom. Lanie showed her where to swipe the card, but was honest when she said, "I don't know where the vault is. I haven't been there."

"I know where the vault is," Sabine sniped. She pushed every station name on the top row, and when they were all lit, they flashed three times together and went dark, then the Atom started on its way to the coded destination.

On the elevator trip down, Lanie thought of options for disarming Sabine, but with her hands cuffed, she could only hope to run, not mount any sort of defense, and it frustrated her.

"Was Wanda your mom?" Lanie asked, without emotion.

"Yeah. And she wasted her best years on this place, with nothing to show for it other than a lousy government pension." Dull, tired anger was everywhere on Sabine's face. It was a contorted, ugly anger that she'd kept concealed, and Lanie suddenly felt gullible for having missed making the connection earlier.

"My mom died nearly broke, with a long-dead husband and a head full of Omega stories," Sabine added. There was old disappointment in her voice, carried from her youth. "...Dragged me all over South America to places she thought were paradise, while millions of dollars sat useless up here in this god-forsaken pit." She turned to Lanie, showing a newer, colder expression. "I'm taking what my mother owed us."

The gold Atom slowed at the inky blackness of the command center station, and Sabine pulled out a folded canvas bag from where it had been tucked into her jeans behind her back. "Get out. Keep your hands in your back pockets. If you try to be brave, you'll get shot—and we'll both lose. Do you understand me?"

Lanie nodded, stepping out. The station was silent. She knew that Atom travel and door lock activations were tracked at the larger control rooms and hoped that Amanda's dad—or anyone—would see that they were about to enter the command center.

Using Lanie's new key card, Sabine unlocked the frosted glass doors and pushed Lanie inside. *Sabine's impatience will be a weakness*, Lanie thought, though she wasn't sure how to take advantage of it yet. A black U-shaped console filled the dark reception area, and clusters of buttons were lit on it. Many flashed. It looked like the bridge of a sci-fi spaceship. Black fabric wall panels absorbed their sound as the pair moved through the darkness; only the focused light over the console provided any peripheral visibility. Above the doors they'd entered, a wall of sleeping television screens hung, clustered like the eyes of a spider. Lanie watched Sabine's face; her eyes darted around the room, searching for the doors and halls that she must have been told about verbally. Clutching Lanie's upper arm,

Sabine hauled her down the fabric-lined hall to the left of the reception area.

Fifty feet down the dark hall, they came upon a glass wall on the right. It provided a view into an enormous, theater-like room. There were rows of consoles on the sloping floor, and giant projection screens at the low end. Gold-leaf lettering on the glass identified it as the "Core Operations Room."

As Lanie slowed to look, Sabine jerked her along. "Move it, you little leech." She glanced at Lanie over her shoulder. "If you get near any of the consoles or emergency call stations, I'll *end* you," she hissed.

By then, Lanie had assessed that Sabine was talking tougher than she was. Sabine was flustered and didn't know her way around. Lanie could see it in the occasional twitch of her lip as she decided which door and hallway to try. Lanie doubted whether Sabine would have enough courage to shoot anyone, but it wasn't the time to find out. That was a bet she might have to make later, and it was a sobering thought.

They'd made a couple turns from the main hallway and were headed down a teak-lined corridor with more frosted glass doors. Each door was marked with the name of a different manager. These were the executive offices she'd seen in a floorplan of the command center. But Lanie hadn't seen a vault on any of the drawings.

"I don't know about any vault. How are you so sure there is one?" Lanie asked. Her aim was to cause tension more than be helpful.

"Shut up," Sabine muttered without turning back. "My mother told me where it is. Only the principals and director knew the entry procedure. You're gonna help me get in."

They came to the end of the paneled hallway, where two deceased potted trees stood on either side of a pair of doors. One door was marked LADIES, and the other, MEN.

"You found us the restroom... nice work. I kinda have to go," Lanie quipped.

Sabine backhanded her hostage, and her small ring drew a red scratch on Lanie's cheek. "I guess you're feeling a little feisty now," Sabine sneered. "Don't tangle with me today."

Turning her attention back to the hallway, Sabine forced Lanie to the floor with her free hand. "Sit cross-legged. Don't move an inch.".

Lanie sat on the gold textured carpet and looked around the dead-end hallway. Other than the two restroom doors and their potted trees, there were no furnishings. Framed photos of the Atom stations hung on the wall every few feet. Sabine grabbed the trunk of the dead ficus to the left of the doors and yanked it out of the pot, scattering dry soil everywhere. She then tossed the pot aside, uncovering a small metal tab on the carpet. It looked like the pull tab for a can of soup. When Sabine pulled up on the tab, a circle of carpet came up with it, exposing a cylindrical compartment underneath. She jammed her hand into the opening, then an electric solenoid behind the paneled wall clicked. The framed photo on the wall above Lanie's head leaned outward, and a familiar card tray emerged from over the top edge.

"Get up!" Sabine barked. Shuffling through the key cards she'd taken from Lanie's room, Sabine pulled the red-striped card and inserted it into the reader. The entire wall section unlatched and began pivoting inward, revealing a concrete passage. At the end of the passage was a vault door whose face had a keyhole, card slot, and combination dial. The space between the vault door and the passage where they stood was about thirty feet.

Before they started down the hallway, Sabine yanked Lanie forward to the edge of the carpet. She pointed to the ceiling, at a group of nozzles along the top of each wall. "You're gonna be the guinea pig," she said, glaring at Lanie. "If you move too quickly, the vault doors will automatically close, and you'll be gassed to death through those nozzles."

Sabine gave Lanie a painful jab between her shoulder blades. "GO! No more than three feet per second." She jammed the red-striped card into Lanie's hand.

Lanie winced, then turned back to look at Sabine. "How would I know what three feet per second is?!"

"It's a slow walk, slower than you'll move with a walker if I blow a hole through your hip with this gun." She waved the weapon at Lanie. "Now MOVE it, we can't be here long!"

Lanie watched the nozzles as she crept in and saw many small glass lenses at eye level in the face of the concrete wall. She also noticed that every two feet there were thin gaps in the concrete floor and walls that aligned. Her heartrate quickened. *There were other security features that Sabine didn't know about.*

"Not that slow, idiot, you can go a little faster."

Lanie glowered back at her. Her steps were consistent and deliberate, and soon she was standing on the metal grating in front of the vault door.

Approximating Lanie's speed, Sabine approached behind. "Put in the key card, then get outta the way."

Contorting as best she could with her hands behind her back, Lanie stood on her toes and bit her lip as she maneuvered the key card into position. The reader took the striped card, and a cover slid over the tray. It's indicator light turned green, then a red light illuminated on the key lock.

Sabine pulled up the silver chain she always wore around her neck. On the end was a silver key very much like Lanie's, though its crystal was blue. She slipped it into the key slot, but it didn't turn. Huffing, she withdrew her key, then dug in her pocket for Lanie's. When she turned the copper key in the lock, a beam shone through the crystal, projecting an entirely different set of numbers than those Lanie had seen at the Regents rotunda near the waterfall. Displayed on the floor at the foot of the door, each number was preceded by an "L" or an "R." With sweat beading on the skin above her eyebrows, Sabine shoved Lanie aside and started spinning the large chrome combination dial. Lanie watched as Sabine positioned the numbers, mouthing the pattern.

Right, 72... Left, 60... Right, 26... Left, 48.

The last indicator turned green, and a series of squealing, clanking slide bolts withdrew behind the door's face. Stepping back, Sabine again looked at her watch, then waved the gun at Lanie. "Pull it open."

The shock of what was inside temporarily masked Lanie's discomfort and fear. The vault's interior was big enough to park a car inside, with metal shelving on each wall. Dense stacks of fifty- and hundred-dollar bills lay banded in steel trays. *There must be over a hundred trays*, Lanie thought. But more impressive was a large group of gold bars, on the bottom shelf in the back corner. They were stacked in an uneven mound at ankle height, as though they had been in the way, like leftovers in the refrigerator.

Stooping down as she approached, Lanie could see that the bars had been cast with the Omega emblem on their top face, along with their individual weight in grams. Each was about ten inches long and five inches wide, and they gleamed as though they radiated their own energy.

Sabine's eyes glistened; this was what she had come for. She flapped her canvas bag open and pitched it at Lanie. "I'm gonna switch your cuffs to the front, and you're gonna load this bag. If you pull anything while I'm switching the cuffs, you'll rot in here with this money."

Lanie knew better. If she triggered the alarm on the way out, they'd both be locked in and gassed together.

"Put in a few rows of cash on the bottom of the bag, and gold bars on top of that," Sabine said, as she jammed a couple bundles of bills into her back pockets.

After lining the bottom of the bag, Lanie figured she'd loaded over two hundred thousand dollars in bills before she reached for the gold bars.

They were as heavy as they looked, and Lanie realized it was going to be a chore to haul even a pair of them out of the complex.

"Put three in," Sabine demanded. When Lanie had complied, Sabine pushed her out of the way and tried to lift the bag. "Put in another."

With the cash and four bars of gold, the bag easily weighed over fifty pounds. The canvas bag was rated for the weight, but its vinyl-wrapped handles dug into Lanie's palms.

"This is seriously the best bag you could find to rob a vault?!" Lanie asked in a condescending tone.

"I'm not the one carrying it," Sabine said.

"It's too heavy!" Lanie struggled with the bag thumping against her shins as she walked. "I can't carry it in front of me with the cuffs on."

"Keep moving, twit." Sabine swung the vault door closed and spun the combination. The tray ejected Lanie's key card, and Sabine slid it into her pocket with the bundles of bills. Sabine left the copper key, and Lanie quietly backed up to the door and slipped it out of the lock. She shuffled toward the passage entryway with the heavy bag, and she could hear Sabine coming up behind.

Before she reached the doorway, Lanie saw the shadow of an approaching figure on the carpet in the hallway and her frayed nerves sharpened. She knew that whoever was around the corner could only be on her side. Without waiting to see who it was, she dropped the bag and sprinted out of the passage. The lights in the passage immediately went out, and a muffled air horn sounded. She heard a blood-curdling scream behind her as Sabine charged toward the closing door. The hiss of escaping gas came from overhead, and perforated aluminum plates began rising from the floor at each of the gaps Lanie had seen.

When Lanie rounded the corner, she saw Mr. Rinnas standing in the hallway. He held an assault rifle with a short, stumpy barrel. Lanie was so shocked to see him, her head began reeling, but she cleared her thoughts to stay focused.

Mr. Rinnas's expression was cool and focused as Lanie ran toward him. He waved her past, but Lanie slid on the dead tree remains and tumbled onto the carpet, rolling past him in a heap. He lifted the rifle just in time to see the heavy bag fly from the closing passage, and Sabine exploded out just behind it. She'd barely cleared the last metal plate, and it tore the sleeve from her shirt as it sealed against the ceiling. Her eyes were wild, like an attacking animal. Lanie didn't have time to run; she feared being hit in the back by a bullet. When Sabine saw that Mr. Rinnas was armed, she raised her gun to fire at him.

Mr. Rinnas shot first with a deafening blast, hitting Sabine in the chest. She stumbled backwards, falling to the floor near the restroom doors. Lanie was aghast, fearing that she would see blood and human entrails all over the hallway, but this was not the case. Specks of blood appeared all over Sabine's shirt, and on the bare skin of her forearms, but she was alive and looking very shocked. Mr. Rinnas grabbed Lanie by the wrist and dragged her to her feet.

"I hit her with rubber buckshot. When she figures that out, she's gonna fire at us," he said calmly. This was not the Larry Rinnas Lanie knew, and she stared at him. "You need to focus—and engage!" he said, shoving Lanie through the doorway of the nearest office. Then he turned to face Sabine. Lanie stumbled against the desk and spun around, just in time to see Mr. Rinnas cower as Sabine took her first shot. The crack of the handgun sounded, and the wooden door jamb over Mr. Rinnas's right shoulder burst in a shower of splinters.

Sabine was screaming expletives at the end of the hall, and Lanie could hear she was running toward them. Without looking through the door, Mr. Rinnas shrank down and said, "I'm going to draw her away. You run into the Ops Room as soon as we're around the cor...." He was drowned out by a second shot of the gun. This time the bullet perforated his right forearm, throwing it backward in an involuntary spasm. Lanie saw blood begin to soak into the sleeve of his shirt.

Unfazed, Mr. Rinnas fired at Sabine again, just as she appeared in the doorway. The rubber beads hit her waist and thighs at close range, doubling her over. She fell to the floor, looking in at Lanie with spots of blood covering her cheeks. The expression on her face was of frantic frustration, then a grimace of pain as her wounds began to burn.

Lanie didn't wait. She charged at Sabine, intending to tackle her. Mr. Rinnas threw himself on top of Sabine first, attempting to smother the gun from her hand. Lanie was committed and couldn't stop, and she tripped over the two of them, flying across the hall into the opposite door. The frosted pane shattered as her cuffed hands slammed against it. She passed through and landed over the arm of a chair, with shards of glass scattering around her. Mr. Rinnas was pulling at Sabine's ankles, preventing her from standing up. She screamed in anger and flopped onto her back, then pointed the gun straight into Mr. Rinnas's face. Lanie's blood froze. She didn't want to see her neighbor killed before her eyes.

With all the breath in her lungs, Lanie yelled "STOP!" Sabine's eyes didn't flinch; she focused only on Mr. Rinnas's face.

"That's ENOUGH!" Sabine yelled, with white spittle flying from the corners of her mouth. Her eyes were reddened, and her cheeks were swelling. Mr. Rinnas was aware she had the upper hand, and he sat motionless, focusing on Sabine's moves.

Some of the gas from the vault passage had escaped into the hallway, and everyone's eyes watered. Lanie's throat burned, and she stifled the urge to cough. Sabine stood up. Her jeans and shirt were perforated as though a piranha had attacked, and she was obviously in pain.

"YOU—STAY!" She pointed at Lanie without looking at her. "DON'T GET HIM SHOT!" She kept the gun aimed at Mr. Rinnas. Whisps of smoke trailed out of the gun's hot barrel. "Some rescue *that* was... you morons nearly got yourselves killed." Sabine picked up the hot rifle and threw it into the office opposite Lanie. "Stand up!" she yelled, then positioned Lanie between herself and Mr. Rinnas. Dragging over the canvas bag on the carpet, she poked the handgun into Lanie's ribs. "Let's go," she said, then she kicked Mr. Rinnas's thigh. "You too, tough guy, get up. Get into the car at the station. Walk—NOW!"

Lanie was forced to carry the heavy bag again, following behind Mr. Rinnas. He looked helpless and annoyed but said nothing to Lanie. When they reached the Atom station, Sabine demanded that Mr. Rinnas get into the all-black unit that he'd arrived in. She made him climb into the third row at the back of the carriage and pressed a destination on its console. Once the Atom left the station, it wouldn't stop until the next evacuation platform, even if Mr. Rinnas pressed the emergency button. Lanie was about to lose her rescuer. As the black carriage swept him away, Mr. Rinnas stared through the back window in disgust, clutching his arm. Lanie watched as he disappeared into the dark tunnel.

Sabine thumped the side of Lanie's head with the gun's barrel and motioned for her to climb into their gold Atom. She'd only gotten one foot into the carriage when she detected motion in the corner of her eye. Sabine had sensed the same motion, and both women looked back. Amanda burst from behind a parked black Atom and spun off a brutal leg sweep, taking Sabine down in one shot. Lanie's captor landed face-first on the floor— again. The gun's grip crushed Sabine's knuckles on the concrete deck, and she yelped in frustrated pain. Amanda stood and quickly heel-kicked Sabine in the center of her back.

Shaking off the blow, Sabine spun around on her hip, deflecting Amanda's next kick. Amanda lost her balance and fell against the Atom. Infuriated, Sabine raised the gun and aimed at Amanda, whose eyes were fearless and confident. Before she had a chance to squeeze the trigger, Lanie swung the bag of gold bars like a wrecking ball, plowing Sabine across the floor and into the motorway ahead of their gold Atom. Amanda tried to attack, but Sabine raised the gun. Baring her teeth and breathing heavily,

Sabine carefully inched herself away from the Atom track's energized bus bar, then glowered at the two girls.

"Don't move, either of you!" Amanda was closer, and Sabine slapped her fiercely on the side of her face, then grabbed her collar and forced her into the Atom. "You, you're going with me," she said. "You wanted to get involved, huh? Well now you're involved."

Sabine dragged the bag of gold into the Atom, then closed the door. She punched the button on the Atom's console while she pointed the gun at Amanda's back. They both watched Lanie as the Atom disappeared into the opposite tunnel. Lanie suddenly felt a wave of panic crash over her. She was worried about what Sabine would do to Amanda. But she was also worried that her dad and Isaiah might be home at any time. There wasn't time to be hysterical, though—Lanie knew she needed to stay focused. Amanda's key card lay on the concrete, along with a set of keys. Lanie scooped them up, then scrambled into a black Atom and headed toward her house. Scenarios of what horror might be waiting at home flashed through Lanie's head during the dark trip in the elevator. She tried to push them aside, thinking of what her plan would be.

At the executive residence, Lanie confirmed what she feared—Amanda's card wouldn't open the big steel door. Lanie took the Atom back to the other end of the corridor, and while the carriage was stopped at the elevator door, she jumped out. Sabine had Lanie's key cards, but Lanie had the copper principal key, which she inserted into the lock. When she turned it in the glass door's lock, the lights in the room came on, and the door swung open. When she closed the door behind her, she heard a chirp of escaping air, and a second door against the elevator shaft wall opened.

It was pitch-dark beyond the door. Based on the musty breeze coming through the opening, Lanie figured she was standing on the edge of the thousand-foot shaft. A black metal platform extended into the dark space, with a spiral staircase that led up. Relying on the faith that her hunch was correct, Lanie stepped out into the darkness and let the door close.

With her hands cuffed, the ascent was tough. She couldn't use the handrail. There were no lights, so all Lanie could do was trust that the stairs led to a landing somewhere higher up. The howling draft in the bottomless space swirled, pushing her hair into her face. Lanie figured she'd gone up five or six levels when she finally bumped into a door. She was thankful to find it had a conventional knob, and she pushed her way into the room. She had entered a small stone room that was lined with dust and cobwebs. A lone, dim bulb hung from the ceiling. Powdery dust covered the floor and hand-cut timbers stood in the corners, propping up the stone ceiling. In the farthest corner was a second, pear-shaped door with a horizontal push bar. Lanie ran to it, throwing her weight against the bar. When the disguised, stone-clad door swung open, she found she was standing under the rock overhang of a shallow cave, in the night air. A dense shrub blocked the cave entry, and Lanie was about to push through it when she heard a growly, throaty meow from around her feet.

Wide-eyed, she looked down and saw two little furry tan balls with ears. They looked like muscular house cats. They were pawing each other playfully and batting at Lanie's shoelaces. She knew right away that they were mountain lion cubs. If Lanie hadn't been so worried about her family and Amanda, she'd have marveled at how cute the cubs were, but then her blood went ice cold at her next thought: *If the cubs are here, mom's not far away.*

There were no other animals in the small cave, so Lanie inched cautiously through the shrub, looking around. As she anticipated, she was standing in the rocky corner of the mountain ridge, inside the fenced mine compound. The old mine elevator headframe stood only twenty feet away. Lanie swung her head both directions, then she saw what she was hoping she wouldn't. A large mountain lion was watching her from above the mine entrance, with its head lowered. Lanie kept walking, trying to put distance between her and the big cat. Its paws were nearly as big as Lanie's face, and the cat's round cheeks were flared up, exposing sharp teeth. It stood and started to walk along the ridge above the mine's timber-framed entrance, tracking Lanie. *This is absolutely ridiculous*, Lanie thought to herself. *Of all the danger and adventure in my life right now, a mountain lion is gonna be how I die?*

Besides the horror of the situation, it was also terribly inconvenient. Lanie needed to get to the house—she needed to run. But breaking into a sprint would probably get her attacked, so Lanie did what she'd heard was the right thing to do: She started making a huge amount of noise. Clapping her hands and stomping her feet, Lanie barked and yelled at the animal, which seemed to surprise it. Its yellow eyes were dilated, and the giant black pupils watched as Lanie backed away.

Figuring that Lanie might not be worth the trouble, the mountain lion turned and disappeared over the ridge. Lanie didn't wait to confirm the big cat was gone for good; she scaled the fence and started sprinting up the trail toward her house. The waning full moon was still high in the sky, so the familiar desert was easy to cross for Lanie—even in handcuffs.

When she crested the hill, she saw no light in the windows of the house below. Lanie stumbled and fell as she descended the trail. The pebbles stung her already-bruised knees and palms. Upon reaching the house, she found the back door was open, which led Lanie to assume that Hudson was inside somewhere. She feared for his safety but also hoped he had something up his sleeve. Lanie had only been gone for forty-five minutes, though it felt like hours. Sabine had a ten-minute head start. She and Amanda should have been up into the house already, and Lanie became nervous. The oven passage was closed, and she was just about to reach for the switch when she heard the bookcase swing open.

Ducking down, Lanie watched over the countertop. Amanda emerged from the front room first, with Sabine behind. Sabine was still holding the gun. In the grayish wash of moonlight from the entryway's clerestory, Lanie could see that Amanda's nose was bloodied and her shirt was ripped. Sabine's hair was also scrambled, and she was limping.

"Sit!" Sabine said to Amanda. "No more stupidosity tonight. You're lucky I didn't shoot you in the head after what you pulled on the ride over here." She strode over to the breakfast bar, just over the counter from where Lanie was hiding. Lanie stayed hidden while Sabine dug in her purse, flinging items onto the counter.

"We're going for a ride—a long ride," Sabine said as she pulled her BMW's key fob from the pile of items. Lanie assumed that she planned to take Amanda along as collateral. Without wasting time collecting her other personal effects, Sabine tossed her empty purse into the kitchen and turned toward the door, and that's when Lanie jumped up. She grabbed a long knife from the wood block near the stove and vaulted onto the countertop, screaming at Sabine.

Both Amanda and Sabine were startled, and Sabine lurched back, falling down the step into the den. She dropped the gun onto the carpet. Lanie saw the gun bounce under the coffee table and seized the opportunity to try to gain control of the situation. On her knees atop the counter, Lanie looked at the carving knife she held, deciding it was her best option. She grabbed the blade end and arched her arm back, preparing to launch it toward Sabine as though she were performing in a circus stunt show.

Sabine's eyes went wide, and she ducked as Lanie made her first attempt. Aware of Lanie's reputation for bad coordination, Amanda scrambled toward the wall, giving the flying blade a wide berth. The knife pegged itself to the arm of the reading chair several feet from Sabine. Realizing that she was likely safe, Sabine scrambled to grab the gun.

"Don't do it!" Lanie warned, then grabbed a second knife from the block. She whipped her arm and sent a paring knife straight into the coffee table's leg—only inches from Sabine's head. The knife made a gratifying "*thok*" as it stuck solidly in the teak. Sabine's expression changed as she focused on the knife at the tip of her nose, then she hastened her sweep for the gun. Lanie pulled out a large butcher's cleaver and raised her arm over her head.

351

"Oh my God, Lanie, no more knives!" Amanda said from her position near the kitchen table. She was covering the bottom of her face with both hands, looking both scared and stunned.

Even Lanie was surprised at her own ability to make the throws while in handcuffs, but the aggression was working, so she went with it. She dove at Sabine while holding the gleaming blade over her head with both hands, like a slasher movie villain, even though she had no intention of stabbing anyone. In fact, Lanie wasn't exactly sure what she planned to do next but knew she needed to keep her offensive position. Sabine's face betrayed her fear, and in a move of self-preservation she raised the gun and fired. The bullet whizzed past Lanie's left shoulder and shattered the skylight over the breakfast bar.

As the jewels of tempered glass rained around her in the dim light, Lanie took a broad swipe with the knife and nicked Sabine's trigger finger. Her same stroke also disemboweled the side of the sofa, leaving a gash that spilled foam padding onto the carpet. Before she could make another swipe, Sabine had pointed the gun barrel into Lanie's face.

"DROP IT!" Sabine yelled.

Lanie was lucky the first shot had missed, so she complied and backed up to the breakfast bar.

"What is WRONG with you two?! Do you really want me to shoot you? Do you really want to lose your lives to protect this stupid secret under your house?!" She pulled Lanie away from the sofa and directed her to pick up the bag of gold. It was then that they both noticed Amanda was gone.

Sabine thrust Lanie toward the front door. The bag's handles had chafed her palms raw, and Lanie could feel blisters forming.

"Get over there! To the door!" Sabine barked. Glancing both directions beyond the front door, Sabine didn't see anyone around. She unlocked her car with the remote while she prodded Lanie down the path. "Let's go; get in!"

Approaching the circular drive, Lanie saw that both tires on the right side of Sabine's BMW were flat. She looked around, hoping to see Hudson, or anyone, but was jabbed from behind by Sabine.

"GO!" Sabine said. "Stupid kid."

Sabine then noticed the tires and paused. She ran to the street side, finding all four tires were flat. She began mumbling something foul, trying to think of a new plan. Lanie could see unease in Sabine's expression. Her eyes darted from left to right; she knew as well as Lanie that they were probably being watched. She forced Lanie back up the path and through the front door. Sabine slammed and locked the front door, then closed the doors to the three rooms off the entryway. Wearing an expression of agitation and hysteria, Sabine scanned the living room to ensure she wasn't about to be attacked.

"Get to the garage—MOVE!" Sabine stomped around the corner, dragging Lanie by her shirt sleeve. She ripped the door off the key cabinet in the hallway then growled in frustration. There wasn't a single set of keys in the box, and Lanie knew right away that Hudson was responsible, but he still hadn't shown himself.

Sabine shook her head, then hauled Lanie to her bedroom. She watched Lanie closely as she backed into the reading niche. From the wall over the desk, she grabbed the shadow box that Mrs. Speros had made, including Lanie's set of keys to the Cadillac. She slammed it onto the desktop and its contents spread all over, mixed with shattered glass and split wood. Sabine tore the keys from the satin backing, and Lanie felt like her own heart had been ripped loose.

The garage was pitch dark when Sabine flung the door open. She hesitated to enter at first. Lanie couldn't blame her—she knew this was where Hudson would attack. As soon as Sabine stepped through the doorway, the hiss of pepper spray accompanied a hidden stream from the direction of the workbench. Sabine began screaming as her eyes were inflamed by the liquid. Lanie could see Amanda crouched on her knees on top of the workbench.

Hudson stepped out of the shadows from the other direction wearing safety goggles and quickly lowered a looped cargo strap around Sabine's arms. He yanked the loose end through the turnbuckle, cinching her arms against her torso. Sabine fired the gun randomly into the darkness and the muzzle flash briefly lit the garage. Lanie's own eyes burned from the spray mist, but she lunged forward, ramming Sabine with her shoulder. The two of them smashed against the grille of the Rambler, then Lanie blacked out.

# Chapter 23

# UNHAPPY TRAVELERS

The sky was still dark when Lanie started to regain her consciousness. Her stomach was nauseous, and her head throbbed in pain—as did her wrists. Without lifting her head, her eyes began to focus on the chrome window switches of the Cadillac's door. She heard the highway rushing outside. Her hands were cuffed tightly to the pull handle on the door panel. Even the dim, greenish light inside the car hurt Lanie's eyes. She raised her dizzy head, blinking her eyes in hopes her view would stabilize. Her glasses were gone.

Sabine was at the wheel, focused on the road. Lit by the instrument panel, her bloodshot eyes looked tired, and Lanie could see her face was swollen from the rubber shot and pepper spray. The night's brawl had made an ugly mess of the woman that her dad was smitten with. Lanie then thought of Amanda and Hudson, and sat up, looking into the back seat—it was empty.

"They're not dead," Sabine said, without taking her eyes off the road. Her voice was cold. "I'm not a killer; I'm only in this to get what I want."

Lanie assumed the only reason for Sabine's humane statement was that she believed her plan had been a success, and that she was feeling comfortable in her escape.

"What did you do with them, witch?" Lanie said with a hoarse voice.

"I don't know why you thought a bunch of eighth-graders would get the drop on me." Sabine turned to face Lanie. Her eyelid was twitching. It was hard for Lanie to read her expression through her accumulated injuries. "I would laugh at you with your fat lip and bruises, but I'm sure I look worse," Sabine added. "Just shut your face so this drive can be at least a *little* peaceful; we have a long way to go."

Lanie looked at the road ahead. They were on a two-lane highway, away from any city lights. Very few headlights passed from cars going the other direction. A small green shield on a passing signpost read 79 South, and Lanie realized they were headed toward Tucson the back way, east of the busy route from Phoenix.

"Where are we going?"

"*I'm* going to live the rest of my life wealthy—far from you and your troupe of crazies." Sabine brushed her fingers at Lanie. "I don't care what happens to *you*. When they find this car, they'll find you."

Lanie adjusted her feet; the heavy bag of cash and gold was crowding the footwell.

"I have to pee," Lanie said.

Sabine chuffed, and her face twisted. "We're not stopping until we get where we're going. Your stupid ambushes and stunts back home set us back two hours."

Lanie kicked the bag away from her feet as best she could. "You're an idiot," she rasped at Sabine. "What do you think you're gonna do with forty pounds of gold bars? You gonna take that to the bank?!"

With the hint of a smile, Sabine said, "I haven't even thought much about that yet, but where I'm going it's not going to be a problem."

Lanie figured that they were at least two hours, maybe more, from Tucson. The Cadillac didn't have any sort of GPS equipment, so Lanie brainstormed ways she could leave markers or signals. Both her phone and her Omega com device were at home. Her mind was foggy—like the time she'd crashed into a tree while snow-sledding on Mount Lemmon. Just like that day, she didn't know what happened before she blacked out.

Another sign. Eighty-four miles to Tucson.

Lanie's mouth was dry and her throat burned. She thought of the cozy reading table at the Red Rocks cafe. She thought of her shady, safe spot on the hill behind her house. She wanted to sit on the sofa and watch a movie with her dad and Isaiah. Anywhere sounded better than where she was, and her spirit began to sink lower. Lanie wondered if the challenge was over, and if she'd lost. Her new journey had only just begun, and already she'd failed. A surge of discouragement overcame her, and her eyes filled with tears. She cast her view into the sleeping desert beyond her window—she didn't want Sabine to see her emotion. What if she never saw Isaiah's sneaky smile again? Was the previous night's embrace with her dad going to be the last time she saw him?

Just when Lanie was slipping into enough of a depression to want to give up, she remembered Amanda and Hudson—and Mr. Rinnas. It hurt her split lip, but she smiled through her welling tears, thinking of Hudson in his safety goggles, attempting to rope Sabine. She was proud of Amanda for taking down a grown woman with a leg sweep. Right then, Lanie also thought of the motorhome trip, their family dinner in Tonopah, Esther's smile, and everything else that had happened that autumn—and how far she'd come. She suddenly felt ashamed about feeling defeated, and her spirit was offended that she had considered giving up. In that moment, she was overtaken by a feeling of flaming empowerment. *Lanie Speros wasn't giving up.* The story couldn't—it *wasn't*—going to end that way. She wouldn't let it. If this flimsy escape plot was all Sabine had, Lanie could do better. She clenched her fists and stiffened her legs. Her limbs still worked, and as long as they did, she would continue to fight.

She looked at the Cadillac script on the dashboard in front of her. This was her mom's car, and she was going to take it home. Lanie stared up at the road ahead and her eyes narrowed. She pursed her lips in a determined smile. Her blood started to warm. She felt like Lanie Speros again.

"You're *toast*," she said to Sabine, without looking over. Her voice was calm, and she projected her words clearly and deliberately. "You and I aren't done yet. You're goin' *down*—so you'd better watch your back, 'cause it's gonna be *me* who takes you out." It felt good to issue such a clear threat, and Lanie believed with all her soul that she'd make good on it.

Sabine glanced over, then Lanie looked her straight in the face. She snuffled, attempting to dismiss Lanie's threat. But now, more than ever, Lanie could see uncertainty and doubt in Sabine's eyes, and that only multiplied the courage Lanie felt. Sabine either figured Lanie's promise was a bluff, or she was pondering what Lanie might have up her sleeve. Either way, she said nothing.

For the next two hours, the two women didn't speak. Lanie kept a peripheral eye on speed and fuel level as well as their location. She thought of what their range would be, where they might have to stop for gas, and what was available to her in the car. At half-past ten o'clock Tucson passed by and Lanie wondered what the plan was. By that time, Lanie expected that her dad and Esther had cast a wide net looking for her. She wondered what resources Esther would have at her disposal. *Would they send the police? Did Esther have her own strike team?*

Lanie didn't trust Sabine at all but did believe that she'd left Amanda and Hudson alive. She had to keep shifting in her seat, continuously adjusting her arms so that her hands didn't go numb. Only fifteen minutes later Sabine left the interstate, driving onto a southbound highway—toward the mountainside mining town of Bisbee.

Near midnight, they passed the ghost town of Tombstone, Arizona. Lanie realized then that Sabine could be headed for the Mexican border. *How clichéd*, she thought. Such a predictable escape plan only reinforced Lanie's opinion that Sabine was neither creative nor effective at managing a situation. The signs on the highway showed Bisbee as twelve miles ahead, and Lanie knew the border was nearly walking distance from there. The Fleetwood had less than an eighth tank of fuel when they passed through Bisbee, and Sabine hadn't stopped. The historic stone and brick buildings were dark as the Cadillac crawled up, then down, the sleeping town's steep streets.

On the southern edge of Bisbee, Sabine finally pulled off the highway into a small strip mall with a convenience store. Only the convenience store was open, otherwise the strip mall was empty except for a local transient on the curb who was drinking from a bottle in a brown paper bag. Without a word, Sabine shut off the engine and locked Lanie in the car. If Lanie opened the door from the inside, the car's alarm would go off and draw attention. But she didn't want to escape; she wanted to deal with Sabine—and even looked forward to it. She'd only been alone a few moments when Lanie heard a subtle knocking.

"Lanie!" The muffled call came from behind. Stumped at first, Lanie soon realized that someone was in the trunk. "Lanie, are you there?" the distant voice repeated.

Lanie's tired eyes widened. "Amanda! Is that you!? Are you OK?!"

"I'm OK," the voice said. "I'm a little beat up but I'm OK! Get me out as soon as you can. I'll help you out."

Lanie was worried. "Can you breathe OK? Are you safe there?"

"Uhh, have you ever *been* in the trunk of this car? It's bigger than my bedroom at home." Amanda sneezed, then continued. "I'm fine, girl, just deal with that rotten woman so I can get out."

"OK, shhh, keep quiet, she's coming. I don't want her to know we found each other." There was a trunk release button in the glove box, but, while cuffed to the door, Lanie would never be able to reach it.

Sabine approached the car carrying a white plastic bag. She yanked Lanie's door open, aggravating her bruised wrists. Lanie stayed silent, pinching her eyes closed.

"Scrap whatever attack plan you may have brewing," Sabine said as she unlocked the cuffs. "I'm giving you some slack so you can have a drink; don't make me wish I didn't do it." She released Lanie's right hand, and kept her left wrist cuffed to the door.

"I still gotta go," Lanie said, between gulps of water.

"Then you're gonna do it right here, next to the car."

Lanie looked at her in disgusted horror, then down at the dirty asphalt. "Are you serious?"

"You either *do* or you *don't*, it's up to you."

The drunk on the curb was watching them. Lanie declined, pulling her feet back into the car. Sabine cuffed Lanie's hands together again and slammed the door. When she sat into the driver's seat, she checked her watch. She shook her head in disappointment and started the engine. Sabine drove along the highway a few miles then slowed to a crawl, hunched over the steering wheel. The blacktop was dark and empty. After creeping along for several yards, she spotted the turn she wanted and swung the Cadillac onto a dirt road.

A mile down the rough road, Sabine stopped and shut the engine off. She sat back in her seat and drew in a deep breath, then scowled at Lanie.

"I can't meet my ride until first light, so we're here for the night." She reclined her seat and lay back, running a bruised hand through her tangled hair.

Lanie looked around the car, finding moonlit desert in every direction. She was exhausted and hurt all over and still didn't have any viable escape options. In the morning she'd need to be alert and rested, so she used the switch on the door to slide the power seat forward, which at least allowed her the comfort of laying against the seatback.

The sound of the Cadillac's engine starting woke Lanie a few hours later. Purplish dawn lit the desert around the car. Where it sat on the ruddy dirt road, the car seemed small—a toy placed in the middle of a vast sandy diorama. The dim light revealed some scattered saguaro cacti and sparse brush, but otherwise the rocky valley was devoid of life. Sabine didn't look rested, only more disheveled, but she was alert. She pulled out her phone and called a stored number. Lanie could hear the line ringing with no answer, until a man's voice started speaking on the voicemail greeting. Sabine impatiently hung up without leaving a message and accelerated down the dirt road.

Moments later her phone rang.

"I'm here, where are you? How long?" she said into the phone, then looked up through the top of the windshield. "Fine, I'll be there in five. I'm in a greenish car. I'm not driving my car."

The man's voice on the other end sounded excited, but she interrupted him. "Don't worry about that. I got here. You just manage your own part," she said, then hung up.

The road ahead straightened out, and Sabine drove very fast. The Fleetwood's suspension heaved and shuddered as the tires pounded the rocky trail underneath. Occasionally, the car's electronics would step in, reducing the engine's power while a light on the dash warned of low traction. The wreath-and-crest ornament standing at the hood's tip trembled every time the undercarriage grazed the earth below. A rumbling in the distance became louder and Lanie suspected one of the car's mild tires was about to succumb to the rough terrain, but then a small airplane shot overhead, only a couple hundred feet up. It disappeared over a rise in the road ahead.

At the top of the rise Lanie saw a long strip of graded dirt in the valley beyond. The plane had looped wide, touching down there. Near the end of the makeshift airfield, the little plane turned around and started back toward the Cadillac as Sabine stopped in a cloud of dust. Lanie recognized the aircraft as a Cessna 172. Her late grandpa on her mom's side had flown one for years.

A man with rugged, sun-aged skin and black wavy hair was at the controls of the Cessna. He was a little older than Sabine but had the same secretive eyes and angular jaw. Sabine slammed the driver's door behind her after the plane's propeller stopped. The man approached her and the two hugged each other. The rising sun lit them orange against the plane's cab, and they stared at Lanie across the hood of the car. They appeared to be discussing Sabine's delays and trouble as well as their hostages.

The man shook his head at Lanie, then looked at Sabine. They murmured and pointed fingers at each other, then at Lanie, and Sabine headed back to the car. Lanie's pulse quickened. Whatever she was going to do, it would happen soon. Her blood ran hot, and she tried to keep her mind clear.

Sabine pulled open the passenger door, pointing the gun into Lanie's face again. Staring into the black barrel, Lanie swore that when she got home, she'd make her dad throw the gun into a lake. Sabine released the right handcuff, leaving the set to hang from Lanie's left wrist.

"You're going to move the money and gold into the plane, two bars at a time," Sabine said. A condescending smile crossed her tattered face. "If you aren't stupid, I'll let you live, and if you're lucky, a Border Patrol plane will spot you before you die of dehydration."

While Lanie rubbed her wrists, Sabine continued, "Your half-wit dad obviously was of no use to you. He left his only daughter in my hands without a second thought." She yanked Lanie out of the car by her collar. "And obviously your mommy isn't gonna help you either. Looks like you're on your own. Now MOVE!"

Lanie's blood was boiling now; her face flushed with fury. She knew Sabine had made those spiteful comments just to get her upset, but Lanie soaked it up. It was almost time to make her move. Sabine stepped back as Lanie passed and stumbled just a bit. Lanie glared, using eye contact as a reminder of her earlier threat. Sabine knew that without the help of guns and handcuffs, she'd already be defeated—they *both* knew it. Lanie's jaw clenched and she considered attacking Sabine savagely right then. But she knew she needed to stay calm and think ahead. She walked two of the heavy gold bars to the open passenger door on the plane. The man sat in the left seat staring back at her.

"Poot dem on da plat-form," he snapped in his best approximation of English. He pointed to a small shelf behind the two seats. Lanie assumed the nameless pilot was Sabine's half-brother, based on their family resemblance.

She reached through the door opening, and her back popped and snapped as she muscled the two bars into place. Sabine stood near the car's dusty hood, holding the gun with both hands as Lanie returned.

"Come on. Last two, then the bag of cash."

During the second trip, Lanie identified the outline of the car's keys bulging in Sabine's left pocket. She looked at the plane's small hooded wheels as she reached in to deposit the bars. Turning back, she sized up the plane's tail in relation to the car's nose. While Lanie stuffed the bundles of bills back into the canvas bag, Sabine backed up to the plane's door, waiting. She held the door open when Lanie returned, pointing the gun at her as she shoved the bag of cash behind the seat. Stepping back as told, Lanie watched while Sabine eased around the edge of the door. The nameless pilot started the plane's big four-cylinder engine and it settled into a steady, loping beat, its propeller chopping at the sun on the horizon.

"Say goodbye to your dad for me. Maybe he'll find some sucker to replace your mom one of these days," Sabine said and turned to the plane.

That final insult was Lanie's invitation. The rage that had been simmering in her veins had gathered into a steady stream of volcanic power. In the split second that Sabine looked down at the seat of the plane, Lanie surged at her. With a cracked and ghoulish howl, Lanie grabbed Sabine's hair and rammed her face into the door jamb of the plane's fuselage. Sabine dropped the gun, screaming in pain as blood dribbled down her forehead. Lanie ripped Sabine's hair backward and swung her left hand up in a wild punch, striking Sabine's jaw. The loose handcuffs slapped across her face, drawing blood from Sabine's nose.

Dazed, Sabine fell back against the wing's diagonal brace, raising an arm to defend herself. Lanie then attacked with her maximum energy, quickly throwing a second punch with her other hand. Her fist connected squarely with Sabine's temple, spinning her head to the side. Sabine dropped on top of the plane's landing wheel, reeling. Without waiting for a reaction, Lanie reached around and clamped Sabine in a headlock with her left arm.

Realizing the tables had turned, the man in the plane throttled the engine up and prepared to pull away without Sabine. He looked back at Lanie and she pointed a rigid finger at him, mouthing, "You're next."

Horrified and scared, Sabine flared with as much effort as she could muster. She elbowed Lanie in the ribs, then landed a punch over her shoulder that smashed Lanie's ear. But Lanie only tightened her grip around Sabine's neck, knowing that she had control—the situation was hers to steer. Sabine was gasping for air as the plane pulled away, and she reached weakly for the door. Lanie kicked it closed, denting its aluminum skin— and sealing Sabine's fate.

The propeller pelted them both with sand and dust while Lanie yelled into Sabine's ear, "I TOLD YOU, YOU'RE DONE!" She punched Sabine as hard as she could with her free hand and let her fall to the dirt. Nearly passed out from Lanie's choke hold, Sabine lay on the ground gasping as the plane started down the airstrip. Resisting the urge to kick her, Lanie instead reached down and yanked on Sabine's left pocket with all her might, tearing the stitching clean out of her jeans. From the breach, Lanie pulled the car keys, then released the trunk with the remote. She stepped over the top of the disabled woman and knelt on her chest, clamping her throat. The handcuffs clinked against Sabine's bare teeth. With her right hand, Lanie ripped the silver chain and key from Sabine's neck as Amanda ran up.

Lanie checked on the plane. The pilot had to taxi to the end of the airstrip and turn back in order to take off, and Lanie was going to prevent that. She looked up at Amanda with flaming determination.

"Can you handle her?"

"Go!" Amanda yelled. "I'll deal with her!"

From Sabine's other pocket, Lanie extracted the handcuff keys and key cards. She first released her own wrist before tossing everything in the dirt at Amanda's feet. Lanie bumped fists with Amanda, then ran to the Cadillac. She jumped into the driver's seat and twisted the key, firing the Fleetwood's V8. As Lanie slid the seat forward she saw Sabine stirring, try-ing to sit up as Amanda collected the items from the desert floor. Lanie was about to honk the horn to warn her, but Amanda had spotted the escape attempt and executed a textbook flying body slam on Sabine, flattening her into the dirt.

The first thing Lanie did was reach into the glovebox and disable the Cadillac's traction control with the button hidden there. Then she cranked the steering wheel hard right and dumped the shift lever into *drive*, stomp-ing the gas pedal into the carpet. Dirt and gravel sprayed every direction from the rear wheels as the car pirouetted around its nose, aligning in the direction of the plane. She spun the wheel with her palm, and dust fun-neled through the open windows past her face. The back of the car squatted as she tore off down the airstrip with the throttle wide open. When Lanie passed the two women on the ground, she could hear Amanda yelling, "YEAHH!" She was kneeling on Sabine and punched her fist in the air.

Feeling like she had the energy of a nuclear reactor radiating from her skin, Lanie gritted her teeth as the Cessna came closer. The pilot had already turned the plane around and was accelerating toward the car. Lanie intended to block his path. She jabbed the parking brake pedal with her left foot and pitched the Fleetwood into a lurid slide, obstructing the whole width of the airstrip. The plane came so close that Lanie could see the panic on the pilot's face. He steered into the brush around the car, and the plane bounced and teetered over the rocks. Lanie floored the accelerator again as the Cessna resumed its takeoff attempt. She used the throttle to bring the car's tail around and aimed the hood ornament at the plane's rudder.

The Cessna's engine was at full power, roaring as the plane accelerated down the strip. But the Cadillac was much faster—at least up until about 65mph. Lanie was closing on the plane quickly when she passed the women on the ground in a rooster tail of dust. At fifty miles per hour, Lanie caught the plane and rammed the car up under its tail. The rudder creased the hood, but Lanie knew the Cessna's tail was too high... she was aiming for the wheels.

She pushed the car up close along the left side of the fuselage and the plane's stabilizer flap cracked the windshield. The pilot was frantic, looking through his window as the long hood rode up next to his door. They were exceeding seventy miles per hour, and Lanie had to make her move. She steered right, swiping the fuselage. The Cadillac's bumper climbed over the plane's left wheel skirt and snapped its wheel spindle, causing the wing to crash down onto the hood.

The impact slowed the plane significantly—the man's escape attempt was terminated. The Cessna was crippled and running out of runway. Sabine's brother steered and pulled up on the stalk but was unable to control his speed or direction. Lanie used the car's nose to force the Cessna's tail to the side, using the same pit maneuver that police use to end car chases. The plane slid sideways, pointing the car's grille straight into the pilot's door. Lanie smiled; this was exactly the position she wanted, and she pushed the gas pedal all the way to the floor. The car downshifted, and the engine howled as Lanie plowed the plane toward the end of the airstrip. The left wing's edge had buckled, and the right-hand wing tip was grazing the ground ahead. The right landing wheel failed next, and the body of the plane dropped in front of the car. They were nearing the end of the airstrip, so Lanie stomped the brake pedal, sending the plane cartwheeling into a rocky ravine.

She watched until the plane came to rest. It was over now. The adrenaline rush started to sicken Lanie's empty stomach, and she put the car into *park*. She stepped out and walked toward the wreckage, seeing no motion. The Cessna lay on its belly, supported only by its tattered wing tip. The propeller was mangled and wrapped around the nose and the engine smoked. The smell of spilled aviation fuel surrounded the plane's carcass. She found the pilot lying across the front seats inside—he wasn't moving. The plastic windows had been shed from the fuselage. Lanie could hear the pilot moaning as she pulled the door open. As much as she wanted to punch him where he lay, she was glad he was alive. One of his arms was twisted in an unnatural kink behind his back—he had broken bones.

The gold bars had scattered during the wreck, and two were lying in the desert among the debris. She contemplated abandoning them. Lanie had no need for gold bars. But as she approached the idling car, she looked back at the wreckage. Esther would expect an Omega representative to bring them back.

Amanda was standing on the airstrip when Lanie returned. She slowly stopped the car next to her and, after the dust cleared, said, "Hey girl, need a lift?"

With a smile as broad as the sunrise, Amanda hitched out her thumb. "Wherever you're going, I'm in," she said, leaning through the window. "Whatcha wanna do with Wicked Stepmother here?"

Sabine was handcuffed, lying face down in the dirt, looking most uncomfortable. Cactus needles littered her purple top, and dust was mottled with the dried blood on her face and arms. Her right eyelid had swollen shut. Lanie's initial inclination was to leave her for the hawks and coyotes. But she looked into Amanda's blue eyes and nodded her head. They needed to be responsible—and merciful—and she knew Amanda agreed.

"We can't leave her out here—not like this." She put the car into *park* and shut off the engine, then popped the trunk open. "But we can give her a taste of her own medicine."

## Chapter 24

# THE RETURN HOME

The sun was still low in the morning sky when Lanie pulled off the highway and into a lonely roadside gas station near Bisbee. The gravel chattered under the tires as the car coasted slowly up to the gas pump. The Cadillac's engine had started stumbling four miles back. When it stalled, starved of fuel a half-mile away, the two girls thought they might have to push.

Lanie sprinted inside to use the restroom and left Amanda to pump gas. She had slapped down a fifty-dollar bill on the cashier's counter on her way through the store. When she returned to the car, Amanda went inside and Lanie stood under the blazing sun, gazing either direction down the deserted highway. Like the gas stations of the 1930s, the pump island had no canopy—and the pumps weren't much more modern. While she held the fuel nozzle, Lanie looked down at her blistered hand. Her wrist was swelling up. Punching a person was much more painful than she'd expected. Her burgundy nail polish from the formal still shined, but was as scratched and nicked as the car.

Amanda emerged from the convenience store with two bags full of snacks and bottled water, and she held them up for Lanie to see. The two young women sat back into the car while the store clerk watched with wide eyes from the counter inside.

"His mind is blown," Amanda said, smiling crookedly.

"Yeah, well let's hope he doesn't call anybody with his story," Lanie said as she accelerated onto the highway. "You never finished telling me about Hudson—is he OK or what?"

"Oh yeah," Amanda said, chuckling as she waved her hand. "Sabine clocked him good with a right hook, then locked him in the trunk of your dad's Rambler. She was gonna put me in there too—but I wouldn't fit!" They shared a laugh while Amanda passed Lanie a bottle of cold brew coffee. Amanda was developing an ugly black eye on the left side of her face, and it looked painful, but Lanie noticed that it wasn't affecting her new friend's smile.

The weather was cool, and the sky was clear as they sped north across the desert. The girls each wore a pair of flimsy gas station sunglasses that Amanda had bought during their fuel stop. Lanie found some suitable country music from a station in a distant city, and the two friends nodded with the beat as the wind whipped their hair. Lanie felt wonderfully alive, and her senses were all sharp—she was excited. The open road stretched into the distance ahead of them, and the huge Cadillac seemed to fit Lanie like a glove. She looked over at her navigator and couldn't help but feel proud.

"This doesn't suck," she said to Amanda, waving her curls out of her view.

"Today is *definitely* getting better," Amanda agreed.

In a small town called Kearny, Lanie pulled off into a gas station with an outside phone booth. She felt sheepish for having missed the first turnoff toward Phoenix, but the drive was nicer on their new route. They'd stopped at a couple places to attempt a call, but in the age of cellular phones, working telephone booths were becoming scarce. With a handful of quarters, Lanie first called 9-1-1. She told the Highway Patrol dispatcher that she'd been attacked at a gas station by a crazy woman who claimed to have kidnapped a person from Fountain Hills.

CHRIS CONTES

"You'll find her handcuffed to the flagpole at the cemetery in the town of Winkelman," she told the dispatcher. Amanda had made a similar call from a cafe near Tombstone, advising that a smuggler had crashed his plane southeast of Bisbee.

Next, Lanie called her dad's cell phone. He answered and was immediately frantic, asking so many questions that she couldn't even insert a word. Amanda stood near the booth looking on.

"DAD!" she said, cutting him off. "Yes, we're fine—I'm fine," she added, touching the huge bruise on the side of her face. She licked the split on her lip. "We're on our way home—the situation is handled." Lanie grimaced and held the receiver away from her ear after she spoke, because it was clear Mr. Speros wasn't satisfied with her condensed report.

Realizing that her dad must be near a nervous breakdown, Lanie interrupted him again. "Dad, listen. We're coming home, and we're safe. There's no more danger."

"You heard me, Lanie Marion, you stay right where you're standing, and we'll send help—tell me where you are!" said the voice over the phone.

She looked up at Amanda. "No, Dad, sorry, we're not gonna wait. We're driving home on our own. I'll see you soon, OK? Probably around 3 p.m. I love you a lot. Give a hug to Isaiah. And call Esther too, so she can call Mr. Reyes." She hung up the phone while her dad was still pleading for her to stay put.

"He wants to send the police to bring us home?" Amanda asked.

"Yeah. What good is that gonna do," Lanie mumbled. "We'll be sitting in a sheriff's office out here for hours, stepping around questions that we're not supposed to answer, waiting for our parents to come get us." Lanie kicked away a pebble from the dirt under the phone kiosk. "Nah. Let's go."

Coasting down the mountain approaching Phoenix, Lanie slowed to the speed limit, attempting to blend with highway traffic. She was pacing a J.B. Hunt freight semi in the right lane as a stream of faster traffic passed on

370

the left. The last car in the group was a black Chevy Suburban with tinted windows. As the Suburban overtook them, its speed leveled off alongside. Lanie looked over to see the rear window rolling down. Esther peered at her from inside, wearing her familiar smile. Lanie's eyes widened, and she sat up in her seat. With a jeweled finger, Esther pointed toward the road-side and rolled her window up. The Suburban dropped back and fell in behind the Cadillac.

The girls glanced at each other, wondering if they were about to be excommunicated from the Omega program. Lanie pulled off at a rest area a mile ahead and shut off the engine. The two girls stepped out of the car as the Suburban parked behind. The Cadillac's hot exhaust system ticked and pinged in the quiet of the desert.

Adam emerged first, dressed in a crisp gray suit. He greeted the girls with a nod, hiding a smile. Esther's door swung wide before Adam had the chance to open it, and she stepped out without his assistance. When she approached the girls, she shook her head. She lifted off her sunglasses and stared at the two young women with her lips pursed. Esther looked serious, but Lanie could see admiration behind her eyes.

"Well, just *look* at the two of you. Each time I think you kids are all *done* with surprises, you pitch me a new one." She leaned against the Chevy's grille. "Out crashing airplanes, driving across the desert like escaped assassins, and stopping at convenience stores with four *million* dollars of gold in the trunk." She shook her head again but looked up with a taut smile. "I'm gonna call you all the Wrecking Crew." She looked up at Adam, who stood near the Cadillac with his hands folded. "I don't know what I need *you* for, if these kids are gonna roll this heavy."

Adam smiled and looked toward the highway, trying to mask his expression. He knocked on the trunk lid, so Lanie pressed the remote release. Without any strain, Adam lifted the dust-covered canvas bag out and walked behind the Suburban. Lanie realized she was not about to be destroyed, but resisted the urge to throw her arms around Esther.

Tightening her face, Esther continued. "But ladies, as impressed as I am, your parents are an absolute wreck. I can't have you running this kind of operation. And you have no idea how long it's gonna take me to cover your tracks today." She walked over to Amanda and looked closer at her black eye. Then she lifted Lanie's bangs, sizing up her injuries.

Esther pointed fingers at both of the girls independently, then dropped her hand, glancing around. "This rest stop is not the place to get into it. But when we are past this episode you're all going to spend a few days in specialized training. You need to sharpen some of these skills you've got." She turned to Lanie. "Ms. Speros, your propensity for grue-some self-defense is both alarming and fascinating, but it needs to be chan-neled. Both...," she stopped to amend her statement, *"all three of you*—I'm afraid you're not gonna be as fortunate next time, and these half-baked, hurricane-like defenses that you mount must be tightened up." She turned to walk back to her door.

Lanie held up the copper key. "Do you want this?"

Esther paused, then waved her hand. "Keep it. Lock it up. You will need it again soon."

Lanie then pulled the silver chain out of her pocket—with Sabine's stainless-steel key. "I think you'll want this one though."

Esther appeared taken aback. "My, my, my... now *there's* a surprise." She gave a nod to Adam, who gently took the key from Lanie.

"Wanda disappeared—and married a Regent... didn't she?" Lanie asked, smiling smartly.

The cool expression on Esther's face revealed nothing. "We'll revisit Sabine's story soon, after I've had time to collect more facts. Just the same, I appreciate your attention to cleaning up details," she said, letting her smile crack through.

Lanie was sure that Esther was going to have her and Amanda get into the SUV, but instead she swirled her finger in the air, signaling Adam to roll out.

"You wanted to make the drive, so finish it," she said to the girls from her position on the Suburban's running board. "Don't get yourselves pulled over."

Adam walked back to his door, where he turned and saluted the girls. "Mad skills, ladies; nice work," he said as he climbed in. They watched as the Suburban sped up the highway ramp.

At 3:30 that afternoon, Lanie and Amanda arrived in Fountain Hills as afternoon rush hour was starting to pick up. Only a few blocks from her house, Lanie stopped at a traffic light and checked her look in the visor mirror. She was a mess, with dried blood around her lip and tender, throbbing bruises everywhere. Her face was dirty and her hair a tangled mat. She flipped the visor back up, figuring she ought to worry more about what her dad was going to say. Her mom's car had also taken a beating, though Lanie knew that under the layers of dust, the damage was superficial. Afternoon sun warmed her cheek, and her hand dangled from the window. Her mind was far away as she watched the red traffic light. Then she heard Amanda gasp.

"Oh SNAP," her passenger said, looking out Lanie's window.

Lanie followed Amanda's gaze to her left, and her heart jumped. The broad side of a school bus was coasting up next to them at the traffic light. It was marked with big black letters:

FOUNTAIN HILLS UNION SCHOOL DISTRICT

Looking up over the top of her sunglasses, Lanie saw rows of heads and arms protruding from the bus windows. All eyes were on her and Amanda. The students of Superstition Canyon Junior High were crowding against the right side of the bus to get a better view. Jaws were hanging open and many kids were pointing. Danny Austin's face was among the group.

"Ohhh danggg," Lanie said, pulling her arm inside the window. She stared straight ahead with both hands on the wheel. The chatter and disbelief of the students on the bus was audible over the idling engines.

*"That's Lanie Speros, look at her!"*

*"Holy cow, she's driving—whose car is that?!"*

*"Look how busted up she is, what's going on?"*

*"Who is that other girl?"*

Lanie could tell her face was beet red, but her blush likely wasn't visible to the spectators. When the light turned green, she quickly rounded the corner at the intersection, leaving the gawking students behind. Both girls were quiet for the last minutes of the drive. When Lanie turned onto Constellation Way she felt elated to be home. Up the street, she saw several vehicles parked in the cul-de-sac near her house, including a Fountain Hills police cruiser.

"Oh, that's my dad's truck," Amanda said, pointing to a Ford F350 pickup.

A group of people were assembled in the open garage when Lanie pulled into the driveway, and all faces turned to watch. Lanie picked out her grandparents, Isaiah, Mr. Reyes, the whole Newman family, Mr. & Mrs. Rinnas, two Fountain Hills police officers, and a couple men in suits that she didn't recognize. Mr. Rinnas's arm was in a cast. When his eyes met Lanie's, he winked and held a finger up to his lips. She understood his signal... the site executive's identity needed to remain concealed. She shut the engine off, and the two girls looked at each other. Lanie's eyes returned to the crowd in the garage. Hudson stood with the group and he was smiling, but he was the only one.

Isaiah ran up to the car. "LAY-LAY!" he yelled, reaching through the open window. "We're glad you're home! You look junky. Did you miss us? Why did you crash up mom's car? Did you get your drivers' license?"

"Hi buddy," she said, grabbing his hand as he continued his line of questions. Her dad was walking toward the car, looking tired and relieved.

"Well, we can do this one of two ways," Amanda said. "We can slither up there expecting to be busted or we can be proud of what we did, and walk up like *we* are the ones who pulled this thing off." She raised her eyebrows at Lanie and threw her sunglasses on the dusty dash. "I can tell you what *I'm* gonna do," she said, and swung the car door open.

Lanie knew Amanda was right. With a crooked smile, she opened her door as her dad approached and hooked her arm over the windshield.

Check in at **www.LanieSperos.com** to see additional illustrations and more information about Lanie's story.

# ABOUT THE AUTHOR

Seeking a more upbeat, fast-paced reading experience for his young boys, Chris Contes began fiction writing later in his career—at age forty-five. With years of history in the automotive and theme park industries, Chris taps a diverse and eclectic range of work experiences that share a common thread—a love of making a day job out of his passions. His background also provides an engaging and technically accurate source for unique scene setting and storytelling. An avid fiction reader himself, Chris gravitates toward stories that are motivating, energetic, and faithful to technical details.

Chris has a business degree from Arizona State University and spent ten years working at automotive test facilities for General Motors and Nissan. In 2005, he followed his dream and left the auto industry for a behind-the-scenes career leading ride maintenance projects and programs at Disneyland, Universal Studios Hollywood, and Knott's Berry Farm. He lives with his family near Los Angeles.